Favorite Tales from The Arabian Nights' Entertainments

Translated by
RICHARD F. BURTON

D0168386

DOVER PUBLICATIONS, INC.
Mineola, New York

Bibliographical Note

This Dover edition, first published in 2001, is a new selection of stories from a standard edition of *The Arabian Nights*, first published 1885–1888. A new Note has been written specially for this edition.

Library of Congress Cataloging-in-Publication Data

Arabian nights. English. Selections.
　　Favorite tales from the Arabian nights' entertainments / translated by Richard F. Burton.
　　　　p. cm.
　　ISBN 0-486-41917-7 (pbk.)
　　1. Burton, Richard Francis, Sir, 1821–1890. II. Title.

PJ7716.A1 B813 2001
398.22—dc21

2001047815

Manufactured in the United States by Courier Corporation
41917703
www.doverpublications.com

Note

RICHARD BURTON, the soldier, explorer, linguist, diplomat, poet, and translator extraordinaire who was prolifically active during five decades of the 19th century, was the foremost translator into English of the stories variously known as the Arabian Nights and the Thousand and One Nights. Associated with the name of the artful and bewitching Scheherazade or Sheherazade, as she often is called by Europeans and by English speakers, the stories first were published in 1717, in a French translation made from Arabic manuscript collections. Burton's definitive, uncensored English translation, praised for its authenticity, virility, and elegance, was published in ten volumes in 1885, with six additional volumes published in the following three years. Some of the tales, notably those relating the adventures of Aladdin, Ali Baba, and Sinbad the Sailor, have been adopted as part of European folklore, despite their chiefly Asian origins.

The hundreds of stories included in the Arabian Nights were collected in several groups, at various times ranging from the 8th through the 16th centuries. The tales originated in Egypt, Iran, Iraq, Turkey, and possibly Greece, as well as China, India, and Central Asia (the latter group being added last, and brought to the Middle East by Mongol soldiers). Scheherazade is the focal figure of the frame story that encompasses all of the tales.

According to the frame story that "explains" the genesis of all of the thousand and one tales, King Shahryar has had his wife and her lovers executed, after discovering that she was unfaithful to him with several men. He then begins taking a different bride each night, and having her beheaded the following morning. The young female population is being decimated. Then Shahrazad (Scheherazade), the older of the two daughters of the king's grand vizier, volunteers to be the ruler's bride, so she can implement her plan to save herself and many other women. The young woman's plan is simple. On her wedding night, which is to be the last night of her life, she tells the sleepless king a story so entertaining (promising to finish it the next night) that he spares her life. Each night, she completes the previous tale and begins a new one, thus prolonging her life indefinitely and sparing other women from the series of bridal executions. Eventually the enthralled king revokes his decree regarding the killing of a bride each morning after a single night of wedded life, and settles down to enjoy life with the entrancing Shahrazad.

Burton's translations of the stories of Aladdin, Ali Baba, and Sinbad, in adapted forms, have been beloved in the folklore traditions and popular culture of many European and American countries for several generations. This Dover edition also includes Burton's translations of three other popular stories from the Arabian Nights that are not as widely known in adaptations. "The Fisherman and the Jinni" was the first story Shahrazad told to King Shahryar as she put into effect her creative plan to avoid decapitation. "Judar and His Brethren" and "Khalifah the Fisherman of Baghdad" are tales from later "layers" of the Arabian Nights.

Burton made his uncensored translation of the Arabian Nights in the 1840s, during his active years in India as an officer in the Bombay Army (the military arm of the British East India Company), during which he also learned several of the languages of India and wrote three valuable ethnological studies. It was not until 1884 that he reorganized, edited, and annotated his translations, when he was well into his long tenure as British consul in the quiet diplomatic post of Trieste (then the main port of the Austro-Hungarian Empire, now Italy's northeasternmost city). During the 1880s new literary translations from Latin, Italian, Hindustani, and Arabic were among his other major accomplishments. Although the Arabian Nights translations were praised by many for their vigor and skill, they also were excoriated by some as "an appalling collection of degrading customs," among other things. Burton, a notable exception to the Victorian prudery of his era, remained in an unlikely-seeming marriage with a devout Roman Catholic, Isabel Arundell, for three decades. His translations of the Arabian Nights, published during his lifetime, escaped the extensive destruction of his journals and other manuscripts undertaken by his widow after his death in 1890.

Contents

SINBAD THE SEAMAN
AND SINBAD THE LANDSMAN

THERE LIVED IN the city of Baghdad, during the reign of the Commander of the Faithful, Harun al-Rashid, a man named Sinbad the Hammal, one in poor case who bore burdens on his head for hire. It happened to him one day of great heat that whilst he was carrying a heavy load, he became exceeding weary and sweated profusely, the heat and the weight alike oppressing him. Presently, as he was passing the gate of a merchant's house, before which the ground was swept and watered, and there the air was temperate, he sighted a broad bench beside the door; so he set his load thereon, to take rest and smell the air. He sat down on the edge of the bench, and at once heard from within the melodious sound of lutes and other stringed instruments, and mirth-exciting voices singing and reciting, together with the song of birds warbling and glorifying Almighty Allah in various tunes and tongues; turtles, mocking-birds, merles, nightingales, cushats and stone-curlews, whereat he marvelled in himself and was moved to mighty joy and solace. Then he went up to the gate and saw within a great flower-garden wherein were pages and black slaves and such a train of servants and attendants and so forth as is found only with Kings and Sultans; and his nostrils were greeted with the savoury odours of all manner meats rich and delicate, and delicious and generous wines. So he raised his eyes heavenwards and said, "Glory to Thee, O Lord, O Creator and Provider, who providest whomso Thou wilt without count or stint! O mine Holy One, I cry Thee pardon for all sins and turn to Thee repenting of all offences."

How many by my labours, that evermore endure,
All goods of life enjoy and in cooly shade recline?
Each morn that dawns I wake in travail and in woe,
And strange is my condition and my burden gars me pine:

1

Many others are in luck and from miseries are free,
And Fortune never load them with loads the like o' mine:
They live their happy days in all solace and delight;
Eat, drink and dwell in honour 'mid the noble and the digne:
All living things were made of a little drop of sperm,
Thine origin is mine and my provenance is thine;
Yet the difference and distance 'twixt the two of us are far
As the difference of savour 'twixt vinegar and wine:
But at Thee, O God All-wise! I venture not to rail
Whose ordinance is just and whose justice cannot fail.

When Sinbad the Porter had made an end of reciting his verses, he bore up his burden and was about to fare on, when there came forth to him from the gate a little foot-page, fair of face and shapely of shape and dainty of dress who caught him by the hand saying, "Come in and speak with my lord, for he calleth for thee." The Porter would have excused himself to the page but the lad would take no refusal; so he left his load with the doorkeeper in the vestibule and followed the boy into the house, which he found to be a goodly mansion, radiant and full of majesty, till he brought him to a grand sitting-room wherein he saw a company of nobles and great lords, seated at tables garnished with all manner of flowers and sweet-scented herbs, besides great plenty of dainty viands and fruits dried and fresh and confections and wines of the choicest vintages. There also were instruments of music and mirth and lovely slave-girls playing and singing. All the company was ranged according to rank; and in the highest place sat a man of worshipful and noble aspect whose beard-sides hoariness had stricken; and he was stately of stature and fair of favour, agreeable of aspect and full of gravity and dignity and majesty. So Sinbad the Porter was confounded at that which he beheld and said in himself, "By Allah, this must be either a piece of Paradise or some King's palace!" Then he saluted the company with much respect praying for their prosperity, and kissing the ground before them, stood with his head bowed down in humble attitude. The master of the house bade him draw near and be seated and bespoke him kindly, bidding him welcome. Then he set before him various kinds of viands, rich and delicate and delicious, and the Porter, after saying his Bismillah, fell to and ate his fill, after which he exclaimed, "Praised be Allah whatso be our case!" and, washing his hands, returned thanks to the company for his entertainment. Quoth the host, "Thou art welcome and thy day is a blessed. But what is thy name and calling?" Quoth the other, "O my lord, my name is Sinbad the Hammal, and I carry folk's goods on my head for hire." The housemaster smiled and rejoined, "Know, O Porter, that thy name is even as mine, for I am Sinbad the Seaman; and now, O Porter, I would have thee let me hear the couplets thou recitedst at the gate anon." The Porter was abashed and replied, "Allah upon thee! Excuse me, for toil and travail and lack of luck when the hand is empty, teach a man ill manners and boorish ways." Said the host, "Be not ashamed; thou art become my brother; but repeat to me the verses, for they pleased me whenas I heard thee recite them at the gate." Hereupon the Porter repeated the couplets and they delighted the merchant, who said to him:—Know, O Hammal, that my story is a wonderful one, and thou shalt hear all that befel me and all I underwent ere I rose to this state of prosperity and became the lord of this place wherein thou seest me; for I came not to this high estate save after travail sore and perils galore, and how much toil and trouble have I not suffered in days of yore! I have made seven voyages, by each of which hangeth a marvellous tale, such as confoundeth the reason, and all this came to pass by doom of fortune and fate; for from what destiny doth write there is neither refuge nor flight. Know, then, good my lords (continued he), that I am about to relate the

First Voyage of Sinbad Hight the Seaman

My father was a merchant, one of the notables of my native place, a monied man and ample of means, who died whilst I was yet a child, leaving me much wealth in money and lands and farmhouses. When I grew up, I laid hands on the whole and ate of the best and drank freely and wore rich clothes and lived lavishly, companioning and consorting with youths of my own age, and considering that this course of life would continue for ever and ken no change. Thus did I for a long time, but at last I awoke from my heedlessness and, returning to my senses, I found my wealth had become unwealth and my condition ill-conditioned and all I once hent had left my hand. And recovering my reason I was stricken with dismay and confusion and bethought me of a saying of our lord Solomon, son of David (on whom be peace!), which I had heard aforetime from my father, "Three things are better than other three; the day of death is better than the day of birth, a live dog is better than a dead lion and the grave is better than want." Then I got together my remains of estates and property and sold all, even my clothes, for three thousand dirhams, with which I resolved to travel to foreign parts, remembering the saying of the poet:—

> By means of toil man shall scale the height;
> Who to fame aspires mustn't sleep o' night;
> Who seeketh pearl in the deep must dive,
> Winning weal and wealth by his main and might:

And who seeketh Fame without toil and strife
Th' impossible seeketh and wasteth life.

So taking heart I bought me goods, merchandise and all needed for a voyage and, impatient to be at sea, I embarked, with a company of merchants, on board a ship bound for Bassorah. There we again embarked and sailed many days and nights, and we passed from isle to isle and sea to sea and shore to shore, buying and selling and bartering everywhere the ship touched, and continued our course till we came to an island as it were a garth of the gardens of Paradise. Here the captain cast anchor and making fast to the shore, put out the landing planks. So all on board landed and made furnaces and lighting fires therein, busied themselves in various ways, some cooking and some washing, whilst other some walked about the island for solace, and the crew fell to eating and drinking and playing and sporting. I was one of the walkers but, as we were thus engaged, behold the master who was standing on the gunwale cried out to us at the top of his voice, saying, "Ho there! passengers, run for your lives and hasten back to the ship and leave your gear and save yourselves from destruction, Allah preserve you! For this island whereon ye stand is no true island, but a great fish stationary a-middlemost of the sea, whereon the sand hath settled and trees have sprung up of old time, so that it is become like unto an island; but, when ye lighted fires on it, it felt the heat and moved; and in a moment it will sink with you into the sea and ye will all be drowned. So leave your gear and seek your safety ere ye die!" All who heard him left gear and goods, clothes washed and unwashed, fire pots and brass cooking-pots, and fled back to the ship for their lives, and some reached it while others (amongst whom was I) did not, for suddenly the island shook and sank into the abysses of the deep, with all that were thereon, and the dashing sea surged over it with clashing waves. I sank with the others down, down into the deep, but Almighty Allah preserved me from drowning and threw in my way a great wooden tub of those that had served the ship's company for tubbing. I gripped it for the sweetness of life and, bestriding it like one riding, paddled with my feet like oars, whilst the waves tossed me as in sport right and left. Meanwhile the captain made sail and departed with those who had reached the ship, regardless of the drowning and the drowned; and I ceased not following the vessel with my eyes, till she was hid from sight and I made sure of death. Darkness closed in upon me while in this plight and the winds and waves bore me on all that night and the next day, till the tub brought to with me under the lee of a lofty island, with trees overhanging the tide. I caught hold of a branch and by its aid clambered up on to the land, after coming nigh upon death; but when I reached the shore, I found my legs cramped and numbed and my feet bore traces of the nibbling of fish upon their soles; withal I had felt nothing for excess of anguish and fatigue. I threw myself down on the island ground, like a dead man, and drowned in desolation swooned away, nor did I return to my senses till next morning, when the sun rose and revived me. But I found my feet swollen, so made shift to move by shuffling on my breech and crawling on my knees, for in that island were found store of fruits and springs of sweet water. I ate of the fruits which strengthened me: and thus I abode days and nights, till my life seemed to return and my spirits began to revive and I was better able to move about. So, after due consideration, I fell to exploring the island and diverting myself with gazing upon all things that Allah Almighty had created there; and rested under the trees from one of which I cut me a staff to lean upon. One day as I walked along the marge, I caught sight of some object in the distance and thought it a wild beast or one of the monster-creatures of the sea; but, as I drew near it, looking hard the while, I saw that it was a noble mare, tethered on the beach. Presently I went up to her, but she cried out against me with a great cry, so that I trembled for fear and turned to go away, when there came forth a man from under the earth and followed me, crying out and saying, "Who and whence art thou, and what caused thee to come hither?" "O my lord," answered I, "I am in very sooth, a waif, a stranger, and was left to drown with sundry others by the ship we voyaged in; but Allah graciously sent me a wooden tub; so I saved myself thereon and it floated with me, till the waves cast me up on this island." When he heard this, he took my hand and saying, "Come with me," carried me into a great Sardab, or underground chamber, which was spacious as a saloon. He made me sit down at its upper end; then he brought me somewhat of food and, being anhungered, I ate till I was satisfied and refreshed; and when he had put me at mine ease he questioned me of myself, and I told him all that had befallen me from first to last; and, as he wondered at my adventure, I said, "By Allah, O my lord, excuse me; I have told thee the truth of my case and the accident which betided me; and now I desire that thou tell me who thou art and why thou abidest here under the earth and why thou hast tethered yonder mare on the brink of the sea." Answered he, "Know, that I am one of the several who are stationed in different parts of this island, and we are of the grooms of King Mihrjan and under our hand are all his horses. Every month, about new-moon tide we bring hither our best mares which have never been covered, and picket them on the sea-shore and hide ourselves in this place under the ground, so that none may espy us. Presently, the stallions of the sea scent the mares and come up out of the water and seeing no one, leap the mares and do their will of them. When they have covered them, they try to drag them away with them, but cannot, by reason of the leg-ropes; so they cry out at them and butt at them and kick them, which we hearing, know that the stallions have dismounted; so we run out and shout at them, whereupon they are startled and return in fear to the sea. Then the mares conceive by them and bear colts and fillies worth a mint of money, nor is their like to be found on earth's face. This is the time of the coming forth of the sea-stallions; and Inshallah! I will bear thee to King Mihrjan and show thee our country. And know that hadst thou not happened on us thou hadst perished miserably and none had known of thee: but I will be the means of the saving of thy life and of thy return to thine own land." I called down blessings on him and thanked him for his kindness and courtesy; and, while we were yet talking, behold, the stallion came up out of the sea; and, giving a great cry, sprang upon the mare and covered her. When he had done his will of her, he dismounted and would have carried her away with him, but could not by reason of the tether. She kicked and cried out at him, whereupon the groom took a sword and target and ran out of the underground saloon, smiting the buckler with the blade and calling to his company, who came up shouting and brandishing spears; and the stallion took fright at them and plunging into the sea, like a buffalo, disappeared under the waves. After this we sat awhile, till the rest of the grooms came up, each leading a mare, and seeing me with their fellow-Syce, questioned me of my case and I repeated my story to them. Thereupon they drew near me and spreading the table, ate and invited me to eat; so I ate with them, after which they took horse and mounting me on one of the mares, set out with me and fared on without ceasing, till we came to the capital city of King Mihrjan, and going in to him acquainted him with my story. Then he sent for me, and when they set me before him and salams had been exchanged, he gave me a cordial welcome and wishing me long life bade me tell him my tale. So I related to him all that I had seen and all that had befallen me from first to last, whereat he marvelled and said to me, "By Allah, O my son, thou hast indeed been miraculously preserved! Were not the term of thy life a long one, thou hadst not escaped from these straits; but praised be Allah for safety!" Then he spoke cheerily to me and entreated me with kindness and consideration: moreover, he made me his agent for the port and registrar of all ships that entered the harbour. I attended him regularly, to receive his commandments, and he favoured me and did me all manner of kindness and invested me with costly and splendid robes. Indeed, I was high in credit with him, as an intercessor for the folk and an intermediary between them and him, when they wanted aught of him. I abode thus a great while and, as often as I passed through the city to the port, I

questioned the merchants and travellers and sailors of the city of
Baghdad; so haply I might hear of an occasion to return to my native
land, but could find none who knew it or knew any who resorted
thither. At this I was chagrined, for I was weary of long strangerhood;
and my disappointment endured for a time till one day, going in to
King Mihrjan, I found him with a company of Indians. I saluted them
and they returned my salam; and politely welcomed me and asked me
of my country. When they asked me of my country I questioned them
of theirs and they told me that they were of various castes, some being
called Shakiriyah who are the noblest of their castes and neither
oppress nor offer violence to any, and others Brahmans, a folk who
abstain from wine, but live in delight and solace and merriment and
own camels and horses and cattle. Moreover, they told me that the
people of India are divided into two-and-seventy castes, and I marvelled
at this with exceeding marvel. Amongst other things that I saw in King
Mihrjan's dominions was an island called Kasil, wherein all night is
heard the beating of drums and tabrets; but we were told by the neigh-
boring islanders and by travellers that the inhabitants are people of diligence and judgment. In this sea I saw also a fish two hundred cubits
long and the fishermen fear it; so they strike together pieces of wood
and put it to flight. I also saw another fish, with a head like that of an
owl, besides many other wonders and rarities, which it would be
tedious to recount. I occupied myself thus in visiting the islands till,
one day, as I stood in the port, with a staff in my hand, according to my
custom, behold, a great ship, wherein were many merchants, came sailing for the harbour. When it reached the small inner port where ships
anchor under the city, the master furled his sails and making fast to the
shore, put out the landing-planks, whereupon the crew fell to breaking
bulk and landing cargo whilst I stood by, taking written note of them.
They were long in bringing the goods ashore so I asked the master, "Is
there aught left in thy ship?"; and he answered, "O my lord, there are
divers bales of merchandise in the hold, whose owner was drowned
from amongst us at one of the islands on our course; so his goods
remained in our charge by way of trust and we purpose to sell them and
note their price, that we may convey it to his people in the city of
Baghdad, the Home of Peace." "What was the merchant's name?"
quoth I, and quoth he, "Sinbad the Seaman;" whereupon I straitly considered him and knowing him, cried out to him with a great cry, saying, "O captain, I am that Sinbad the Seaman who travelled with other
merchants; and when the fish heaved and thou calledst to us some
saved themselves and others sank, I being one of them. But Allah
Almighty threw in my way a great tub of wood, of those the crew had
used to wash withal, and the winds and waves carried me to this island,

where by Allah's grace, I fell in with King Mihrjan's grooms and they brought me hither to the King their master. When I told him my story, he entreated me with favour and made me his harbour-master, and I have prospered in his service and found acceptance with him. These bales, therefore are mine, the goods which God hath given me." The other exclaimed, "There is no Majesty and there is no Might save in Allah, the Glorious, the Great! Verily, there is neither conscience nor good faith left among men!" Said I, "O Rais,[1] what mean these words, seeing that I have told thee my case?" And he answered, "Because thou heardest me say that I had with me goods whose owner was drowned, thou thinkest to take them without right; but this is forbidden by law to thee, for we saw him drown before our eyes, together with many other passengers, nor was one of them saved. So how canst thou pretend that thou art the owner of the goods?" "O captain," said I, "Listen to my story and give heed to my words, and my truth will be manifest to thee; for lying and leasing are the letter-marks of the hypocrites." Then I recounted to him all that had befallen me since I sailed from Baghdad with him to the time when we came to the fish-island where we were nearly drowned; and I reminded him of certain matters which had passed between us; whereupon both he and the merchants were certified of the truth of my story and recognised me and gave me joy of my deliverance, saying, "By Allah, we thought not that thou hadst escaped drowning! But the Lord hath granted thee new life." Then they delivered my bales to me, and I found my name written thereon, nor was aught thereof lacking. So I opened them and making up a present for King Mihrjan of the finest and costliest of the contents, caused the sailors carry it up to the palace, where I went in to the King and laid my present at his feet, acquainting him with what had happened, especially concerning the ship and my goods; whereat he wondered with exceeding wonder and the truth of all that I had told him was made manifest to him. His affection for me redoubled after that and he showed me exceeding honour and bestowed on me a great present in return for mine. Then I sold my bales and what other matters I owned making a great profit on them, and bought me other goods and gear of the growth and fashion of the island-city. When the merchants were about to start on their homeward voyage, I embarked on board the ship all that I possessed, and going in to the King, thanked him for all his favours and friendship and craved his leave to return to my own land and friends. He farewelled me and bestowed on me great store of the country-stuffs and produce; and I took leave of him and embarked.

---

[1] The captain or master (not owner) of a ship.

Then we set sail and fared on nights and days, by the permission of
Allah Almighty; and Fortune served us and Fate favoured us, so that we
arrived in safety at Bassorah-city where I landed rejoiced at my safe
return to my natal soil. After a short stay, I set out for Baghdad, the
House of Peace, with store of goods and commodities of great price.
Reaching the city in due time, I went straight to my own quarter and
entered my house where all my friends and kinsfolk came to greet me.
Then I bought me eunuchs and concubines, servants and negro slaves
till I had a large establishment, and I bought me houses, and lands and
gardens, till I was richer and in better case than before, and returned to
enjoy the society of my friends and familiars more assiduously than
ever, forgetting all I had suffered of fatigue and hardship and strangerhood and every peril of travel; and I applied myself to all manner joys
and solaces and delights, eating the daintiest viands and drinking the
deliciousest wines; and my wealth allowed this state of things to
endure. This, then, is the story of my first voyage, and to-morrow,
Inshallah! I will tell you the tale of the second of my seven voyages.
(Saith he who telleth the tale), Then Sinbad the Seaman made Sinbad
the Landsman sup with him and bade give him an hundred gold
pieces, saying, "Thou hast cheered us with thy company this day." The
Porter thanked him and, taking the gift, went his way, pondering that
which he had heard and marvelling mightily at what things betide
mankind. He passed the night in his own place and with early morning
repaired to the abode of Sinbad the Seaman, who received him with
honour and seated him by his side. As soon as the rest of the company
was assembled, he set meat and drink before them and, when they had
well eaten and drunken and were merry and in cheerful case, he took
up his discourse and recounted to them in these words the narrative of

The Second Voyage of Sinbad the Seaman

Know, O my brother, that I was living a most comfortable and enjoy-
able life, in all solace and delight, as I told you yesterday, until one day
my mind became possessed with the thought of travelling about the
world of men and seeing their cities and islands; and a longing seized
me to traffic and to make money by trade. Upon this resolve I took a
great store of cash and, buying goods and gear fit for travel, bound them
up in bales. Then I went down to the river-bank, where I found a noble
ship and brand-new about to sail, equipped with sails of fine cloth and
well manned and provided; so I took passage in her, with a number of
other merchants, and after embarking our goods we weighed anchor
the same day. Right fair was our voyage and we sailed from place to
place and from isle to isle; and whenever we anchored we met a crowd

of merchants and notables and customers, and we took to buying and selling and bartering. At last Destiny brought us to an island, fair and verdant, in trees abundant, with yellow-ripe fruits luxuriant, and flowers fragrant and birds warbling soft descant; and streams crystalline and radiant; but no sign of man showed to the descrier, no, not a blower of the fire. The captain made fast with us to this island, and the merchants and sailors landed and walked about, enjoying the shade of the trees and the song of the birds, that chanted the praises of the One, the Victorious, and marvelling at the works of the Omnipotent King. I landed with the rest; and, sitting down by a spring of sweet water that welled up among the trees, took out some vivers I had with me and ate of that which Allah Almighty had allotted unto me. And so sweet was the zephyr and so fragrant were the flowers, that presently I waxed drowsy and, lying down in that place, was soon drowned in sleep. When I awoke, I found myself alone, for the ship had sailed and left me behind, nor had one of the merchants or sailors bethought himself of me. I searched the island right and left, but found neither man nor Jinn, whereat I was beyond measure troubled and my gall was like to burst for stress of chagrin and anguish and concern, because I was left quite alone, without aught of worldly gear or meat or drink, weary and heart-broken. So I gave myself up for lost and said, "Not always doth the crock escape the shock. I was saved the first time by finding one who brought me from the desert island to an inhabited place, but now there is no hope for me." Then I fell to weeping and wailing and gave myself up to an access of rage, blaming myself for having again ventured upon the perils and hardships of voyage, whenas I was at my ease in mine own house in mine own land, taking my pleasure with good meat and good drink and good clothes and lacking nothing, neither money nor goods. And I repented me of having left Baghdad, and this the more after all the travails and dangers I had undergone in my first voyage, wherein I had so narrowly escaped destruction, and exclaimed "Verily we are Allah's and unto Him we are returning!" I was indeed even as one mad and Jinn-struck and presently I rose and walked about the island, right and left and every whither, unable for trouble to sit or tarry in any one place. Then I climbed a tall tree and looked in all directions, but saw nothing save sky and sea and trees and birds and isles and sands. However, after a while my eager glances fell upon some great white thing, afar off in the interior of the island; so I came down from the tree and made for that which I had seen; and behold, it was a huge white dome rising high in air and of vast compass. I walked all around it, but found no door thereto, nor could I muster strength or nimbleness by reason of its exceeding smoothness and slipperiness. So I marked the spot where I stood and went round about the dome to measure its circumference which I found fifty good paces. And as I stood, casting about how to gain an entrance the day being near its fall and the sun being near the horizon, behold, the sun was suddenly hidden from me and the air became dull and dark. Methought a cloud had come over the sun, but it was the season of summer; so I marvelled at this and lifting my head looked steadfastly at the sky, when I saw that the cloud was none other than an enormous bird, of gigantic girth and inordinately wide of wing which, as it flew through the air, veiled the sun and hid it from the island. At this sight my wonder redoubled and I remembered a story I had heard aforetime of pilgrims and travellers, how in a certain island dwelleth a huge bird, called the "Rukh" which feedeth its young on elephants; and I was certified that the dome which caught my sight was none other than a Rukh's egg. As I looked and wondered at the marvellous works of the Almighty, the bird alighted on the dome and brooded over it with its wings covering it and its legs stretched out behind it on the ground, and in this posture it fell asleep, glory be to Him who sleepeth not! When I saw this, I arose and, unwinding my turband from my head, doubled it and twisted it into a rope, with which I girt my middle and bound my waist fast to the legs of the Rukh, saying in myself, "Peradventure, this bird may carry me to a land of cities and inhabitants, and that will be better than abiding in this desert island." I passed the night watching and fearing to sleep, lest the bird should fly away with me unawares; and, as soon as the dawn broke and morn shone, the Rukh rose off its egg and spreading its wings with a great cry flew up into the air dragging me with it; nor ceased it to soar and to tower till I thought it had reached the limit of the firmament; after which it descended, earthwards, little by little, till it lighted on the top of a high hill. As soon as I found myself on the hard ground, I made haste to unbind myself, quaking for fear of the bird, though it took no heed of me nor even felt me; and, loosing my turband from its feet, I made off with my best speed. Presently, I saw it catch up in its huge claws something from the earth and rise with it high in air, and observing it narrowly I saw it to be a serpent big of bulk and gigantic of girth, wherewith it flew away clean out of sight. I marvelled at this and faring forwards found myself on a peak overlooking a valley, exceeding great and wide and deep, and bounded by vast mountains that spired high in air: none could descry their summits, for the excess of their height, nor was any able to climb up thereto. When I saw this, I blamed myself for that which I had done and said, "Would Heaven I had tarried in the island! It was better than this wild desert; for there I had at least fruits to eat and water to drink, and here are neither trees nor fruits nor streams. But there is no Majesty and there is no Might save in Allah, the Glorious, the Great! Verily, as often as I am quit of one peril,

I fall into a worse danger and a more grievous." However, I took courage and walking along the Wady found that its soil was of diamond, the stone wherewith they pierce minerals and precious stones and porcelain and the onyx, for that it is a dense stone and a dure, whereon neither iron nor hardhead hath effect, neither can we cut off aught therefrom nor break it, save by means of leadstone. Moreover, the valley swarmed with snakes and vipers, each big as a palm tree, that would have made but one gulp of an elephant; and they came out by night, hiding during the day, lest the Rukhs and eagles pounce on them and tear them to pieces, as was their wont, why I wot not. And I repented of what I had done and said, "By Allah, I have made haste to bring destruction upon myself!" The day began to wane as I went along and I looked about for a place where I might pass the night, being in fear of the serpents; and I took no thought of meat and drink in my concern for my life. Presently, I caught sight of a cave nearhand, with a narrow doorway; so I entered and seeing a great stone close to the mouth, I rolled it up and stopped the entrance, saying to myself, "I am safe here for the night; and as soon as it is day, I will go forth and see what destiny will do." Then I looked within the cave and saw at the upper end a great serpent brooding on her eggs, at which my flesh quaked and my hair stood on end; but I raised my eyes to Heaven and, committing my case to fate and lot, abode all that night without sleep till daybreak, when I rolled back the stone from the mouth of the cave and went forth, staggering like a drunken man and giddy with watching and fear and hunger. As in this sore case I walked along the valley, behold, there fell down before me a slaughtered beast; but I saw no one, whereat I marvelled with great marvel and presently remembered a story I had heard aforetime of traders and pilgrims and travellers; how the mountains where are the diamonds are full of perils and terrors, nor can any fare through them; but the merchants who traffic in diamonds have a device by which they obtain them, that is to say, they take a sheep and slaughter and skin it and cut it in pieces and cast them down from the mountain-tops into the valley-sole, where the meat being fresh and sticky with blood, some of the gems cleave to it. There they leave it till mid-day, when the eagles and vultures swoop down upon it and carry it in their claws to the mountain-summits, whereupon the merchants come and shout at them and scare them away from the meat. Then they come and, taking the diamonds which they find sticking to it, go their ways with them and leave the meat to the birds and beasts; nor can any come at the diamonds but by this device. So, when I saw the slaughtered beast fall (he pursued) and bethought me of the story, I went up to it and filled my pockets and shawlgirdle and turband and the folds of my clothes with the choicest diamonds; and, as I was thus

engaged, down fell before me another great piece of meat. Then with
my unrolled turband and lying on my back, I set the bit on my breast
so that I was hidden by the meat, which was thus raised above the
ground. Hardly had I gripped it, when an eagle swooped down upon
the flesh and, seizing it with his talons, flew up with it high in air and
me clinging thereto, and ceased not its flight till it alighted on the head
of one of the mountains where, dropping the carcass he fell to rending
it; but, behold, there arose behind him a great noise of shouting and
clattering of wood, whereat the bird took fright and flew away. Then I
loosed off myself the meat, with clothes daubed with blood therefrom,
and stood up by its side; whereupon up came the merchant, who had
cried out at the eagle, and seeing me standing there, bespoke me not,
but was affrighted at me and shook with fear. However, he went up to
the carcass and turning it over, found no diamonds sticking to it,
whereat he gave a great cry and exclaimed, "Harrow, my disappointment! There is no Majesty and there is no Might save in Allah with
whom we seek refuge from Satan the stoned!" And he bemoaned himself and beat hand upon hand, saying, "Alas, the pity of it! How cometh
this?" Then I went up to him and he said to me, "Who art thou and
what causeth thee to come hither?" And I, "Fear not, I am a man and
a good man and a merchant. My story is wondrous and my adventures
marvellous and the manner of my coming hither is prodigious. So be
of good cheer, thou shalt receive of me what shall rejoice thee, for I
have with me great plenty of diamonds and I will give thee thereof what
shall suffice thee; for each is better than aught thou couldst get otherwise. So fear nothing." The man rejoiced thereat and thanked and
blessed me; then we talked together till the other merchants, hearing
me in discourse with their fellow, came up and saluted me; for each of
them had thrown down his piece of meat. And I went off with them
and told them my whole story, how I had suffered hardships at sea and
the fashion of my reaching the valley. But I gave the owner of the meat
a number of the stones I had by me, so they all wished me joy of my
escape, saying, "By Allah a new life hath been decreed to thee, for none
ever reached yonder valley and came off thence alive before thee; but
praised be Allah for thy safety!" We passed the night together in a safe
and pleasant place, beyond measure rejoiced at my deliverance from
the Valley of Serpents and my arrival in an inhabited land; and on the
morrow we set out and journeyed over the mighty range of mountains,
seeing many serpents in the valley, till we came to a fair great island,
wherein was a garden of huge camphor trees under each of which an
hundred men might take shelter. When the folk have a mind to get
camphor, they bore into the upper part of the bole with a long iron;
whereupon the liquid camphor, which is the sap of the tree, floweth

out and they catch it in vessels, where it concreteth like gum; but, after this, the tree dieth and becometh firewood. Moreover, there is in this island a kind of wild beast, called "Rhinoceros," that pastureth as do steers and buffaloes with us; but it is a huge brute, bigger of body than the camel and like it feedeth upon the leaves and twigs of trees. It is a remarkable animal with a great and thick horn, ten cubits long, amiddleward its head; wherein, when cleft in twain, is the likeness of a man. Voyagers and pilgrims and travellers declare that this beast called "Karkadan" will carry off a great elephant on its horn and graze about the island and the sea-coast therewith and take no heed of it, till the elephant dieth and its fat, melting in the sun, runneth down into the rhinoceros's eyes and blindeth him, so that he lieth down on the shore. Then comes the bird Rukh and carrieth off both the rhinoceros and that which is on its horn to feed its young withal. Moreover, I saw in this island many kinds of oxen and buffaloes, whose like are not found in our country. Here I sold some of the diamonds which I had by me for gold dinars and silver dirhams and bartered others for the produce of the country; and, loading them upon beasts of burden, fared on with the merchants from valley to valley and town to town, buying and selling and viewing foreign countries and the works and creatures of Allah, till we came to Bassorah-city, where we abode a few days, after which I continued my journey to Baghdad. I arrived at home with great store of diamonds and money and goods, and foregathered with my friends and relations and gave alms and largesse and bestowed curious gifts and made presents to all my friends and companions. Then I betook myself to eating well and drinking well and wearing fine clothes and making merry with my fellows, and forgot all my sufferings in the pleasures of return to the solace and delight of life, with light heart and broadened breast. And every one who heard of my return came and questioned me of my adventures and of foreign countries, and I related to them all that had befallen me, and the much I had suffered, whereat they wondered and gave me joy of my safe return. This, then, is the end of the story of my second voyage; and to-morrow, Inshallah! I will tell you what befel me in my third voyage. The company marvelled at his story and supped with him; after which he ordered an hundred dinars of gold to be given to the Porter, who took the sum with many thanks and blessings (which he stinted not even when he reached home) and went his way, wondering at what he had heard. Next morning as soon as day came in its sheen and shone, he rose and praying the dawn-prayer, repaired to the house of Sinbad the Seaman, even as he had bidden him, and went in and gave him good-morrow. The merchant welcomed him and made him sit with him, till the rest of the company arrived; and when they had well eaten and drunken and were merry with joy and jollity, their host began by saying: — Hearken, O my brothers, to what I am about to tell you; for it is even more wondrous than what you have already heard; but Allah alone kenneth what things His Omniscience concealed from man! And listen to

The Third Voyage of Sinbad the Seaman

As I told you yesterday, I returned from my second voyage overjoyed at my safety and with great increase of wealth, Allah having requited me all that I had wasted and lost, and I abode awhile in Baghdad-city savouring the utmost ease and prosperity and comfort and happiness, till the carnal man was once more seized with longing for travel and diversion and adventure, and yearned after traffic and lucre and emolument, for that the human heart is naturally prone to evil. So making up my mind I laid in great plenty of goods suitable for a sea-voyage and repairing to Bassorah, went down to the shore and found there a fine ship ready to sail, with a full crew and a numerous company of merchants, men of worth and substance, faith, piety and consideration. I embarked with them and we set sail on the blessing of Allah Almighty and on His aidance and His favour to bring our voyage to a safe and prosperous issue and already we congratulated one another on our good fortune and boon voyage. We fared on from sea to sea and from island to island and city to city, in all delight and contentment, buying and selling wherever we touched, and taking our solace and our pleasure, till one day when, as we sailed athwart the dashing sea, swollen with clashing billows, behold, the master (who stood on the gunwale examining the ocean in all directions) cried out with a great cry, and buffeted his face and pluckt out his beard and rent his raiment, and bade furl the sail and cast the anchors. So we said to him, "O Rais, what is the matter?" "Know, O my brethren (Allah preserve you!), that the wind hath gotten the better of us and hath driven us out of our course into mid-ocean, and destiny, for our ill luck, hath brought us to the Mountain of the Zughb, a hairy folk like apes, among whom no man ever fell and came forth alive; and my heart presageth that we all be dead men." Hardly had the master made an end of his speech when the apes were upon us. They surrounded the ship on all sides swarming like locusts and crowding the shore. They were the most frightful of wild creatures, covered with black hair like felt, foul of favour and small of stature, being but four spans high, yellow-eyed and blackfaced; none knoweth their language nor what they are, and they shun the company of men. We feared to slay them or strike them or drive them away, because of their inconceivable multitude; lest, if we hurt one, the rest fall on us and slay us, for numbers prevail over courage; so we let them do their will, albeit we feared they would plunder our goods and gear. They swarmed up the cables and gnawed them asunder, and on like wise they did with all the ropes of the ship, so that it fell off from the wind and stranded upon their mountainous coast. Then they laid hands on all the merchants and crew, and landing us on the island, made off with the ship and its cargo and went their ways, we wot not whither. We were thus left on the island, eating of its fruits and pot-herbs and drinking of its streams till, one day, we espied in its midst what seemed an inhabited house. So we made for it as fast as our feet could carry us and behold, it was a castle strong and tall, compassed about with a lofty wall, and having a two-leaved gate of ebony-wood both of which leaves open stood. We entered and found within a space wide and bare like a great square, round which stood many high doors open thrown, and at the farther end a long bench of stone and brasiers, with cooking gear hanging thereon and about it great plenty of bones; but we saw no one and marvelled thereat with exceeding wonder. Then we sat down in the courtyard a little while and presently falling asleep, slept from the forenoon till sundown, when lo! the earth trembled under our feet and the air rumbled with a terrible tone. Then there came down upon us, from the top of the castle, a huge creature in the likeness of a man, black of colour, tall and big of bulk, as he were a great date-tree, with eyes like coals of fire and eye-teeth like boar's tusks and a vast big gape like the mouth of a well. Moreover, he had long loose lips like camels', hanging down upon his breast, and ears like two Jarms falling over his shoulder-blades and the nails of his hands were like the claws of a lion. When we saw this frightful giant, we were like to faint and every moment increased our fear and terror; and we became as dead men for excess of horror and affright. And after tram- pling upon the earth, he sat awhile on the bench; then he arose and coming to us seized me by the arm, choosing me out from among my comrades the merchants. He took me up in his hand and turning me over felt me, as a butcher feeleth a sheep he is about to slaughter, and I but a little mouthful in his hands; but finding me lean and fleshless for stress of toil and trouble and weariness, let me go and took up another, whom in like manner he turned over and felt and let go; nor did he cease to feel and turn over the rest of us, one after another, till he came to the master of the ship. Now he was a sturdy, stout, broad- shouldered wight, fat and in full vigour; so he pleased the giant, who seized him, as a butcher seizeth a beast, and throwing him down, set his foot on his neck and brake it; after which he fetched a long spit and thrusting it up his backside, brought it forth of the crown of his head. Then, lighting a fierce fire, he set over it the spit with the Rais thereon, and turned it over the coals, till the flesh was roasted, when he took the

spit off the fire and set it like a Kabab-stick before him. Then he tare
the body, limb from limb, as one jointeth a chicken and, rending the
flesh with his nails, fell to eating of it and gnawing the bones, till there
was nothing left but some of these, which he threw on one side of the
wall. This done, he sat for a while; then he lay down on the stone-
bench and fell asleep, snarking and snoring like the gurgling of a lamb
or a cow with its throat cut; nor did he awake till morning, when he rose
and fared forth and went his ways. As soon as we were certified that he
was gone, we began to talk with one another, weeping and bemoaning
ourselves for the risk we ran, and saying, "Would Heaven we had been
drowned in the sea or that the apes had eaten us! That were better than
to be roasted over the coals; by Allah, this is a vile, foul death! But
whatso the Lord willeth must come to pass and there is no Majesty and
there is no Might, save in Him, the Glorious, the Great! We shall
assuredly perish miserably and none will know of us; as there is no
escape for us from this place." Then we arose and roamed about the
island, hoping that haply we might find a place to hide us in or a means
of flight, for indeed death was a light matter to us, provided we were not
roasted over the fire and eaten. However, we could find no hiding-
place and the evening overtook us; so, of the excess of our terror, we
returned to the castle and sat down awhile. Presently, the earth trembled under our feet and the black ogre came up to us and turning us
over, felt one after other, till he found a man to his liking, whom he
took and served as he had done the captain, killing and roasting and
eating him: after which he lay down on the bench and slept all night,
snarking and snoring like a beast with its throat cut, till daybreak, when
he arose and went out as before. Then we drew together and conversed
and said one to other, "By Allah, we had better throw ourselves into the
sea and be drowned than die roasted; for this is an abominable death!"
Quoth one of us, "Hear ye my words! let us cast about to kill him, and
be at peace from the grief of him and rid the Moslems of his barbarity
and tyranny." Then said I, "Hear me, O my brothers; if there is nothing for it but to slay him, let us carry some of this firewood and planks
down to the sea-shore and make us a boat wherein, if we succeed in
slaughtering him, we may either embark and let the waters carry us
whither Allah willeth, or else abide here till some ship pass, when we
will take passage in it. If we fail to kill him, we will embark in the boat
and put out to sea; and if we be drowned, we shall at least escape being
roasted over a kitchen fire with sliced weasands; whilst, if we escape, we
escape, and if we be drowned, we die martyrs." "By Allah," said they all,
"this rede is a right;" and we agreed upon this, and set about carrying it
out. So we haled down to the beach the pieces of wood which lay about
the bench; and, making a boat, moored it to the strand, after which we

stowed therein somewhat of victual and returned to the castle. As soon as evening fell the earth trembled under our feet and in came the blackamoor upon us, snarling like a dog about to bite. He came up to us and feeling us and turning us over one by one, took one of us and did with him as he had done before and ate him, after which he lay down on the bench and snored and snorted like thunder. As soon as we were assured that he slept, we arose and taking two iron spits of those standing there, heated them in the fiercest of the fire, till they were red-hot, like burning coals, when we gripped fast hold of them and going up to the giant, as he lay snoring on the bench, thrust them into his eyes and pressed upon them, all of us, with our united might, so that his eyeballs burst and he became stone blind. Thereupon he cried with a great cry, whereat our hearts trembled, and springing up from the bench, he fell a-groping after us, blind-fold. We fled from him right and left and he saw us not, for his sight was altogether blent; but we were in terrible fear of him and made sure we were dead men despairing of escape. Then he found the door, feeling for it with his hands and went out roaring aloud; and behold, the earth shook under us, for the noise of his roaring, and we quaked for fear. As he quitted the castle we followed him and betook ourselves to the place where we had moored our boat, saying to one another, "If this accursed abide absent till the going down of the sun and come not to the castle, we shall know that he is dead; and if he come back, we will embark in the boat and paddle till we escape, committing our affair to Allah." But, as we spoke, behold, up came the blackamoor with other two as they were Ghuls, fouler and more frightful than he, with eyes like red-hot coals; which when we saw, we hurried into the boat and casting off the moorings paddled away and pushed out to sea. As soon as the ogres caught sight of us, they cried out at us and running down to the sea-shore, fell a-pelting us with rocks, whereof some fell amongst us and others fell into the sea. We paddled with all our might till we were beyond their reach, but the most part of us were slain by the rock-throwing, and the winds and waves sported with us and carried us into the midst of the dashing sea, swollen with billows clashing. We knew not whither we went and my fellows died one after another, till there remained but three, myself and two others, for, as often as one died, we threw him into the sea. We were sore exhausted for stress and hunger, but we took courage and heartened one another and worked for dear life and paddled with main and might, till the winds cast us upon an island, as we were dead men for fatigue and fear and famine. We landed on the island and walked about it for a while, finding that it abounded in trees and streams and birds; and we ate of the fruits and rejoiced in our escape from the black and our deliverance from the perils of the sea; and thus we did till nightfall, when we lay down and fell asleep for excess of fatigue. But we had hardly closed our eyes before we were aroused by a hissing sound, like the sough of wind, and awakening, saw a serpent like a dragon, a seld-seen sight, of monstrous make and belly of enormous bulk which lay in a circle around us. Presently it reared its head and, seizing one of my companions, swallowed him up to his shoulders; then it gulped down the rest of him, and we heard his ribs crack in its belly. Presently it went its way, and we abode in sore amazement and grief for our comrade and mortal fear for ourselves, saying, "By Allah, this is a marvellous thing! Each kind of death that threateneth us is more terrible than the last. We were rejoicing in our escape from the black ogre and our deliverance from the perils of the sea; but now we have fallen into that which is worse. There is no Majesty and there is no Might save in Allah! By the Almighty, we have escaped from the blackamoor and from drowning: but how shall we escape from this abominable and viperish monster?" Then we walked about the island, eating of its fruits and drinking of its streams till dusk, when we climbed up into a high tree and went to sleep there, I being on the topmost bough. As soon as it was dark night, up came the serpent, looking right and left; and, making for the tree whereon we were, climbed up to my comrade and swallowed him down to his shoulders. Then it coiled about the bole with him, whilst I, who could not take my eyes off the sight, heard his bones crack in its belly, and it swallowed him whole, after which it slid down from the tree. When the day broke and the light showed me that the serpent was gone, I came down, as I were a dead man for stress of fear and anguish, and thought to cast myself into the sea and be at rest from the woes of the world; but could not bring myself to this, for verily life is dear. So I took five pieces of wood, broad and long, and bound one crosswise to the soles of my feet and others in like fashion on my right and left sides and over my breast; and the broadest and largest I bound across my head and made them fast with ropes. Then I lay down on the ground on my back, so that I was completely fenced in by the pieces of wood, which enclosed me like a bier. So as soon as it was dark, up came the serpent, as usual, and made towards me, but could not get at me to swallow me for the wood that fenced me in. So it wriggled round me on every side, whilst I looked on, like one dead by reason of my terror; and every now and then it would glide away and come back; but as often as it tried to come at me, it was hindered by the pieces of wood wherewith I had bound myself on every side. It ceased not to beset me thus from sundown till dawn, but when the light of day shone upon the beast it made off, in the utmost fury and extreme disappointment. Then I put out my hand and unbound myself, well-nigh down among the dead men for fear and suffering; and went down to the island-shore, whence a ship afar off in the midst of the waves suddenly struck my sight. So I tore off a great branch of a tree and made signs with it to the crew, shouting out the while; which when the ship's company saw they said to one another, "We must stand in and see what this is; peradventure 'tis a man." So they made for the island and presently heard my cries, whereupon they took me on board and questioned me of my case. I told them all my adventures from first to last, whereat they marvelled mightily and covered my shame with some of their clothes. Moreover, they set before me somewhat of food and I ate my fill and I drank cold sweet water and was mightily refreshed; and Allah Almighty quickened me after I was virtually dead. So I praised the Most Highest and thanked Him for His favours and exceeding mercies, and my heart revived in me after utter despair, till meseemed as if all I had suffered were but a dream I had dreamed. We sailed on with a fair wind the Almighty sent us till we came to an island, called Al-Salahitah, which aboundeth in sandal-wood when the captain cast anchor. And when we had cast anchor, the merchants and the sailors landed with their goods to sell and to buy. Then the captain turned to me and said, "Hark'ee, thou art a stranger and a pauper and tellest us that thou hast undergone frightful hardships; wherefore I have a mind to benefit thee with somewhat that may further thee to thy native land, so thou wilt ever bless me and pray for me." "So be it," answered I; "thou shalt have my prayers." Quoth he, "Know then that there was with us a man, a traveller, whom we lost, and we know not if he be alive or dead, for we had no news of him; so I purpose to commit his bales of goods to thy charge, that thou mayst sell them in this island. A part of the proceeds we will give thee as an equivalent for thy pains and service, and the rest we will keep till we return to Baghdad, where we will enquire for his family and deliver it to them, together with the unsold goods. Say me then, wilt thou undertake the charge and land and sell them as other merchants do?" I replied, "Hearkening and obedience to thee, O my lord; and great is thy kindness to me," and thanked him; whereupon he bade the sailors and porters bear the bales in question ashore and commit them to my charge. The ship's scribe asked him, "O master, what bales are these and what merchant's name shall I write upon them?"; and he answered, "Write on them the name of Sinbad the Seaman, him who was with us in the ship and whom we lost at the Rukh's island, and of whom we have no tidings; for we mean this stranger to sell them; and we will give him a part of the price for his pains and keep the rest till we return to Baghdad where, if we find the owner we will make it over to him, and if not, to his family." And the clerk said, "Thy words are apposite and thy rede is right." Now when I heard the captain give orders for the bales to be inscribed with my name, I said to myself, "By

Allah, I am Sinbad the Seaman!" So I armed myself with courage and
patience and waited till all the merchants had landed and were gathered together, talking and chaffering about buying and selling; then I
went up to the captain and asked him, "O my lord, knowest thou what
manner of man was this Sinbad, whose goods thou hast committed to
me for sale?"; and he answered, "I know of him naught save that he was
a man from Baghdad-city, Sinbad hight the Seaman, who was drowned
with many others when we lay anchored at such an island and I have
heard nothing of him since then." At this I cried out with a great cry
and said, "O captain, whom Allah keep! know that I am that Sinbad the
Seaman and that I was not drowned, but when thou castest anchor at
the island, I landed with the rest of the merchants and crew; and I sat
down in a pleasant place by myself and ate somewhat of food I had with
me and enjoyed myself till I became drowsy and was drowned in sleep;
and when I awoke, I found no ship and none near me. These goods are
my goods and these bales are my bales; and all the merchants who
fetch jewels from the Valley of Diamonds saw me there and will bear
me witness that I am the very Sinbad the Seaman; for I related to them
everything that had befallen me and told them how you forgot me and
left me sleeping on the island, and that betided me which betided me."
When the passengers and crew heard my words, they gathered about
me and some of them believed me and others disbelieved; but
presently, behold, one of the merchants, hearing me mention the
Valley of the Diamonds, came up to me and said to them, "Hear what
I say, good people! When I related to you the most wonderful thing in
my travels, and I told you that, at the time we cast down our slaughtered
animals into the Valley of Serpents (I casting with the rest as was my
wont), there came up a man hanging to mine, ye believed me not and
gave me the lie." "Yes," quoth they, "thou didst tell us some such tale,
but we had no call to credit thee." He resumed, "Now this is the very
man, by token that he gave me diamonds of great value, and high price
whose like are not to be found, requiting me more than would have
come up sticking to my quarter of meat; and I companied with him to
Bassorah-city, where he took leave of us and went on to his native stead,
whilst we returned to our own land. This is he; and he told us his name,
Sinbad the Seaman, and how the ship left him on the desert island.
And know ye that Allah hath sent him hither, so might the truth of my
story be made manifest to you. Moreover, these are his goods for, when
he first foregathered with us, he told us of them; and the truth of his
words is patent." Hearing the merchant's speech the captain came up
to me and considered me straitly awhile, after which he said, "What
was the mark on thy bales?" "Thus and thus," answered I, and
reminded him of somewhat that had passed between him and me,

when I shipped with him from Bassorah. Thereupon he was convinced that I was indeed Sinbad the Seaman and took me round the neck and gave me joy of my safety, saying, "By Allah, O my lord, thy case is indeed wondrous and thy tale marvellous; but lauded be Allah who hath brought thee and me together again, and who hath restored to thee thy goods and gear!" Then I disposed of my merchandise to the best of my skill, and profited largely on them whereat I rejoiced with exceeding joy and congratulated myself on my safety and the recovery of my goods. We ceased not to buy and sell at the several islands till we came to the land of Hind, where we bought cloves and ginger and all manner spices; and thence we fared on to the land of Sind, where also we bought and sold. In these Indian seas, I saw wonders without number or count, amongst others a fish like a cow which bringeth forth its young and suckleth them like human beings; and of its skin bucklers are made. There were eke fishes like asses and camels and tortoises twenty cubits wide. And I saw also a bird that cometh out of a sea-shell and layeth eggs and hatcheth her chicks on the surface of the water, never coming up from the sea to the land. Then we set sail again with a fair wind and the blessing of Almighty Allah; and, after a prosperous voyage, arrived safe and sound at Bassorah. Here I abode a few days and presently returned to Baghdad where I went at once to my quarter and my house and saluted my family and familiars and friends. I had gained on this voyage what was beyond count and reckoning, so I gave alms and largesse and clad the widow and the orphan, by way of thanksgiving for my happy return, and fell to feasting and making merry with my companions and intimates and forgot, while eating well and drinking well and dressing well, everything that had befallen me and all the perils and hardships I had suffered. These, then, are the most admirable things I sighted on my third voyage, and tomorrow, an it be the will of Allah, you shall come to me and I will relate the adventures of my fourth voyage, which is still more wonderful than those you have already heard. (Saith he who telleth the tale), Then Sinbad the Seaman bade give Sinbad the Landsman an hundred golden dinars as of wont and called for food. So they spread the tables and the company ate the night-meal and went their ways, marvelling at the tale they had heard. The Porter after taking his gold passed the night in his own house, also wondering at what his namesake the Seaman had told him, and as soon as day broke and the morning showed with its sheen and shone, he rose and praying the dawn-prayer betook himself to Sinbad the Seaman, who returned his salute and received him with an open breast and cheerful favour and made him sit with him till the rest of the company arrived, when he caused to be set on food and they ate and drank and made merry. Then Sinbad bespake them and related to them the narrative of

The Fourth Voyage of Sinbad the Seaman

Know, O my brethren that after my return from my third voyage and foregathering with my friends, and forgetting all my perils and hardships in the enjoyment of ease and comfort and repose, I was visited one day by a company of merchants who sat down with me and talked of foreign travel and traffic, till the old bad man within me yearned to go with them and enjoy the sight of strange countries, and I longed for the society of the various races of mankind and for traffic and profit. So I resolved to travel with them and buying the necessaries for a long voyage, and great store of costly goods, more than ever before, transported them from Baghdad to Bassorah where I took ship with the merchants in question, who were of the chief of the town. We set out, trusting in the blessing of Almighty Allah; and with a favouring breeze and the best conditions we sailed from island to island and sea to sea, till one day, there arose against us a contrary wind and the captain cast out his anchors and brought the ship to a standstill, fearing lest she should founder in mid-ocean. Then we all fell to prayer and humbling ourselves before the Most High; but, as we were thus engaged there smote us a furious squall which tore the sails to rags and tatters: the anchor-cable parted and, the ship foundering, we were cast into the sea, goods and all. I kept myself afloat by swimming half the day, till, when I had given myself up for lost, the Almighty threw in my way one of the planks of the ship, whereon I and some others of the merchants scrambled, and, mounting it as we would a horse, paddled with our feet in the sea. We abode thus a day and a night, the wind and waves helping us on, and on the second day shortly before the midtime between sunrise and noon the breeze freshened and the sea wrought and the rising waves cast us upon an island, well-nigh dead bodies for weariness and want of sleep, cold and hunger and fear and thirst. We walked about the shore and found abundance of herbs, whereof we ate enough to keep breath in body and to stay our failing spirits, then lay down and slept till morning hard by the sea. And when morning came with its sheen and shone, we arose and walked about the island to the right and left, till we came in sight of an inhabited house afar off. So we made towards it, and ceased not walking till we reached the door thereof when lo! a number of naked men issued from it and without saluting us or a word said, laid hold of us masterfully and carried us to their king, who signed us to sit. So we sat down and they set food before us such as we knew not and whose like we had never seen in all our lives. My companions ate of it, for stress of hunger, but my stomach revolted from it and I would not eat; and my refraining from it was, by Allah's favour, the cause of my being alive till now: for no sooner had my comrades tasted of it than their reason fled and their condition changed and they began to devour it like madmen possessed of an evil spirit. Then the savages gave them to drink of cocoa-nut oil and anointed them therewith; and straightway after drinking thereof, their eyes turned into their heads and they fell to eating greedily, against their wont. When I saw this, I was confounded and concerned for them, nor was I less anxious about myself, for fear of the naked folk. So I watched them narrowly, and it was not long before I discovered them to be a tribe of Magian cannibals whose King was a Ghul. All who came to their country or whoso they caught in their valleys or on their roads they brought to this King and fed them upon that food and anointed them with that oil, whereupon their stomachs dilated that they might eat largely, whilst their reason fled and they lost the power of thought and became idiots. Then they stuffed them with cocoa-nut oil and the aforesaid food, till they became fat and gross, when they slaughtered them by cutting their throats and roasted them for the King's eating; but, as for the savages themselves, they ate human flesh raw. When I saw this, I was sore dismayed for myself and my comrades, who were now become so stupefied that they knew not what was done with them and the naked folk committed them to one who used every day to lead them out and pasture them on the island like cattle. And they wandered amongst the trees and rested at will, thus waxing very fat. As for me, I wasted away and became sickly for fear and hunger and my flesh shrivelled on my bones; which when the savages saw, they left me alone and took no thought of me and so far forgot me that one day I gave them the slip and walking out of their place made for the beach which was distant and there espied a very old man seated on a high place, girt by the waters. I looked at him and knew him for the herdsman, who had charge of pasturing my fellows, and with him were many others in like case. As soon as he saw me, he knew me to be in possession of my reason and not afflicted like the rest whom he was pasturing; so signed to me from afar, as who should say, "Turn back and take the right-hand road, for that will lead thee into the King's highway." So I turned back, as he bade me, and followed the right-hand road, now running for fear and then walking leisurely to rest me, till I was out of the old man's sight. By this time, the sun had gone down and the darkness set in; so I sat down to rest and would have slept, but sleep came not to me that night, for stress of fear and famine and fatigue. When the night was half spent, I rose and walked on, till the day broke in all its beauty and the sun rose over the heads of the lofty hills and athwart the low gravelly plains. Now I was weary and hungry and thirsty; so I ate my fill of herbs and grasses that grew in the island and kept life in body and stayed my stomach, after which I set out again and fared on all that day and the next night, staying my greed with roots and herbs; nor did I cease walking for seven days and their nights, till the morn of the eighth day, when I caught sight of a faint object in the distance. So I made towards it, though my heart quaked for all I had suffered first and last, and behold it was a company of men gathering pepper-grains. As soon as they saw me, they hastened up to me and surrounding me on all sides, said to me, "Who art thou and whence come?" I replied, "Know, O folk, that I am a poor stranger," and acquainted them with my case and all the hardships and perils I had suffered, whereat they marvelled and gave me joy of my safety, saying, "By Allah, this is wonderful! But how didst thou escape from these blacks who swarm in the island and devour all who fall in with them; nor is any safe from them, nor can any get out of their clutches?" And after I had told them the fate of my companions, they made me sit by them, till they got quit of their work; and fetched me somewhat of good food, which I ate, for I was hungry, and rested awhile, after which they took ship with me and carrying me to their island-home brought me before the King, who returned my salute and received me honourably and questioned me of my case. I told him all that had befallen me, from the day of my leaving Baghdad-city, whereupon he wondered with great wonder at my adventures, he and his courtiers, and bade me sit by him; then he called for food and I ate with him what sufficed me and washed my hands and returned thanks to Almighty Allah for all His favours praising Him and glorifying Him. Then I left the King and walked for solace about the city, which I found wealthy and populous, abounding in market-streets well stocked with food and merchandise and full of buyers and sellers. So I rejoiced at having reached so pleasant a place and took my ease there after my fatigues; and I made friends with the townsfolk, nor was it long before I became more in honour and favour with them and their King than any of the chief men of the realm. Now I saw that all the citizens, great and small, rode fine horses, high-priced and thoroughbred, without saddles or housings, whereat I wondered and said to the King, "Wherefore, O my lord, dost thou not ride with a saddle? Therein is ease for the rider and increase of power." "What is a saddle?" asked he: "I never saw nor used such a thing in all my life;" and I answered, "With thy permission I will make thee a saddle, that thou mayst ride on it and see the comfort thereof." And quoth he, "Do so." So quoth I to him, "Furnish me with some wood," which being brought, I sought me a clever carpenter and sitting by him showed him how to make the saddle-tree, portraying for him the fashion thereof in ink on the wood. Then I took wool and teased it and made felt of it, and, covering the saddle-tree with leather, stuffed it and polished it and attached the girth and stirrup leathers; after which I fetched a blacksmith and described to him the fashion of the stirrups and bridle-bit. So he forged a fine pair of stirrups and a bit, and filed them smooth and tinned them. Moreover, I made fast to them fringes of silk and fitted bridle-leathers to the bit. Then I fetched one of the best of the royal horses and saddling and bridling him, hung the stirrups to the saddle and led him to the King. The thing took his fancy and he thanked me; then he mounted and rejoiced greatly in the saddle and rewarded me handsomely for my work. When the King's Wazir saw the saddle, he asked of me one like it and I made it for him. Furthermore, all the grandees and officers of state came for saddles to me; so I fell to making saddles (having taught the craft to the carpenter and blacksmith), and selling them to all who sought, till I amassed great wealth and became in high honour and great favour with the King and his household and grandees. I abode thus till, one day, as I was sitting with the King in all respect and contentment, he said to me, "Know thou, O such an one, thou art become one of us, dear as a brother, and we hold thee in such regard and affection that we cannot part with thee nor suffer thee to leave our city; wherefore I desire of thee obedience in a certain matter, and I will not have thee gainsay me." Answered I, "O King, what is it thou desirest of me? Far be it from me to gainsay thee in aught, for I am indebted to thee for many favours and bounties and much kindness, and (praised be Allah!) I am become one of thy servants." Quoth he, "I have a mind to marry thee to a fair, clever and agreeable wife who is wealthy as she is beautiful; so thou mayst be naturalised and domiciled with us: I will lodge thee with me in my palace; wherefore oppose me not neither cross me in this." When I heard these words I was ashamed and held my peace nor could make him any answer, by reason of my much bashfulness before him. Asked he, "Why dost thou not reply to me, O my son?"; and I answered, saying, "O my master, it is thine to command, O king of the age!" So he summoned the Kazi and the witnesses and married me straightway to a lady of a noble tree and high pedigree; wealthy in moneys and means; the flower of an ancient race; of surpassing beauty and grace, and the owner of farms and estates and many a dwelling-place. Now after the King my master had married me to this choice wife, he also gave me a great and goodly house standing alone, together with slaves and officers, and assigned me pay and allowances. So I became in all ease and contentment and delight and forgot everything which had befallen me of weariness and trouble and hardship; for I loved my wife with fondest love and she

loved me no less, and we were as one and abode in the utmost comfort
of life and in its happiness. And I said in myself, "When I return to my
native land, I will carry her with me." But whatso is predestined to a
man, that needs must be, and none knoweth what shall befal him. We
lived thus a great while, till Almighty Allah bereft one of my neighbours
of his wife. Now he was a gossip of mine; so hearing the cry of the keen-
ers I went in to condole him on his loss and found him in very ill
plight, full of trouble and weary of soul and mind. I condoled with him
and comforted him, saying, "Mourn not for thy wife who hath now
found the mercy of Allah; the Lord will surely give thee a better in her
stead and thy name shall be great and thy life shall be long in the land,
Inshallah!" But he wept bitter tears and replied, "O my friend, how can
I marry another wife and how shall Allah replace her to me with a better than she, whenas I have but one day left to live?" "O my brother,"
said I, "return to thy senses and announce not the glad tidings of thine
own death, for thou art well, sound and in good case." "By thy life, O
my friend," rejoined he, "to-morrow thou wilt lose me and wilt never
see me again till the Day of Resurrection." I asked, "How so?" and he
answered, "This very day they bury my wife, and they bury me with her
in one tomb; for it is the custom with us, if the wife die first, to bury the
husband alive with her and in like manner the wife, if the husband die
first; so that neither may enjoy life after losing his or her mate." "By
Allah," cried I, "this is a most vile, lewd custom and not to be endured
of any!" Meanwhile, behold, the most part of the townsfolk came in
and fell to condoling with my gossip for his wife and for himself.
Presently they laid the dead woman out, as was their wont; and, setting
her on a bier, carried her and her husband without the city, till they
came to a place in the side of a mountain at the end of the island by
the sea; and here they raised a great rock and discovered the mouth of
a stone-rivetted pit or well, leading down into a vast underground cavern that ran beneath the mountain. Into this pit they threw the corpse,
then tying a rope of palm-fibres under the husband's armpits, they let
him down into the cavern, and with him a great pitcher of fresh water
and seven scones by way of viaticum. When he came to the bottom, he
loosed himself from the rope and they drew it up; and, stopping the
mouth of the pit with the great stone, they returned to the city, leaving
my friend in the cavern with his dead wife. When I saw this, I said to
myself, "By Allah, this fashion of death is more grievous than the first!"
And I went in to the King and said to him, "O my lord, why do ye bury
the quick with the dead?" Quoth he, "It hath been the custom, thou
must know, of our forebears and our olden Kings from time immemo-
rial, if the husband die first, to bury his wife with him, and the like with
the wife, so we may not sever them, alive or dead." I asked, "O King of

the age, if the wife of a foreigner like myself die among you, deal ye
with him as with yonder man?"; and he answered, "Assuredly, we do
with him even as thou hast seen." When I heard this, my gall-bladder
was like to burst, for the violence of my dismay and concern for myself:
my wit became dazed; I felt as if in a vile dungeon; and hated their society; for I went about in fear lest my wife should die before me and they
bury me alive with her. However, after a while, I comforted myself, saying, "Haply I shall predecease her, or shall have returned to my own
land before she die, for none knoweth which shall go first and which
shall go last." Then I applied myself to diverting my mind from this
thought with various occupations; but it was not long before my wife
sickened and complained and took to her pillow and fared after a few
days to the mercy of Allah; and the King and the rest of the folk came,
as was their wont, to condole with me and her family and to console us
for her loss and not less to condole with me for myself. Then the
women washed her and arraying her in her richest raiment and golden
ornaments, necklaces and jewellery, laid her on the bier and bore her
to the mountain aforesaid, where they lifted the cover of the pit and
cast her in; after which all my intimates and acquaintances and my
wife's kith and kin came round me, to farewell me in my lifetime and
console me for my own death, whilst I cried out among them, saying,
"Almighty Allah never made it lawful to bury the quick with the dead!
I am a stranger, not one of your kind; and I cannot abear your custom,
and had I known it I never would have wedded among you!" They
heard me not and paid no heed to my words, but laying hold of me,
bound me by force and let me down into the cavern, with a large gugglet of sweet water and seven cakes of bread, according to their custom.
When I came to the bottom, they called out to me to cast myself loose
from the cords, but I refused to do so; so they threw them down on me
and, closing the mouth of the pit with the stones aforesaid, went their
ways. I looked about me and found myself in a vast cave full of dead
bodies, that exhaled a fulsome and loathsome smell and the air was
heavy with the groans of the dying. Thereupon I fell to blaming myself
for what I had done, saying, "By Allah, I deserve all that hath befallen
me and all that shall befall me! What curse was upon me to take a wife
in this city? There is no Majesty and there is no Might save in Allah,
the Glorious, the Great! As often as I say, I have escaped from one
calamity, I fall into a worse. By Allah, this is an abominable death to
die! Would Heaven I had died a decent death and been washed and
shrouded like a man and a Moslem. Would I had been drowned at sea
or perished in the mountains! It were better than to die this miserable
death!" And on such wise I kept blaming my own folly and greed of
gain in that black hole, knowing not night from day; and I ceased not

to ban the Foul Fiend and to bless the Almighty Friend. Then I threw myself down on the bones of the dead and lay there, imploring Allah's help and in the violence of my despair, invoking death which came not to me, till the fire of hunger burned my stomach and thirst set my throat aflame when I sat up and feeling for the bread, ate a morsel and upon it swallowed a mouthful of water. After this, the worst night I ever knew, I arose, and exploring the cavern, found that it extended a long way with hollows in its sides; and its floor was strewn with dead bodies and rotten bones, that had lain there from olden time. So I made myself a place in a cavity of the cavern, afar from the corpses lately thrown down and there slept. I abode thus a long while, till my provision was like to give out; and yet I ate not save once every day or second day; nor did I drink more than an occasional draught, for fear my victual should fail me before my death; and I said to myself, "Eat little and drink little; belike the Lord shall vouchsafe deliverance to thee!" One day, as I sat thus, pondering my case and bethinking me how I should do, when my bread and water should be exhausted, behold, the stone that covered the opening was suddenly rolled away and the light streamed down upon me; Quoth I, "I wonder what is the matter: haply they have brought another corpse." Then I espied folk standing about the mouth of the pit, who presently let down a dead man and a live woman, weeping and bemoaning herself, and with her an ampler supply of bread and water than usual. I saw her and she was a beautiful woman; but she saw me not; and they closed up the opening and went away. Then I took the leg-bone of a dead man and, going up to the woman, smote her on the crown of the head; and she cried one cry and fell down in a swoon. I smote her a second and a third time, till she was dead, when I laid hands on her bread and water and found on her great plenty of ornaments and rich apparel, necklaces, jewels and gold trinkets;[1] for it was their custom to bury women in all their finery. I carried the vivers to my sleeping place in the cavern-side and ate and drank of them sparingly, no more than sufficed to keep the life in me, lest the provaunt come speedily to an end and I perish of hunger and thirst. Yet did I never wholly lose hope in Almighty Allah. I abode thus a great while, killing all the live folk they let down into the cavern and taking their provisions of meat and drink; till one day, as I slept, I was awakened by something scratching and burrowing among the bodies in a corner of the cave and said, "What can this be?" fearing wolves or hyænas. So I sprang up and seizing the leg-bone aforesaid, made for the

---

[1] The confession is made with true Eastern sang-froid and probably none of the hearers "disapproved" of the murders which saved the speaker's life.

noise. As soon as the thing was ware of me, it fled from me into the
inward of the cavern, and lo! it was a wild beast. However, I followed it
to the further end, till I saw afar off a point of light not bigger than a
star, now appearing and then disappearing. So I made for it, and as I
drew near, it grew larger and brighter, till I was certified that it was a
crevice in the rock, leading to the open country; and I said to myself,
"There must be some reason for this opening: either it is the mouth of
a second pit, such as that by which they let me down, or else it is a natural fissure in the stonery." So I bethought me awhile and nearing the
light, found that it came from a breach in the back side of the mountain, which the wild beasts had enlarged by burrowing, that they might
enter and devour the dead and freely go to and fro. When I saw this,
my spirits revived and hope came back to me and I made sure of life,
after having died a death. So I went on, as in a dream, and making shift
to scramble through the breach found myself on the slope of a high
mountain, overlooking the salt sea and cutting off all access thereto
from the island, so that none could come at that part of the beach from
the city. I praised my Lord and thanked Him, rejoicing greatly and
heartening myself with the prospect of deliverance; then I returned
through the crack to the cavern and brought out all the food and water
I had saved up and donned some of the dead folk's clothes over my
own; after which I gathered together all the collars and necklaces of
pearls and jewels and trinkets of gold and silver set with precious stones
and other ornaments and valuables I could find upon the corpses; and,
making them into bundles with the grave clothes and raiment of the
dead, carried them out to the back of the mountain facing the sea-
shore, where I established myself, purposing to wait there till it should
please Almighty Allah to send me relief by means of some passing ship.
I visited the cavern daily and as often as I found folk buried alive there,
I killed them all indifferently, men and women, and took their victual
and valuables and transported them to my seat on the sea-shore. Thus
I abode a long while till one day I caught sight of a ship passing in the
midst of the clashing sea, swollen with dashing billows. So I took a
piece of a white shroud I had with me and, tying it to a staff, ran along
the sea-shore, making signals therewith and calling to the people in the
ship, till they espied me and hearing my shouts, sent a boat to fetch me
off. When it drew near, the crew called out to me, saying, "Who art
thou and how camest thou to be on this mountain, whereon never saw
we any in our born days?" I answered, "I am a gentleman and a merchant, who hath been wrecked and saved myself on one of the planks
of the ship, with some of my goods; and by the blessing of the Almighty
and the decrees of Destiny and my own strength and skill, after much
toil and moil I have landed with my gear in this place where I awaited

some passing ship to take me off." So they took me in their boat
together with the bundles I had made of the jewels and valuables from
the cavern, tied up in clothes and shrouds, and rowed back with me to
the ship, where the captain said to me, "How camest thou, O man, to
yonder place on yonder mountain behind which lieth a great city? All
my life I have sailed these seas and passed to and fro hard by these
heights; yet never saw I here any living thing save wild beasts and
birds." I repeated to him the story I had told the sailors, but acquainted
him with nothing of that which had befallen me in the city and the cavern, lest there should be any of the islandry in the ship. Then I took out
some of the best pearls I had with me and offered them to the captain,
saying, "O my lord, thou hast been the means of saving me off this
mountain. I have no ready money; but take this from me in requital of
thy kindness and good offices." But he refused to accept it of me, saying, "When we find a shipwrecked man on the seashore or an island,
we take him up and give him meat and drink, and if he be naked we
clothe him; nor take we aught from him; nay, when we reach a port of
safety, we set him ashore with a present of our own money and entreat
him kindly and charitably, for the love of Allah the Most High." So I
prayed that his life be long in the land and rejoiced in my escape, trusting to be delivered from my stress and to forget my past mishaps; for
every time I remembered being let down into the cave with my dead
wife I shuddered in horror. Then we pursued our voyage and sailed
from island to island and sea to sea, till we arrived at the Island of the
Bell, which containeth a city two days' journey in extent whence after
a six days' run we reached the Island Kala, hard by the land of Hind.
This place is governed by a potent and puissant King and it produceth
excellent camphor and an abundance of the Indian rattan: here also is
a lead mine. At last by the decree of Allah, we arrived in safety at
Bassorah-town where I tarried a few days, then went on to Baghdad-
city, and, finding my quarter, entered my house with lively pleasure.
There I foregathered with my family and friends, who rejoiced in my
happy return and gave me joy of my safety. I laid up in my storehouses
all the goods I had brought with me, and gave alms and largesse to
Fakirs and beggars and clothed the widow and the orphan. Then I gave
myself up to pleasure and enjoyment, returning to my old merry mode
of life. Such, then, be the most marvellous adventures of my fourth voyage, but to-morrow if you will kindly come to me, I will tell you that
which befel me in my fifth voyage, which was yet rarer and more marvellous than those which forewent it. And thou, O my brother Sinbad
the Landsman, shalt sup with me as thou art wont. (Saith he who telleth the tale), When Sinbad the Seaman had made an end of his story,
he called for supper; so they spread the table and the guests ate the

evening meal; after which he gave the Porter an hundred dinars as usual, and he and the rest of the company went their ways, glad at heart and marvelling at the tales they had heard, for that each story was more extraordinary than that which forewent it. The porter Sinbad passed the night in his own house, in all joy and cheer and wonderment; and, as soon as morning came with its sheen and shone, he prayed the dawn-prayer and repaired to the house of Sinbad the Seaman, who welcomed him and bade him sit with him till the rest of the company arrived, when they ate and drank and made merry and the talk went round amongst them. Presently, their host began the narrative of

The Fifth Voyage of Sinbad the Seaman

Know, O my brothers, that when I had been awhile on shore after my fourth voyage; and when, in my comfort and pleasures and merry-makings and in my rejoicing over my large gains and profits, I had forgotten all I had endured of perils and sufferings, the carnal man was again seized with the longing to travel and to see foreign countries and islands. Accordingly I bought costly merchandise suited to my purpose and, making it up into bales, repaired to Bassorah, where I walked about the river-quay till I found a fine tall ship, newly builded with gear unused and fitted ready for sea. She pleased me; so I bought her and, embarking my goods in her, hired a master and crew, over whom I set certain of my slaves and servants as inspectors. A number of merchants also brought their outfits and paid me freight and passage-money; then, after reciting the Fatihah we set sail over Allah's pool in all joy and cheer, promising ourselves a prosperous voyage and much profit. We sailed from city to city and from island to island and from sea to sea viewing the cities and countries by which we passed, and selling and buying in not a few till one day we came to a great uninhabited island, deserted and desolate, whereon was a white dome of biggest bulk half buried in the sands. The merchants landed to examine this dome, leaving me in the ship; and when they drew near, behold, it was a huge Rukh's egg. They fell a-beating it with stones, knowing not what it was, and presently broke it open, whereupon much water ran out of it and the young Rukh appeared within. So they pulled it forth of the shell and cut its throat and took of it great store of meat. Now I was in the ship and knew not what they did; but presently one of the passengers came up to me and said, "O my lord, come and look at the egg that we thought to be a dome." So I looked and seeing the merchants beating it with stones, called out to them, "Stop, stop! do not meddle with that egg, or the bird Rukh will come out and break our ship and destroy us." But they paid no heed to me and gave not over smiting upon the egg, when behold, the day grew dark and dun and the sun was hidden from us, as if some great cloud had passed over the firmament. So we raised our eyes and saw that what we took for a cloud was the Rukh poised between us and the sun, and it was his wings that darkened the day. When he came and saw his egg broken, he cried a loud cry, whereupon his mate came flying up and they both began circling about the ship crying out at us with voices louder than thunder. I called to the Rais and crew, "Put out to sea and seek safety in flight, before we be all destroyed." So the merchants came on board and we cast off and made haste from the island to gain the open sea. When the Rukhs saw this, they flew off and we crowded all sail on the ship, thinking to get out of their country; but presently the two re-appeared and flew after us and stood over us, each carrying in its claws a huge boulder which it had brought from the mountains. As soon as the he-Rukh came up with us, he let fall upon us the rock he held in his pounces; but the master put about ship, so that the rock missed her by some small matter and plunged into the waves with such violence, that the ship pitched high and then sank into the trough of the sea and the bottom of the ocean appeared to us. Then the she-Rukh let fall her rock, which was bigger than that of her mate, and as Destiny had decreed, it fell on the poop of the ship and crushed it, the rudder flying into twenty pieces; whereupon the vessel foundered and all and everything on board were cast into the main. As for me I struggled for sweet life, till Almighty Allah threw in my way one of the planks of the ship, to which I clung and bestriding it, fell a-paddling with my feet. Now the ship had gone down hard by an island in the midst of the main and the winds and waves bore me on till, by permission of the Most High, they cast me up on the shore of the island, at the last gasp for toil and distress and half dead with hunger and thirst. So I landed more like a corpse than a live man and throwing myself down on the beach, lay there awhile, till I began to revive and recover spirits, when I walked about the island and found it as it were one of the garths and gardens of Paradise. Its trees, in abundance dight, bore ripe-yellow fruit for freight; its streams ran clear and bright; its flowers were fair to scent and to sight and its birds warbled with delight the praises of Him to whom belong permanence and all-might. So I ate my fill of the fruits and slaked my thirst with the water of the streams till I could no more and I returned thanks to the Most High and glorified Him; after which I sat till nightfall, hearing no voice and seeing none inhabitant. Then I lay down, well-nigh dead for travail and trouble and terror, and slept without surcease till morning, when I arose and walked about under the trees, till I came to the channel of a draw-well fed by a spring of running water, by which well sat an old man of venerable aspect, girt about with a waist-cloth made of the fibre of palm-fronds. Quoth I to myself, "Haply this Shaykh is of those who were wrecked in the ship and hath made his way to the island." So I drew near to him and saluted him, and he returned my salam by signs, but spoke not; and I said to him, "O nuncle mine, what causeth thee to sit here?" He shook his head and moaned and signed to me with his hand as who should say, "Take me on thy shoulders and carry me to the other side of the well-channel." And quoth I in my mind, "I will deal kindly with him and do what he desireth; it may be I shall win me a reward in Heaven for he may be a paralytic." So I took him on my back and carrying him to the place whereat he pointed, said to him, "Dismount at thy leisure." But he would not get off my back and wound his legs about my neck. I looked at them and seeing that they were like a buffalo's hide for blackness and roughness, was affrighted and would have cast him off; but he clung to me and gripped my neck with his legs, till I was well-nigh choked, the world grew black in my sight and I fell senseless to the ground like one dead. But he still kept his seat and raising his legs drummed with his heels and beat harder than palm-rods my back and shoulders, till he forced me to rise for excess of pain. Then he signed to me with his hand to carry him hither and thither among the trees which bore the best fruits; and if ever I refused to do his bidding or loitered or took my leisure he beat me with his feet more grievously than if I had been beaten with whips. He ceased not to signal with his hand wherever he was minded to go; so I carried him about the island, like a captive slave, and he dismounted not night or day; and whenas he wished to sleep he wound his legs about my neck and leaned back and slept awhile, then arose and beat me; whereupon I sprang up in haste, unable to gainsay him because of the pain he inflicted on me. And indeed I blamed myself and sore repented me of having taken compassion on him and continued in this condition, suffering fatigue not to be described, till I said to myself, "I wrought him a weal and he requited me with my ill; by Allah, never more will I do any man a service so long as I live!" And again and again I besought the Most High that I might die, for stress of weariness and misery; and thus I abode a long while till, one day, I came with him to a place wherein was abundance of gourds, many of them dry. So I took a great dry gourd and, cutting open the head, scooped out the inside and cleaned it; after which I gathered grapes from a vine which grew hard by and squeezed them into the gourd, till it was full of the juice. Then I stopped up the mouth and set it in the sun, where I left it for some days, until it became strong wine; and every day I used to drink of it, to comfort and sustain me under my fatigues with that froward and obstinate fiend; and as often as I drank myself drunk, I forgot my troubles and took new heart. One day he saw me drinking and signed to me with his hand, as who should say, "What is that?" Quoth I, "It is an excellent cordial, which cheereth the heart and reviveth the spirits." Then, being heated with wine, I ran and danced with him among the trees, clapping my hands and singing and making merry; and I staggered under him by design. When he saw this, he signed to me to give him the gourd that he might drink, and I feared him and gave it him. So he took it and, draining it to the dregs, cast it on the ground, whereupon he grew frolicsome and began to clap his hands and jig to and fro on my shoulders and he made water upon me so copiously that all my dress was drenched. But presently the fumes of the wine rising to his head, he became helplessly drunk and his side-muscles and limbs relaxed and he swayed to and fro on my back. When I saw that he had lost his senses for drunkenness, I put my hand to his legs and, loosing them from my neck, stooped down well-nigh to the ground and threw him at full length. Then I took up a great stone from among the trees and coming up to him smote him therewith on the head with all my might and crushed in his skull as he lay dead drunk. Thereupon his flesh and fat and blood being in a pulp, he died and went to his deserts, The Fire, no mercy of Allah be upon him! I then returned, with a heart at ease, to my former station on the sea-shore and abode in that island many days, eating of its fruits and drinking of its waters and keeping a look-out for passing ships; till one day, as I sat on the beach, recalling all that had befallen me and saying, "I wonder if Allah will save me alive and restore me to my home and family and friends!" behold, a ship was making for the island through the dashing sea and clashing waves. Presently, it cast anchor and the passengers landed; so I made for them, and when they saw me all hastened up to me and gathering round me questioned me of my case and how I came thither. I told them all that had betided me, whereat they marvelled with exceeding marvel and said, "He who rode on thy shoulder is called the 'Shaykh al-Bahr' or Old Man of the Sea, and none ever felt his legs on neck and came off alive but thou; and those who die under him he eateth: so praised be Allah for thy safety!" Then they set somewhat of food before me, whereof I ate my fill, and gave me somewhat of clothes wherewith I clad myself anew and covered my nakedness; after which they took me up into the ship, and we sailed days and nights, till fate brought us to a place called the City of Apes, builded with lofty houses, all of which gave upon the sea and it had a single gate studded and strengthened with iron nails. Now every night, as soon as it is dusk the dwellers in this city use to come forth of the gates and, putting out to sea in boats and ships, pass the night upon the waters in their fear lest the apes should come down on them from the mountains. Hearing this I was sore troubled remembering what I had before suffered from the ape-kind. Presently I landed to solace myself in the city, but meanwhile the ship set sail without me and I repented of having gone ashore, and calling to mind my companions and what had befallen me with the apes, first and after, sat down and fell a-weeping and lamenting. Presently one of the townsfolk accosted me and said to me, "O my lord, meseemeth thou art a stranger to these parts?" "Yes," answered I, "I am indeed a stranger and a poor one, who came hither in a ship which cast anchor here, and I landed to visit the town; but when I would have gone on board again, I found they had sailed without me." Quoth he, "Come and embark with us, for if thou lie the night in the city, the apes will destroy thee." "Hearkening and obedience," replied I, and rising, straightway embarked with him in one of the boats, whereupon they pushed off from shore and anchoring a mile or so from the land, there passed the night. At daybreak, they rowed back to the city and landing, went each about his business. Thus they did every night, for if any tarried in the town by night the apes came down on him and slew him. As soon as it was day, the apes left the place and ate of the fruits of the gardens, then went back to the mountains and slept there till nightfall, when they again came down upon the city. Now this place was in the farthest part of the country of the blacks, and one of the strangest things that befel me during my sojourn in the city was on this wise. One of the company with whom I passed the night in the boat, asked me, "O my lord, thou art apparently a stranger in these parts; hast thou any craft whereat thou canst work?"; and I answered, "By Allah, O my brother, I have no trade nor know I any handicraft, for I was a merchant and a man of money and substance and had a ship of my own, laden with great store of goods and merchandise; but it foundered at sea and all were drowned excepting me who saved myself on a piece of plank which Allah vouchsafed to me of His favour." Upon this he brought me a cotton bag and giving it to me, said, "Take this bag and fill it with pebbles from the beach and go forth with a company of the townsfolk to whom I will give a charge respecting thee. Do as they do and belike thou shalt gain what may further thy return voyage to thy native land." Then he carried me to the beach, where I filled my bag with pebbles large and small, and presently we saw a company of folk issue from the town, each bearing a bag like mine, filled with pebbles. To these he committed me, commending me to their care, and saying, "This man is a stranger, so take him with you and teach him how to gather, that he may get his daily bread, and you will earn your reward and recompense in Heaven." "On our head and eyes be it!" answered they and bidding me welcome, fared on with me till we came to a spacious Wady, full of lofty trees with trunks so smooth that none might climb them. Now sleeping under these trees were many apes, which when they saw us rose and fled from us and swarmed up among the branches; whereupon my companions began to pelt them with what they had in their bags, and the apes fell to plucking of the fruit of the trees and casting them at the folk. I looked at the fruits they cast at us and found them to be Indian or cocoa nuts; so I chose out a great tree, full of apes, and going up to it, began to pelt them with stones, and they in return pelted me with nuts, which I collected, as did the rest; so that even before I had made an end of my bagful of pebbles, I had gotten great plenty of nuts; and as soon as my companions had in like manner gotten as many nuts as they could carry, we returned to the city, where we arrived at the fag-end of day. Then I went into the kindly man who had brought me in company with the nut-gatherers and gave him all I had gotten, thanking him for his kindness; but he would not accept them, saying, "Sell them and make profit by the price;" and presently he added (giving me the key of a closet in his house) "Store thy nuts in this safe place and go thou forth every morning and gather them as thou hast done today, and choose out the worst for sale and supplying thyself; but lay up the rest here, so haply thou mayst collect enough to serve thee for thy return home." "Allah requite thee!" answered I and did as he advised me, going out daily with the cocoa-nut gatherers, who commended me to one another and showed me the best-stocked trees. Thus did I for some time, till I had laid up great store of excellent nuts, besides a large sum of money, the price of those I had sold. I became thus at my ease and bought all I saw and had a mind to, and passed my time pleasantly greatly enjoying my stay in the city, till, as I stood on the beach, one day, a great ship steering through the heart of the sea presently cast anchor by the shore and landed a company of merchants, who proceeded to sell and buy and barter their goods for cocoa-nuts and other commodities. Then I went to my friend and told him of the coming of the ship and how I had a mind to return to my own country; and he said, "'Tis for thee to decide." So I thanked him for his bounties and took leave of him; then, going to the captain of the ship, I agreed with him for my passage and embarked my cocoa-nuts and what else I possessed. We weighed anchor the same day and sailed from island to island and sea to sea; and whenever we stopped, I sold and traded with my cocoa-nuts, and the Lord requited me more than I erst had and lost. Amongst other places, we came to an island abounding in cloves and cinnamon and pepper; and the country people told me that by the side of each pepper-bunch groweth a great leaf which shadeth it from the sun and casteth the water off it in the wet season; but, when the rain ceaseth the leaf turneth over and droopeth down by the side of the bunch. Here I took in great store of pepper and cloves and cinnamon, in exchange for cocoa-nuts, and we passed thence to the Island of Al-Usirat, whence cometh the Comorin aloes-wood and thence to another island, five days' journey in length, where grows the Chinese lign-aloes, which is better than the Comorin; but the people of this island are fouler of condition and religion than those of the other, for that they love fornication and wine-bibbing, and know not prayer nor call to prayer. Thence we came to the pearl-fisheries, and I gave the divers some of my cocoa-nuts and said to them, "Dive for my luck and lot!" They did so and brought up from the deep bight great store of large and priceless pearls; and they said to me, "By Allah, O my master, thy luck is a lucky!" Then we sailed on, with the blessing of Allah (whose name be exalted!); and ceased not sailing till we arrived safely at Bassorah. There I abode a little and then went on to Baghdad, where I entered my quarter and found my house and foregathered with my family and saluted my friends who gave me joy of my safe return, and I laid up all my goods and valuables in my storehouses. Then I distributed alms and largesse and clothed the widow and the orphan and made presents to my relations and comrades; for the Lord had requited me fourfold that I had lost. After which I returned to my old merry way of life and forgot all I had suffered in the great profit and gain I had made. Such, then, is the history of my fifth voyage and its wonderments, and now to supper; and to-morrow, come again and I will tell you what befel me in my sixth voyage; for it was still more wonderful than this. (Saith he who telleth the tale), Then he called for food; and the servants spread the table, and when they had eaten the evening-meal, he bade give Sinbad the porter an hundred golden dinars and the Landsman returned home and lay him down to sleep, much marvelling at all he had heard. Next morning, as soon as it was light, he prayed the dawn-prayer; and, after blessing Mohammed the Cream of all creatures, betook himself to the house of Sinbad the Seaman and talked with him, till the rest of the company arrived. Then the servants spread the table and when they had well eaten and drunken and were mirthful and merry, Sinbad the Seaman began in these words the narrative of

The Sixth Voyage of Sinbad the Seaman

Know, O my brothers and friends and companions all, that I abode some time, after my return from my fifth voyage, in great solace and satisfaction and mirth and merriment, joyance and enjoyment; and I forgot what I had suffered, seeing the great gain and profit I had made till, one day, as I sat making merry and enjoying myself with my friends, there came in to me a company of merchants whose case told tales of travel, and talked with me of voyage and adventure and greatness of pelf and lucre. Hereupon I remembered the days of my return from abroad, and my joy at once more seeing my native land and foregathering with my family and friends; and my soul yearned for travel and traffic. So compelled by Fate and Fortune I resolved to undertake another voyage; and, buying me fine and costly merchandise meet for foreign trade, made it up into bales, with which I journeyed from Baghdad to Bassorah. Here I found a great ship ready for sea and full of merchants and notables, who had with them goods of price; so I embarked my bales therein. And we left Bassorah in safety and good spirits under the safeguard of the King, the Preserver and continued our voyage from place to place and from city to city, buying and selling and profiting and diverting ourselves with the sight of countries where strange folks dwell. And Fortune and the voyage smiled upon us, till one day, as we went along, behold, the captain suddenly cried with a great cry and cast his turband on the deck. Then he buffeted his face like a woman and plucked out his beard and fell down in the waist of the ship well nigh fainting for stress of grief and rage, and crying, "Oh and alas for the ruin of my house and the orphanship of my poor children!" So all the merchants and sailors came round about him and asked him, "O master, what is the matter?"; for the light had become night before their sight. And he answered, saying, "Know, O folk, that we have wandered from our course and left the sea whose ways we wot, and come into a sea whose ways I know not; and unless Allah vouchsafe us a means of escape, we are all dead men; wherefore pray ye to the Most High, that He deliver us from this strait. Haply amongst you is one righteous whose prayers the Lord will accept." Then he arose and clomb the mast to see an there were any escape from that strait; and he would have loosed the sails; but the wind redoubled upon the ship and whirled her round thrice and drave her backwards; whereupon her rudder brake and she fell off towards a high mountain. With this the captain came down from the mast, saying, "There is no Majesty and there is no Might save in Allah, the Glorious, the Great; nor can man prevent that which is fore-ordained of fate! By Allah, we are fallen on a place of sure destruction, and there is no way of escape for us, nor can any of us be saved!" Then we all fell a-weeping over ourselves and bidding one another farewell for that our days were come to an end, and we had lost all hopes of life. Presently the ship struck the mountain and broke up, and all and everything on board of her were plunged into the sea. Some of the merchants were drowned and others made shift to reach the shore and save themselves upon the mountain; I amongst the number, and when we got ashore, we found a great island, or rather peninsula whose base was strewn with wreckage of crafts and goods and gear cast up by the sea from broken ships whose passengers had been drowned; and the quantity confounded compt and calculation. So I climbed the cliffs into the inward of the isle and walked on inland, till I came to a stream of sweet water, that welled up at the nearest foot of the mountains and disappeared in the earth under the range of hills on the opposite side. But all the other passengers went over the mountains to the inner tracts; and, dispersing hither and thither, were confounded at what they saw and became like madmen at the sight of the wealth and treasures wherewith the shores were strewn. As for me I looked into the bed of the stream aforesaid and saw therein great plenty of rubies, and great royal pearls and all kinds of jewels and precious stones which were as gravel in the bed of the rivulets that ran through the fields, and the sands sparkled and glittered with gems and precious ores. Moreover we found in the island abundance of the finest lign-aloes, both Chinese and Comorin; and there also is a spring of crude ambergris which floweth like wax or gum over the stream-banks, for the great heat of the sun, and runneth down to the sea-shore, where the monsters of the deep come up and swallowing it, return into the sea. But it burneth in their bellies; so they cast it up again and it congealeth on the surface of the water, whereby its colour and quantities are changed; and at last, the waves cast it ashore, and the travellers and merchants who know it, collect it and sell it. But as to the raw ambergris which is not swallowed, it floweth over the channel and congealeth on the banks and when the sun shineth on it, it melteth and scenteth the whole valley with a musk-like fragrance: then, when the sun ceaseth from it, it congealeth again. But none can get to this place where is the crude ambergris, because of the mountains which enclose the island on all sides and which foot of man cannot ascend.[1] We continued thus to explore the island, marvelling at the wonderful works of Allah and the riches we found there, but sore troubled for our own case, and dismayed at our prospects. Now we had picked up on the beach some small matter of victual from the wreck and husbanded it carefully, eating but once every day or two, in our fear lest it should fail us and we die miserably of famine and affright. Moreover, we were weak for colic brought on by sea-sickness and low diet, and my companions deceased, one after other, till there was but a small company of us left. Each that died we washed and shrouded in some of the clothes and linen cast ashore by the tides; and after a little, the rest of my fellows perished, one by one, till I had buried the last of the party and abode alone on the island, with but a little provision left, I who was

---

[1] The tale-teller forgets that Sinbad and his companions have just ascended it; but this *inconsequence* is a characteristic of the Eastern Saga. I may note that the description of ambergris in the text tells us admirably well what it is not.

wont to have so much. And I wept over myself, saying, "Would Heaven I had died before my companions and they had washed me and buried me! It had been better than I should perish and none wash me and shroud me and bury me. But there is no Majesty and there is no Might save in Allah, the Glorious, the Great!" Now after I had buried the last of my party and abode alone on the island, I arose and dug me a deep grave on the sea-shore, saying to myself, "Whenas I grow weak and know that death cometh to me, I will cast myself into the grave and die there, so the wind may drift the sand over me and cover me and I be buried therein." Then I fell to reproaching myself for my little wit in leaving my native land and betaking me again to travel, after all I had suffered during my first five voyages, and when I had not made a single one without suffering more horrible perils and more terrible hardships than in its forerunner and having no hope of escape from my present stress; and I repented me of my folly and bemoaned myself, especially as I had no need of money, seeing that I had enough and more than enough and could not spend what I had, no, nor a half of it in all my life. However, after a while Allah sent me a thought and I said to myself, "By God, needs must this stream have an end as well as a beginning; ergo an issue somewhere, and belike its course may lead to some inhabited place; so my best plan is to make me a little boat big enough to sit in, and carry it and launching it on the river, embark therein and drop down the stream. If I escape, I escape, by God's leave; and if I perish, better die in the river than here." Then, sighing for myself, I set to work collecting a number of pieces of Chinese and Comorin aloes-wood and I bound them together with ropes from the wreckage; then I chose out from the broken up ships straight planks of even size and fixed them firmly upon the aloes-wood, making me a boat-raft a little narrower than the channel of the stream; and I tied it tightly and firmly as though it were nailed. Then I loaded it with the goods, precious ores and jewels: and the union pearls which were like gravel and the best of the ambergris crude and pure, together with what I had collected on the island and what was left me of victual and wild herbs. Lastly I lashed a piece of wood on either side, to serve me as oars; and launched it, and embarking, did according to the saying of the poet: —

> Fly, fly with life whenas evils threat;
> Leave the house to tell of its builder's fate!
> Land after land shalt thou seek and find
> But no other life on thy wish shall wait:
> Fret not thy soul in thy thoughts o' night;
> All woes shall end or sooner or late.
> Whoso is born in one land to die,
> There and only there shall gang his gait:

> Nor trust great things to another wight,
> Soul hath only soul for confederate.

My boat-raft drifted with the stream, I pondering the issue of my affair; and the drifting ceased not till I came to the place where it disappeared beneath the mountain. I rowed my conveyance into the place which was intensely dark; and the current carried the raft with it down the underground channel. The thin stream bore me on through a narrow tunnel where the raft touched either side and my head rubbed against the roof, return therefrom being impossible. Then I blamed myself for having thus risked my life, and said, "If this passage grow any straiter, the raft will hardly pass, and I cannot turn back; so I shall inevitably perish miserably in this place." And I threw myself down upon my face on the raft, by reason of the narrowness of the channel, whilst the stream ceased not to carry me along, knowing not night from day, for the excess of the gloom which encompassed me about and my terror and concern for myself lest I should perish. And in such condition my course continued down the channel which now grew wider and then straiter till, sore aweary by reason of the darkness which could be felt, I fell asleep, as I lay prone on the craft, and I slept knowing not an the time were long or short. When I awoke at last, I found myself in the light of Heaven and opening my eyes I saw myself in a broad of the stream and the raft moored to an island in the midst of a number of Indians and Abyssinians. As soon as these blackamoors saw that I was awake, they came up to me and bespoke me in their speech; but I understood not what they said and thought that this was a dream and a vision which had betided me for stress of concern and chagrin. But I was delighted at my escape from the river. When they saw I understood them not and made them no answer, one of them came forward and said to me in Arabic, "Peace be with thee, O my brother! Who art thou and whence faredst thou hither? How camest thou into this river and what manner of land lies behind yonder mountains, for never knew we any one make his way thence to us?" Quoth I, "And upon thee be peace and the ruth of Allah and His blessing! Who are ye and what country is this?" "O my brother," answered he, "we are husband-men and tillers of the soil, who came out to water our fields and plantations; and, finding thee asleep on this raft, laid hold of it and made it fast by us, against thou shouldst awake at thy leisure. So tell us how thou camest hither?" I answered, "For Allah's sake, O my lord, ere I speak give me somewhat to eat, for I am starving, and after ask me what thou wilt." So he hastened to fetch me food and I ate my fill, till I was refreshed and my fear was calmed by a good belly-full and my life returned to me. Then I rendered thanks to the Most High for mercies great and small, glad to be out of the river and rejoicing to be amongst

them, and I told them all my adventures from first to last, especially my
troubles in the narrow channel. They consulted among themselves and
said to one another, "There is no help for it but we carry him with us
and present him to our King, that he may acquaint him with his adventures." So they took me, together with the raft-boat and its lading of
monies and merchandise; jewels, minerals and golden gear, and
brought me to their King, who was King of Sarandib, telling him what
had happened; whereupon he saluted me and bade me welcome.
Then he questioned me of my condition and adventures through the
man who had spoken Arabic and I repeated to him my story from
beginning to end, whereat he marvelled exceedingly and gave me joy
of my deliverance; after which I arose and fetched from the raft great
store of precious ores and jewels and ambergris and lign-aloes and presented them to the King, who accepted them and entreated me with
the utmost honour, appointing me a lodging in his own palace. So I
consorted with the chief of the islanders, and they paid me the utmost
respect. And I quitted not the royal palace. Now the Island Sarandib
lieth under the equinoctial line, its night and day both numbering
twelve hours. It measureth eighty leagues long by a breadth of thirty
and its width is bounded by a lofty mountain and a deep valley. The
mountain is conspicuous from a distance of three days and it containeth many kinds of rubies and other minerals, and spice-trees of all
sorts. The surface is covered with emery wherewith gems are cut and
fashioned; diamonds are in its rivers and pearls arc in its valleys. I
ascended that mountain and solaced myself with a view of its marvels
which are indescribable and afterwards I returned to the King.
Thereupon, all the travellers and merchants who came to the place
questioned me of the affairs of my native land and of the Caliph Harun
al-Rashid and his rule and I told them of him and of that wherefor he
was renowned, and they praised him because of this; whilst I in turn
questioned them of the manners and customs of their own countries
and got the knowledge I desired. One day, the King himself asked me
of the fashions and form of government of my country, and I
acquainted him with the circumstance of the Caliph's sway in the city
of Baghdad and the justice of his rule. The King marvelled at my
account of his appointments and said, "By Allah, the Caliph's ordinances are indeed wise and his fashions of praiseworthy guise and thou
hast made me love him by what thou tellest me; wherefore I have a
mind to make him a present and send it by thee." Quoth I,
"Hearkening and obedience, O my lord; I will bear thy gift to him and
inform him that thou art his sincere lover and true friend." Then I
abode with the King in great honour and regard and consideration for
a long while till, one day, as I sat in his palace, I heard news of a company of merchants, that were fitting out a ship for Bassorah, and said to

myself, "I cannot do better than voyage with these men." So I rose without stay or delay and kissed the King's hand and acquainted him with my longing to set out with the merchants, for that I pined after my people and mine own land. Quoth he, "Thou art thine own master; yet, if it be thy will to abide with us, on our head and eyes be it, for thou gladdenest us with thy company." "By Allah, O my lord," answered I, "thou hast indeed overwhelmed me with thy favours and well-doings; but I weary for a sight of my friends and family and native country." When he heard this, he summoned the merchants in question and commended me to their care, paying my freight and passage-money. Then he bestowed on me great riches from his treasuries and charged me with a magnificent present for the Caliph Harun al-Rashid. Moreover he gave me a sealed letter, saying, "Carry this with thine own hand to the Commander of the Faithful and give him many salutations from us!" "Hearing and obedience," I replied. The missive was written on the skin of the Khawi (which is finer than lamb-parchment and of yellow colour), with ink of ultramarine and the contents were as follows. "Peace be with thee from the King of Al-Hind, before whom are a thousand elephants and upon whose palace-crenelles are a thousand jewels. But after (laud to the Lord and praises to His Prophet!): we send thee a trifling gift which be thou pleased to accept. Thou art to us a brother and a sincere friend; and great is the love we bear for thee in heart; favour us therefore with a reply. The gift besitteth not thy dignity: but we beg of thee, O our brother, graciously to accept it and peace be with thee." And the present was a cup of ruby a span high the inside of which was adorned with precious pearls; and a bed covered with the skin of the serpent which swalloweth the elephant, which skin hath spots each like a dinar and whoso sitteth upon it never sickeneth; and an hundred thousand miskals of Indian lign-aloes and a slave-girl like a shining moon. Then I took leave of him and of all my intimates and acquaintances in the island and embarked with the merchants aforesaid. We sailed with a fair wind, committing ourselves to the care of Allah (be He extolled and exalted!) and by His permission arrived at Bassorah, where I passed a few days and nights equipping myself and packing up my bales. Then I went on to Baghdad-city, the House of Peace, where I sought an audience of the Caliph and laid the King's presents before him. He asked me whence they came and I said to him, "By Allah, O Commander of the Faithful, I know not the name of the city nor the way thither!" He then asked me, "O Sinbad, is this true which the King writeth?"; and I answered, after kissing the ground, "O my lord, I saw in his kingdom much more than he hath written in his letter. For state processions a throne is set for him upon a huge elephant, eleven cubits high: and upon this he sitteth having his great lords and officers and guests standing in two ranks, on his right hand

and on his left. At his head is a man hending in hand a golden javelin
and behind him another with a great mace of gold whose head is an
emerald a span long and as thick as a man's thumb. And when he
mounteth horse there mount with him a thousand horsemen clad in
gold brocade and silk; and as the King proceedeth a man precedeth
him, crying, This is the King of great dignity, of high authority! And he
continueth to repeat his praises in words I remember not, saying at the
end of his panegyric, This is the King owning the crown whose like nor
Solomon nor the Mihraj ever possessed. Then he is silent and one
behind him proclaimeth, saying, He will die! Again I say he will die!;
and the other addeth, Extolled be the perfection of the Living who
dieth not! Moreover by reason of his justice and ordinance and intelligence, there is no Kazi in his city, and all his lieges distinguish between
Truth and Falsehood." Quoth the Caliph, "How great is this King! His
letter hath shown me this; and as for the mightiness of his dominion
thou hast told us what thou hast eye-witnessed. By Allah, he hath been
endowed with wisdom as with wide rule." Then I related to the
Commander of the Faithful all that had befallen me in my last voyage;
at which he wondered exceedingly and bade his historians record my
story and store it up in his treasuries, for the edification of all who might
see it. Then he conferred on me exceeding great favours, and I repaired
to my quarter and entered my home, where I warehoused all my goods
and possessions. Presently, my friends came to me and I distributed
presents among my family and gave alms and largesse; after which I
yielded myself to joyance and enjoyment, mirth and merry-making,
and forgot all that I had suffered. Such, then, O my brothers, is the history of what befel me in my sixth voyage, and to-morrow, Inshallah! I
will tell you the story of my seventh and last voyage, which is still more
wondrous and marvellous than that of the first six. (Saith he who telleth the tale), Then he bade lay the table, and the company supped
with him; after which he gave the Porter an hundred dinars, as of wont,
and they all went their ways, marvelling beyond measure at that which
they had heard. Sinbad the Landsman went home and slept as of wont.
Next day he rose and prayed the dawn-prayer and repaired to his namesake's house where, after the company was all assembled, the host
began to relate

The Seventh Voyage of Sinbad the Seaman

Know, O company, that after my return from my sixth voyage, which
brought me abundant profit, I resumed my former life in all possible
joyance and enjoyment and mirth and making merry day and night;
and I tarried some time in this solace and satisfaction till my soul
began once more to long to sail the seas and see foreign countries and

company with merchants and hear new things. So having made up my mind, I packed up in bales a quantity of precious stuffs suited for sea-trade and repaired with them from Baghdad-city to Bassorah-town, where I found a ship ready for sea, and in her a company of considerable merchants. I shipped with them and becoming friends, we set forth on our venture, in health and safety; and sailed with a fair wind, till we came to a city called Madinat-al-Sin; but after we had left it, as we fared on in all cheer and confidence, devising of traffic and travel, behold, there sprang up a violent head-wind and a tempest of rain fell on us and drenched us and our goods. So we covered the bales with our cloaks and garments and drugget and canvas, lest they be spoiled by the rain, and betook ourselves to prayer and supplication to Almighty Allah and humbled ourselves before Him for deliverance from the peril that was upon us. But the captain arose and tightening his girdle tucked up his skirts and, after taking refuge with Allah from Satan the Stoned, clomb to the mast-head, whence he looked out right and left and gazing at the passengers and crew fell to buffeting his face and plucking out his beard. So we cried to him, "O Rais, what is the matter?"; and he replied saying, "Seek ye deliverance of the Most High from the strait into which we have fallen and bemoan yourselves and take leave of one another; for know that the wind hath gotten the mastery of us and hath driven us into the uttermost of the seas of the world." Then he came down from the mast-head and opening his sea-chest, pulled out a bag of blue cotton, from which he took a powder like ashes. This he set in a saucer wetted with a little water and, after waiting a short time, smelt and tasted it; and then he took out of the chest a booklet, wherein he read awhile and said weeping, "Know, O ye passengers, that in this book is a marvellous matter, denoting that whoso cometh hither shall surely die, without hope of escape; for that this ocean is called the Sea of the Clime of the King, wherein is the sepulchre of our lord Solomon, son of David (on both be peace!) and therein are serpents of vast bulk and fearsome aspect: and what ship soever cometh to these climes there riseth to her a great fish out of the sea and swalloweth her up with all and everything on board her." Hearing these words from the captain great was our wonder, but hardly had he made an end of speaking, when the ship was lifted out of the water and let fall again and we applied to praying the death-prayer and committing our souls to Allah. Presently we heard a terrible great cry like the loud-pealing thunder, whereat we were terror-struck and became as dead men, giving ourselves up for lost. Then behold, there came up to us a huge fish, as big as a tall mountain, at whose sight we became wild for affright and, weeping sore, made ready for death, marvelling at its vast size and gruesome semblance; when lo! a second fish made its appearance than which we had seen naught more monstrous. So we bemoaned

ourselves of our lives and farewelled one another; but suddenly up
came a third fish bigger than the two first; whereupon we lost the power
of thought and reason and were stupefied for the excess of our fear and
horror. Then the three fish began circling round about the ship and the
third and biggest opened his mouth to swallow it, and we looked into
its mouth and behold, it was wider than the gate of a city and its throat
was like a long valley. So we besought the Almighty and called for succour upon His Apostle (on whom be blessing and peace!), when suddenly a violent squall of wind arose and smote the ship, which rose out
of the water and settled upon a great reef, the haunt of sea-monsters,
where it broke up and fell asunder into planks and all and everything
on board were plunged into the sea. As for me, I tore off all my clothes
but my gown and swam a little way, till I happened upon one of the
ship's planks whereto I clung and bestrode it like a horse, whilst the
winds and the waters sported with me and the waves carried me up and
cast me down; and I was in most piteous plight for fear and distress and
hunger and thirst. Then I reproached myself for what I had done
and my soul was weary after a life of ease and comfort; and I said to
myself, "O Sinbad, O Seaman, thou repentest not and yet thou art ever
suffering hardships and travails; yet wilt thou not renounce sea-travel;
or, an thou say, 'I renounce,' thou liest in thy renouncement. Endure
then with patience that which thou sufferest, for verily thou deservest
all that betideth thee!" And I ceased not to humble myself before
Almighty Allah and weep and bewail myself, recalling my former estate
of solace and satisfaction and mirth and merriment and joyance; and
thus I abode two days, at the end of which time I came to a great island
abounding in trees and streams. There I landed and ate of the fruits of
the island and drank of its waters, till I was refreshed and my life
returned to me and my strength and spirits were restored and I
recited: —

> Oft when thy case shows knotty and tangled skein,
> Fate downs from Heaven and straightens every ply:
> In patience keep thy soul till clear thy lot
> For He who ties the knot can eke untie.

Then I walked about, till I found on the further side, a great river of
sweet water, running with a strong current; whereupon I called to mind
the boat-raft I had made aforetime and said to myself, "Needs must I
make another; haply I may free me from this strait. If I escape, I have
my desire and I vow to Allah Almighty to forswear travel; and if I perish I shall be at peace and shall rest from toil and moil." So I rose up
and gathered great store of pieces of wood from the trees (which were
all of the finest sanders-wood, whose like is not albe I knew it not), and

made shift to twist creepers and tree-twigs into a kind of rope, with which I bound the billets together and so contrived a raft. Then saying, "An I be saved, 'tis of God's grace," I embarked thereon and committed myself to the current, and it bore me on for the first day and the second and the third after leaving the island; whilst I lay in the raft, eating not and drinking, when I was athirst, of the water of the river, till I was weak and giddy as a chicken, for stress of fatigue and famine and fear. At the end of this time I came to a high mountain, whereunder ran the river; which when I saw, I feared for my life by reason of the straitness I had suffered in my former journey, and I would fain have stayed the raft and landed on the mountainside; but the current overpowered me and drew it into the subterranean passage like an archway; whereupon I gave myself up for lost and said, "There is no Majesty and there is no Might save in Allah, the Glorious, the Great!" However, after a little, the raft glided into open air and I saw before me a wide valley, whereinto the river fell with a noise like the rolling of thunder and a swiftness as the rushing of the wind. I held on to the raft, for fear of falling off it, whilst the waves tossed me right and left; and the craft continued to descend with the current nor could I avail to stop it nor turn it shorewards, till it stopped with me at a great and goodly city, grandly edified and containing much people. And when the townsfolk saw me on the raft, dropping down with the current, they threw me out ropes which I had not strength enough to hold; then they tossed a net over the craft and drew it ashore with me, whereupon I fell to the ground amidst them, as I were a dead man, for stress of fear and hunger and lack of sleep. After a while, there came up to me out of the crowd an old man of reverend aspect, well stricken in years, who welcomed me and threw over me abundance of handsome clothes, wherewith I covered my nakedness. Then he carried me to the Hammam-bath and brought me cordial sherbets and delicious perfumes; moreover, when I came out, he bore me to his house, where his people made much of me and, seating me in a pleasant place, set rich food before me, whereof I ate my fill and returned thanks to God the Most High for my deliverance. Thereupon his pages fetched me hot water, and I washed my hands, and his handmaids brought me silken napkins, with which I dried them and wiped my mouth. Also the Shaykh set apart for me an apartment in a part of his house and charged his pages and slave-girls to wait upon me and do my will and supply my wants. They were assiduous in my service, and I abode with him in the guest-chamber three days, taking my ease of good eating and good drinking and good scents till life returned to me and my terrors subsided and my heart was calmed and my mind was eased. On the fourth day the Shaykh, my host, came in to me and said, "Thou cheerest us with thy company, O my son, and praised be Allah for thy safety! Say: wilt thou now come down with me to the beach and the bazar and sell thy goods and take their price? Belike thou mayst buy thee wherewithal to traffic. I have ordered my servants to remove thy stock-in-trade from the sea and they have piled it on the shore." I was silent awhile and said to myself, "What mean these words and what goods have I?" Then he said, "O my son, be not troubled nor careful, but come with me to the market and if any offer for thy goods what price contenteth thee, take it; but, an thou be not satisfied, I will lay them up for thee in my warehouse, against a fitting occasion for sale." So I bethought me of my case and said to myself, "Do his bidding and see what are these goods!"; and I said to him, "O my nuncle the Shaykh, I hear and I obey; I may not gainsay thee in aught for Allah's blessing is on all thou dost." Accordingly he guided me to the market-street, where I found that he had taken in pieces the raft which carried me and which was of sandal-wood and I heard the broker crying it for sale. Then the merchants came and opened the gate of bidding for the wood and bid against one another till its price reached a thousand dinars, when they left bidding and my host said to me, "Hear, O my son, this is the current price of thy goods in hard times like these: wilt thou sell them for this or shall I lay them up for thee in my storehouses, till such time as prices rise?" "O my lord," answered I, "the business is in thy hands: do as thou wilt." Then asked he, "Wilt thou sell the wood to me, O my son, for an hundred gold pieces over and above what the merchants have bidden for it?" and I answered, "Yes: I have sold it to thee for monies received." So he bade his servants transport the wood to his storehouses and, carrying me back to his house, seated me and counted out to me the purchase money; after which he laid it in bags and setting them in a privy place, locked them up with an iron padlock and gave me its key. Some days after this, the Shaykh said to me, "O my son, I have somewhat to propose to thee, wherein I trust thou wilt do my bidding." Quoth I, "What is it?" Quoth he, "I am a very old man and have no son; but I have a daughter who is young in years and fair of favour and endowed with abounding wealth and beauty. Now I have a mind to marry her to thee, that thou mayst abide with her in this our country, and I will make thee master of all I have in hand for I am an old man and thou shalt stand in my stead." I was silent for shame and made him no answer, whereupon he continued, "Do my desire in this, O my son, for I wish but thy weal; and if thou wilt but do as I say, thou shalt have her at once and be as my son; and all that is under my hand or that cometh to me shall be thine. If thou have a mind to traffic and travel to thy native land, none shall hinder thee, and thy property will be at thy sole disposal; so do as thou wilt." "By Allah, O my uncle," replied I, "thou art become to me even as my father, and I am a stranger and have undergone many hardships: while for stress of that which I have suffered naught of judgment or knowledge is left to me. It is for thee, therefore, to decide what I shall do." Hereupon he sent his servants for the Kazi and the witnesses and married me to his daughter making for us a noble marriage-feast and high festival. When I went in to her, I found her perfect in beauty and loveliness and symmetry and grace, clad in rich raiment and covered with a profusion of ornaments and necklaces and other trinkets of gold and silver and precious stones, worth a mint of money, a price none could pay. She pleased me and we loved each other; and I abode with her in all solace and delight of life, till her father was taken to the mercy of Allah Almighty. So we shrouded him and buried him, and I laid hands on the whole of his property and all his servants and slaves became mine. Moreover, the merchants installed me in his office, for he was their Shaykh and their Chief; and none of them purchased aught but with his knowledge and by his leave. And now his rank passed on to me. When I became acquainted with the townsfolk, I found that at the beginning of each month they were transformed, in that their faces changed and they became like unto birds and they put forth wings wherewith they flew unto the upper regions of the firmament and none remained in the city save the women and children; and I said in my mind, "When the first of the month cometh, I will ask one of them to carry me with them, whither they go." So when the time came and their complexion changed and their forms altered, I went in to one of the townsfolk and said to him, "Allah upon thee! carry me with thee, that I might divert myself with the rest and return with you." "This may not be," answered he; but I ceased not to solicit him and I importuned him till he consented. Then I went out in his company, without telling any of my family or servants or friends, and he took me on his back and flew up with me so high in air, that I heard the angels glorifying God in the heavenly dome, whereat I wondered and exclaimed, "Praised be Allah! Extolled be the perfection of Allah!" Hardly had I made an end of pronouncing the Tasbih—praised be Allah!—when there came out a fire from heaven and all but consumed the company; whereupon they fled from it and descended with curses upon me and, casting me down on a high mountain, went away, exceeding wroth with me, and left me there alone. As I found myself in this plight, I repented of what I had done and reproached myself for having undertaken that for which I was unable, saying, "There is no Majesty and there is no Might, save in Allah, the Glorious, the Great! No sooner am I delivered from one affliction than I fall into a worse." And I continued in this case knowing not whither I should go, when lo! there came up two young men, as they were moons, each using as a staff a rod of red gold. So I approached them and saluted them; and when they returned my salam, I said to them, "Allah upon you twain; who are ye and what are ye?" Quoth they, "We are of the servants of the

Most High Allah, abiding in this mountain;" and, giving me a rod of red gold they had with them, went their ways and left me. I walked on along the mountain-ridge staying my steps with the staff and pondering the case of the two youths, when behold, a serpent came forth from under the mountain, with a man in her jaws, whom she had swallowed even to below his navel, and he was crying out and saying, "Whoso delivereth me, Allah will deliver him from all adversity!" So I went up to the serpent and smote her on the head with the golden staff, whereupon she cast the man forth of her mouth. Then I smote her a second time, and she turned and fled; whereupon he came up to me and said, "Since my deliverance from yonder serpent hath been at thy hands I will never leave thee, and thou shalt be my comrade on this mountain." "And welcome," answered I; so we fared on along the mountain, till we fell in with a company of folk, and I looked and saw amongst them the very man who had carried me and cast me down there. I went up to him and spake him fair, excusing myself to him and saying, "O my comrade, it is not thus that friend should deal with friend." Quoth he, "It was thou who well-nigh destroyed us by thy Tasbih and thy glorifying God on my back." Quoth I, "Pardon me, for I had no knowledge of this matter; but, if thou wilt take me with thee, I swear not to say a word." So he relented and consented to carry me with him, but he made an express condition that, so long as I abode on his back, I should abstain from pronouncing the Tasbih or otherwise glorifying God. Then I gave the wand of gold to him whom I had delivered from the serpent and bade him farewell, and my friend took me on his back and flew with me as before, till he brought me to the city and set me down in my own house. My wife came to meet me and saluting me gave me joy of my safety and then said, "Beware of going forth hereafter with yonder folk, neither consort with them, for they are brethren of the devils, and know not how to mention the name of Allah Almighty; neither worship they Him." "And how did thy father with them?" asked I; and she answered, "My father was not of them, neither did he as they; and as now he is dead methinks thou hadst better sell all we have and with the price buy merchandise and journey to thine own country and people, and I with thee; for I care not to tarry in this city, my father and my mother being dead." So I sold all the Shaykh's property piecemeal, and looked for one who should be journeying thence to Bassorah that I might join myself to him. And while thus doing I heard of a company of townsfolk who had a mind to make the voyage, but could not find them a ship; so they bought wood and built them a great ship wherein I took passage with them, and paid them all the hire. Then we embarked, I and my wife, with all our moveables, leaving our houses and domains and so forth, and set sail, and ceased not sailing from island to island and from sea to sea, with a fair wind and a favouring, till we arrived at Bassorah safe and sound. I made no stay there, but freighted another vessel and, transferring my goods to her, set out forthright for Baghdad-city, where I arrived in safety, and entering my quarter and repairing to my house, foregathered with my family and friends and familiars and laid up my goods in my warehouses. When my people who, reckoning the period of my absence on this my seventh voyage, had found it to be seven and twenty years, and had given up all hope of me, heard of my return, they came to welcome me and to give joy of my safety; and I related to them all that had befallen me; whereat they marvelled with exceeding marvel. Then I forswore travel and vowed to Allah the Most High I would venture no more by land or sea, for that this seventh and last voyage had surfeited me of travel and adventure; and I thanked the Lord (be He praised and glorified!), and blessed Him for having restored me to my kith and kin and country and home. "Consider, therefore, O Sinbad, O Landsman," continued Sinbad the Seaman, "what sufferings I have undergone and what perils and hardships I have endured before coming to my present state." "Allah upon thee, O my Lord!" answered Sinbad the Landsman, "pardon me the wrong I did thee." And they ceased not from friendship and fellowship, abiding in all cheer and pleasures and solace of life, till there came to them the Destroyer of Delights and the Sunderer of Societies and the Shatterer of Palaces and the Caterer for Cemeteries to wit, the Cup of Death, and glory be to the Living One who dieth not! And there is a tale touching

ALADDIN OR THE WONDERFUL LAMP

IT HATH REACHED me, O King of the Age, that there dwelt in a city of the cities of China a man which was a tailor, withal a pauper, and he had one son, Aladdin hight. Now this boy had been from his babyhood a ne'er-do-well, a scapegrace; and, when he reached his tenth year, his father inclined to teach him his own trade; and, for that he was over indigent to expend money upon his learning other work or craft or apprenticeship, he took the lad into his shop that he might be taught tailoring. But, as Aladdin was a scapegrace and a ne'er-do-well and wont to play at all times with the gutter boys of the quarter, he would not sit in the shop for a single day; nay, he would await his father's leaving it for some purpose, such as to meet a creditor, when he would run off at once and fare forth to the gardens with the other scapegraces and low companions, his fellows. Such was his case; counsel and castigation were of no avail, nor would he obey either parent in aught or learn any trade and presently, for his sadness and sorrowing because of his son's vicious indolence, the tailor sickened and died. Aladdin continued in his former ill courses and, when his mother saw that her spouse had deceased, and that her son was a scapegrace and good for nothing at all she sold the shop and whatso was to be found therein and fell to spinning cotton yarn. By this toilsome industry she fed herself and found food for her son Aladdin the scapegrace who, seeing himself freed from bearing the severities of his sire, increased in idleness and low habits; nor would he ever stay at home save at meal-hours while his miserable wretched mother lived only by what her hands could spin until the youth had reached his fifteenth year. It befel, one day of the days, that as he was sitting about the quarter at play with the vagabond boys behold, a Darwaysh from the Maghrib, the Land of the Setting Sun, came up and stood gazing for solace upon the lads and he looked hard at Aladdin and carefully considered his semblance, scarcely noticing his companions the while. Now this Darwaysh was a Moorman from Inner Marocco and he was a magician who could upheap by his magic hill upon hill, and he was also an adept in astrology. So after narrowly considering Aladdin he said in himself, "Verily, this is the lad I need and to find whom I have left my natal land." Presently he led one of the children apart and questioned him anent the scapegrace saying, "Whose son is he?" And he sought all information concerning his condition and whatso related to him. After this he walked up to Aladdin and drawing him aside asked, "O my son, haply thou art the child of Such-an-one the tailor?" and the lad answered, "Yes, O my lord, but 'tis long since he died." The Maghrabi, the Magician, hearing these words threw himself upon Aladdin and wound his arms around his neck and fell to bussing him, weeping the while with tears trickling adown his cheeks. But when the lad saw the Moorman's case he was seized with surprise thereat and questioned him, saying, "What causeth thee to weep, O my lord; and how camest thou to know my father?" "How canst thou, O my son," replied the Moorman, in a soft voice saddened by emotion, "question me with such query after informing me that thy father and my brother is deceased; for that he was my brother-german and now I come from my adopted country and after long exile I rejoiced with exceeding joy in the hope of looking upon him once more and condoling with him over the past; and now thou hast announced to me his demise. But blood hideth not from blood and it hath revealed to me that thou art my nephew, son of my brother, and I knew thee amongst all the lads, albeit thy father, when I parted from him, was yet unmarried." Then he again clasped Aladdin to his bosom crying, "O my son, I have none to condole with now save thyself; and thou standest in stead of thy sire, thou being his issue and representative and 'whoso leaveth issue dieth not,' O my child!" So saying, the Magician put hand to purse and pulling out ten gold pieces gave them to the lad asking, "O my son, where is your house and where dwelleth she, thy mother, and my brother's

widow?" Presently Aladdin arose with him and showed him the way to
their home and meanwhile quoth the Wizard, "O my son, take these
moneys and give them to thy mother, greeting her from me, and let her
know that thine uncle, thy father's brother, hath reappeared from his
exile and that Inshallah—God willing—on the morrow I will visit her
to salute her with the salam and see the house wherein my brother was
homed and look upon the place where he lieth buried." Thereupon
Aladdin kissed the Maghrabi's hand, and, after running in his joy at
fullest speed to his mother's dwelling, entered to her clean contrariwise
to his custom, inasmuch as he never came near her save at meal-times
only. And when he found her, the lad exclaimed in his delight, "O my
mother, I give thee glad tidings of mine uncle who hath returned from
his exile and who now sendeth me to salute thee." "O my son," she
replied, "meseemeth thou mockest me! Who is this uncle and how
canst thou have an uncle in the bonds of life?" He rejoined, "How
sayest thou, O my mother, that I have nor living uncles nor kinsmen,
when this man is my father's own brother? Indeed he embraced me
and bussed me, shedding tears the while, and bade me acquaint thee
herewith." She retorted, "O my son, well I wot thou haddest an uncle,
but he is now dead nor am I ware that thou hast other eme." The
Maroccan Magician fared forth next morning and fell to finding out
Aladdin, for his heart no longer permitted him to part from the lad;
and, as he was to-ing and fro-ing about the city-highways, he came face
to face with him disporting himself, as was his wont, amongst the
vagabonds and the scapegraces. So he drew near to him and, taking
his hand, embraced him and bussed him; then pulled out of his poke
two dinars and said, "Hie thee to thy mother and give her these couple
of ducats and tell her that thine uncle would eat the evening-meal
with you; so do thou take these two gold pieces and prepare for us a
succulent supper. But before all things show me once more the way to
your home." "On my head and mine eyes be it, O my uncle," replied
the lad and forewent him, pointing out the street leading to the house.
Then the Moorman left him and went his ways and Aladdin ran home
and, giving the news and the two sequins to his parent, said, "My uncle
would sup with us." So she arose straightway and going to the market-
street bought all she required; then, returning to her dwelling she borrowed from the neighbours whatever was needed of pans and platters
and so forth and when the meal was cooked and suppertime came she
said to Aladdin, "O my child, the meat is ready but peradventure thine
uncle wotteth not the way to our dwelling; so do thou fare forth and
meet him on the road." He replied, "To hear is to obey," and before the
twain ended talking a knock was heard at the door. Aladdin went out
and opened when, behold, the Maghrabi, the Magician, together with
an eunuch carrying the wine and the dessert-fruits; so the lad led them

in and the slave went about his business. The Moorman on entering saluted his sister-in-law with the salam; then began to shed tears and to question her saying, "Where be the place whereon my brother went to sit?" She showed it to him, whereat he went up to it and prostrated himself in prayer and kissed the floor crying, "Ah, how scant is my satisfaction and how luckless is my lot, for that I have lost thee, O my brother, O vein of my eye!" And after such fashion he continued weeping and wailing till he swooned away for excess of sobbing and lamentation; wherefor Aladdin's mother was certified of his soothfastness. So coming up to him she raised him from the floor and said, "What gain is there in slaying thyself?" As soon as he was seated at his ease and before the food-trays were served up, he fell to talking with her and saying, "O wife of my brother, it must be a wonder to thee how in all thy days thou never sawest me nor learnedst thou aught of me during the life-time of my brother who hath found mercy. Now the reason is that forty years ago I left this town and exiled myself from my birth-place and wandereth forth over all the lands of Al-Hind and Al-Sind and entered Egypt and settled for a long time in its magnificent city, which is one of the world-wonders, till at last I fared to the regions of the Setting Sun and abode for a space of thirty years in the Maroccan interior. Now one day of the days, O wife of my brother, as I was sitting alone at home, I fell to thinking of mine own country and of my birth-place and of my brother (who hath found mercy); and my yearning to see him waxed excessive and I bewept and bewailed my strangerhood and distance from him. And at last my longings drave me homewards until I resolved upon travelling to the region which was the falling-place of my head and my homestead, to the end that I might again see my brother. Then quoth I to myself: — O man, how long wilt thou wander like a wild Arab from thy place of birth and native stead? Moreover, thou hast one brother and no more; so up with thee and travel and look upon him ere thou die; for who wotteth the woes of the world and the changes of the days? 'Twould be saddest regret an thou lie down to die without beholding thy brother and Allah (laud be to the Lord!) hath vouchsafed thee ample wealth; and belike he may be straitened and in poor case, when thou wilt aid thy brother as well as see him. So I arose at once and equipped me for wayfare and recited the Fatihah; then, whenas Friday prayers ended, I mounted and travelled to this town, after suffering manifold toils and travails which I patiently endured whilst the Lord (to whom be honour and glory!) veiled me with the veil of His protection. So I entered and whilst wandering about the streets, the day before yesterday, I beheld my brother's son Aladdin disporting himself with the boys and, by God the Great, O wife of my brother, the moment I saw him this heart of mine went forth to him (for blood yearneth unto blood!), and my soul felt and informed me that he was my very nephew.

So I forgot all my travails and troubles at once on sighting him and I was like to fly for joy; but, when he told me of the dear one's departure to the ruth of Allah Almighty, I fainted for stress of distress and disappointment. Perchance, however, my nephew hath informed thee of the pains which prevailed upon me; but after a fashion I am consoled by the sight of Aladdin, the legacy bequeathed to us by him who hath found mercy for that 'whoso leaveth issue is not wholly dead.'" And when he looked at his sister-in-law she wept at these his words; so he turned to the lad that he might cause her to forget the mention of her mate, as a means of comforting her and also of completing his deceit, and asked him, saying, "O my son Aladdin, what hast thou learned in the way of work and what is thy business? Say me, hast thou mastered any craft whereby to earn a livelihood for thyself and for thy mother?" The lad was abashed and put to shame and he hung down his head and bowed his brow groundwards; but his parent spake out, "How, forsooth? By Allah, he knoweth nothing at all, a child so ungracious as this I never yet saw; no, never! All the day long he idleth away his time with the sons of the quarter, vagabonds like himself, and his father (O regret of me!) died not save of dolour for him. And I also am now in piteous plight: I spin cotton and toil at my distaff, night and day, that I may earn me a couple of scones of bread which we eat together. This is his condition. O my brother-in-law; and, by the life of thee, he cometh not near me save at meal-times and none other. Indeed, I am thinking to lock the house-door nor ever open to him again but leave him to go and seek a livelihood whereby he can live, for that I am now grown a woman in years and have no longer strength to toil and go about for a maintenance after this fashion. O Allah, I am compelled to provide him with daily bread when I require to be provided!" Hereat the Moorman turned to Aladdin and said, "Why is this, O son of my brother, thou goest about in such ungraciousness? 'Tis a disgrace to thee and unsuitable for men like thyself. Thou art a youth of sense, O my son, and the child of honest folk, so 'tis for thee a shame that thy mother, a woman in years, should struggle to support thee. And now that thou hast grown to man's estate it becometh thee to devise thee some device whereby thou canst live, O my child. Look around thee and Alhamdolillah—praise be to Allah—in this our town are many teachers of all manner of crafts and nowhere are they more numerous; so choose thee some calling which may please thee to the end that I stablish thee therein; and, when thou growest up, O my son, thou shalt have some business whereby to live. Haply thy father's industry may not be to thy liking; and, if so it be, choose thee some other handicraft which suiteth thy fancy; then let me know and I will aid thee with all I can, O my son." But when the Maghrabi saw that Aladdin kept silence and made him no reply, he knew that the lad wanted none other occupation than a scapegrace-life, so he said to him, "O son of my brother, let not my words seem hard and harsh to thee, for, if despite all I say, thou still dislike to learn a craft, I will open thee a merchant's store furnished with costliest stuffs and thou shalt become famous amongst the folk and take and give and buy and sell and be well known in the city." Now when Aladdin heard the words of his uncle the Moorman, and the design of making him a Khwajah— merchant and gentleman,—he joyed exceedingly knowing that such folk dress handsomely and fare delicately. So he looked at the Maghrabi smiling and drooping his head groundwards and saying with the tongue of the case that he was content. The Maghrabi, the Magician, looked at Aladdin and saw him smiling, whereby he understood that the lad was satisfied to become a trader. So he said to him, "Since thou art content that I open thee a merchant's store and make thee a gentleman, do thou, O son of my brother, prove thyself a man and Inshallah—God willing—to-morrow I will take thee to the Bazar in the first place and will have a fine suit of clothes cut out for thee, such gear as merchants wear; and, secondly, I will look after a store for thee and keep my word." Now Aladdin's mother had somewhat doubted the Maroccan being her brother-in-law; but as soon as she heard his promise of opening a merchant's store for her son and setting him up with stuffs and capital and so forth, the woman decided and determined in her mind that this Maghrabi was in very sooth her husband's brother, seeing that no stranger man would do such goodly deed by her son. So she began directing the lad to the right road and teaching him to cast ignorance from out his head and to prove himself a man; moreover she bade him ever obey his excellent uncle as though he were his son and to make up for the time he had wasted in frowardness with his fellows. After this she arose and spread the table, then served up supper; so all sat down and fell to eating and drinking, while the Maghrabi conversed with Aladdin upon matters of business and the like, rejoicing him to such degree that he enjoyed no sleep that night. But when the Moorman saw that the dark hours were passing by, and the wine was drunken, he arose and sped to his own stead; but, ere going, he agreed to return next morning and take Aladdin and look to his suit of merchant's clothes being cut out for him. And as soon as it was dawn, behold, the Maghrabi rapped at the door which was opened by Aladdin's mother: the Moorman, however, would not enter, but asked to take the lad with him to the market-street. Accordingly Aladdin went forth to his uncle and, wishing him good morning, kissed his hand; and the Maroccan took him by the hand and fared with him to the Bazar. There he entered a clothier's shop containing all kinds of clothes and called for a suit of the most sumptuous; whereat the merchant brought him out his need, all wholly fashioned and ready sewn;

and the Moorman said to the lad, "Choose, O my child, whatso pleaseth thee." Aladdin rejoiced exceedingly seeing that his uncle had given him his choice, so he picked out the suit most to his own liking and the Maroccan paid to the merchant the price thereof in ready money. Presently he led the lad to the Hammam-baths where they bathed; then they came out and drank sherbets, after which Aladdin arose and, donning his new dress in huge joy and delight, went up to his uncle and kissed his hand and thanked him for his favours. The Maghrabi, the Magician, after leaving the Hammam with Aladdin, took him and trudged with him to the Merchant's bazar; and, having diverted him by showing the market and its sellings and buyings, said to him, "O my son, it besitteth thee to become familiar with the folk, especially with the merchants, so thou mayst learn of them merchant-craft, seeing that the same hath now become thy calling." Then he led him forth and showed him the city and its cathedral-mosques together with all the pleasant sights therein; and, lastly, made him enter a cook's shop. Here dinner was served to them on platters of silver and they dined well and ate and drank their sufficiency, after which they went their ways. Presently the Moorman pointed out to Aladdin the pleasances and noble buildings, and went in with him to the Sultan's Palace and diverted him with displaying all the apartments which were mighty fine and grand; and led him finally to the Khan of stranger merchants where he himself had his abode. Then the Maroccan invited sundry traders which were in the Caravanserai; and they came and sat down to supper, when he notified to them that the youth was his nephew, Aladdin by name. And after they had eaten and drunken and night had fallen, he rose up and taking the lad with him led him back to his mother, who no sooner saw her boy as he were one of the merchants than her wits took flight and she waxed sad for very gladness. Then she fell to thanking her false connection, the Moorman, for all his benefits and said to him, "O my brother-in-law, I can never say enough though I expressed my gratitude to thee during the rest of thy days and praised thee for the good deeds thou hast done by this my child." Thereupon quoth the Maroccan, "O wife of my brother, deem this not mere kindness of me, for that the lad is mine own son and 'tis incumbent on me to stand in the stead of my brother, his sire. So be thou fully satisfied!" And quoth she, "I pray Allah by the honour of the Hallows, the ancients and the moderns, that He preserve thee and cause thee continue, O my brother-in-law, and prolong for me thy life; so shalt thou be a wing overshadowing this orphan lad; and he shall ever be obedient to thine orders nor shall he do aught save whatso thou biddest him thereunto." The Maghrabi replied, "O wife of my brother, Aladdin is now a man of sense and the son of goodly folk, and I hope to Allah that he will follow in the footsteps of his sire and cool thine eyes. But I regret that, to-morrow

being Friday, I shall not be able to open his shop, as 'tis meeting-day
when all the merchants, after congregational prayer, go forth to the gardens and pleasances. On the Sabbath, however, Inshallah!—an it
please the Creator—we will do our business. Meanwhile tomorrow I
will come to thee betimes and take Aladdin for a pleasant stroll to the
gardens and pleasances without the city which haply he may hitherto
not have beheld. There also he shall see the merchants and notables
who go forth to amuse themselves, so shall he become acquainted with
them and they with him." The Maghrabi went away and lay that night
in his quarters; and early next morning he came to the tailor's house
and rapped at the door. Now Aladdin (for stress of his delight in the
new dress he had donned and for the past day's enjoyment in the
Hammam and in eating and drinking and gazing at the folk; expecting
furthermore his uncle to come at dawn and carry him off on pleasur-
ing to the gardens) had not slept a wink that night, nor closed his eyelids, and would hardly believe it when day broke. But hearing the
knock at the door he went out at once in hot haste, like a spark of fire,
and opened and saw his uncle, the Magician, who embraced him and
kissed him. Then, taking his hand, the Moorman said to him as they
fared forth together, "O son of my brother, this day will I show thee a
sight thou never sawest in all thy life," and he began to make the lad
laugh and cheer him with pleasant talk. So doing they left the city gate,
and the Maroccan took to promenading with Aladdin amongst the gardens and to pointing out for his pleasure the mighty fine pleasances
and the marvellous high-builded pavilions. And whenever they stood to
stare at a garth or a mansion or a palace the Maghrabi would say to his
companion, "Doth this please thee, O son of my brother?" Aladdin was
nigh to fly with delight at seeing sights he had never seen in all his born
days; and they ceased not to stroll about and solace themselves until
they waxed aweary, when they entered a mighty grand garden which
was nearhand, a place that the heart delighted and the sight belighted;
for that its swift-running rills flowed amidst the flowers and the waters
jetted from the jaws of lions moulded in yellow brass like unto gold. So
they took seat over against a lakelet and rested a little while, and
Aladdin enjoyed himself with joy exceeding and fell to jesting with his
uncle and making merry with him as though the Magician were really
his father's brother. Presently the Maghrabi arose and loosing his girdle
drew forth from thereunder a bag full of victual, dried fruits and so
forth, saying to Aladdin, "O my nephew, haply thou art become anhungered; so come forward and eat what thou needest." Accordingly the
lad fell upon the food and the Moorman ate with him and they were
gladdened and cheered by rest and good cheer. Then quoth the
Magician, "Arise, O son of my brother, an thou be reposed and let us
stroll onwards a little and reach the end of our walk." Thereupon

Aladdin arose and the Maroccan paced with him from garden to garden until they left all behind them and reached the base of a high and
naked hill; when the lad who, during all his days, had never issued
from the city-gate and never in his life had walked such a walk as this,
said to the Maghrabi, "O uncle mine, whither are we wending? We
have left the gardens behind us one and all and have reached the bar-
ren hill-country; and, if the way be still long, I have no strength left for
walking: indeed I am ready to fall with fatigue. There are no gardens
before us, so let us hark back and return to town." Said the Magician,
"No, O my son; this is the right road, nor are the gardens ended for we
are going to look at one which hath ne'er its like amongst those of the
Kings and all thou hast beheld are naught in comparison therewith.
Then gird thy courage to walk; thou art now a man, Alhamdolillah —
praise be to Allah!" Then the Maghrabi fell to soothing Aladdin with
soft words and telling him wondrous tales, lies as well as truth, until
they reached the site intended by the African Magician who had travelled from the Sunset-land to the regions of China for the sake thereof.
And when they made the place, the Moorman said to Aladdin, "O son
of my brother, sit thee down and take thy rest, for this is the spot we are
now seeking and, Inshallah, soon will I divert thee by displaying marvel-matters whose like not one in the world ever saw; nor hath any
solaced himself with gazing upon that which thou art about to behold.
But when thou art rested, arise and seek some wood-chips and fuel
sticks which be small and dry, wherewith we may kindle a fire: then
will I show thee, O son of my brother, matters beyond the range of matter." Now, when the lad heard these words, he longed to look upon
what his uncle was about to do and, forgetting his fatigue, he rose forthright and fell to gathering small wood-chips and dry sticks, and continued until the Moorman cried to him, "Enough, O son of my brother!"
Presently the Magician brought out from his breast-pocket a casket
which he opened, and drew from it all he needed of incense; then he
fumigated and conjured and adjured, muttering words none might
understand. And the ground straightway clave asunder after thick
gloom and quake of earth and bellowings of thunder. Hereat Aladdin
was startled and so affrighted that he tried to fly; but, when the African
Magician saw his design, he waxed wroth with exceeding wrath, for that
without the lad his work would profit him naught, the hidden hoard
which he sought to open being not to be opened save by means of
Aladdin. So noting this attempt to run away, the Magician arose and
raising his hand smote Aladdin on the head a buffet so sore that well-
nigh his back-teeth were knocked out, and he fell swooning to the
ground. But after a time he revived by the magic of the Magician, and
cried, weeping the while, "O my uncle, what have I done that
deserveth from thee such a blow as this?" Hereat the Maghrabi fell to

soothing him, and said, "O my son, 'tis my intent to make thee a man; therefore, do thou not gainsay me, for that I am thine uncle and like unto thy father. Obey me, therefore, in all I bid thee, and shortly thou shalt forget all this travail and toil whenas thou shalt look upon the marvel-matters I am about to show thee." And soon after the ground had cloven asunder before the Maroccan it displayed a marble slab wherein was fixed a copper ring. The Maghrabi, striking a geomantic table, turned to Aladdin, and said to him, "An thou do all I shall bid thee, indeed thou shalt become wealthier than any of the kings, and for this reason, O my son, I struck thee, because here lieth a hoard which is stored in thy name; and yet thou designedst to leave it and to levant. But now collect thy thoughts, and behold how I opened earth by my spells and adjurations. Under yon stone wherein the ring is set lieth the treasure wherewith I acquainted thee: so set thy hand upon the ring and raise the slab, for that none other amongst the folk, thyself excepted, hath power to open it, nor may any of mortal birth, save thyself, set foot within this Enchanted Treasury which hath been kept for thee. But 'tis needful that thou learn of me all wherewith I would charge thee; nor gainsay e'en a single syllable of my words. All this, O my child, is for thy good; the hoard being of immense value, whose like the kings of the world never accumulated, and do thou remember that 'tis for thee and me." So poor Aladdin forgot his fatigue and buffet and tear-shedding, and he was dumbed and dazed at the Maghrabi's words and rejoiced that he was fated to become rich in such measure that not even the Sultans would be richer than himself. Accordingly, he cried, "O my uncle, bid me do all thou pleasest, for I will be obedient unto thy bidding." The Maghrabi replied, "O my nephew, thou art to me as my own child and even dearer, for being my brother's son and for my having none other kith and kin except thyself; and thou, O my child, art my heir and successor." So saying, he went up to Aladdin and kissed him and said, "For whom do I intend these my labours? Indeed, each and every are for thy sake, O my son, to the end that I may leave thee a rich man and one of the very greatest. So gainsay me not in all I shall say to thee, and now go up to yonder ring and uplift it as I bade thee." Aladdin answered, "O uncle mine, this ring is over heavy for me: I cannot raise it single-handed, so do thou also come forward and lend me strength and aidance towards uplifting it, for indeed I am young in years." The Moorman replied, "O son of my brother, we shall find it impossible to do aught if I assist thee, and all our efforts would be in vain. But do thou set thy hand upon the ring and pull it up, and thou shalt raise the slab forthright, and in very sooth I told thee that none can touch it save thyself. But whilst haling at it cease not to pronounce thy name and the names of thy father and mother, so 'twill rise at once to thee nor shalt thou feel its weight." Thereupon the lad mustered up strength and girt the loins of resolution and did as the Maroccan had bidden him, and hove up the slab with all ease when he pronounced his name and the names of his parents, even as the Magician had bidden him. And as soon as the stone was raised he threw it aside and there appeared before him a Sardab, a souterrain, whereunto led a case of some twelve stairs and the Maghrabi said, "O Aladdin, collect thy thoughts and do whatso I bid thee to the minutest detail nor fail in aught thereof. Go down with all care into yonder vault until thou reach the bottom and there shalt thou find a space divided into four halls, and in each of these thou shalt see four golden jars and others of virgin or and silver. Beware, however, lest thou take aught therefrom or touch them, nor allow thy gown or its skirts even to brush the jars or the walls. Leave them and fare forwards until thou reach the fourth hall without lingering for a single moment on the way; and, if thou do aught contrary thereto thou wilt at once be transformed and become a black stone. When reaching the fourth hall thou wilt find therein a door which do thou open, and pronouncing the names thou spakest over the slab, enter therethrough into a garden adorned everywhere with fruit-bearing trees. This thou must traverse by a path thou wilt see in front of thee measuring some fifty cubits long, beyond which thou wilt come upon an open saloon and therein a ladder of some thirty rungs. Thou shalt there find a Lamp hanging from its ceiling; so mount the ladder and take that Lamp and place it in thy breast-pocket after pouring out its contents; nor fear evil from it for thy clothes because its contents are not common oil. And on return thou art allowed to pluck from the trees whatso thou pleasest, for all is thine so long as the Lamp is in thy hand." Now when the Moorman ended his charge to Aladdin, he drew off a seal-ring and put it upon the lad's forefinger saying, "O my son, verily this signet shall free thee from all hurt and fear which may threaten thee, but only on condition that thou bear in mind all I have told thee. So arise straightway and go down the stairs, strengthening thy purpose and girding the loins of resolution: moreover fear not for thou art now a man and no longer a child. And in shortest time, O my son, thou shalt win thee immense riches and thou shalt become the wealthiest of the world." Accordingly, Aladdin arose and descended into the souterrain, where he found the four halls, each containing four jars of gold and these he passed by, as the Maroccan had bidden him, with the utmost care and caution. Thence he fared into the garden and walked along its length until he entered the saloon, where he mounted the ladder and took the Lamp which he extinguished, pouring out the oil which was therein, and placed it in his breast-pocket. Presently, descending the ladder he returned to the garden where he fell to gazing at the trees whereupon sat birds glorifying with loud voices their Great Creator. Now he had not observed them as he went in, but all these trees bare for fruitage costly gems; moreover each had its own kind of growth and jewels of its peculiar sort; and these were of every colour, green and white; yellow, red and other such brilliant hues and the radiance flashing from these gems paled the rays of the sun in forenoon sheen. Furthermore the size of each stone so far surpassed description that no King of the Kings of the world owned a single gem equal to the larger sort nor could boast of even one half the size of the smaller kind of them. Aladdin walked amongst the trees and gazed upon them and other things which surprised the sight and bewildered the wits; and, as he considered them, he saw that in lieu of common fruits the produce was of mighty fine jewels and precious stones, such as emeralds and diamonds; rubies, spinels and balasses, pearls and similar gems astounding the mental vision of man. And forasmuch as the lad had never beheld things like these during his born days nor had reached those years of discretion which would teach him the worth of such valuables (he being still but a little lad), he fancied that all these jewels were of glass or crystal. So he collected them until he had filled his breast-pockets and began to certify himself if they were or were not common fruits, such as grapes, figs and such like edibles. But seeing them of glassy substance, he, in his ignorance of precious stones and their prices, gathered into his breast-pockets every kind of growth the trees afforded; and, having failed of his purpose in finding them food, he said in his mind, "I will collect a portion of these glass fruits for playthings at home." So he fell to plucking them in quantities and cramming them in his pokes and breast-pockets till these were stuffed full; after which he picked others which he placed in his waist-shawl and then, girding himself therewith, carried off all he availed to, purposing to place them in the house by way of ornaments and, as hath been mentioned, never imagining that they were other than glass. Then he hurried his pace in fear of his uncle, the Maghrabi, until he had passed through the four halls and lastly on his return reached the souterrain where he cast not a look at the jars of gold, albeit he was able and allowed to take of the contents on his way back. But when he came to the souterrain-stairs and climbed the steps till naught remained but the last; and, finding this higher than all the others, he was unable alone and unassisted, burthened moreover as he was, to mount it. So he said to the Maghrabi, "O my uncle, lend me thy hand and aid me to climb;" but the Moorman answered, "O my son, give me the Lamp and lighten thy load; belike 'tis that weigheth thee down." The lad rejoined, "O my uncle, 'tis not the Lamp downweigheth me at all; but do thou lend me a hand and as soon as I reach ground I will give it to thee." Hereat the Maroccan, the Magician, whose only object was the Lamp and none other, began to insist upon Aladdin giving it to him at once; but the lad (forasmuch as he had placed it at the bottom of his breast-pocket and his other pouches being full of gems bulged outwards) could not reach it with his fingers to hand it over, so the wizard after much vain persistency in requiring what his nephew was unable to give, fell to raging with furious rage and to demanding the Lamp whilst Aladdin could not get at it. Yet had the lad promised truthfully that he would give it up as soon as he might reach ground, without lying thought or ill-intent. But when the Moorman saw that he would not hand it over, he waxed wroth with wrath exceeding and cut off all his hopes of winning it; so he conjured and adjured and cast incense amiddlemost the fire, when forthright the slab made a cover of itself, and by the might of magic lidded the entrance; the earth buried the stone as it was aforetime and Aladdin, unable to issue forth, remained underground. Now the Sorcerer was a stranger, and, as we have mentioned, no uncle of Aladdin's, and he had misrepresented himself and preferred a lying claim, to the end that he might obtain the Lamp by means of the lad for whom this Hoard had been upstored. So the Accursed heaped the earth over him and left him to die of hunger. For this Maghrabi was an African of Afrikiyah proper, born in the Inner Sunset-land, and from his earliest age upwards he had been addicted to witchcraft and had studied and practised every manner of occult science, for which unholy lore the city of Africa is notorious. And he ceased not to read and hear lectures until he had become a past-master in all such knowledge. And of the abounding skill in spells and conjurations which he had acquired by the perusing and the lessoning of forty years, one day of the days he discovered by devilish inspiration that there lay in an extreme city of the cities of China, named Al-Kal'as, an immense Hoard, the like whereof none of the Kings in this world had ever accumulated: moreover, that the most marvellous article in this Enchanted Treasure was a wonderful Lamp which, whoso possessed, could not possibly be surpassed by any man upon earth, either in high degree or in wealth and opulence; nor could the mightiest monarch of the universe attain to the all-sufficiency of this Lamp with its might of magical means. When the Maghrabi assured himself by his science and saw that this Hoard could be opened only by the presence of a lad named Aladdin, of pauper family and abiding in that very city, and learnt how taking it would be easy and without hardships, he straightway and without stay or delay equipped himself for a voyage to China (as we have already told), and he did what he did with Aladdin fancying that he would become Lord of the Lamp. But his attempt and his hopes were baffled and his work was clean wasted; whereupon, determining to do the lad die, he heaped up the earth over him by gramarye to the end that the unfortunate might perish, reflecting that "The live man hath no murtherer." Secondly, he did so with the design that, as Aladdin could not come forth from underground, he would

also be impotent to bring out the Lamp from the souterrain. So
presently he wended his ways and retired to his own land, Africa, a sad-
der man and disappointed of all his expectations. Such was the case
with the Wizard; but as regards Aladdin when the earth was heaped
over him, he began shouting to the Moorman whom he believed to be
his uncle, and praying him to lend a hand that he might issue from the
souterrain and return to earth's surface; but, however loudly he cried,
none was found to reply. At that moment he comprehended the sleight
which the Maroccan had played upon him, and that the man was no
uncle but a liar and a wizard. Then the unhappy despaired of life, and
learned to his sorrow that there was no escape for him; so he fell to
beweeping with sore weeping the calamity that had befallen him; and
after a little while he stood up and descended the stairs to see if Allah
Almighty had lightened his grief-load by leaving a door of issue. So he
turned him to the right and to the left but he saw naught save darkness
and four walls closed upon him, for that the Magician had by his magic
locked all the doors and had shut up even the garden, where through
the lad erst had passed, lest it offer him the means of issuing out upon
earth's surface, and that he might surely die. Then Aladdin's weeping
waxed sorer, and his wailing louder whenas he found all the doors fast
shut, for he had thought to solace himself awhile in the garden. But
when he felt that all were locked, he fell to shedding tears and lamenting like unto one who hath lost his every hope, and he returned to sit
upon the stairs of the flight whereby he had entered the souterrain. But
it is a light matter for Allah (be He exalted and extolled!) whenas He
designeth aught to say, "Be" and it becometh; for that He createth joy
in the midst of annoy; and on this wise it was with Aladdin. Whilst the
Maghrabi, the Magician, was sending him down into the souterrain he
set upon his finger by way of a gift, a seal-ring and said, "Verily this
signet shall save thee from every strait an thou fall into calamity and ill
shifts of time; and it shall remove from thee all hurt and harm, and aid
thee with a strong arm whereso thou mayst be set." Now this was by destiny of God the Great, that it might be the means of Aladdin's escape;
for whilst he sat wailing and weeping over his case and cast away all
hope of life, and utter misery overwhelmed him, he rubbed his hands
together for excess of sorrow, as is the wont of the woeful; then, raising
them in supplication to Allah, he cried, "I testify that there is no
God save Thou alone, The Most Great, the Omnipotent, the All-
conquering, Quickener of the dead, Creator of man's need and
Granter thereof, Resolver of his difficulties and duresse and Bringer of
joy not of annoy. Thou art my sufficiency and Thou art the Truest of
Trustees. And I bear my witness that Mohammed is Thy servant and
Thine Apostle and I supplicate Thee, O my God, by his favour with
Thee to free me from this my foul plight." And whilst he implored the

Lord and was chafing his hands in the soreness of his sorrow for that had befallen him of calamity, his fingers chanced to rub the Ring when, lo and behold! forthright its Familiar rose upright before him and cried, "Adsum; thy slave between thy hands is come! Ask whatso thou wantest, for that I am the thrall of him on whose hand is the Ring, the Signet of my lord and master." Hereat the lad looked at him and saw standing before him a Marid like unto an Ifrit of our lord Solomon's Jinns. He trembled at the terrible sight; but, hearing the Slave of the Ring say, "Ask whatso thou wantest, verily, I am thy thrall, seeing that the signet of my lord be upon thy finger," he recovered his spirits and remembered the Moorman's saying when giving him the Ring. So he rejoiced exceedingly and became brave and cried, "Ho thou, Slave of the Lord of the Ring, I desire thee to set me upon the face of the earth." And hardly had he spoken this speech when suddenly the ground clave asunder and he found himself at the door of the Hoard and outside it in full view of the world. Now for three whole days he had been sitting in the darkness of the Treasury underground and when the sheen of day and the shine of sun smote his face he found himself unable to keep his eyes open; so he began to unclose the lids a little and to close them a little until his eyeballs regained force and got used to the light and were purged of the noisome murk. Withal he was astounded at finding himself without the Hoard-door whereby he had passed in when it was opened by the Maghrabi, the Magician; especially as the adit had been lidded and the ground had been smoothed, showing no sign whatever of entrance. Thereat his surprise increased until he fancied himself in another place, nor was his mind convinced that the stead was the same until he saw the spot whereupon they had kindled the fire of wood-chips and dried sticks, and where the African Wizard had conjured over the incense. Then he turned him rightwards and leftwards and sighted the gardens from afar and his eyes recognised the road whereby he had come. So he returned thanks to Allah Almighty who had restored him to the face of earth and had freed him from death after he had cut off all hopes of life. Presently he arose and walked along the way to the town, which now he knew well, until he entered the streets and passed on to his own home. Then he went in to his mother and on seeing her, of the overwhelming stress of joy at his escape and the memory of past affright and the hardships he had borne and the pangs of hunger, he fell to the ground before his parent in a fainting-fit. Now his mother had been passing sad since the time of his leaving her and he found her moaning and crying about him; however on sighting him enter the house she joyed with exceeding joy, but soon was overwhelmed with woe when he sank upon the ground swooning before her eyes. Still, she did not neglect the matter or treat it lightly, but at once hastened to sprinkle water upon his face and after she asked of the neighbours some scents which she made him snuff up. And when he came round a little, he prayed her to bring him somewhat of food saying, "O my mother, 'tis now three days since I ate anything at all." Thereupon she arose and brought him what she had by her; then, setting it before him, said, "Come forward, O my son; eat and be cheered and, when thou shalt have rested, tell me what hath betided and affected thee, O my child; at this present I will not question thee for thou art aweary in very deed." Aladdin ate and drank and was cheered and after he had rested and had recovered spirits he cried, "Ah O my mother, I have a sore grievance against thee for leaving me to that accursed wight who strave to compass my destruction and designed to take my life. Know thou that I beheld Death with mine own eyes at the hand of this damned wretch, whom thou didst certify to be my uncle; and, had not Almighty Allah rescued me from him, I and thou, O my mother, had been cozened by the excess of this Accursed's promises to work my welfare, and by the great show of affection which he manifested to us. Learn, O my mother, that this fellow is a sorcerer, a Moorman, an accursed, a liar, traitor, a hypocrite; nor deem I that the devils under the earth are damnable as he. Allah abase him in his every book! Hear thee, O my mother, what this abominable one did, and all that I shall tell thee will be soothfast and certain. See how the damned villain brake every promise he made, certifying that he would soon work all good with me; and do thou consider the fondness which he displayed to me and the deeds which he did by me; and all this only to win his wish, for his design was to destroy me; and Alhamdolillah— laud to the Lord—for my deliverance. Listen and learn, O my mother, how this Accursed entreated me." Then Aladdin informed his mother of all that had befallen him (weeping the while for stress of gladness); how the Maghrabi had led him to a hill wherein was hidden the Hoard and how he had conjured and fumigated, adding, "After which, O my mother, mighty fear gat hold of me when the hill split and the earth gaped before me by his wizardry; and I trembled with terror at the rolling of thunder in mine ears and the murk which fell upon us when he fumigated and muttered spells. Seeing these horrors I in mine affright designed to fly; but, when he understood mine intent he reviled me and smote me a buffet so sore that it caused me to swoon. However, inasmuch as the Treasury was to be opened only by means of me, O my mother, he could not descend therein himself, it being in my name and not in his; and, for that he is an ill-omened magician, he under- stood that I was necessary to him and this was his need of me." Aladdin acquainted his mother with all that had befallen him from the Maghrabi, the Magician, and said, "After he had buffeted me, he judged it advisable to soothe me in order that he might send me down into the Enchanted Treasury; and first he drew from his finger a Ring which he placed upon mine. So I descended and found four halls all full of gold and silver which counted as naught, and the Accursed had charged me not to touch aught thereof. Then I entered a mighty fine flower-garden every where bedecked with tall trees whose foliage and fruitage bewildered the wits, for all, O my mother, were of vari-coloured glass, and lastly I reached the Hall wherein hung this Lamp. So I took it straightway and put it out and poured forth its contents." And so saying, Aladdin drew the Lamp from his breast-pocket and showed it to his mother, together with the gems and jewels which he had brought from the garden; and there were two large bag-pockets full of precious stones, whereof not one was to be found amongst the kings of the world. But the lad knew naught anent their worth deeming them glass or crystal; and presently he resumed, "After this, O mother mine, I reached the Hoard-door carrying the Lamp and shouted to the accursed Sorcerer, which called himself my uncle, to lend me a hand and hale me up, I being unable to mount of myself the last step for the over-weight of my burthen. But he would not and said only:—First hand me the Lamp! As, however, I had placed it at the bottom of my breast-pocket and the other pouches bulged out beyond it, I was unable to get at it and said:—O my uncle, I cannot reach thee the Lamp, but I will give it to thee when outside the Treasury. His only need was the Lamp and he designed, O my mother, to snatch it from me and after that slay me, as indeed he did his best to do by heaping the earth over my head. Such then is what befel me from this foul Sorcerer." Hereupon Aladdin fell to abusing the Magician in hot wrath and with a burning heart and crying, "Well-away! I take refuge from this damned wight, the ill-omened, the wrong-doer, the forswearer, the lost to all humanity, the arch-traitor, the hypocrite, the annihilator of ruth and mercy." When Aladdin's mother heard his words and what had befallen him from the Maghrabi, the Magician, she said, "Yea, verily, O my son, he is a miscreant, a hypocrite who murthereth the folk by his magic; but 'twas the grace of Allah Almighty, O my child, that saved thee from the tricks and the treachery of this accursed Sorcerer whom I deemed to be truly thine uncle." Then, as the lad had not slept a wink for three days and found himself nodding, he sought his natural rest, his mother doing on like wise; nor did he awake till about noon on the second day. As soon as he shook off slumber he called for somewhat of food being sore anhungered, but said his mother, "O my son, I have no victual for thee inasmuch as yesterday thou atest all that was in the house. But wait patiently a while: I have spun a trifle of yarn which I will carry to the market-street and sell it and buy with what it may be worth some vict-ual for thee." "O my mother," said he, "keep your yarn and sell it not; but fetch me the Lamp I brought hither that I may go vend it and with its price purchase provaunt, for that I deem 'twill bring more money than the spinnings." So Aladdin's mother arose and fetched the Lamp for her son; but, while so doing, she saw that it was dirty exceedingly; so she said, "O my son, here is the Lamp, but 'tis very foul: after we shall have washed it and polished it 'twill sell better." Then, taking a handful of sand she began to rub therewith, but she had only begun when appeared to her one of the Jann whose favour was frightful and whose bulk was horrible big, and he was gigantic as one of the Jababirah. And forthright he cried to her, "Say whatso thou wantest of me. Here am I, thy Slave and Slave to whoso holdeth the Lamp; and not I alone, but all the Slaves of the Wonderful lamp which thou hendest in hand." She quaked and terror was sore upon her when she looked at that frightful form and her tongue being tied she could not return aught reply, never having been accustomed to espy similar semblances. Now her son was standing afar off and he had already seen the Jinni of the Ring which he had rubbed within the Treasury; so when he heard the Slave speaking to his parent, he hastened forwards and snatching the Lamp from her hand, said, "O Slave of the Lamp, I am anhungered and 'tis my desire that thou fetch me somewhat to eat and let it be something toothsome beyond our means." The Jinni disappeared for an eye-twinkle and returned with a mighty fine tray and precious of price, for that 'twas all in virginal silver and upon it stood twelve golden platters of meats manifold and dainties delicate, with bread snowier than snow; also two silvern cups and as many black jacks full of wine clear-strained and long-stored. And after setting all these before Aladdin, he evanished from vision. Thereupon the lad went and sprinkled rose water upon his mother's face and caused her to snuff up perfumes pure and pungent and said to her when she revived, "Rise, O mother mine, and let us eat of these meats wherewith Almighty Allah hath eased our poverty." But when she saw that mighty fine silvern tray she fell to marvelling at the matter and quoth she, "O my son, who be this generous, this beneficent one who hath abated our hunger-pains and our penury? We are indeed under obligation to him and, meseemeth, 'tis the Sultan who, hearing of our mean condition and our misery, hath sent us this food-tray." Quoth he, "O my mother, this be no time for questioning: arouse thee and let us eat for we are both a-famished." Accordingly, they sat down to the tray and fell to feeding when Aladdin's mother tasted meats whose like in all her time she had never touched; so they devoured them with sharpened appetites and all the capacity engendered by stress of hunger; and, secondly, the food was such that marked the tables of the Kings. But neither of them knew whether the tray was or was not valuable, for never in their born days had they looked upon aught like it. As soon as they had finished the meal (withal leaving victual enough for supper and eke for the next day), they arose and washed their hands and sat at chat, when the mother turned to her son and

said, "Tell me, O my child, what befel thee from the Slave, the Jinni,
now that Alhamdolillah—laud to the Lord!—we have eaten our full of
the good things wherewith He hath favoured us and thou hast no pretext for saying to me, 'I am anhungered.'" So Aladdin related to her all
that took place between him and the Slave what while she had sunk
upon the ground aswoon for sore terror; and at this she, being seized
with mighty great surprise, said, "'Tis true; for the Jinns do present
themselves before the Sons of Adam but I, O my son, never saw them
in all my life and meseemeth that this be the same who saved thee
when thou wast within the Enchanted Hoard." "This is not he, O my
mother: this who appeared before thee is the Slave of the Lamp!"
"Who may this be, O my son?" "This be a Slave of sort and shape other
than he; that was the Familiar of the Ring and this his fellow thou
sawest was the Slave of the Lamp thou hendest in hand." And when his
parent heard these words she cried, "There! there! so this Accursed,
who showed himself to me and went nigh unto killing me with affright,
is attached to the Lamp." "Yes," he replied, and she rejoined, "Now I
conjure thee, O my son, by the milk wherewith I suckled thee, to throw
away from thee this Lamp and this Ring; because they can cause us
only extreme terror and I especially can never abear a second glance at
them. Moreover all intercourse with them is unlawful, for that the
Prophet (whom Allah save and assain!) warned us against them with
threats." He replied, "Thy commands, O my mother, be upon my head
and mine eyes; but, as regards this saying thou saidest, 'tis impossible
that I part or with Lamp or with Ring. Thou thyself hast seen what good
the Slave wrought us whenas we were famishing; and know, O my
mother, that the Maghrabi, the liar, the Magician, when sending me
down into the Hoard, sought nor the silver nor the gold wherewith the
four halls were fulfilled, but charged me to bring him only the Lamp
(naught else), because in very deed he had learned its priceless value;
and, had he not been certified of it, he had never endured such toil and
trouble nor had he travelled from his own land to our land in search
thereof; neither had he shut me up in the Treasury when he despaired
of the Lamp which I would not hand to him. Therefore it befitteth us,
O my mother, to keep the Lamp and take all care thereof nor disclose
its mysteries to any; for this is now our means of livelihood and this it
is shall enrich us. And likewise as regards the Ring, I will never with-
draw it from my finger, inasmuch as but for this thou hadst nevermore
seen me on life; nay I should have died within the Hoard underground.
How then can I possibly remove it from my finger? And who wotteth
that which may betide me by the lapse of Time, what trippings or
calamities or injurious mishaps wherefrom this Ring may deliver me?
However, for regard to thy feelings I will stow away the Lamp nor ever
suffer it to be seen of thee hereafter." Now when his mother heard his

words and pondered them she knew they were true and said to him, "Do, O my son, whatso thou willest; for my part I wish never to see them nor ever sight that frightful spectacle I erst saw." Aladdin and his mother continued eating of the meats brought them by the Jinni for two full told days till they were finished; but when he learned that nothing of food remained for them, he arose and took a platter of the platters which the Slave had brought upon the tray. Now they were all of the finest gold but the lad knew naught thereof; so he bore it to the Bazar and there, seeing a man which was a peddler, a viler than the Satans, offered it to him for sale. When the peddler espied it he took the lad aside that none might see him, and he looked at the platter and considered it till he was certified that it was of gold refined. But he knew not whether Aladdin was acquainted with its value or he was in such matters a raw laddie; so he asked him, "For how much, O my lord, this platter?" and the other answered, "Thou wottest what be its worth." The peddler debated with himself as to how much he should offer, because Aladdin had returned him a craftsman-like reply; and he thought of the smallest valuation; at the same time he feared lest the lad haply knowing its worth, should expect a considerable sum. So he said in his mind, "Belike the fellow is an ignoramus in such matters nor is ware of the price of the platter." Whereupon he pulled out of his pocket a dinar, and Aladdin eyed the gold piece lying in his palm and hastily taking it went his way; whereby the peddler was certified of his customer's innocence of all such knowledge, and repented with entire repentance that he had given him a golden dinar in lieu of a copper carat, a bright-polished groat. However, Aladdin made no delay but went at once to the baker's where he bought him bread and changed the ducat; then, going to his mother, he gave her the scones and the remaining small coin and said, "O my mother, hie thee and buy thee all we require." So she arose and walked to the Bazar and laid in the necessary stock; after which they ate and were cheered. And whenever the price of the platter was expended, Aladdin would take another and carry it to the accursed peddler who bought each and every at a pitiful price; and even this he would have minished but, seeing how he had paid a dinar for the first, he feared to offer a lesser sum, lest the lad go and sell to some rival in trade and thus he lose his usurious gains. Now when all the golden platters were sold, there remained only the silver tray whereupon they stood; and, for that it was large and weighty, Aladdin brought the peddler to his house and produced the article, when the buyer, seeing its size gave him ten dinars and these being accepted went his ways. Aladdin and his mother lived upon the sequins until they were spent; then he brought out the Lamp and rubbed it and straightway appeared the Slave who had shown himself aforetime. And said the lad, "I desire that thou bring me a tray of food like unto that thou broughtest me erewhiles, for indeed I am famisht." Accordingly, in the glance of an eye the Slave produced a similar tray supporting twelve platters of the most sumptuous, furnished with requisite cates; and thereon stood clean bread and sundry glass bottles of strained wine. Now Aladdin's mother had gone out when she knew he was about to rub the Lamp that she might not again look upon the Jinni; but after a while she returned and, when she sighted the tray covered with silvern platters and smelt the savour of the rich meats diffused over the house, she marvelled and rejoiced. Thereupon quoth he, "Look, O my mother! Thou badest me throw away the Lamp, see now its virtues;" and quoth she, "O my son, Allah increase his weal, but I would not look upon him." Then the lad sat down with his parent to the tray and they ate and drank until they were satisfied; after which they removed what remained for use on the morrow. As soon as the meats had been consumed, Aladdin arose and stowed away under his clothes a platter of the platters and went forth to find the Jew, purposing to sell it to him; but by fiat of Fate he passed by the shop of an ancient jeweller, an honest man and a pious who feared Allah. When the Shaykh saw the lad, he asked him saying, "O my son, what dost thou want? for that times manifold have I seen thee passing hereby and having dealings with a Jewish man; and I have espied thee handing over to him sundry articles; now also I fancy thou hast somewhat for sale and thou seekest him as a buyer thereof. But thou wottest not, O my child, that the Jews ever hold lawful to them the good of Moslems, the Confessors of Allah Almighty's unity, and always defraud them; especially this accursed Jew with whom thou hast relations and into whose hands thou hast fallen. If then, O my son, thou have aught thou wouldest sell show the same to me and never fear, for I will give thee its full price by the truth of Almighty Allah." Thereupon Aladdin brought out the platter which when the ancient goldsmith saw, he took and weighed it in his scales and asked the lad saying, "Was it the fellow of this thou soldest to the Jew?" "Yes, its fellow and its brother," he answered, and quoth the old man, "What price did he pay thee?" Quoth the lad, "One dinar." The ancient goldsmith, hearing from Aladdin how the Jew used to give only one dinar as the price of the platter, cried, "Ah! I take refuge from this Accursed who cozeneth the servants of Allah Almighty!" Then, looking at the lad, he exclaimed, "O my son, verily yon tricksy Jew hath cheated thee and laughed at thee, this platter being pure silver and virginal. I have weighed it and found it worth seventy dinars; and, if thou please to take its value, take it." Thereupon the Shaykh counted out to him seventy gold pieces, which he accepted and presently thanked him for his kindness in exposing the Jew's rascality. And after this, whenever the price of a platter was expended, he would bring another, and on such wise he and his mother were soon in better circumstances; yet they ceased not to live after their olden fashion as middle class folk without spending on diet overmuch or squandering money. But Aladdin had now thrown off the ungraciousness of his boyhood; he shunned the society of scapegraces and he began to frequent good men and true, repairing daily to the market-street of the merchants and there companying with the great and small of them, asking about matters of merchandise and learning the price of investments and so forth; he likewise frequented the Bazars of the Goldsmiths and the Jewellers where he would sit and divert himself by inspecting their precious stones and by noting how jewels were sold and bought therein. Accordingly, he presently became ware that the tree-fruits, wherewith he had filled his pockets what time he entered the Enchanted Treasury, were neither glass nor crystal but gems rich and rare; and he understood that he had acquired immense wealth such as the Kings never can possess. He then considered all the precious stones which were in the Jewellers' Quarter, but found that their biggest was not worth his smallest. On this wise he ceased not every day repairing to the Bazar and making himself familiar with the folk and winning their loving will; and enquiring anent selling and buying, giving and taking, the dear and the cheap, until one day of the days when, after rising at dawn and donning his dress he went forth, as was his wont, to the Jewellers' Bazar; and, as he passed along it he heard the crier crying as follows: "By command of our magnificent master, the King of the Time and the Lord of the Age and the Tide, let all the folk lock up their shops and stores and retire within their houses, for that the Lady Badr al-Budur, daughter of the Sultan, designeth to visit the Hammam; and whoso gainsayeth the order shall be punished with death-penalty and be his blood upon his own neck!" But when Aladdin heard the proclamation, he longed to look upon the King's daughter and said in his mind, "Indeed all the lieges talk of her beauty and loveliness and the end of my desires is to see her." Then Aladdin fell to contriving some means whereby he might look upon the Princess Badr al-Budur and at last judged best to take his station behind the Hammam-door whence he might see her face as she entered. Accordingly, without stay or delay he repaired to the Baths before she was expected and stood a-rear of the entrance, a place whereat none of the folk happened to be looking. Now when the Sultan's daughter had gone the rounds of the city and its main streets and had solaced herself by sight-seeing, she finally reached the Hammam and whilst entering she raised her veil, and when Aladdin saw her favour he said, "In very truth her fashion magnifieth her Almighty Fashioner and glory be to Him who created her and adorned her with this beauty and loveliness." His strength was struck down from the moment he saw her and his thoughts were distraught; his gaze was dazed, the love of her gat hold of the whole of his heart; and, when he returned home to his mother, he was as one in ecstasy. His parent addressed him, but he neither replied nor denied; and, when she set before him the morning meal he continued in like case; so quoth she, "O my son, what is 't may have befallen thee? Say me, doth aught ail thee? Let me know what ill hath betided thee for, unlike thy custom, thou speakest not when I bespeak thee." Thereupon Aladdin (who used to think that all women resembled his mother and who, albeit he had heard of the charms of Badr al-Budur, daughter of the Sultan, yet knew not what "beauty" and "loveliness" might signify) turned to his parent and exclaimed, "Let me be!" However, she persisted in praying him to come forwards and eat, so he did her bidding but hardly touched food; after which he lay at full length on his bed all the night through in cogitation deep until morning morrowed. The same was his condition during the next day, when his mother was perplexed for the case of her son and unable to learn what had happened to him. So, thinking that belike he might be ailing, she drew near him and asked him saying, "O my son, an thou sense aught of pain or such like, let me know that I may fare forth and fetch thee the physician; and to-day there be in this our city a leech from the Land of the Arabs whom the Sultan hath sent to summon and the bruit abroad reporteth him to be skilful exceedingly. So, an be thou ill let me go and bring him to thee." Aladdin, hearing his parent's offer to summon the mediciner, said, "O my mother, I am well in body and on no wise ill. But I ever thought that all women resembled thee until yesterday, when I beheld the Lady Badr al-Budur, daughter of the Sultan, as she was faring for the Baths." Then he related to her all and everything that had happened to him adding, "Haply thou also hast heard the crier a-crying:—Let no man open shop or stand in street that the Lady Badr al-Budur may repair to the Hammam without eye seeing her. But I have looked upon her even as she is, for she raised her veil at the door; and, when I viewed her favour and beheld that noble work of the Creator, a sore fit of ecstasy, O my mother, fell upon me for love of her and firm resolve to win her hath opened its way into every limb of me, nor is repose possible for me except I win her. Wherefore I purpose asking her to wife from the Sultan her sire in lawful wedlock." When Aladdin's mother heard her son's words, she belittled his wits and cried, "O my child, the name of Allah upon thee! meseemeth thou hast lost thy senses. But be thou rightly guided, O my son, nor be thou as the men Jinn-maddened!" He replied, "Nay, O mother of mine, I am not out of my mind nor am I of the maniacs; nor shall this thy saying alter one jot of what is in my thoughts, for rest is impossible to me until I shall have won the darling of my heart's core, the beautiful Lady Badr al-Budur. And now I am resolved to ask her of her sire the Sultan." She rejoined, "O my son, by my life upon thee speak not such speech, lest any overhear thee and say thou be insane: so cast away from thee such nonsense! Who shall undertake a matter like this or make such request to the King? Indeed, I know not how, supposing thy speech to be soothfast, thou shalt manage to crave such grace of the Sultan or through whom thou desirest to propose it." He retorted, "Through whom shall I ask it, O my mother, when thou art present? And who is there fonder and more faithful to me than thyself? So my design is that thou thyself shalt proffer this my petition." Quoth she, "O my son, Allah remove me far therefrom! What! have I lost my wits like thyself? Cast the thought away and a long way from thy heart. Remember whose son thou art, O my child, the orphan boy of a tailor, the poorest and meanest of the tailors toiling in this city; and I, thy mother, am also come of pauper folk and indigent. How then durst thou ask to wife the daughter of the Sultan, whose sire would not deign marry her with the sons of the Kings and the Sovrans, except they were his peers in honour and grandeur and majesty; and, were they but one degree lower, he would refuse his daughter to them." Aladdin took patience until his parent had said her say, when quoth he, "O my mother, everything thou hast called to mind is known to me; moreover 'tis thoroughly well known to me that I am the child of pauper parents; withal do not these words of thee divert me from my design at all, at all. Nor the less do I hope of thee, an I be thy son and thou truly love me, that thou grant me this favour, otherwise thou wilt destroy me; and present Death hovereth over my head except I win my will of heart's dearling; and I, O my mother, am in every case thy child." Hearing these words, his parent wept of her sorrow for him and said, "O my child! Yes, in very deed I am thy mother, nor have I any son or life's blood of my liver except thyself, and the end of my wishes is to give thee a wife and rejoice in thee. But suppose that I would seek a bride of our likes and equals, her people will at once ask an thou have any land or garden, merchandise or handicraft, wherewith thou canst support her; and what is the reply I can return? Then, if I cannot possibly answer the poor like ourselves, how shall I be bold enough, O my son, to ask for the daughter of the Sultan of China-land who hath no peer or behind or before him? Therefore do thou weigh this matter in thy mind. Also who shall ask her to wife for the son of a snip? Well indeed I wot that my saying aught of this kind will but increase our misfortunes; for that it may be the cause of our incurring mortal danger from the Sultan; peradventure even death for thee and me. And, as concerneth myself, how shall I venture upon such rash deed and perilous, O my son? and in what way shall I ask the Sultan for his daughter to be thy wife; and, indeed, how ever shall I even get access to him? And should I succeed therein, what is to be my answer an they ask me touching thy means? Haply the King will hold me to be a madwoman. And, lastly, suppose that I obtain audience of the Sultan, what offering is there I can submit to the King's majesty? 'Tis true, O my child, that the Sultan is mild and merciful, never rejecting any who approach him to require justice or ruth or protection, nor any who pray him for a present; for he is liberal and lavisheth favour upon near and far. But he dealeth his boons to those deserving them, to men who have done some derring-do in battle under his eyes or have rendered as civilians great service to his estate. But thou! do thou tell me what feat thou hast performed in his presence or before the public that thou meritest from him such grace? And, secondly, this boon thou ambitionest is not for one of our condition, nor is it possible that the King grant to thee the bourne of thine aspiration; for whoso goeth to the Sultan and craveth of him a favour, him it besitteth to take in hand somewhat that suiteth the royal majesty, as indeed I warned thee aforetime. How, then, shalt thou risk thyself to stand before the Sultan and ask his daughter in marriage, when thou hast with thee naught to offer him of that which beseemeth his exalted station?" Hereto Aladdin replied, "O my mother, thou speakest to the point and hast reminded me aright and 'tis meet that I revolve in mind the whole of thy remindings. But, O my mother, the love of Princess Badr al-Budur hath entered into the core of my heart; nor can I rest without I win her. However, thou hast also recalled to me a matter which I forgot and 'tis this emboldeneth me to ask his daughter of the King. Albeit thou, O my mother, declarest that I have no gift which I can submit to the Sultan, as is the wont of the world, yet in very sooth I have an offering and a present whose equal, O my mother, I hold none of the Kings to possess; no, nor even aught like it. Because verily that which I deemed glass or crystal was nothing but precious stones and I hold that all the Kings of the World have never possessed any thing like one of the smallest thereof. For, by frequenting the jeweller-folk, I have learned that they are the costliest gems and these are what I brought in my pockets from the Hoard, whereupon, an thou please, compose thy mind. We have in our house a bowl of China porcelain; so arise thou and fetch it, that I may fill it with these jewels, which thou shalt carry as a gift to the King, and thou shalt stand in his presence and solicit him for my requirement. I am certified that by such means the matter will become easy to thee; and, if thou be unwilling, O my mother, to strive for the winning of my wish as regards the Lady Badr al-Budur, know thou that surely I shall die. Nor do thou imagine that this gift is of aught save the costliest of stones and be assured, O my mother, that in my many visits to the Jewellers' Bazar I have observed the merchants selling for sums man's judgment may not determine jewels whose beauty is not worth one quarter carat of what we possess; seeing which I was certified that ours are beyond all price. So arise, O my mother, as I bade thee and bring me the porcelain bowl aforesaid, that I may arrange therein some of these gems and we will see what semblance they show." So she brought him the China bowl saying in herself, "I shall know what to do when I find out if the words of my child concerning these jewels be soothfast or not;" and she set it before her son who pulled the stones out of his pockets and disposed them in the bowl and ceased not arranging therein gems of sorts till such time as he had filled it. And when it was brimful she could not fix her eyes firmly upon it; on the contrary, she winked and blinked for the dazzle of the stones and their radiance and excess of lightning-like glance; and her wits were bewildered thereat; only she was not certified of their value being really of the enormous extent she had been told. Withal she reflected that possibly her son might have spoken aright when he declared that their like was not to be found with the Kings. Then Aladdin turned to her and said, "Thou hast seen, O my mother, that this present intended for the Sultan is magnificent, and I am certified that it will procure for thee high honour with him and that he will receive thee with all respect. And now, O my mother, thou hast no excuse; so compose thy thoughts and arise; take thou this bowl and away with it to the palace." His mother rejoined, "O my son, 'tis true that the present is high-priced exceedingly and the costliest of the costly; also that according to thy word none owneth its like. But who would have the boldness to go and ask the Sultan for his daughter, the Lady Badr al-Budur? I indeed dare not say to him: — I want thy daughter! when he shall ask me: — What is thy want? for know thou, O my son, that my tongue will be tied. And, granting that Allah assist me and I embolden myself to say to him: — My wish is to become a connection of thine through the marriage of thy daughter the Lady Badr al-Budur, to my son Aladdin, they will surely decide at once that I am demented and will thrust me forth in disgrace and despised. I will not tell thee that I shall thereby fall into danger of death, for 'twill not be I only but thou likewise. However, O my son, of my regard for thine inclination, I needs must embolden myself and hie thither; yet, O my child, if the King receive me and honour me on account of the gift and enquire of me what thou desirest, and in reply I ask of him that which thou desirest in the matter of thy marriage with his daughter, how shall I answer him an he ask me, as is man's wont, What estates hast thou, and what income? And perchance, O my son, he will question me of this before questioning me of thee." Aladdin replied, "'Tis not possible that the Sultan should make such demand what time he considereth the jewels and their magnificence; nor is it meet to think of such things as these which may never occur. Now do thou but arise and set before him this present of precious stones and ask of him his daughter for me, and sit not yonder making much of the difficulty in thy fancy. Ere this thou hast learned, O mother mine, that the Lamp which we possess hath become to us a stable income and that whatso I want of it the same is supplied to me; and my hope is that by means thereof I shall learn how to answer the Sultan should he ask me of that thou sayest." Then Aladdin and his mother fell to talking over the subject all that night long and when morning morrowed, the dame arose and heartened her heart, especially as her son had expounded to her some little of the powers of the Lamp and the virtues thereof; to wit, that it would supply all they required of it. Aladdin, however, seeing his parent take courage when he explained to her the workings of the Lamp, feared lest she might tattle to the folk thereof; so he said to her, "O my mother, beware how thou talk to any of the properties of the Lamp and its profit, as this is our one great good. Guard thy thoughts lest thou speak over much concerning it before others, whoso they be; haply we shall lose it and lose the boon fortune we possess and the benefits we expect, for that 'tis of him." His mother replied, "Fear not therefor, O my son," and she arose and took the bowl full of jewels, which she wrapped up in a fine kerchief, and went forth betimes that she might reach the Divan ere it became crowded. When she passed into the Palace, the levée not being fully attended, she saw the Wazirs and sundry of the Lords of the land going into the presence-room and after a short time, when the Divan was made complete by the Ministers and high Officials and Chieftains and Emirs and Grandees, the Sultan appeared and the Wazirs made their obeisance and likewise did the Nobles and the Notables. The King seated himself upon the throne of his kingship, and all present at the levée stood before him with crossed arms awaiting his commandment to sit; and, when they received it, each took his place according to his degree; then the claimants came before the Sultan who delivered sentence, after his wonted way, until the Divan was ended, when the King arose and withdrew into the palace and the others all went their ways. And when Aladdin's mother saw the throne empty and the King passing into his Harem, she also wended her ways and returned home. But as soon as her son espied her, bowl in hand, he thought that haply something untoward had befallen her, but he would not ask of aught until such time as she had set down the bowl, when she acquainted him with that had occurred and ending by adding, "Alhamdolillah, — laud to the Lord! — O my child, that I found courage enough and secured for myself standing-place in the levée this day; and, albe I dreaded to bespeak the King yet (Inshallah!) on the morrow I will address him. Even to-day were many who, like myself, could not get audience of the Sultan. But be of good cheer, O my son, and to-morrow needs must I bespeak him for thy sake; and what happened not may happen." When Aladdin heard his parent's words, he joyed with excessive joy; and, although he expected the matter to be managed hour by hour, for excess of his love and longing to the Lady Badr al-Budur yet he possessed his soul in patience. They slept well

that night and betimes next morning the mother of Aladdin arose and
went with her bowl to the King's court which she found closed. So she
asked the people and they told her that the Sultan did not hold a levée
every day but only thrice in the se'nnight; wherefor she determined to
return home; and, after this, whenever she saw the court open she
would stand before the King until the reception ended and when it was
shut she would go to make sure thereof; and this was the case for the
whole month. The Sultan was wont to remark her presence at every
levée, but, on the last day when she took her station, as was her wont,
before the Council, she allowed it to close and lacked boldness to come
forwards and speak even a syllable. Now as the King having risen was
making for his Harem accompanied by the Grand Wazir, he turned to
him and said, "O Wazir, during the last six or seven levée days I see
yonder old woman present herself at every reception and I also note
that she always carrieth a something under her mantilla. Say me, hast
thou, O Wazir, any knowledge of her and her intention?" "O my lord
the Sultan," said the other, "verily women be weakly of wits, and haply
this goodwife cometh hither to complain before thee against her good-
man or some of her people." But this reply was far from satisfying the
Sultan; nay, he bade the Wazir, in case she should come again, set her
before him; and forthright the Minister placed hand on head and
exclaimed, "To hear is to obey, O our lord the Sultan!" Now one day
of the days, when she did according to her custom, the Sultan cast his
eyes upon her as she stood before him, and said to his Grand Wazir,
"This be the very woman whereof I spake to thee yesterday, so do thou
straightway bring her before me, that I may see what be her suit and fulfil her need." Accordingly, the Minister at once introduced her and
when in the presence she saluted the King by kissing her finger-tips and
raising them to her brow; and, praying for the Sultan's glory and con-
tinuance and the permanence of his prosperity, bussed ground before
him. Thereupon, quoth he, "O woman, for sundry days I have seen
thee attend the levée sans a word said; so tell me an thou have any
requirement I may grant." She kissed ground a second time and after
blessing him, answered, "Yea, verily, as thy head liveth, O King of the
Age, I have a want; but first of all, do thou deign grant me a promise of
safety that I may prefer my suit to the ears of our lord the Sultan; for
haply thy Highness may find it a singular." The King, wishing to know
her need, and being a man of unusual mildness and clemency, gave his
word for her immunity and bade forthwith dismiss all about him,
remaining without other but the Grand Wazir. Then he turned towards
his suppliant and said, "Inform me of thy suit: thou hast the safeguard
of Allah Almighty." "O King of the Age," replied she, "I also require of
thee pardon;" and quoth he, "Allah pardon thee even as I do." Then,
quoth she, "O our lord the Sultan, I have a son, Aladdin hight; and he,

one day of the days, having heard the crier commanding all men to shut shop and shun the streets, for that the Lady Badr al-Budur, daughter of the Sultan, was going to the Hammam, felt an uncontrollable longing to look upon her, and hid himself in a stead whence he could sight her right well, and that place was behind the door of the Baths. When she entered he beheld her and considered her as he wished, and but too well; for, since the time he looked upon her, O King of the Age, unto this hour, life hath not been pleasant to him. And he hath required of me that I ask her to wife for him from thy Highness, nor could I drive this fancy from his mind because love of her hath mastered his vitals and to such degree that he said to me: Know thou, O mother mine, that an I win not my wish surely I shall die. Accordingly I hope that thy Highness will deign be mild and merciful and pardon this boldness on the part of me and my child and refrain to punish us therefor." When the Sultan heard her tale he regarded her with kindness and, laughing aloud, asked her, "What may be that thou carriest and what be in yonder kerchief?" And she seeing the Sultan laugh in lieu of waxing wroth at her words, forthright opened the wrapper and set before him the bowl of jewels, whereby the audience-hall was illumined as it were by lustres and candelabra; and he was dazed and amazed at the radiance of the rare gems, and he fell to marvelling at their size and beauty and excellence and cried, "Never at all until this day saw I anything like these jewels for size and beauty and excellence: nor deem I that there be found in my treasury a single one like them." Then he turned to his Minister and asked, "What sayest thou, O Wazir? Tell me, hast thou seen in thy time such mighty fine jewels as these?" The other answered, "Never saw I such, O our lord the Sultan, nor do I think that there be in the treasures of my lord the Sultan the fellow of the least thereof." The King resumed, "Now indeed whoso hath presented to me such jewels meriteth to become bridegroom to my daughter, Badr al-Budur; because, as far as I see, none is more deserving of her than he." When the Wazir heard the Sultan's words he was tongue-tied with concern and he grieved with sore grief, for the King had promised to give the Princess in marriage to his son; so after a little while he said, "O King of the Age, thy Highness deigned promise me that the Lady Badr al-Budur should be spouse to my son; so 'tis but right that thine exalted Highness vouchsafe us a delay of three months, during which time, Inshallah! my child may obtain and present an offering yet costlier than this." Accordingly the King, albeit he knew that such a thing could not be done, or by the Wazir or by the greatest of his Grandees, yet of his grace and kindness granted him the required delay. Then he turned to the old woman, Aladdin's mother, and said, "Go to thy son and tell him I have pledged my word that my daughter shall be in his name; only 'tis needful that I make the requisite preparations of nuptial furniture for her use; and 'tis only meet that he take patience for the next three months." Receiving this reply, Aladdin's mother thanked the Sultan and blessed him; then, going forth in hottest haste, as one flying for joy, she went home; and when her son saw her entering with a smiling face, he was gladdened at the sign of good news, especially because she had returned without delay as on the past days, and had not brought back the bowl. Presently he asked her saying, "Inshallah, thou bearest me, O my mother, glad tidings; and peradventure the jewels and their value have wrought their work and belike thou hast been kindly received by the King and he hath shown thee grace and hath given ear to thy request?" So she told him the whole tale, how the Sultan had entreated her well and had marvelled at the extraordinary size of the gems and their surpassing water as did also the Wazir, adding, "And he promised that his daughter should be thine. Only, O my child, the Wazir spake of a secret contract made with him by the Sultan before he pledged himself to me and, after speaking privily, the King put me off to the end of three months: therefore I have become fearful lest the Wazir be evilly disposed to thee and perchance he may attempt to change the Sultan's mind." When Aladdin heard his mother's words and how the Sultan had promised him his daughter, deferring, however, the wedding until after the third month, his mind was gladdened and he rejoiced exceedingly and said, "Inasmuch as the King hath given his word after three months (well, it *is* a long time!), at all events my gladness is mighty great." Then he thanked his parent, showing her how her good work had exceeded her toil and travail; and said to her, "By Allah, O my mother, hitherto I was as 'twere in my grave and therefrom thou hast withdrawn me; and I praise Allah Almighty because I am at this moment certified that no man in the world is happier than I or more fortunate." Then he took patience until two of the three months had gone by. Now one day of the days his mother fared forth about sundown to the Bazar that she might buy somewhat of oil; and she found all the market shops fast shut and the whole city decorated, and the folk placing waxen tapers and flowers at their casements; and she beheld the soldiers and household troops and Aghas riding in procession and flambeaux and lustres flaming and flaring, and she wondered at the marvellous sight and the glamour of the scene. So she went in to an oilman's store which stood open still and bought her need of him and said, "By thy life, O uncle, tell me what be the tidings in town this day, that people have made all these decorations and every house and market-street are adorned and the troops all stand on guard?" The oilman asked her, "O woman, I suppose thou art a stranger and not one of this city?" and she answered, "Nay, I am thy townswoman." He rejoined, "Thou a townswoman, and yet wottest not that this very night the son of the Grand Wazir goeth in to the Lady

Badr al-Budur, daughter of the Sultan! He is now in the Hammam and all this power of soldiery is on guard and standing under arms to await his coming forth, when they will bear him in bridal procession to the palace where the Princess expecteth him." As the mother of Aladdin heard these words, she grieved and was distraught in thought and perplexed how to inform her son of this sorrowful event, well knowing that the poor youth was looking, hour by hour, to the end of the three months. But she returned straightway home to him and when she entered she said, "O my son, I would give thee certain tidings, yet hard to me will be the sorrow they shall occasion thee." He cried, "Let me know what be thy news;" and she replied, "Verily the Sultan hath broken his promise to thee in the matter of the Lady Badr al-Budur, and this very night the Grand Wazir's son goeth in to her. And for some time, O my son, I have suspected that the Minister would change the King's mind, even as I told thee how he had spoken privily to him before me." Aladdin asked, "How learnedst thou that the Wazir's son is this night to pay his first visit to the Princess?" So she told him the whole tale, how when going to buy oil she had found the city decorated and the eunuch-officials and Lords of the land with the troops under arms awaiting the bridegroom from the Baths; and that the first visit was appointed for that very night. Hearing this Aladdin was seized with a fever of jealousy brought on by his grief: however, after a short while he remembered the Lamp and, recovering his spirits said, "By thy life, O my mother, do thou believe that the Wazir's son will not enjoy her as thou thinkest. But now leave we this discourse and arise thou and serve up supper and after eating let me retire to my own chamber and all will be well and happy." After he had supped Aladdin retired to his chamber and, locking the door, brought out the Lamp and rubbed it, whenas forthright appeared to him its Familiar who said, "Ask whatso thou wantest, for I am thy Slave and Slave to him who holdeth the Lamp in hand; I and all the Slaves of the Lamp." He replied, "Hear me! I prayed the Sultan for his daughter to wife and he plighted her to me after three months; but he hath not kept his word; nay, he hath given her to the son of the Wazir and this very night the bridegroom will go in to her. Therefore I command thee (an thou be a trusty Servitor to the Lamp) when thou shalt see bride and bridegroom bedded together this night, at once take them up and bear them hither abed; and this be what I want of thee." The Marid replied, "Hearing and obeying; and if thou have other service but this, do thou demand of me all thou desirest." Aladdin rejoined, "At the present time I require naught save that I bade thee do." Hereupon the Slave disappeared and Aladdin returned to pass the rest of the evening with his mother. But at that hour when he knew that the Servitor would be coming, he arose and retired to his chamber and after a little while, behold, the Marid came bringing to him the newly-wedded couple upon their bridal-bed. Aladdin rejoiced to see them with exceeding joy; then he cried to the Slave, "Carry yonder gallows-bird hence and lay him at full length in the privy." His bidding was done straightway; but, before leaving him, the Slave blew upon the bridegroom a blast so cold that it shrivelled him and the plight of the Wazir's son became piteous. Then the Servitor returning to Aladdin said to him, "An thou require aught else, inform me thereof;" and said the other, "Return a-morn that thou mayst restore them to their stead;" whereto, "I hear and obey," quoth the Marid and evanished. Presently Aladdin arose, hardly believing that the affair had been such a success for him; but whenas he looked upon the Lady Badr al-Budur lying under his own roof, albeit he had long burned with her love yet he preserved respect for her and said, "O Princess of fair ones, think not that I brought thee hither to minish thy honour. Heaven forbid! Nay 'twas only to prevent the wrong man enjoying thee, for that thy sire the Sultan promised thee to me. So do thou rest in peace." When the Lady Badr al-Budur, daughter of the Sultan, saw herself in that mean and darksome lodging, and heard Aladdin's words, she was seized with fear and trembling and waxed clean distraught; nor could she return aught of reply. Presently the youth arose and stripping off his outer dress placed a scymitar between them and lay upon the bed beside the Princess; and he did no villain deed, for it sufficed him to prevent the consummation of her nuptials with the Wazir's son. On the other hand the Lady Badr al Budur passed a night the evillest of all nights; nor in her born days had she seen a worse; and the same was the case with the Minister's son who lay in the chapel of ease and who dared not stir for the fear of the Jinni which overwhelmed him. As soon as it was morning the Slave appeared before Aladdin, without the Lamp being rubbed, and said to him, "O my lord, an thou require aught, command me therefor, that I may do it upon my head and mine eyes." Said the other, "Go, take up and carry the bride and bridegroom to their own apartment;" so the Servitor did his bidding in an eye-glance and bore away the pair, and placed them in the palace as whilome they were and without their seeing any one; but both died of affright when they found themselves being transported from stead to stead. And the Marid had barely time to set them down and wend his ways ere the Sultan came on a visit of congratulation to his daughter; and, when the Wazir's son heard the doors thrown open, he sprang straightway from his couch and donned his dress for he knew that none save the King could enter at that hour. Yet it was exceedingly hard for him to leave his bed wherein he wished to warm himself a trifle after his cold night in the water-closet which he had lately left. The Sultan went in to his daughter Badr al-Budur and kissing her between the eyes gave her good morning and asked her of her bridegroom and whether she was pleased and satisfied with him. But she returned no reply whatever and looked at him with the eye of anger and, although he repeated his words again and again, she held her peace nor bespake him with a single syllable. So the King quitted her and, going to the Queen, informed her of what had taken place between him and his daughter; and the mother, unwilling to leave the Sultan angered with their child, said to him, "O King of the Age, this be the custom of most newly-married couples at least during their first days of marriage, for that they are bashful and somewhat coy. So deign thou excuse her and after a little while she will again become herself and speak with the folk as before, whereas now her shame, O King of the Age, keepeth her silent. However 'tis my wish to fare forth and see her." Thereupon the Queen arose and donned her dress; then, going to her daughter, wished her good morning and kissed her between the eyes. Yet would the Princess make no answer at all, whereat quoth the Queen to herself, "Doubtless some strange matter hath occurred to trouble her with such trouble as this." So she asked her saying, "O my daughter, what hath caused this thy case? Let me know what hath betided thee that, when I come and give thee good morning, thou hast not a word to say to me?" Thereat the Lady Badr al-Budur raised her head and said, "Pardon me, O my mother, 'twas my duty to meet thee with all respect and worship, seeing that thou hast honoured me by this visit. However, I pray thee to hear the cause of this my condition and see how the night I have just spent hath been to me the evillest of the nights. Hardly had we lain down, O my mother, than one whose form I wot not uplifted our bed and transported it to a darksome place, fulsome and mean." Then the Princess related to the Queen-mother all that had befallen her that night; how they had taken away her bridegroom, leaving her lone and lonesome, and how after a while came another youth who lay beside her, in lieu of her bridegroom, after placing his scymitar between her and himself; "and in the morning" (she continued) "he who carried us off returned and bore us straight back to our own stead. But at once when he arrived hither he left us and suddenly my sire the Sultan entered at the hour and moment of our coming and I had nor heart nor tongue to speak him withal, for the stress of the terror and trembling which came upon me. Haply such lack of duty may have proved sore to him, so I hope, O my mother, that thou wilt acquaint him with the cause of this my condition and that he will pardon me for not answering him and blame me not, but rather accept my excuses." When the Queen heard these words of Princess Badr al-Budur, she said to her, "O my child, compose thy thoughts. An thou tell such tale before any, haply shall he say:— Verily, the Sultan's daughter hath lost her wits. And thou hast done right well in not choosing to recount thine adventure to thy father; and beware and again I say beware, O my daughter, lest thou inform him thereof." The Princess replied, "O my mother, I have spoken to thee like one sound in senses nor have I lost my wits: this be what befel me and, if thou believe it not because coming from me, ask my bridegroom." To which the Queen replied, "Rise up straightway, O my daughter, and banish from thy thoughts such fancies as these; and robe thyself and come forth to glance at the bridal feasts and festivities they are making in the city for the sake of thee and thy nuptials; and listen to the drumming and the singing and look at the decorations all intended to honour thy marriage, O my daughter." So saying, the Queen at once summoned the tirewomen who dressed and prepared the Lady Badr al-Budur; and presently she went in to the Sultan and assured him that their daughter had suffered during all her wedding-night from swevens and nightmare and said to him, "Be not severe with her for not answering thee." Then the Queen sent privily for the Wazir's son and asked of the matter, saying, "Tell me, are these words of the Lady Badr al-Budur soothfast or not?" But he, in his fear of losing his bride out of hand, answered, "O my lady, I have no knowledge of that whereof thou speakest." Accordingly the mother made sure that her daughter had seen visions and dreams. The marriage-feasts lasted throughout that day with Almahs and singers and the smiting of all manner instruments of mirth and merriment, while the Queen and the Wazir and his son strave right strenuously to enhance the festivities that the Princess might enjoy herself; and that day they left nothing of what exciteth to pleasure unrepresented in her presence, to the end that she might forget what was in her thoughts and derive increase of joyance. Yet did naught of this take any effect upon her; nay, she sat in silence, sad of thought, sore perplexed at what had befallen her during the last night. It is true that the Wazir's son had suffered even more because he had passed his sleeping hours lying in the water-closet: he, however, had falsed the story and had cast out remembrance of the night; in the first place for his fear of losing his bride and with her the honour of a connection which brought him such excess of consideration and for which men envied him so much; and, secondly, on account of the wondrous loveliness of the Lady Badr al-Budur and her marvellous beauty. Aladdin also went forth that day and looked at the merry-makings which extended throughout the city as well as the palace and he fell a-laughing, especially when he heard the folk prating of the high honour which had accrued to the son of the Wazir and the prosperity of his fortunes in having become son-in-law to the Sultan and the high consideration shown by the wedding fêtes. And he said in his mind, "Indeed ye wot not, O ye miserables, what befel him last night that ye envy him!" But after darkness fell and it was time for sleep, Aladdin arose and, retiring to his chamber, rubbed the Lamp, whereupon the Slave incontinently appeared and was bidden to bring him the Sultan's daughter together with her bridegroom as on the past night ere the Wazir's son could abate her maidenhead. So the Marid without stay or delay evanished for a little while until the appointed time, when he returned carrying the bed whereon lay the Lady Badr al-Budur and the Wazir's son; and he did with the bridegroom as he had done before, to wit, he took him and lay him at full length in the jakes and there left him dried up for excess of fear and trembling. Then Aladdin arose, and placing the scymitar between himself and the Princess, lay down beside her; and when day broke the Slave restored the pair to their own place, leaving Aladdin filled with delight at the state of the Minister's son. Now when the Sultan woke up amorn he resolved to visit his daughter and see if she would treat him as on the past day; so shaking off his sleep he sprang up and arrayed himself in his raiment and, going to the apartment of the Princess bade open the door. Thereat the son of the Wazir arose forthright and came down from his bed and began donning his dress whilst his ribs were wrung with cold; for when the King entered the Slave had but just brought him back. The Sultan, raising the arras, drew near his daughter as she lay abed and gave her good morning; then kissing her between the eyes, he asked her of her case. But he saw her looking sour and sad and she answered him not at all, only glowering at him as one in anger and her plight was pitiable. Hereat the Sultan waxed wroth with her for that she would not reply and he suspected that something evil had befallen her, whereupon he bared his blade and cried to her, brand in hand, saying, "What be this hath betided thee? Either acquaint me with what happened or this very moment I till take thy life! Is such conduct the token of honour and respect I expect of thee, that I address thee and thou answerest me not a word?" When the Lady Badr al-Budur saw her sire in high dudgeon and the naked glaive in his grip, she was freed from her fear of the past, so she raised her head and said to him, "O my beloved father, be not wroth with me nor be hasty in thy hot passion, for I am excusable in what thou shalt see of my case. So do thou lend an ear to what occurred to me and well I wot that after hearing my account of what befel to me during these two last nights, thou wilt pardon me and thy Highness will be softened to pitying me even as I claim of thee affection for thy child." Then the Princess informed her father of all that had betided her adding, "O my sire, an thou believe me not, ask my bridegroom and he will recount to thy Highness the whole adventure; nor did I know either what they would do with him when they bore him away from my side or where they would place him." When the Sultan heard his daughter's words, he was saddened and his eyes brimmed with tears; then he sheathed his sabre and kissed her saying, "O my daughter, wherefore didst thou not tell me what happened on the past night that I might have guarded thee from this torture and and terror which visited

thee a second time? But now 'tis no matter. Rise and cast out all such
care and to-night I will set a watch to ward thee nor shall any mishap
again make thee miserable." Then the Sultan returned to his palace
and straightway bade summon the Grand Wazir and asked him, as he
stood before him in his service, "O Wazir, how dost thou look upon this
matter? Haply thy son hath informed thee of what occurred to him and
to my daughter." The Minister replied, "O King of the Age, I have not
seen my son or yesterday or to-day." Hereat the Sultan told him all that
had afflicted the Princess, adding, "'Tis my desire that thou at once
seek tidings of thy son concerning the facts of the case: peradventure of
her fear my daughter may not be fully aware of what really befel her;
withal I hold all her words to be truthful." So the Grand Wazir arose
and, going forth, bade summon his son and asked him anent all his lord
had told him whether it be true or untrue. The youth replied, "O my
father the Wazir, Heaven forbid that the Lady Badr al-Budur speak
falsely: indeed all she said was sooth and these two nights proved to us
the evillest of our nights instead of being nights of pleasure and mar-
riage-joys. But what befel me was the greatest evil because, instead of
sleeping abed with my bride, I lay in the wardrobe, a black hole, frightful, noisome of stench, truly damnable; and my ribs were bursten with
cold." In fine, the young man told his father the whole tale, adding as
he ended it, "O dear father mine, I implore thee to speak with the
Sultan that he may set me free from this marriage. Yes, indeed 'tis a
high honour for me to be the Sultan's son-in-law and especially the
love of the Princess hath gotten hold of my vitals; but I have no strength
left to endure a single night like unto these two last." The Wazir, hearing the words of his son, was saddened and sorrowful exceedingly, for it
was his design to advance and promote his child by making him son-
in-law to the Sultan. So he became thoughtful and perplexed about the
affair and the device whereby to manage it, and it was sore grievous for
him to break off the marriage, it having been a rare enjoyment to him
that he had fallen upon such high good fortune. Accordingly he said,
"Take patience, O my son, until we see what may happen this night,
when we will set watchmen to ward you; nor do thou give up the
exalted distinction which hath fallen to none save to thyself." Then the
Wazir left him and, returning to the sovran, reported that all told to him
by the Lady Badr al-Budr was a true tale; whereupon quoth the Sultan,
"Since the affair is on this wise, we require no delay," and he at once
ordered all the rejoicings to cease and the marriage to be broken off.
This caused the folk and the citizens to marvel at the matter, especially
when they saw the Grand Wazir and his son leaving the palace in
pitiable plight for grief and stress of passion; and the people fell to asking, "What hath happened and what is the cause of the wedding being
made null and void?" Nor did any know aught of the truth save Aladdin

the lover who claimed the Princess's hand, and he laughed in his sleeve. But even after the marriage was dissolved, the Sultan forgot nor even recalled to mind his promise made to Aladdin's mother; and the same was the case with the Grand Wazir, while neither had any inkling of whence befel them that which had befallen. So Aladdin patiently awaited the lapse of the three months after which the Sultan had pledged himself to give him to wife his daughter; but, soon as ever the term came, he sent his mother to the Sultan for the purpose of requiring him to keep his covenant. So she went to the palace and when the King appeared in the Divan and saw the old woman standing before him, he remembered his promise to her concerning the marriage after a term of three months, and he turned to the Minister and said, "O Wazir, this be the ancient dame who presented me with the jewels and to whom we pledged our word that when the three months had elapsed we would summon her to our presence before all others." So the Minister went forth and fetched her and when she went in to the Sultan's presence she saluted him and prayed for his glory and permanence of prosperity. Hereat the King asked her if she needed aught, and she answered, "O King of the Age, the three months' term thou assignedst to me is finished, and this is thy time to marry my son Aladdin with thy daughter, the Lady Badr al-Budur." The Sultan was distraught at this demand, especially when he saw the old woman's pauper condition, one of the meanest of her kind; and yet the offering she had brought to him was of the most magnificent, far beyond his power to pay the price. Accordingly, he turned to the Grand Wazir and said, "What device is there with thee? In very sooth I did pass my word, yet meseemeth that they be pauper folk and not persons of high condition." The Grand Wazir, who was dying of envy and who was especially saddened by what had befallen his son, said to himself, "How shall one like this wed the King's daughter and my son lose this highmost honour?" Accordingly, he answered his Sovran speaking privily, "O my lord, 'tis an easy matter to keep off a poor devil such as this, for he is not worthy that thy Highness give his daughter to a fellow whom none knoweth what he may be." "By what means," enquired the Sultan, "shall we put off the man when I pledged my promise; and the word of the Kings is their bond?" Replied the Wazir, "O my lord, my rede is that thou demand of him forty platters made of pure sand-gold and full of gems (such as the woman brought thee aforetime), with forty white slave-girls to carry the platters and forty black eunuch-slaves." The King rejoined, "By Allah, O Wazir, thou hast spoken to the purpose, seeing that such thing is not possible and by this way we shall be freed." Then quoth he to Aladdin's mother, "Do thou go and tell thy son that I am a man of my word even as I plighted it to him, but on condition that he have power to pay the dower of my daughter; and that which I require of him is a settlement consisting of two score platters of virgin gold, all brimming with gems the like of those thou broughtest to me, and as many white handmaids to carry them and two score black eunuch-slaves to serve and escort the bearers. An thy son avail hereto I will marry him with my daughter." Thereupon she returned home wagging her head and saying in her mind, "Whence can my poor boy procure these platters and such jewels? And granted that he return to the Enchanted Treasury and pluck them from the trees which, however, I hold impossible; yet given that he bring them whence shall he come by the girls and the blacks?" Nor did she leave communing with herself till she reached her home, where she found Aladdin awaiting her, and she lost no time in saying, "O my son, did I not tell thee never to fancy that thy power would extend to the Lady Badr al-Budur, and that such a matter is not possible to folk like ourselves?" "Recount to me the news," quoth he; so quoth she, "O my child, verily the Sultan received me with all honour according to his custom and, meseemeth his intentions towards us be friendly. But thine enemy is that accursed Wazir; for, after I addressed the King in thy name as thou badest me say:—In very sooth the promised term is past, adding:—'Twere well an thy Highness would deign issue commandment for the espousals of thy daughter the Lady Badr al-Budur to my son Aladdin, he turned to and addressed the Minister who answered privily, after which the Sultan gave me his reply." Then she enumerated the King's demand and said, "O my son, he indeed expecteth of thee an instant reply; but I fancy that we have no answer for him." When Aladdin heard these words he laughed and said, "O my mother, thou affirmest that we have no answer and thou deemest the case difficult exceedingly; but compose thy thoughts and arise and bring me somewhat we may eat; and, after we have dined, an the Compassionate be willing, thou shalt see my reply. Also the Sultan thinketh like thyself that he hath demanded a prodigious dower in order to divert me from his daughter, whereas the fact is that he hath required of me a matter far less than I expected. But do thou fare forth at once and purchase the provision and leave me to procure thee a reply." So she went out to fetch her needful from the Bazar and Aladdin retired to his chamber and taking the Lamp rubbed it, when forthright appeared to him its Slave and said, "Ask, O my lord, whatso thou wantest." The other replied, "I have demanded of the Sultan his daughter to wife and he hath required of me forty bowls of purest gold each weighing ten pounds and all to be filled with gems such as we find in the Gardens of the Hoard; furthermore, that they be borne on the heads of as many white handmaids, each attended by her black eunuch-slave, also forty in full rate; so I desire that thou bring all these into my presence." "Hearkening and obeying, O my lord," quoth the Slave, and, disappearing for the space of an hour or so, presently returned bringing the platters and jewels, handmaids and eunuchs; then, setting them before him the Marid cried, "This be what thou demandedst of me: declare now an thou want any matter or service other than this." Aladdin rejoined, "I have need of naught else; but, an I do, I will summon thee and let thee know." The Slave now disappeared and, after a little while, Aladdin's mother returned home and, on entering the house, saw the blacks and the handmaids. Hereat she wondered and exclaimed, "All this proceedeth from the Lamp which Allah perpetuate to my son!" But ere she doffed her mantilla Aladdin said to her, "O my mother, this be thy time before the Sultan enter his Serraglio-palace do thou carry to him what he required and wend thou with it at once, so may he know that I avail to supply all he wanteth and yet more; also that he is beguiled by his Grand Wazir and the twain imagined vainly that they would baffle me." Then he arose forthright and opened the house-door, when the handmaids and blackamoors paced forth in pairs, each girl with her eunuch beside her, until they crowded the quarter, Aladdin's mother foregoing them. And when the folk of that ward sighted such mighty fine sight and marvellous spectacle, all stood at gaze and they considered the forms and figures of the handmaids marvelling at their beauty and loveliness, for each and every wore robes inwrought with gold and studded with jewels, no dress being worth less than a thousand dinars. They stared as intently at the bowls and albeit these were covered with pieces of brocade, also orfrayed and dubbed with precious stones, yet the sheen outshot from them dulled the shine of the sun. Then Aladdin's mother walked forwards and all the handmaids and eunuchs paced behind her in the best of ordinance and disposition, and the citizens gathered to gaze at the beauty of the damsels, glorifying God the Most Great, until the train reached the palace and entered it accompanied by the tailor's widow. Now when the Aghas and Chamberlains and Army-officers beheld them, all were seized with surprise, notably by seeing the handmaids who each and every would ravish the reason of an anchorite. And albeit the royal Chamberlains and Officials were men of family, the sons of Grandees and Emirs, yet they could not but especially wonder at the costly dresses of the girls and the platters borne upon their heads; nor could they gaze at them open-eyed by reason of the exceeding brilliance and radiance. Then the Nabobs went in and reported to the King who forthright bade admit them to the presence-chamber, and Aladdin's mother went in with them. When they stood before the Sultan, all saluted him with every sign of respect and worship and prayed for his glory and prosperity; then they set down from their heads the bowls at his feet and, having removed the brocade covers, rested with arms crossed behind them. The Sultan wondered with exceeding wonder and was distraught by the beauty of the handmaids and their

loveliness which passed praise; and his wits were wildered when he
considered the golden bowls brimful of gems which captured man's
vision, and he was perplexed at the marvel until he became, like the
dumb, unable to utter a syllable for the excess of his wonder. Also his
sense was stupefied the more when he bethought him that within an
hour or so all these treasures had been collected. Presently he commanded the slave-girls to enter, with what loads they bore, the dower of
the Princess; and, when they had done his bidding Aladdin's mother
came forward and said to the Sultan, "O my lord, this be not much
wherewith to honour the Lady Badr al-Budur, for that she meriteth
these things multiplied times manifold." Hereat the Sovran turned to
the Minister and asked, "What sayest thou, O Wazir? is not he who
could produce such wealth in a time so brief, is he not, I say, worthy to
become the Sultan's son-in-law and take the King's daughter to wife?"
Then the Minister (although he marvelled at these riches even more
than did the Sultan), whose envy was killing him and growing greater
hour by hour, seeing his liege lord satisfied with the moneys and the
dower and yet being unable to fight against fact, made answer, "'Tis not
worthy of her." Withal he fell to devising a device against the King that
he might withhold the Lady Badr al-Budur from Aladdin and accordingly he continued, "O my liege, the treasures of the universe all of
them are not worth a nail-pairing of thy daughter: indeed thy Highness
hath prized these things overmuch in comparison with her." When the
King heard the words of his Grand Wazir, he knew that the speech was
prompted by excess of envy, so turning to the mother of Aladdin he
said, "O woman, go to thy son and tell him that I have accepted of him
the dower and stand to my bargain, and that my daughter be his bride
and he my son-in-law: furthermore, bid him at once make act of presence that I may become familiar with him: he shall see naught from
me save all honour and consideration, and this night shall be the beginning of the marriage-festivities. Only, as I said to thee, let him come to
me and tarry not." Thereupon Aladdin's mother returned home with
the speed of the stormwinds that she might hasten her utmost to con-
gratulate her son; and she flew with joy at the thought that her boy was
about to become son-in-law to the Sultan. After her departure the King
dismissed the Divan and, entering the palace of the Princess, bade
them bring the bowls and the handmaids before him and before her,
that she also might inspect them. But when the Lady Badr al-Budur
considered the jewels, she waxed distraught and cried, "Meseemeth
that in the treasures of the world there be not found one jewel rivalling
these jewels." Then she looked at the handmaids and marvelled at their
beauty and loveliness, and knew that all this came from her new bridegroom who had sent them in her service. So she was gladdened, albeit
she had been grieved and saddened on account of her former husband,

the Wazir's son, and she rejoiced with exceeding joy when she gazed upon the damsels and their charms; nor was her sire, the Sultan, less pleased and inspirited when he saw his daughter relieved of all her mourning and melancholy and his own vanished at the sight of her enjoyment. Then he asked her, "O my daughter, do these things divert thee? Indeed I deem that this suitor of thine be more suitable to thee than the son of the Wazir; and right soon, (Inshallah!) O my daughter, thou shalt have fuller joy with him." Such was the case with the King; but as regards Aladdin, as soon as he saw his mother entering the house with face laughing for stress of joy he rejoiced at the sign of glad tidings and cried, "To Allah alone be lauds! Perfected is all I desired." Rejoined his mother, "Be gladdened at my good news, O my son, and hearten thy heart and cool thine eyes for the winning of thy wish. The Sultan hath accepted thine offering, I mean the moneys and the dower of the Lady Badr al-Budur, who is now thine affianced bride; and, this very night, O my child, is your marriage and thy first visit to her; for the King, that he might assure me of his word, hath proclaimed to the world thou art his son-in-law and promised this night to be the night of going in. But he also said to me: — Let thy son come hither forthright that I may become familiar with him and receive him with all honour and worship. And now here am I, O my son, at the end of my labours: happen whatso may happen the rest is upon thy shoulders." Thereupon Aladdin arose and kissed his mother's hand and thanked her, enhancing her kindly service: then he left her and entering his chamber took the Lamp and rubbed it when, lo and behold! its Slave appeared and cried, "Adsum! Ask whatso thou wantest." The young man replied, "'Tis my desire that thou take me to a Hammam whose like is not in the world; then, fetch me a dress so costly and kingly that no royalty ever owned its fellow." The Marid replied, "I hear and I obey," and carried him to Baths such as were never seen by the Kings of the Chosroes, for the building was all of alabaster and carnelian and it contained marvellous limnings which captured the sight; and the great hall was studded with precious stones. Not a soul was therein but, when Aladdin entered, one of the Jann in human shape washed him and bathed him to the best of his desire. Aladdin, after having been washed and bathed, left the Baths and went into the great hall where he found that his old dress had been removed and replaced by a suit of the most precious and princely. Then he was served with sherbets and ambergris'd coffee and, after drinking, he arose and a party of black slaves came forwards and clad him in the costliest of clothing, then perfumed and fumigated him. It is known that Aladdin was the son of a tailor, a pauper, yet now would none deem him to be such; nay, all would say, "This be the greatest that is of the progeny of the Kings: praise be to Him who changeth and who is not changed!" Presently came the Jinni and lifting him up bore him to his home and asked, "O my lord, tell me hast thou aught of need?" He answered, "Yes, 'tis my desire that thou bring me eight and forty Mamelukes, of whom two dozen shall forego me and the rest follow me, the whole number with their war-chargers and clothing and accoutrements; and all upon them and their steeds must be of naught save of highest worth and the costliest, such as may not be found in treasuries of the Kings. Then fetch me a stallion fit for the riding of the Chosroes and let his furniture, all thereof, be of gold crusted with the finest gems: fetch me also eight and forty thousand dinars that each white slave may carry a thousand gold pieces. 'Tis now my intent to fare to the Sultan, so delay thou not, for that without all these requisites whereof I bespake thee I may not visit him. Moreover set before me a dozen slave-girls unique in beauty and dight with the most magnificent dresses, that they wend with my mother to the royal palace; and let every handmaid be robed in raiment that befitteth Queen's wearing." The Slave replied, "To hear is to obey;" and, disappearing for an eye-twinkling, brought all he was bidden bring and led by hand a stallion whose rival was not amongst the Arabian Arabs, and its saddle cloth was of splendid brocade gold-inwrought. Thereupon, without stay or delay, Aladdin sent for his mother and gave her the garments she should wear and committed to her charge the twelve slave-girls forming her suite to the palace. Then he sent one of the Mamelukes, whom the Jinni had brought, to see if the Sultan had left the Serraglio or not. The white slave went forth lighter than the lightning and returning in like haste, said, "O my lord, the Sultan awaiteth thee!" Hereat Aladdin arose and took horse, his Mamelukes riding a-van and arear of him, and they were such that all must cry, "Laud to the Lord who created them and clothed them with such beauty and loveliness." And they scattered gold amongst the crowd in front of their master who surpassed them all in comeliness and seemlihead nor needest thou ask concerning the sons of the Kings,—praise be to the Bountiful, the Eternal! All this was of the virtues of the Wonderful Lamp, which, whoso possessed, him it gifted with fairest favour and finest figure, with wealth and with wisdom. The folk admired Aladdin's liberality and exceeding generosity and all were distraught seeing his charms and elegance, his gravity and his good manners, they glorified the Creator for this noble creation, they blessed him each and every and, albeit they knew him for the son of Such-an-one, the tailor, yet no man envied him; nay, all owned that he deserved his great good fortune. Now the Sultan had assembled the Lords of the land and, informing them of the promise he had passed to Aladdin, touching the marriage of his daughter, had bidden them await his approach and then go forth, one and all, to meet him and greet him. Hereupon the Emirs and Wazirs, the Chamberlains, the Nabobs and the Army-officers took their stations expecting him at the palace gate. Aladdin would fain have dismounted at the outer entrance; but one of the Nobles, whom the King had deputed for such duty, approached him and said, "O my lord, 'tis the Royal Command that thou enter riding thy steed nor dismount except at the Divan-door." Then they all forewent him in a body and conducted him to the appointed place where they crowded about him, these to hold his stirrup and those supporting him on either side whilst others took him by the hands and helped him dismount; after which all the Emirs and Nobles preceded him into the Divan and led him close up to the royal throne. Thereupon the Sultan came down forthright from his seat of estate and, forbidding him to buss the carpet, embraced and kissed and seated him to the right of and beside himself. Aladdin did whatso is suitable, in the case of the Kings, of salutation and offering of blessings, and said, "O our lord the Sultan, indeed the generosity of thy Highness demanded that thou deign vouchsafe to me the hand of thy daughter, the Lady Badr al-Budur, albeit I undeserve the greatness of such gift, I being but the humblest of thy slaves. I pray Allah grant thee prosperity and perpetuance; but in very sooth, O King, my tongue is helpless to thank thee for the fullness of the favour, passing all measure, which thou hast bestowed upon me. And I hope of thy Highness that thou wilt give me a piece of ground fitted for a pavilion which shall besit thy daughter, the Lady Badr al-Budur." The Sultan was struck with admiration when he saw Aladdin in his princely suit and looked upon him and considered his beauty and loveliness, and noted the Mamelukes standing to serve him in their comeliness and seemlihead; and still his marvel grew when the mother of Aladdin approached him in costly raiment and sumptuous, clad as though she were a Queen, and when he gazed upon the twelve handmaids standing before her with crossed arms and with all worship and reverence doing her service. He also considered the eloquence of Aladdin and his delicacy of speech and he was astounded thereat, he and all his who were present at the levée. Thereupon fire was kindled in the Grand Wazir's heart for envy of Aladdin until he was like to die: and it was worse when the Sultan, after hearing the youth's succession of prayers and seeing his high dignity of demeanour, respectful withal, and his eloquence and elegance of language, clasped him to his bosom and kissed him and cried, "Alas, O my son, that I have not enjoyed thy converse before this day!" He rejoiced in him with mighty great joy and straightway bade the music and the bands strike up; then he arose and, taking the youth led him into the palace where supper had been prepared and the Eunuchs at once laid the tables. So the Sovran sat down and seated his son-in-law on his right side and the Wazirs and high officials and Lords of the land took places each according to his degree, whereupon the bands played and a mighty fine marriage-feast was dispread in the palace. The King now applied himself to making friendship with Aladdin and conversed with the youth, who answered him with all courtesy and eloquence, as though he had been bred in the palaces of the Kings or he had lived with them his daily life. And the more the talk was prolonged between them, the more did the Sultan's pleasure and delight increase, hearing his son-in-law's readiness of reply and his sweet flow of language. But after they had eaten and drunken and the trays were removed, the King bade summon the Kazis and witnesses who presently attended and knitted the knot and wrote out the contract-writ between Aladdin and the Lady Badr al-Budur. And presently the bridegroom arose and would have fared forth, when his father-in-law withheld him and asked, "Whither away, O my child? The bride-fêtes have begun and the marriage is made and the tie is tied and the writ is written." He replied, "O my lord the King, 'tis my desire to edify, for the Lady Badr al-Budur, a pavilion befitting her station and high degree, nor can I visit her before so doing. But, Inshallah! the building shall be finished within the shortest time, by the utmost endeavour of thy slave and by the kindly regard of thy Highness; and, although I do (yes indeed!) long to enjoy the society of the Lady Badr al-Budur, yet 'tis incumbent on me first to serve her and it becometh me to set about the work forthright." "Look around thee, O my son," replied the Sultan, "for what ground thou deemest suitable to thy design and do thou take all things into thy hands; but I deem the best for thee will be yonder broad plain facing my palace; and, if it please thee, build thy pavilion thereupon." "And this," answered Aladdin, "is the sum of my wishes that I may be nearhand to thy Highness." So saying he farewelled the King and took horse, with his Mamelukes riding before him and behind him, and all the world blessed him and cried, "By Allah he is deserving," until such time as he reached his home. Then he alighted from his stallion and repairing to his chamber, rubbed the Lamp and behold, the Slave stood before him and said, "Ask, O my lord, whatso thou wantest;" and Aladdin rejoined, "I require of thee a service grave and important which thou must do for me, and 'tis that thou build me with all urgency a pavilion fronting the palace of the Sultan; and it must be a marvel for it shall be provided with every requisite, such as royal furniture and so forth." The Slave replied, "To hear is to obey" and evanished and, before the next dawn brake, returned to Aladdin and said, "O my lord, the pavilion is finished to the fullest of thy fancy; and, if thou wouldst inspect it, arise forthright and fare with me." Accordingly, he rose up and the Slave carried him in the space of an eye-glance to the pavilion which, when Aladdin looked upon it, struck him with surprise at such building, all its stones being of jasper and alabaster, Sumaki-marble and mosaic-work. Then the Slave led him into the treasury which was full of all manner of gold and silver and costly gems, not to be counted or computed, priced or estimated. Thence to another place, where Aladdin saw all requisites for the table, plates and dishes, spoons and ladles, basins and covers, cups and tasses, the whole of precious metal: thence to the kitchen, where they found the kitcheners provided with their needs and cooking batteries, likewise golden and silvern; thence to a warehouse piled up with chests full-packed of royal raiment, stuffs that captured the reason, such as gold-wrought brocades from Indian and China and kimcobs or orfrayed cloths; thence to many apartments replete with appointments which beggar description; thence to the stables containing coursers whose like was not to be met with amongst the kings of the universe; and, lastly, they went to the harness-rooms all hung with housings, costly saddles and other furniture, everywhere studded with pearls and precious stones. And all this was the work of one night. Aladdin was wonderstruck and astounded by that magnificent display of wealth which not even the mightiest monarch on earth could produce; and more so to see his pavilion fully provided with eunuchs and handmaids whose beauty would seduce a saint. Yet the prime marvel of the pavilion was an upper kiosque or belvedere of four-and-twenty windows all made of emeralds and rubies and other gems; and one window remained unfinished at the requirement of Aladdin that the Sultan might prove him impotent to complete it. When the youth had inspected the whole edifice, he was pleased and gladdened exceedingly: then, turning to the Slave he said, "I require of thee still one thing which is yet wanting and whereof I had forgotten to tell thee." "Ask, O my lord, thy want," quoth the Servitor; and quoth the other, "I demand of thee a carpet of the primest brocade all gold-inwrought which, when unrolled and outstretched, shall extend hence to the Sultan's palace in order that the Lady Badr al-Budur may, when coming hither, pace upon it and not tread common earth." The Slave departed for a short while and said on his return, "O my lord, verily that which thou demandest is here." Then he took him and showed him a carpet which wildered the wits, and it extended from palace to pavilion; and after this the Servitor bore off Aladdin and set him down in his own home. Now day was brightening so the Sultan rose from his sleep and throwing open the casement looked out and espied, opposite his palace, a palatial pavilion ready edified. Thereupon he fell to rubbing his eyes and opening them their widest and considering the scene, and he soon was certified that the new edifice was mighty fine and grand enough to bewilder the wits. Moreover, with amazement as great he saw the carpet dispread between palace and pavilion: like their lord also the royal doorkeepers and the household, one and all, were dazed and amazed at the spectacle. Meanwhile the Wazir came in and, as he entered, espied the newly-builded pavilion and the carpet, whereat he

also wondered; and, when he went in to the Sultan the twain fell to
talking on this marvellous matter with great surprise at a sight which
distracted the gazer and attracted the heart. They said finally, "In very
truth, of this pavilion we deem that none of the royalties could build its
fellow;" and the King, turning to the Minister, asked him, "Hast thou
seen now that Aladdin is worthy to be the husband of the Princess my
daughter? Hast thou looked upon and considered this right royal building, this magnificence of opulence, which thought of man can not contain?" But the Wazir in his envy of Aladdin replied, "O King of the Age,
indeed this foundation and this building and this opulence may not be
save by means of magic nor can any man in the world, be he the richest in goods or the greatest in governance, avail to found and finish in
a single night such edifice as this." The Sultan rejoined, "I am surprised to see in thee how thou dost continually harp on evil opinion of
Aladdin; but I hold that 'tis caused by thine envy and jealousy. Thou
wast present when I gave him the ground at his own prayer for a place
whereon he might build a pavilion wherein to lodge my daughter, and
I myself favoured him with a site for the same and that too before thy
very face. But however that be, shall one who could send me as dower
for the Princess such store of such stones whereof the kings never
obtained even a few, shall he, I say, be unable to edify an edifice like
this?" When the Wazir heard the Sultan's words, he knew that his lord
loved Aladdin exceedingly; so his envy and malice increased; only, as
he could do nothing against the youth, he sat silent and impotent to
return a reply. But Aladdin seeing that it was broad day, and the
appointed time had come for his repairing to the palace (where his
wedding was being celebrated and the Emirs and Wazirs and Grandees
were gathered together about the Sultan to be present at the ceremony), arose and rubbed the Lamp, and when its Slave appeared and
said, "O my lord, ask whatso thou wantest, for I stand before thee and
at thy service," said he, "I mean forthright to seek the palace, this day
being my wedding-festival and I want thee to supply me with ten thousand dinars." The Slave evanished for an eye-twinkling and returned
bringing the moneys, when Aladdin took horse with his Mamelukes a-
van and arear and passed on his way, scattering as he went gold pieces
upon the lieges until all were fondly affected towards him and his dignity was enhanced. But when he drew near the palace, and the Emirs
and Aghas and Army-officers who were standing to await him noted his
approach, they hastened straightway to the King and gave him the tidings thereof; whereupon the Sultan rose and met his son-in-law and,
after embracing and kissing him, led him still holding his hand into his
own apartment where he sat down and seated him by his right side.
The city was all decorated and music rang through the palace and
the singers sang until the King bade bring the noon-meal, when the

eunuchs and Mamelukes hastened to spread the tables and trays which are such as are served to the kings. Then the Sultan and Aladdin and the Lords of the land and the Grandees of the realm took their seats and ate and drank until they were satisfied. And it was a mighty fine wedding in city and palace and the high nobles all rejoiced therein and the commons of the kingdom were equally gladdened, while the Governors of provinces and Nabobs of districts flocked from far regions to witness Aladdin's marriage and its processions and festivities. The Sultan also marvelled in his mind to look at Aladdin's mother and recall to mind how she was wont to visit him in pauper plight, while her son could command all this opulence and magnificence. And when the spectators, who crowded the royal palace to enjoy the wedding-feasts, looked upon Aladdin's pavilion and the beauties of the building, they were seized with an immense surprise that so vast an edifice as this could be reared on high during a single night; and they blessed the youth and cried, "Allah gladden him! By Allah, he deserveth all this! Allah bless his days!" When dinner was done, Aladdin rose and, farewelling the Sultan, took horse with his Mamelukes and rode to his own pavilion that he might prepare to receive therein his bride, the Lady Badr al-Badur. As he passed, all the folk shouted their good wishes with one voice and their words were, "Allah gladden thee! Allah increase thy glory. Allah grant thee length of life!" while immense crowds of people gathered to swell the marriage procession and they conducted him to his new home, he showering gold upon them during the whole time. When he reached his pavilion, he dismounted and walked in and sat him down on the divan, whilst his Mamelukes stood before him with arms afolded; also after a short delay they brought him sherbets and, when these were drunk, he ordered his white slaves and handmaids and eunuchs and all who were in the pavilion to make ready for meeting the Lady Badr al-Budur. Moreover, as soon as mid-afternoon came and the air had cooled and the great heat of the sun was abated, the Sultan bade his Army-officers and Emirs and Wazirs go down into the Maydan-plain whither he likewise rode. And Aladdin also took horse with his Mamelukes, he mounting a stallion whose like was not among the steeds of the Arab al-Arba, and he showed his horsemanship in the hippodrome and so played with the Jarid that none could withstand him, while his bride sat gazing upon him from the latticed balcony of her bower and, seeing him in such beauty and cavalarice, she fell headlong in love of him and was like to fly for joy. And after they had ringed their horses on the Maydan and each had displayed whatso he could of horsemanship, Aladdin proving himself the best man of all, they rode in a body to the Sultan's palace and the youth also returned to his own pavilion. But when it was evening, the Wazirs and Nobles took the bridegroom and, falling in, escorted him to the royal Hammam (known as the Sultani), when he was bathed and perfumed. As soon as he came out he donned a dress more magnificent than the former and took horse with the Emirs and the soldier-officers riding before him and forming a grand cortège, wherein four of the Wazirs bore naked swords round about him. All the citizens and the strangers and the troops marched before him in ordered throng carrying wax candles and kettle drums and pipes and other instruments of mirth and merriment, until they conducted him to his pavilion. Here he alighted and walking in took his seat and seated the Wazirs and Emirs who had escorted him, and the Mamelukes brought sherbets and sugared drinks, which they also passed to the people who had followed in his train. It was a world of folk whose tale might not be told; withal Aladdin bade his Mamelukes stand without the pavilion-doors and shower gold upon the crowd. When the Sultan returned from the Maydan-plain to his palace he ordered the household, men as well as women, straightway to form a cavalcade for his daughter, with all ceremony, and bear her to her bridegroom's pavilion. So the nobles and soldier-officers, who had followed and escorted the bridegroom, at once mounted, and the handmaids and eunuchs went forth with wax candles and made a mighty fine procession for the Lady Badr al-Budur and they paced on preceding her till they entered the pavilion of Aladdin whose mother walked beside the bride. In front of the Princess also fared the wives of the Wazirs and Emirs, Grandees and Notables, and in attendance on her were the eight and forty slave-girls presented to her aforetime by her bridegroom, each hending in hand a huge cierge scented with camphor and ambergris and set in a candlestick of gem-studded gold. And reaching Aladdin's pavilion they led her to her bower in the upper storey and changed her robes and enthroned her; then, as soon as the displaying was ended, they accompanied her to Aladdin's apartments and presently he paid her the first visit. Now his mother was with the bride and, when the bridegroom came up and did off her veil, the ancient dame fell to considering the beauty of the Princess and her loveliness; and she looked around at the pavilion which was all litten up by gold and gems besides the manifold candelabra of precious metals encrusted with emeralds and jacinths; so she said in her mind, "Once upon a time I thought the Sultan's palace mighty fine, but this pavilion is a thing apart; nor do I deem that any of the greatest Kings or Chosroes attained in his day to aught like thereof; also am I certified that all the world could not build anything evening it." Nor less did the Lady Badr al-Budur fall to gazing at the pavilion and marvelling for its magnificence. Then the tables were spread and they all ate and drank and were gladdened; after which fourscore damsels came before them each holding in hand an instrument of mirth and merriment; then they deftly moved their finger-tips and touched the strings smiting them into song, most musical, most melancholy, till they rent the hearts of the hearers. Hereat the Princess increased in marvel and quoth she to herself, "In all my life ne'er heard I songs like these," till she forsook food, the better to listen. And at last Aladdin poured out for her wine and passed it to her with his own hand; so great joy and jubilee went round amongst them and it was a notable night, such an one as Iskandar, Lord of the Two Horns, had never spent in his time. When they had finished eating and drinking and the tables were removed from before them, Aladdin arose and went in to his bride.[1] As soon as morning morrowed he left his bed and the treasurer brought him a costly suit and a mighty fine, of the most sumptuous robes worn by the Kings. Then, after drinking coffee flavoured with ambergris, he ordered the horses be saddled and, mounting with his Mamelukes before and behind him, rode to the Sultan's palace and on his entering its court the eunuchs went in and reported his coming to their lord. When the Sultan heard of Aladdin's approach, he rose up forthright to receive him and embraced and kissed him as though he were his own son: then, seating him on his right, he blessed and prayed for him, as did the Wazirs and Emirs, the Lords of the land and the Grandees of the realm. Presently, the King commanded bring the morning-meal which the attendants served up and all broke their fast together, and when they had eaten and drunken their sufficiency and the tables were removed by the eunuchs, Aladdin turned to the Sultan and said, "O my lord, would thy Highness deign honour me this day at dinner, in the house of the Lady Badr al-Budur thy beloved daughter, and come accompanied by all thy Ministers and Grandees of the reign?" The King replied (and he was delighted with his son-in-law,) "Thou art surpassing in liberality, O my son!" Then he gave orders to all invited and rode forth with them (Aladdin also riding beside him) till they reached the pavilion and as he entered it and considered its construction, its architecture and its stonery, all jasper and carnelian, his sight was dazed and his wits were amazed at such grandeur and magnificence of opulence. Then turning to the Minister he thus addressed him, "What sayest thou? Tell me hast thou seen in all thy time aught like this amongst the mightiest of earth's monarchs for the abundance of gold and gems we are now beholding?" The Grand Wazir replied, "O my lord the King, this be a feat which cannot be accomplished by might of monarch amongst Adam's sons; nor could the collected peoples of the universal world build a palace like unto

---

[1]The exceptional reserve of this and other descriptions makes M. H. Zotenberg suspect that the tale was written for one of the Mameluke Princesses: I own to its modesty but I doubt that such virtue would have recommended it to the dames in question.

this; nay, even builders could not be found to make aught resembling it, save (as I said to thy Highness) by force of sorcery." These words certified the King that his Minister spake not except in envy and jealousy of Aladdin, and would stablish in the royal mind that all this splendour was not made of man but by means of magic and with the aid of the Black Art. So quoth he to him, "Suffice thee so much, O Wazir: thou hast none other word to speak and well I know what cause urgeth thee to say this say." Then Aladdin preceded the Sultan till he conducted him to the upper Kiosque where he saw its skylights, windows and latticed casements and jalousies wholly made of emeralds and rubies and other costly gems; whereat his mind was perplexed and his wits were bewildered and his thoughts were distraught. Presently he took to strolling round the Kiosque and solacing himself with these sights which captured the vision, till he chanced to cast a glance at the window which Aladdin by design had left unwrought and not finished like the rest; and, when he noted its lack of completion, he cried, "Woe and well-away for thee, O window, because of thine imperfection;" and, turning to his Minister he asked, "Knowest thou the reason of leaving incomplete this window and its framework?" The Wazir said, "O my lord, I conceive that the want of finish in this window resulteth from thy Highness having pushed on Aladdin's marriage and he lacked the leisure to complete it." Now at that time, Aladdin had gone in to his bride, the Lady Badr al-Budur, to inform her of her father's presence; and, when he returned, the King asked him, "O my son what is the reason why the window of this Kiosque was not made perfect?" "O King of the Age, seeing the suddenness of my wedding," answered he, "I failed to find artists for finishing it." Quoth the Sultan, "I have a mind to complete it myself;" and quoth Aladdin, "Allah perpetuate thy glory, O thou the King; so shall thy memory endure in thy daughter's pavilion." The Sultan forthright bade summon jewellers and goldsmiths and ordered them be supplied from the treasury with all their needs of gold and gems and noble ores; and, when they were gathered together he commanded them to complete the work still wanting in the Kiosque-window. Meanwhile the Princess came forth to meet her sire the Sultan who noticed, as she drew near, her smiling face; so he embraced her and kissed her, then led her to the pavilion and all entered in a body. Now this was the time of the noon-day meal and one table had been spread for the Sovran, his daughter and his son-in-law and a second for the Wazirs, the Lords of the land, the Grandees of the realm, the Chief Officers of the host, the Chamberlains and the Nabobs. The King took seat between the Princess and her husband; and, when he put forth his hand to the food and tasted it, he was struck with surprise by the flavour of the dishes and their savoury and sumptuous cooking. Moreover, there stood before him the four-score damsels

each and every saying to the full moon, "Rise that I may seat myself
in thy stead!" All held instruments of mirth and merriment and they
tuned the same and deftly moved their finger-tips and smote the strings
into song, most musical, most melodious, which expanded the
mourner's heart. Hereby the Sultan was gladdened and time was good
to him and for high enjoyment he exclaimed, "In very sooth the thing
is beyond the compass of King and Kaysar." Then they fell to eating
and drinking; and the cup went round until they had drunken enough,
when sweetmeats and fruits of sorts and other such edibles were served,
the dessert being laid out in a different salon whither they removed and
enjoyed of these pleasures their sufficiency. Presently the Sultan arose
that he might see if the produce of his jewellers and goldsmiths
favoured that of the pavilion; so he went upstairs to them and inspected
their work and how they had wrought; but he noted a mighty great difference and his men were far from being able to make anything like the
rest of Aladdin's pavilion. They informed him how all the gems stored
in the Lesser Treasury had been brought to them and used by them but
that the whole had proved insufficient; wherefor he bade open the
Greater Treasury and gave the workmen all they wanted of him.
Moreover he allowed them, an it sufficed not, to take the jewels wherewith Aladdin had gifted him. They carried off the whole and pushed on
their labours but they found the gems fail them, albeit they had not finished half the part wanting to the Kiosque-window. Herewith the King
commanded them to seize all the precious stones owned by the Wazirs
and Grandees of the realm; but, although they did his bidding, the supply still fell short of their requirements. Next morning Aladdin arose to
look at the jewellers' work and remarked that they had not finished a
moiety of what was wanting to the Kiosque-window: so he at once
ordered them to undo all they had done and restore the jewels to their
owners. Accordingly, they pulled out the precious stones and sent the
Sultan's to the Sultan and the Wazirs' to the Wazirs. Then the jewellers
went to the King and told him of what Aladdin had bidden; so he asked
them, "What said he to you, and what was his reason and wherefore
was he not content that the window be finished and why did he undo
the work ye wrought?" They answered, "O our lord, we know not at all,
but he bade us deface whatso we had done." Hereupon the Sultan at
once called for his horse, and mounting, took the way pavilion-wards,
when Aladdin, after dismissing the goldsmiths and jewellers had retired
into his closet and had rubbed the Lamp. Hereat straightway its
Servitor appeared to him and said, "Ask whatso thou wantest: thy Slave
is between thy hands;" and said Aladdin, "'Tis my desire that thou finish the window which was left unfinished." The Marid replied, "On my
head be it and also upon mine eyes!" then he vanished and after a little

while returned saying, "O my lord, verily that thou commandedst me do is completed." So Aladdin went upstairs to the Kiosque and found the whole window in wholly finished state; and, whilst he was still considering it, behold, a castrato came in to him and said, "O my lord, the Sultan hath ridden forth to visit thee and is passing through the pavilion-gate." So Aladdin at once went down and received his father-in-law. The Sultan, on sighting his son-in-law, cried to him, "Wherefore, O my child, hast thou wrought on this wise and sufferedst not the jewellers to complete the Kiosque-window leaving in the pavilion an unfinished place?" Aladdin replied, "O King of the Age, I left it not imperfect save for a design of mine own; nor was I incapable of perfecting it nor could I purpose that thy Highness should honour me with visiting a pavilion wherein was aught of deficiency. And, that thou mayst know I am not unable to make it perfect, let thy Highness deign walk upstairs with me and see if anything remain to be done therewith or not." So the Sultan went up with him and, entering the Kiosque, fell to looking right and left, but he saw no default at all in any of the windows; nay, he noted that all were perfect. So he marvelled at the sight and embraced Aladdin and kissed him, saying, "O my son, what be this singular feat? Thou canst work in a single night what in months the jewellers could not do. By Allah, I deem thou hast nor brother nor rival in this world." Quoth Aladdin, "Allah prolong thy life and preserve thee to perpetuity! thy slave deserveth not this encomium;" and quoth the King, "By Allah, O my child, thou meritest all praise for a feat whereof all the artists of the world were incapable." Then the Sultan came down and entered the apartments of his daughter, the Lady Badr al-Budur, to take rest beside her, and he saw her joyous exceedingly at the glory and grandeur wherein she was; then, after reposing awhile he returned to his palace. Now Aladdin was wont every day to thread the city-streets with his Mamelukes riding a-van and arear of him showering rightwards and leftwards gold upon the folk; and all the world, stranger and neighbour, far and near, were fulfilled of his love for the excess of his liberality and generosity. Moreover he increased the pensions of the poor Religious and the paupers and he would distribute alms to them with his own hand; by which good deed, he won high renown throughout the realm and most of the Lords of the land and Emirs would eat at his table; and men swore not at all save by his precious life. Nor did he leave faring to the chase and the Maydan-plain and the riding of horses and playing at javelin-play in presence of the Sultan; and, whenever the Lady Badr al-Budur beheld him disporting himself on the backs of steeds, she loved him much the more, and thought to herself that Allah had wrought her abundant good by causing to happen whatso happened with the son of the Wazir and by preserving her virginity intact for her true bridegroom, Aladdin. Aladdin won for himself day by day a fairer fame and a rarer report, while affection for him increased in the hearts of all the lieges and he waxed greater in the eyes of men. Moreover it chanced that in those days certain enemies took horse and attacked the Sultan, who armed and accounted an army to repel them and made Aladdin commander thereof. So he marched with his men nor ceased marching until he drew near the foe whose forces were exceeding many; and, presently, when the action began he bared his brand and charged home upon the enemy. Then battle and slaughter befel and violent was the hurly-burly, but at last Aladdin broke the hostile host and put all to flight, slaying the best part of them and pillaging their coin and cattle, property and possessions; and he despoiled them of spoils that could not be counted nor computed. Then he returned victorious after a noble victory and entered the capital which had decorated herself in his honour, of her delight in him; and the Sultan went forth to meet him and giving him joy embraced him and kissed him; and throughout the kingdom was held high festival with great joy and gladness. Presently, the Sovran and his son-in-law repaired to the pavilion where they were met by the Princess Badr al-Budur who rejoiced in her husband and, after kissing him between the eyes, led him to her apartments. After a time the Sultan also came and they sat down while the slave-girls brought them sherbets and confections which they ate and drank. Then the Sultan commanded that the whole kingdom be decorated for the triumph of his son-in-law and his victory over the invader: and the subjects and soldiery and all the people knew only Allah in heaven and Aladdin on earth; for that their love, won by his liberality, was increased by his noble horsemanship and his successful battling for the country and putting to flight the foe. Such then was the high fortune of Aladdin; but as regards the Maghrabi, the Magician, after returning to his native country, he passed all this space of time in bewailing what he had borne of toil and travail to win the Lamp and mostly that his trouble had gone vain and that the morsel when almost touching his lips had flown from his grasp. He pondered all this and mourned and reviled Aladdin for the excess of his rage against him and at times he would exclaim, "For this bastard's death underground I am well satisfied and hope only that some time or other I may obtain the Lamp, seeing how 'tis yet safe." Now one day of the days he struck a table of sand and dotted down the figures and carefully considered their consequence; then he transferred them to paper that he might study them and make sure of Aladdin's destruction and the safety of the Lamp preserved beneath the earth. Presently, he firmly stablished the sequence of the figures, mothers as well as daughters, but still he saw not the Lamp. Thereupon rage overrode him and he made another

trial to be assured of Aladdin's death; but he saw him not in the
Enchanted Treasure. Hereat his wrath still grew, and it waxed greater
when he ascertained that the youth had issued from underground and
was now upon earth's surface alive and alert: furthermore, that he had
become owner of the Lamp, for which he had himself endured such
toil and travail and troubles as man may not bear save for so great an
object. Accordingly quoth he to himself, "I have suffered sore pains and
penalties which none else could have endured for the Lamp's sake in
order that other than I may carry it off; and this Accursed hath taken it
without difficulty. And who knoweth an he wot the virtues of the Lamp,
than whose owner none in the world should be wealthier? There is no
help but that I work for his destruction." He then struck another geomantic table and examining the figures saw that the lad had won for
himself unmeasurable riches and had wedded the daughter of his
King; so of his envy and jealousy he was fired with the flame of wrath;
and, rising without let or stay, he equipped himself and set forth for
China-land, where he arrived in due season. Now when he had
reached the King's capital wherein was Aladdin, he alighted at one of
the Khans; and, when he had rested from the weariness of wayfare, he
donned his dress and went down to wander about the streets, where he
never passed a group without hearing them prate about the pavilion
and its grandeur and vaunt the beauty of Aladdin and his lovesomeness,
his liberality and generosity, his fine manners and his good morals.
Presently he entered an establishment wherein men were drinking a
certain warm beverage; and going up to one of those who were loud in
their lauds, he said to him, "O fair youth, who may be the man ye
describe and commend?" "Apparently thou art a foreigner, O man,"
answered the other, "and thou comest from a far country; but, even this
granted, how happeneth it thou hast not heard of the Emir Aladdin
whose renown, I fancy, hath filled the universe and whose pavilion,
known by report to far and near, is one of the Wonders of the World?
How, then, never came to thine ears aught of this or the name of
Aladdin (whose glory and enjoyment our Lord increase!) and his
fame?" The Moorman replied, "The sum of my wishes is to look upon
this pavilion and, if thou wouldest do me a favour, prithee guide me
thereunto, for I am a foreigner." The man rejoined, "To hear is to
obey;" and, foregoing him, pointed out Aladdin's pavilion whereupon
the Maroccan fell to considering it and at once understood that it was
the work of the Lamp. So he cried, "Ah! Ah! needs must I dig a pit for
this Accursed, this son of a snip, who could not earn for himself even
an evening meal: and, if the Fates abet me, I will assuredly destroy his
life and send his mother back to spinning at the wheel, e'en as she was
wont erewhiles to do." So saying, he returned to his caravanserai in a

sore state of grief and melancholy and regret bred by his envy and hate
of Aladdin. He took his astrological gear and geomantic table to discover where might be the Lamp; and he found that it was in the pavilion and not upon Aladdin's person. So he rejoiced thereat with joy
exceeding and exclaimed, "Now indeed 'twill be an easy task to take
the life of this Accursed and I see my way to getting the Lamp." Then
he went to a coppersmith and said to him, "Do thou make me a set of
lamps and take from me their full price and more; only I would have
thee hasten to finish them." Replied the smith, "Hearing and obeying,"
and fell aworking to keep his word; and when they were ready the
Moorman paid him what price he required; then taking them he carried them to the Khan and set them in a basket. Presently he began
wandering about the highways and market-streets of the capital crying
aloud, "Ho! who will exchange old lamps for new lamps?" But when
the folk heard him cry on this wise, they derided him and said,
"Doubtless this man is Jinn-mad, for that he goeth about offering new
for old;" and a world followed him and the children of the quarter
caught him up from place to place, laughing at him the while, nor did
he forbid them or care for their maltreatment. And he ceased not
strolling about the streets till he came under Aladdin's pavilion, where
he shouted with his loudest voice and the boys screamed at him, "A
madman! A madman!" Now Destiny had decreed that the Lady Badr
al-Budur be sitting in her Kiosque whence she heard one crying like a
crier, and the children bawling at him; only she understood not what
was going on; so she gave orders to one of her slave-girls saying, "Go
thou and see who 'tis that crieth and what be his cry." The girl fared
forth and looked on when she beheld a man crying, "Ho! who will
exchange old lamps for new lamps?" and the little ones pursuing and
laughing at him; and as loudly laughed the Princess when this strange
case was told to her. Now Aladdin had carelessly left the lamp in his
pavilion without hiding it and locking it up in his strong box;[1] and one
of the slave-girls who had seen it said, "O my lady, I think to have
noticed, in the apartment of my lord Aladdin, an old lamp: so let us
give it in change for a new lamp to this man, and see if his cry be truth
or lie." Whereupon the Princess said to the slave-girl, "Bring the old
lamp which thou saidst to have seen in thy lord's apartment." Now the
Lady Badr al-Budur knew naught of the Lamp and of the specialities

---

[1]Nothing can be more improbable than this detail, but upon such abnormal
situations almost all stories, even in our most modern "Society-novels,"
depend and the cause is clear—without them there would be no story. And
the modern will, perhaps, suggest that "the truth was withheld for a higher
purpose, for the working out of certain ends."

thereof which had raised Aladdin her spouse to such high degree and grandeur; and her only end and aim was to understand by experiment the mind of a man who would give in exchange the new for the old. So the handmaid fared forth and went up to Aladdin's apartment and returned with the Lamp to her lady who, like all the others, knew nothing of the Maghrabi's cunning tricks and his crafty device. Then the Princess bade an Agha of the eunuchry go down and barter the old Lamp for a new lamp. So he obeyed her bidding and, after taking a new lamp from the man, he returned and laid it before his lady who looking at it and seeing that it was brand-new, fell to laughing at the Moorman's wits. But the Maroccan, when he held the article in hand and recognised it for the Lamp of the Enchanted Treasury, at once placed it in his breast-pocket and left all the other lamps to the folk who were bartering of him. Then he went forth running till he was clear of the city, when he walked leisurely over the level grounds and he took patience until night fell on him in desert ground where was none other but himself. There he brought out the Lamp when suddenly appeared to him the Marid who said "Adsum! thy slave between thy hands is come: ask of me what so thou wantest." "'Tis my desire," the Moorman replied, "that thou upraise from its present place Aladdin's pavilion with its inmates and all that be therein, not forgetting myself, and set it down upon my own land, Africa. Thou knowest my town and I want the building placed in the gardens hard by it." The Marid-slave replied, "Hearkening and obedience: close thine eyes and open thine eyes whenas thou shalt find thyself together with the pavilion in thine own country." This was done; and, in an eye-twinkling, the Maroccan and the pavilion with all therein were transported to the African land. Such then was the work of the Maghrabi, the Magician; but now let us return to the Sultan and his son-in-law. It was the custom of the King, because of his attachment to and his affection for his daughter, every morning when he had shaken off sleep, to open the latticed casement and look out therefrom that he might catch sight of her abode. So that day he arose and did as he was wont. But when he drew near the latticed casement of his palace, and looked out at Aladdin's pavilion he saw naught; nay, the site was smooth as a well-trodden highway and like unto what it had been aforetime; and he could find nor edifice nor offices. So astonishment clothed him as with a garment, and his wits were wildered and he began to rub his eyes, lest they be dimmed or darkened, and to gaze intently; but at last he was certified that no trace of the pavilion remained nor sign of its being; nor wist he the why and the wherefore of its disappearance. So his surprise increased and he smote hand upon hand and the tears trickled down his cheeks over his beard, for that he knew not what had become of his daughter. Then he sent out officials forthright and summoned the Grand Wazir who at once attended; and, seeing him in this piteous plight said, "Pardon, O King of the Age, may Allah avert from thee every ill! Wherefore art thou in such sorrow?" Exclaimed the Sovran, "Methinketh thou wottest not my case?" and quoth the Minister, "On no wise, O our lord: by Allah, I know of it nothing at all." "Then," resumed the Sultan, "'tis manifest thou hast not looked this day in the direction of Aladdin's pavilion." "True, O my lord," quoth the Wazir, "it must still be locked and fast shut;" and quoth the King, "Forasmuch as thou hast no inkling of aught, arise and look out at the window and see Aladdin's pavilion whereof thou sayest 'tis locked and fast shut." The Minister obeyed his bidding but could not see anything, or pavilion or other place; so with mind and thoughts sore perplexed he returned to his liege lord who asked him, "Hast now learned the reason of my distress and noted yon locked-up palace and fast shut?" Answered the Wazir, "O King of the Age, erewhile I represented to thy Highness that this pavilion and these matters be all magical." Hereat the Sultan, fired with wrath, cried, "Where be Aladdin?" and the Minister replied, "He hath gone a-hunting," when the King commanded without stay or delay sundry of his Aghas and Army-officers to go and bring to him his son-in-law chained and with pinioned elbows. So they fared forth until they found Aladdin when they said to him, "O our lord Aladdin, excuse us nor be thou wroth with us; for the King hath commanded that we carry thee before him pinioned and fettered, and we hope pardon from thee because we are under the royal orders which we cannot gainsay." Aladdin, hearing these words, was seized with surprise and not knowing the reason of this remained tongue-tied for a time, after which he turned to them and asked, "O assembly, have you naught of knowledge concerning the motive of the royal mandate? Well I wot my soul to be innocent and that I never sinned against king or against kingdom." "O our lord," answered they, "we have no inkling whatever." So Aladdin alighted from his horse and said to them, "Do ye whatso the Sultan bade you do, for that the King's command is upon the head and the eyes." The Aghas, having bound Aladdin in bonds and pinioned his elbows behind his back, haled him in chains and carried him into the city. But when the lieges saw him pinioned and ironed, they understood that the Sultan purposed to strike off his head; and, forasmuch as he was loved of them exceedingly, all gathered together and seized their weapons; then, swarming out of their houses, followed the soldiery to see what was to do. And when the troops arrived with Aladdin at the palace, they went in and informed the Sultan of this, whereat he forthright commanded the Sworder to cut off the head of his son-in-law. Now as soon as the subjects were aware of this order, they barricaded the gates and closed the doors of the palace and sent a message to the King saying, "At this very moment we will level thine abode over the heads of all it containeth and over thine own, if the least hurt or harm befal Aladdin." So the Wazir went in and reported to the Sultan, "O King of the Age, thy commandment is about to seal the roll of our lives; and 'twere more suitable that thou pardon thy son-in-law lest there chance to us a sore mischance; for that the lieges do love him far more than they love us." Now the Sworder had already dispread the carpet of blood and, having seated Aladdin thereon, had bandaged his eyes; moreover he had walked round him three several times awaiting the last orders of his lord, when the King looked out of the window and saw his subjects, who had suddenly attacked him, swarming up the walls intending to tear them down. So forthright he bade the Sworder stay his hand from Aladdin and commanded the crier fare forth to the crowd and cry aloud that he had pardoned his son-in-law and received him back into favour. But when Aladdin found himself free and saw the Sultan seated on his throne, he went up to him and said, "O my lord, inasmuch as thy Highness hath favoured me throughout my life, so of thy grace now deign let me know the how and the wherein I have sinned against thee." "O traitor," cried the King, "unto this present I knew not any sin of thine;" then, turning to the Wazir he said, "Take him and make him look out at the window and after let him tell us where be his pavilion." And when the royal order was obeyed Aladdin saw the place level as a well-trodden road, even as it had been ere the base of the building was laid, nor was there the faintest trace of edifice. Hereat he was astonished and perplexed knowing not what had occurred; but, when he returned to the presence, the King asked him, "What is it thou hast seen? Where is thy pavilion and where is my daughter, the core of my heart, my only child, than whom I have none other?" Aladdin answered, "O King of the Age, I wot naught thereof nor aught of what hath befallen," and the Sultan rejoined, "Thou must know, O Aladdin, I have pardoned thee only that thou go forth and look into this affair and enquire for me concerning my daughter; nor do thou ever show thyself in my presence except she be with thee; and, if thou bring her not, by the life of my head I will cut off the head of thee." The other replied, "To hear is to obey: only vouchsafe me a delay and respite of some forty days; after which, an I produce her not, strike off my head and do with me whatso thou wishest." The Sultan said to Aladdin, "Verily I have granted thee thy request, a delay of forty days; but think not thou canst fly from my hand, for I would bring thee back even if thou wert above the clouds instead of being only upon earth's surface." Replied Aladdin, "O my lord the Sultan, as I said to thy Highness, an I fail to bring her within the term appointed, I will present

myself for my head to be stricken off." Now when the folk and the
lieges all saw Aladdin at liberty, they rejoiced with joy exceeding and
were delighted for his release; but the shame of his treatment and bashfulness before his friends and the envious exultation of his foes had
bowed down Aladdin's head; so he went forth a-wandering through the
city ways and he was perplexed concerning his case and knew not what
had befallen him. He lingered about the capital for two days, in saddest
state, wotting not what to do in order to find his wife and his pavilion,
and during this time sundry of the folk privily brought him meat and
drink. When the two days were done he left the city to stray about the
waste and open lands outlying the walls, without a notion as to whither
he should wend; and he walked on aimlessly until the path led him
beside a river where, of the stress of sorrow that overwhelmed him, he
abandoned himself to despair and thought of casting himself into the
water. Being, however, a good Moslem who professed the unity of the
Godhead, he feared Allah in his soul; and, standing upon the margin
he prepared to perform the Wuzu-ablution. But as he was baling up the
water in his right hand and rubbing his fingers, it so chanced that he
also rubbed the Ring. Hereat its Marid appeared and said to him,
"Adsum! thy thrall between thy hands is come: ask of me whatso thou
wantest." Seeing the Marid, Aladdin rejoiced with exceeding joy and
cried, "O Slave, I desire of thee that thou bring before me my pavilion
and therein my wife, the Lady Badr al-Budur, together with all and
everything it containeth." "O my lord," replied the Marid, "'tis right
hard upon me that thou demandest a service whereto I may not avail:
this matter dependeth upon the Slave of the Lamp nor dare I even
attempt it." Aladdin rejoined, "Forasmuch as the matter is beyond thy
competence, I require it not of thee, but at least do thou take me up
and set me down beside my pavilion in what land soever that may be."
The Slave exclaimed, "Hearing and obeying, O my lord;" and, uplifting him high in air, within the space of an eye-glance set him down
beside his pavilion in the land of Africa and upon a spot facing his
wife's apartment. Now this was at fall of night yet one look enabled him
to recognise his home; whereby his cark and care were cleared away
and he recovered trust in Allah after cutting off all his hope to look
upon his wife once more. Then he fell to pondering the secret and
mysterious favours of the Lord (glorified be His omnipotence!); and
how, after despair had mastered him the Ring had come to gladden
him, and how, when all his hopes were cut off, Allah had deigned bless
him with the services of its Slave. So he rejoiced and his melancholy
left him; then, as he had passed four days without sleep for the excess
of his cark and care and sorrow and stress of thought, he drew near
his pavilion and slept under a tree hard by the building which (as we

mentioned) had been set down amongst the gardens outlying the city
of Africa. He slumbered till Morning showed her face and, when awakened by the warbling of the small birds, he arose and went down to the
bank of the river which flowed thereby into the city; and here he again
washed his hands and face and after finished his Wuzu-ablution. Then
he prayed the dawn-prayer, and when he had ended his orisons he
returned and sat down under the windows of the Princess's bower. Now
the Lady Badr al-Budur, of her exceeding sorrow for severance from her
husband and her sire the Sultan, and for the great mishap which had
happened to her from the Maghrabi, the Magician, the Accursed, was
wont to rise during the murk preceding dawn and to sit in tears inasmuch as she could not sleep o' nights, and had forsworn meat and
drink. Her favourite slave-girl would enter her chamber at the hour of
prayer-salutation in order to dress her; and this time, by decree of
Destiny, when she threw open the window to let her lady comfort and
console herself by looking upon the trees and rills, and she herself
peered out of the lattice, she caught sight of her master sitting below,
and informed the Princess of this, saying, "O my lady! O my lady!
here's my lord Aladdin seated at the foot of the wall." So her mistress
arose hurriedly and gazing from the casement saw him; and her husband raising his head saw her; so she saluted him and he saluted her,
both being like to fly for joy. Presently quoth she, "Up and come in to
me by the private postern, for now the Accursed is not here;" and she
gave orders to the slave-girl who went down and opened for them.
Then Aladdin passed through it and was met by his wife, when they
embraced and exchanged kisses with all delight until they wept for
overjoy. After this they sat down and Aladdin said to her, "O my lady,
before all things 'tis my desire to ask thee a question. 'Twas my wont to
place an old copper lamp in such a part of my pavilion, what became
of that same?" When the Princess heard these words she sighed and
cried, "O my dearling, 'twas that very Lamp which garred us fall into
this calamity!" Aladdin asked her, "How befel the affair?" and she
answered by recounting to him all that had passed, first and last, especially how they had given in exchange an old lamp for a new lamp,
adding, "And next day we hardly saw one another at dawn before we
found ourselves in this land, and he who deceived us and took the lamp
by way of barter informed me that he had done the deed by might of
his magic and by means of the Lamp; that he is a Moorman from
Africa, and that we are now in his native country." When the Lady Badr
al-Budur ceased speaking, Aladdin resumed, "Tell me the intent of this
Accursed in thy respect, also what he sayeth to thee and what be his
will of thee?" She replied, "Every day he cometh to visit me once and
no more: he would woo me to his love and he sueth that I take him to

spouse in lieu of thee and that I forget thee and be consoled for the loss
of thee. And he telleth me that the Sultan my sire hath cut off my husband's head, adding that thou, the son of pauper parents, wast by him
enriched. And he sootheth me with talk, but he never seeth aught from
me save weeping and wailing; nor hath he heard from me one sugar-
sweet word." Quoth Aladdin, "Tell me where he hath placed the Lamp
an thou know anything thereof;" and quoth she, "He beareth it about
on his body alway, nor is it possible that he leave it for a single hour;
moreover once when he related what I have now recounted to thee, he
brought it out of his breast-pocket and allowed me to look upon it."
When Aladdin heard these words, he joyed with exceeding joy and
said, "O my lady, do thou lend ear to me. 'Tis my design to go from
thee forthright and to return only after doffing this my dress; so wonder
not when thou see me changed, but direct one of thy women to stand
by the private postern alway and, whenever she espy me coming, at
once to open. And now I will devise a device whereby to slay this
damned loon." Herewith he arose and, issuing from the pavilion-door,
walked till he met on the way a Fellah to whom he said, "O man, take
my attire and give me thy garments." But the peasant refused so
Aladdin stripped him of his dress perforce and donned it, leaving to the
man his own rich gear by way of gift. Then he followed the highway
leading to the neighbouring city and entering it went to the Perfumers'
Bazar where he bought of one some rarely potent Bhang, the son of a
minute, paying two dinars for two drachms thereof and he returned in
disguise by the same road till he reached the pavilion. Here the slave-
girl opened to him the private postern wherethrough he went in to the
Lady Badr al-Budur. And said, "Hear me! I desire of thee that thou
dress and dight thyself in thy best and thou cast off all outer show and
semblance of care; also when the Accursed, the Maghrabi, shall visit
thee, do thou receive him with a 'Welcome and fair welcome,' and
meet him with smiling face and invite him to come and sup with thee.
Moreover, let him note that thou hast forgotten Aladdin thy beloved,
likewise thy father; and that thou hast learned to love him with exceeding love, displaying to him all manner joy and pleasure. Then ask him
for wine which must be red and pledge him to his secret in a signifi-
cant draught; and, when thou hast given him two or three cups full and
hast made him wax careless, then drop these drops into his cup and fill
it up with wine: no sooner shall he drink of it than he will fall upon his
back senseless as one dead." Hearing these words, the Princess exclaimed,
"'Tis exceedingly sore to me that I do such deed; withal must I do it that
we escape the defilement of this Accursed who tortured me by severance from thee and from my sire. Lawful and right therefore is the
slaughter of this Accursed." Then Aladdin ate and drank with his wife

what hindered his hunger; then, rising without stay or delay, fared forth the pavilion. So the Lady Badr al-Budur summoned the tirewoman who robed and arrayed her in her finest raiment and adorned her and perfumed her; and, as she was thus, behold, the accursed Maghrabi entered. He joyed much seeing her in such case and yet more when she confronted him, contrary to her custom, with a laughing face; and his love-longing increased and his desire to have her. Then she took him and, seating him beside her, said, "O my dearling, do thou (an thou be willing) come to me this night and let us sup together. Sufficient to me hath been my sorrow for, were I to sit mourning through a thousand years or even two thousand, Aladdin would not return to me from the tomb; and I depend upon thy say of yesterday, to wit, that my sire the Sultan slew him in his stress of sorrow for severance from me. Nor wonder thou an I have changed this day from what I was yesterday; and the reason thereof is I have determined upon taking thee to friend and playfellow in lieu of and succession to Aladdin, for that now I have none other man but thyself. So I hope for thy presence this night, that we may sup together and we may carouse and drink somewhat of wine each with other; and especially 'tis my desire that thou cause me to taste the wine of thy natal soil, the African land, because belike 'tis better than aught of the wine of China we drink: I have with me some wine but 'tis the growth of my country and I vehemently wish to taste the wine produced by thine." When the Maghrabi saw the love lavisht upon him by the Lady Badr al-Budur, and noted her change from the sorrowful, melancholy woman she was wont to be, he thought that she had cut off her hope of Aladdin and he joyed exceedingly and said to her, "I hear and obey, O my lady, whatso thou wishest and all thou biddest. I have at home a jar of our country wine, which I have carefully kept and stored deep in earth for a space of eight years; and I will now fare and fill from it our need and will return to thee in all haste." But the Princess, that she might wheedle him the more and yet more, replied, "O my darling, go not thou, leaving me alone, but send one of the eunuchs to fill for us thereof and do thou remain sitting beside me, that I may find in thee my consolation." He rejoined, "O my lady, none wotteth where the jar be buried save myself nor will I tarry from thee." So saying, the Moorman went out and after a short time he brought back as much wine as they wanted; whereupon quoth the Princess to him, "Thou hast been at pains and trouble to serve me and I have suffered for thy sake, O my beloved." Quoth he, "On no wise, O eyes of me; I hold myself enhonoured by thy service." Then the Lady Badr al-Budur sat with him at table, and the twain fell to eating and presently the Princess expressed a wish to drink, when the handmaid filled her a cup forthright and then crowned another for the Maroccan. So she drank to his long life and his secret wishes and he also drank to her life; then the Princess, who was unique in eloquence and delicacy of speech, fell to making a cup-companion of him and beguiled him by addressing him in the sweetest terms of hidden meaning. This was done only that he might become more madly enamoured of her, but the Maghrabi thought that it resulted from her true inclination for him; nor knew that it was a snare set up to slay him. So his longing for her increased, and he was dying of love for her when he saw her address him in such tenderness of words and thoughts, and his head began to swim and all the world seemed as nothing in his eyes. But when they came to the last of the supper and the wine had mastered his brains and the Princess saw this in him, she said, "With us there be a custom throughout our country, but I know not an it be the usage of yours or not." The Moorman replied, "And what may that be?" So she said to him, "At the end of supper each lover in turn taketh the cup of the beloved and drinketh it off;" and at once she crowned one with wine and bade the handmaid carry to him her cup wherein the drink was blended with the Bhang. Now she had taught the slave-girl what to do and all the handmaids and eunuchs in the pavilion longed for the Sorcerer's slaughter and in that matter were one with the Princess. Accordingly the damsel handed him the cup and he, when he heard her words and saw her drinking from the cup and passing hers to him and noted all that show of love, fancied himself Iskandar, Lord of the Two Horns. Then said she to him, the while swaying gracefully to either side and putting her hand within his hand, "O my life, here is thy cup with me and my cup with thee, and on this wise do lovers drink from each other's cups." Then she bussed the brim and drained it to the dregs and again she kissed its lip and offered it to him. Thereat he flew for joy and meaning to do the like, raised her cup to his mouth and drank off the whole contents, without considering whether there was therein aught harmful or not. And forthright he rolled upon his back in death-like condition and the cup dropped from his grasp, whereupon the Lady Badr al-Budur and the slave-girls ran hurriedly and opened the pavilion door to their lord Aladdin, who, disguised as a Fellah, entered therein. He went up to the apartment of his wife, whom he found still sitting at table; and facing her lay the Maghrabi as one slaughtered; so he at once drew near to her and kissed her and thanked her for this. Then rejoicing with joy exceeding he turned to her and said, "Do thou with thy handmaids betake thyself to the inner-rooms and leave me alone for the present that I may take counsel touching mine affair." The Princess hesitated not but went away at once, she and her women; then Aladdin arose and, after locking the door upon them, walked up to the Moorman and put forth his hand to his breast-pocket and thence drew the Lamp; after which he unsheathed his sword and slew the villain. Presently he rubbed the Lamp and the Marid-slave appeared and said, "Adsum, O my lord, what is it thou wantest?" "I desire of thee," said Aladdin, "that thou take up my pavilion from this country and transport it to the land of China and there set it down upon the site where it was whilome, fronting the palace of the Sultan." The Marid replied, "Hearing and obeying, O my lord." Then Aladdin went and sat down with his wife and throwing his arms round her neck kissed her and she kissed him, and they sat in converse, what while the Jinni transported the pavilion and all therein to the place appointed. Presently Aladdin bade the handmaids spread the table before him and he and the Lady Badr al-Budur took seat thereat and fell to eating and drinking, in all joy and gladness, till they had their sufficiency when, removing to the chamber of wine and cup-converse, they sat there and caroused in fair companionship and each kissed other with all love-liesse. The time had been long and longsome since they enjoyed aught of pleasure; so they ceased not doing thus until the wine-sun arose in their heads and sleep gat hold of them, at which time they went to their bed in all ease and comfort. Early on the next morning Aladdin woke and awoke his wife, and the slave-girls came in and donned her dress and prepared her and adorned her whilst her husband arrayed himself in his costliest raiment and the twain were ready to fly for joy at reunion after parting. Moreover the Princess was especially joyous and glad-some because on that day she expected to see her beloved father. Such was the case of Aladdin and the Lady Badr al-Budur; but as regards the Sultan, after he drove away his son-in-law he never ceased to sorrow for the loss of his daughter; and every hour of every day he would sit and weep for her as women weep, because she was his only child and he had none other to take to heart. And as he shook off sleep, morning after morning, he would hasten to the window and throw it open and peer in the direction where formerly stood Aladdin's pavilion and pour forth tears until his eyes were dried up and their lids were ulcered. Now on that day he arose at dawn and, according to his custom, looked out when, lo and behold! he saw before him an edifice; so he rubbed his eyes and considered it curiously when he became certified that it was the pavilion of his son-in-law. So he called for a horse without let or delay; and as soon as his beast was saddled, he mounted and made for the palace; and Aladdin, when he saw his father-in-law approaching, went down and met him half way: then, taking his hand, aided him to step upstairs to the apartment of his daughter. And the Princess, being as earnestly desirous to see her sire, descended and greeted him at the door of the staircase fronting the ground-floor hall. Thereupon the King folded her in his arms and kissed her, shedding tears of joy; and she did likewise till at last Aladdin led them to the upper saloon where they took seats and the Sultan fell to asking her case and what had betided her. The Lady Badr al-Budur began to inform the Sultan of all which had befallen her, saying, "O my father, I recovered not life save yesterday when I saw my husband, and he it was who freed me from the thraldom of that Maghrabi, that Magician, that Accursed, than whom I believe there be none viler on the face of the earth; and, but for my beloved, I had never escaped him nor hadst thou seen me during the rest of my days. But mighty sadness and sorrow gat about me, O my father, not only for losing thee but also for the loss of a husband, under whose kindness I shall be all the length of my life, seeing that he freed me from that fulsome sorcerer." Then the Princess began repeating to her sire everything that happened to her, and relating to him how the Moorman had tricked her in the guise of a lamp-seller who offered in exchange new for old; how she had given him the Lamp whose worth she knew not, and how she had bartered it away only to laugh at the lampman's folly. "And next morning, O my father," she continued, "we found ourselves and whatso the pavilion contained in Africa-land, till such time as my husband came to us and devised a device whereby we escaped: and, had it not been for Aladdin's hastening to our aid, the Accursed was determined to enjoy me perforce." Then she told him of the Bhang-drops administered in wine to the African and concluded, "Then my husband returned to me and how I know not, but we were shifted from Africa-land to this place." Aladdin in his turn recounted how, finding the wizard dead drunken, he had sent away his wife and her women from the polluted place into the inner apartments; how he had taken the Lamp from the Sorcerer's breast-pocket whereto he was directed by his wife; how he had slaughtered the villain and, finally how, making use of the Lamp, he had summoned its Slave and ordered him to transport the pavilion back to its proper site, ending his tale with, "And, if thy Highness have any doubt anent my words, arise with me and look upon the accursed Magician." The King did accordingly and, having considered the Moorman, bade the carcase be carried away forthright and burned and its ashes scattered in air. Then he took to embracing Aladdin and kissing him said, "Pardon me, O my son, for that I was about to destroy thy life through the foul deeds of this damned enchanter, who cast thee into such pit of peril; and I may be excused, O my child, for what I did by thee, because I found myself forlorn of my daughter; my only one, who to me is dearer than my very kingdom. Thou knowest how the hearts of parents yearn unto their offspring, especially when like myself they have but one and none other to love." And on this wise the Sultan took to excusing himself and kissing his son-in-law. Aladdin said to the Sultan, "O King of the Time, thou didst naught to me contrary to Holy Law, and I also sinned not against thee; but all the trouble came from that Maghrabi, the impure, the Magician." Thereupon the Sultan bade the city be decorated and they obeyed him and held high feast and festivities. He also commanded the crier to cry about the streets saying, "This day is a mighty great fête, wherein public rejoicings must be held throughout the realm, for a full month of thirty days, in honour of the Lady Badr al-Budur and her husband Aladdin's return to their home." On this wise befel it with Aladdin and the Maghrabi; but withal the King's son-in-law escaped not wholly from the Accursed, albeit the body had been burnt and the ashes scattered in air. For the villain had a brother yet more villainous than himself, and a greater adept in necromancy, geomancy and astromancy; and, even as the old saw saith "A bean and 'twas split;" so each one dwelt in his own quarter of the globe that he might fill it with his sorcery, his fraud and his treason. Now, one day of the days it fortuned that the Moorman's brother would learn how it fared with him, so he brought out his sandboard and dotted it and produced the figures which, when he had considered and carefully studied them, gave him to know that the man he sought was dead and housed in the tomb. So he grieved and was certified of his decease, but he dotted a second time seeking to learn the manner of the death and where it had taken place; so he found that the site was the China-land and that the mode was the foulest of slaughter; furthermore, that he who did him die was a young man Aladdin hight. Seeing this he straightway arose and equipped himself for wayfare; then he set out and cut across the wilds and wolds and heights for the space of many a month until he reached China and the capital of the Sultan wherein was the slayer of his brother. He alighted at the so-called Strangers' Khan and, hiring himself a cell, took rest therein for a while; then he fared forth and wandered about the highways that he might discern some path which would aid him unto the winning of his ill-minded wish, to wit, of wreaking upon Aladdin blood-revenge for his brother. Presently he entered a coffee-house, a fine building which stood in the market-place and which collected a throng of folk to play, some at the Mankalah, others at the backgammon and others at the chess and what not else. There he sat down and listened to those seated beside him and they chanced to be conversing about an ancient dame and a holy, by name Fatimah, who dwelt alway at her devotions in a hermitage without the town, and this she never entered save only two days each month. They mentioned also that she had performed many saintly miracles which, when the Maghrabi, the Necromancer, heard he said in himself, "Now have I found that which I sought: Inshallah—God willing—by means of this crone will I win to my wish." The Necromancer went up to the folk who were talking of the miracles performed by the devout old woman and said to one of them, "O my uncle, I heard you all chatting about the prodigies of a certain saintess named Fatimah: who is she and where may be her abode?" "Marvellous!" exclaimed the man: "How canst thou be in our city and yet never have heard about the miracles of the Lady Fatimah? Evidently, O thou poor fellow, thou art a foreigner, since the fastings of this devotee and her asceticism in worldly matters and the beauties of her piety never came to thine ears." The Moorman rejoined, "'Tis true, O my lord: yes, I am a stranger and came to this your city only yesternight; and I hope thou wilt inform me concerning the saintly miracles of this virtuous woman and where may be her wone, for that I have fallen into a calamity, and 'tis my wish to visit her and crave her prayers, so haply Allah (to whom be honour and glory!) will, through her blessings, deliver me from mine evil." Hereat the man recounted to him the marvels of Fatimah the Devotee and her piety and the beauties of her worship; then, taking him by the hand went with him without the city and showed him the way to her abode, a cavern upon a hillock's head. The Necromancer acknowledged his kindness in many words and, thanking him for his good offices, returned to his cell in the caravanserai. Now by the fiat of Fate on the very next day Fatimah came down to the city, and the Maghrabi, the Necromancer, happened to leave his hostelry a-morn, when he saw the folk swarming and crowding; wherefore he went up to discover what was to do and found the Devotee standing amiddlemost the throng, and all who suffered from pain or sickness flocked to her soliciting a blessing and praying for her prayers; and each and every she touched became whole of his illness. The Maroccan, the Necromancer, followed her about until she returned to her antre; then, awaiting till the evening evened, he arose and repaired to a vintner's store where he drank a cup of wine. After this he fared forth the city and finding the Devotee's cavern, entered it and saw her lying prostrate with her back upon a strip of matting. So he came forward and mounted upon her belly; then he drew his dagger and shouted at her; and, when she awoke and opened her eyes, she espied a Moorish man with an unsheathed poniard sitting upon her middle as though about to kill her. She was troubled and sore terrified, but he said to her, "Hearken! an thou cry out or utter a word I will slay thee at this very moment: arise now and do all I bid thee." Then he sware to her an oath that if she obeyed his orders, whatever they might be, he would not do her die. So saying, he rose up from off her and Fatimah also arose, when he said to her, "Give me thy gear and take thou my habit;" whereupon she gave him her clothing and head-fillets, her face-kerchief and her mantilla. Then quoth he, "'Tis also requisite that thou anoint me with somewhat

shall make the colour of my face like unto thine." Accordingly she went
into the inner cavern and, bringing out a gallipot of ointment, spread
somewhat thereof upon her palm and with it besmeared his face until
its hue favoured her own; then she gave him her staff and, showing him
how to walk and what to do when he entered the city, hung her rosary
around his neck. Lastly she handed to him a mirror and said, "Now
look! Thou differest from me in naught;" and he saw himself Fatimah's
counterpart as though she had never gone or come. But after obtaining
his every object he falsed his oath and asked for a cord which she
brought to him; then he seized her and strangled her in the cavern; and
presently, when she was dead, haled the corpse outside and threw it
into a pit hard by and went back to sleep in her cavern; and, when
broke the day, he rose and repairing to the town took his stand under
the walls of Aladdin's pavilion. Hereupon flocked the folk about him,
all being certified that he was Fatimah the Devotee and he fell to doing
whatso she was wont to do: he laid hands on these in pain and recited
for those a chapter of the Koran and made orisons for a third. Presently
the thronging of the folk and the clamouring of the crowd were heard
by the Lady Badr al-Budur, who said to her handmaidens, "Look what
is to do and what be the cause of this turmoil!" Thereupon the Agha of
the eunuchry fared forth to see what might be the matter and presently
returning said, "O my lady, this clamour is caused by the Lady
Fatimah, and if thou be pleased to command, I will bring her to thee;
so shalt thou gain through her a blessing." The Princess answered, "Go
bring her, for since many a day I am always hearing of her miracles and
her virtues, and I do long to see her and get a blessing by her interven-
tion, for the folk recount her manifestations in many cases of difficulty."
The Agha went forth and brought in the Maroccan, the Necromancer,
habited in Fatimah's clothing; and, when the wizard stood before the
Lady Badr al-Budur, he began at first sight to bless her with a string of
prayers; nor did any one of those present doubt at all but that he was
the Devotee herself. The Princess arose and salam'd to him; then seating him beside her, said, "O my Lady Fatimah, 'tis my desire that thou
abide with me alway, so might I be blessed through thee, and also learn
of thee the paths of worship and piety and follow thine example making for salvation." Now all this was foul deceit of the accursed African
and he designed furthermore to complete his guile, so he continued.
"O my Lady, I am a poor woman and a religious that dwelleth in the
desert; and the like of me deserveth not to abide in the palaces of the
kings." But the Princess replied, "Have no care whatever, O my Lady
Fatimah; I will set apart for thee an apartment of my pavilion, that thou
mayest worship therein and none shall ever come to trouble thee; also
thou shalt avail to worship Allah in my palace better than in thy cavern."

The Maroccan rejoined, "Hearkening and obedience, O my lady; I will not oppose thine order for that the commands of the children of the kings may not be gainsaid nor renounced. Only I hope of thee that my eating and my drinking and sitting may be within my own chamber which shall be kept wholly private; nor do I require or desire the delicacies of diet, but do thou favour me by sending thy handmaid every day with a bit of bread and a sup of water; and, when I feel fain of food, let me eat by myself in my own room." Now the Accursed hereby purposed to avert the danger of haply raising his face-kerchief at meal times, when his intent might be baffled by his beard and mustachios discovering him to be a man. The Princess replied, "O my Lady Fatimah, be of good heart; naught shall happen save what thou wishest. But now arise and let me show thee the apartment in the palace which I would prepare for thy sojourn with us." The Lady Badr al-Budur arose and taking the Necromancer who had disguised himself as the Devotee, ushered him into the place which she had kindly promised him for a home and said, "O my Lady Fatimah, here thou shalt dwell with every comfort about thee and in all privacy and repose; and the place shall be named after thy name;" whereupon the Maghrabi acknowledged her kindness and prayed for her. Then the Princess showed him the jalousies and the jewelled Kiosque with its four and twenty windows and said to him, "What thinkest thou, O my Lady Fatimah, of this marvellous pavilion?" The Moorman replied, "By Allah, O my daughter, 'tis indeed passing fine and wondrous exceedingly; nor do I deem that its fellow is to be found in the whole universe; but alas for the lack of one thing which would enhance its beauty and decoration!" The Princess asked her, "O my Lady Fatimah, what lacketh it and what be this thing would add to its adornment? Tell me thereof, inasmuch as I was wont to believe it wholly perfect." The Maroccan answered, "O my lady, all it wanteth is that there be hanging from the middle of the dome the egg of a fowl called the Rukh; and, were this done, the pavilion would lack its peer all the world over." The Princess asked, "What be this bird and where can we find her egg?" and the Maroccan answered, "O my lady, the Rukh is indeed a giant fowl which carrieth off camels and elephants in her pounces and flieth away with them, such is her stature and strength; also this fowl is mostly found in Mount Kaf; and the architect who built this pavilion is able to bring thee one of her eggs." They then left such talk as it was the hour for the noon-day meal and, when the handmaid had spread the table, the Lady Badr al-Budur sent down to invite the Accursed African to eat with her. But he accepted not, and for a reason he would on no wise consent; nay, he rose and retired to the room which the Princess had assigned to him and whither the slave-girls carried his dinner. Now when evening evened, Aladdin returned from the chase and met his wife who salam'd to him and he clasped her to his bosom and kissed her. Presently, looking at her face he saw thereon a shade of sadness and he noted that contrary to her custom, she did not laugh; so he asked her, "What hath betided thee, O my dearling? tell me, hath aught happened to trouble thy thoughts?" "Nothing whatever," answered she, "but, O my beloved, I fancied that our pavilion lacked naught at all; however, O eyes of me, Aladdin, were the dome of the upper story hung with an egg of the fowl called Rukh, there would be naught like it in the universe." Her husband rejoined, "And for this trifle thou art saddened when 'tis the easiest of all matters to me! So cheer thyself; and, whatever thou wantest, 'tis enough thou inform me thereof, and I will bring it from the abyss of the earth in the quickest time and at the earliest hour." Aladdin, after refreshing the spirits of his Princess by promising her all she could desire, repaired straightway to his chamber and taking the Lamp rubbed it, when the Marid appeared without let or delay saying, "Ask whatso thou wantest." Said the other, "I desire thee to fetch me an egg of the bird Rukh and do thou hang it to the dome-crown of this my pavilion." But when the Marid heard these words, his face waxed fierce and he shouted with a mighty loud voice and a frightful, and cried, "O denier of kindly deeds, sufficeth it not for thee that I and all the Slaves of the Lamp are ever at thy service, but thou must also require me to bring thee our Liege Lady for thy pleasure, and hang her up at thy pavilion-dome for the enjoyment of thee and thy wife! Now by Allah, ye deserve, thou and she, that I reduce you to ashes this very moment and scatter you upon the air; but, inasmuch as ye twain be ignorant of this matter, unknowing its inner from its outer significance, I will pardon you for indeed ye are but innocents. The offence cometh from that accursed Necromancer, brother to the Maghrabi, the Magician, who abideth here representing himself to be Fatimah, the Devotee, after assuming her dress and belongings and murthering her in the cavern: indeed he came hither seeking to slay thee by way of blood-revenge for his brother; and 'tis he who taught thy wife to require this matter of me." So saying the Marid evanished. But when Aladdin heard these words, his wits fled his head and his joints trembled at the Marid's terrible shout; but he empowered his purpose and, arising forthright issued from his chamber and went into his wife's. There he affected an ache of head, for that he knew how famous was Fatimah for the art and mystery of healing all such pains; and, when the Lady Badr al-Budur saw him sitting hand to head and complaining of unease, she asked him the cause and he answered, "I know of none other save that my head acheth exceedingly." Hereupon she straightway bade summon Fatimah that the Devotee might impose her hand upon his head; and Aladdin asked her, "Who may this Fatimah be?" So she informed him that it was Fatimah the Devotee to whom she had given a home in the pavilion. Meanwhile the slave-girls had fared forth and summoned the Maghrabi, and when the Accursed made act of presence, Aladdin rose up to him, and, acting like one who knew naught of his purpose, salam'd to him as though he had been the real Fatimah and, kissing the hem of his sleeve, welcomed him and entreated him with honour and said, "O my Lady Fatimah, I hope thou wilt bless me with a boon, for well I wot thy practice in the healing of pains: I have gotten a mighty ache in my head." The Moorman, the Accursed, could hardly believe that he heard such words, this being all that he desired. The Necromancer, habited as Fatimah the Devotee, came up to Aladdin that he might place hand upon his head and heal his ache; so he imposed one hand and, putting forth the other under his gown, drew a dagger wherewith to slay him. But Aladdin watched him and, taking patience till he had wholly unsheathed the weapon, seized him with a forceful grip; and, wrenching the dagger from his grasp plunged it deep into his heart. When the Lady Badr al-Budur saw him do on this wise, she shrieked and cried out, "What hath this virtuous and holy woman done that thou hast charged thy neck with the heavy burthen of her blood shed wrongfully? Hast thou no fear of Allah that thou killest Fatimah, this saintly woman, whose miracles are far-famed?" "No," replied Aladdin, "I have not killed Fatimah. I have slain only Fatimah's slayer, he that is the brother of the Maghrabi, the Accursed, the Magician, who carried thee off by his black art and transported my pavilion to the Africa-land; and this damnable brother of his came to our city and wrought these wiles, murthering Fatimah and assuming her habit, only that he might avenge upon me his brother's blood; and he also 'twas who taught thee to require of me a Rukh's egg, that my death might result from such requirement. But, an thou doubt my speech, come forwards and consider the person I have slain." Thereupon Aladdin drew aside the Moorman's face-kerchief and the Lady Badr al-Budur saw the semblance of a man with a full beard that well-nigh covered his features. She at once knew the truth and said to her husband, "O my beloved, twice have I cast thee into death-risk!" but he rejoined, "No harm in that, O my lady, by the blessing of your loving eyes: I accept with all joy all things thou bringest me." The Princess, hearing these words, hastened to fold him in her arms and kissed him saying, "O my dearling, all this is for my love to thee and I knew naught thereof; but indeed I do not deem lightly of thine affection." So Aladdin kissed her and strained her to his breast; and the love between them waxed but greater. At that moment the Sultan appeared and they told him all that had happened, showing him the corpse of the Maghrabi, the Necromancer, when the King commanded the body to be burned and the ashes scattered on air, even as had befallen the Wizard's brother. And Aladdin abode with his wife, the Lady Badr al-Budur, in all pleasure and joyance of life and thenceforward escaped every danger; and, after a while, when the Sultan deceased, his son-in-law was seated upon the throne of the Kingdom; and he commanded and dealt justice to the lieges so that all the folk loved him and he lived with his wife in all solace and happiness until there came to him the Destroyer of delights and the Severer of societies. And a tale is also told about

ALI BABA AND THE FORTY THIEVES

IN DAYS OF yore and in times and tides long gone before there dwelt in a certain town of Persia two brothers one named Kasim and the other Ali Baba, who at their father's demise had divided the little wealth he had left to them with equitable division, and had lost no time in wasting and spending it all. The elder, however, presently took to himself a wife, the daughter of an opulent merchant; so that when his father-in-law fared to the mercy of Almighty Allah, he became owner of a large shop filled with rare goods and costly wares and of a storehouse stocked with precious stuffs; likewise of much gold that was buried in the ground. Thus was he known throughout the city as a substantial man. But the woman whom Ali Baba had married was poor and needy; they lived, therefore, in a mean hovel and Ali Baba eked out a scanty livelihood by the sale of fuel which he daily collected in the jungle and carried about the town to the Bazar upon his three asses. Now it chanced one day that Ali Baba had cut dead branches and dry fuel sufficient for his need, and had placed the load upon his beasts when suddenly he espied a dust-cloud spireing high in air to his right and moving rapidly towards him; and when he closely considered it he descried a troop of horsemen riding on amain and about to reach him. At this sight he was sore alarmed, and fearing lest perchance they were a band of bandits who would slay him and drive off his donkeys, in his affright he began to run; but forasmuch as they were near hand and he could not escape from out the forest, he drove his animals laden with the fuel into a bye-way of the bushes and swarmed up a thick trunk of a huge tree to hide himself therein; and he sat upon a branch whence he could descry everything beneath him whilst none below could catch a glimpse of him above; and that tree grew close beside a rock which towered high above-head. The horsemen, young, active, and doughty riders, came close up to the rock-face and all dismounted; whereat Ali Baba took good note of them and soon he was fully persuaded by their mien and demeanour that they were a troop of highwaymen who, having fallen upon a caravan had despoiled it and carried off the spoil and brought their booty to this place with intent of concealing it safely in some cache. Moreover he observed that they were forty in number. Ali Baba saw the robbers, as soon as they came under the tree, each unbridle his horse and hobble it; then all took off their saddle-bags which proved to be full of gold and silver. The man who seemed to be the captain presently pushed forwards, load on shoulder, through thorns and thickets, till he came up to a certain spot where he uttered these strange words, "Open, O Simsim!" and forthwith appeared a wide doorway in the face of the rock. The robbers went in and last of all their Chief and then the portal shut of itself. Long while they stayed within the cave whilst Ali Baba was constrained to abide perched upon the tree, reflecting that if he came down peradventure the band might issue forth that very moment and seize him and slay him. At last he had determined to mount one of the horses and driving on his asses to return townwards, when suddenly the portal flew open. The robber-chief was first to issue forth; then, standing at the entrance, he saw and counted his men as they came out, and lastly he spake the magical words, "Shut, O Simsim!" whereat the door closed of itself. When all had passed muster and review, each slung on his saddle-bags and bridled his own horse and as soon as ready they rode off, led by the leader, in the direction whence they came. Ali Baba remained still perched on the tree and watched their departure; nor would he descend until what time they were clean gone out of sight, lest perchance one of them return and look around and descry him. Then he thought within himself, "I too will try the virtue of those magical words and see if at my bidding the door will open and close." So he called out aloud, "Open, O Simsim!" And no sooner had he spoken than straightway the portal flew open and he entered within. He saw a large cavern and a vaulted, in height equalling the stature of a full-grown man and it was hewn in the live stone and lighted up with light that came through air-holes and bulls-eyes in the upper surface of the rock which formed the roof. He had expected to find naught save outer gloom in this robbers' den, and he was surprised to see the whole room filled with bales of all manner stuffs, and heaped up from sole to ceiling with camel-loads of silks and brocades and embroidered cloths and mounds on mounds of vari-coloured carpetings; besides which he espied coins golden and silvern without measure or account, some piled upon the ground and others bound in leathern bags and sacks. Seeing these goods and moneys in such abundance, Ali Baba determined in his mind that not during a few years only but for many generations thieves must have stored their gains and spoils in this place. When he stood within the cave, its door had closed upon him, yet he was not dismayed since he had kept in memory the magical words; and he took no heed of the precious stuffs around him, but applied himself only and wholly to the sacks of Ashrafis. Of these he carried out as many as he judged sufficient burthen for the beasts; then he loaded them upon his animals, and covered his plunder with sticks and fuel, so none might discern the bags, but might think that he was carrying home his usual ware. Lastly he called out, "Shut, O Simsim!" and forthwith the door closed, for the spell so wrought that whensoever any entered the cave, its portal shut of itself behind him; and, as he issued therefrom, the same would neither open nor close again till he had pronounced the words, "Shut, O Simsim!" Presently, having laden his asses Ali Baba urged them before him with all speed to the city and reaching home he drove them into the yard; and, shutting close the outer door, took down first the sticks and fuel and after the bags of gold which he carried in to his wife. She felt them and finding them full of coin suspected that Ali Baba had been robbing and fell to berating and blaming him for that he should do so ill a thing. Quoth Ali Baba to his wife:—"Indeed I am no robber and rather do thou rejoice with me at our good fortune." Hereupon he told her of his adventure and began to pour the gold from the bags in heaps before her, and her sight was dazzled by the sheen and her heart delighted at his recital and adventures. Then she began counting the gold, whereat quoth Ali Baba, "O silly woman, how long wilt thou continue turning over the coin? now let me dig a hole wherein to hide this treasure that none may know its secret." Quoth she, "Right is thy rede! still would I weigh the moneys and have some inkling of their amount;" and he replied, "As thou pleasest, but see thou tell no man." So she went off in haste to Kasim's home to borrow weights and scales wherewith she might balance the Ashrafis and make some reckoning of their value; and when she could not find Kasim she said to his wife, "Lend me, I pray thee, thy scales for a moment." Replied her sister-in-law, "Hast thou need of the bigger balance or the smaller?" and the other rejoined, "I need not the large scales, give me the little;" and her sister-in-law cried, "Stay here a moment whilst I look about and find thy want." With this pretext Kasim's wife went aside and secretly smeared wax and suet over the pan of the balance, that she might know what thing it was Ali Baba's wife would weigh, for she made sure that whatso it be some bit thereof would stick to the wax and fat. So the woman took this opportunity to satisfy her curiosity, and Ali Baba's wife suspecting naught thereof carried home the scales and began to weigh the gold, whilst Ali Baba ceased not digging; and, when the money was weighed, they twain stowed it into the hole which they carefully filled up with earth. Then the good wife took back the scales to her kinswoman, all unknowing that an Ashrafi had adhered to the cup of the scales; but when Kasim's wife espied the gold coin she fumed with envy and wrath, saying to herself, "So ho! they borrowed my balance to weigh out Ashrafis?" and she marvelled greatly whence so poor a man as Ali Baba had gotten such store of wealth that he should be obliged to weigh it with a pair of scales. Now after long pondering the matter, when her husband returned home at eventide, she said to him, "O man, thou deemest thyself a wight of wealth and substance, but lo, thy brother Ali Baba is an Emir by the side of thee and richer far than thou art. He hath such heaps of gold that he must needs weigh his moneys with scales, whilst thou, forsooth, art satisfied to count thy coin." "Whence knowest thou this?" asked Kasim, and in answer his wife related all anent the pair of scales and how she found an Ashrafi stuck to them, and shewed him the gold coin which bore the mark and superscription of some ancient king. No sleep had Kasim all that night by reason of his envy and jealousy and covetise; and next morning he rose betimes and going to Ali Baba said, "O my brother, to all appearance thou art poor and needy; but in effect thou hast a store of wealth so abundant that perforce thou must weigh thy gold with scales." Quoth Ali Baba, "What is this thou sayest? I understand thee not; make clear thy purport;" and quoth Kasim with ready rage, "Feign not that thou art ignorant of what I say and think not to deceive me." Then showing him the Ashrafi he cried, "Thousands of gold coins such as these thou hast put by; and meanwhile my wife found this one stuck to the cup of the scales." Then Ali Baba understood how both Kasim and his wife knew that he had store of Ashrafis, and said in his mind that it would not avail him to keep the matter hidden, but would rather cause ill-will and mischief; and thus he was induced to tell his brother every whit concerning the bandits and also of the treasure trove in the cave. When he had heard the story, Kasim exclaimed, "I would fain learn of thee the certainty of the place where thou foundest the moneys; also the magical words whereby the door opened and closed; and I forewarn thee an thou tell me not the whole truth, I will give notice of those Ashrafis to the Wali; then shalt thou forfeit all thy wealth and be disgraced and thrown into gaol." Thereupon Ali Baba told him his tale not forgetting the magical words; and Kasim who kept careful heed of all these matters next day set out, driving ten mules he had hired, and readily found the place which Ali Baba had described to him. And when he came to the aforesaid rock and to the tree whereon Ali Baba had hidden himself, and he had made sure of the door he cried in great joy, "Open, O Simsim!" The portal yawned wide at once and Kasim went within and saw the piles of jewels and treasures lying ranged all around; and, as soon as he stood amongst them the door shut after him as wont to do. He walked about in ecstasy marvelling at the treasures, and when weary of admiration he gathered together bags of Ashrafis, a sufficient load for his ten mules, and placed them by the entrance in readiness to be carried outside and set upon the beasts. But by the will of Allah Almighty he had clean forgotten the cabalistic words and cried out, "Open, O Barley!" whereat the door refused to move. Astonished and confused beyond measure he named the names of all manner of grains save sesame, which had slipped from his memory as though he had never heard the word; whereat in his dire distress he heeded not the Ashrafis that lay heaped at the entrance and paced to and fro, backwards and forwards, within the cave sorely puzzled and perplexed. The wealth whose sight had erewhile filled his heart with joy and gladness was now the cause of bitter grief and sadness. It came to pass that at noontide the robbers, returning by that way, saw from afar some mules standing beside the entrance and much they marvelled at what had brought the beasts to that place; for, inasmuch as Kasim by mischance had failed to tether or hobble them, they had strayed about the jungle and were browsing hither and thither. However, the thieves paid scant regard to the estrays nor cared they to secure them, but only wondered by what means they had wandered so far from the town. Then, reaching the cave the Captain and his troop dismounted and going up to the door repeated the formula and at once it flew open. Now Kasim had heard from within the cave the horse-hooves drawing nigh and yet nigher; and he fell down to the ground in a fit of fear never doubting that it was the clatter of the banditti who would slaughter him without fail. Howbeit he presently took heart of grace and at the moment when the door flew open he rushed out hoping to make good his escape. But the unhappy ran full tilt against the Captain who stood in front of the band, and felled him to the ground; whereupon a robber standing near his chief at once bared his brand and with one cut clave Kasim clean in twain. Thereupon the robbers rushed into the cavern, and put back as they were before the bags of Ashrafis which Kasim had heaped up at the doorway ready for taking away; nor recked they aught of those which Ali Baba had removed, so dazed and amazed were they to discover by what means the strange man had effected an entrance. All knew that it was not possible for any to drop through the skylights so tall and steep was the rock's face, withal slippery of ascent; and also that none could enter by the portal unless he knew the magical words whereby to open it. However they presently quartered the dead body of Kasim and hung it to the door within the cavern, two parts to the right jamb and as many to the left that the sight might be a warning of approaching doom for all who dared enter the cave. Then coming out they closed the hoard door and rode away upon their wonted work.

Now when night fell and Kasim came not home, his wife waxed uneasy in mind and running round to Ali Baba said, "O my brother, Kasim hath not returned: thou knowest whither he went, and sore I fear me some misfortune hath betided him." Ali Baba also divined that a mishap had happened to prevent his return; not the less, however, he strove to comfort his sister-in-law with words of cheer and said, "O wife of my brother, Kasim haply exerciseth discretion and, avoiding the city, cometh by a roundabout road and will be here anon. This, I do believe, is the reason why he tarrieth." Thereupon comforted in spirit Kasim's wife fared homewards and sat awaiting her husband's return; but when half the night was spent and still he came not, she was as one distraught. She feared to cry aloud for her grief, lest haply the neighbours hearing her should come and learn the secret; so she wept in silence and upbraiding herself fell to thinking, "Wherefore did I disclose this secret to him and beget envy and jealousy of Ali Baba? This be the fruit thereof and hence the disaster that hath come down upon me." She spent the rest of the night in bitter tears and early on the morrow hied in hottest hurry to Ali Baba and prayed that he would go forth in quest of his brother; so he strove to console her and straightway set out with his asses for the forest. Presently, reaching the rock he wondered to see stains of blood freshly shed and not finding his brother or the ten mules he forefelt a calamity from so evil a sign. He then went to the door and saying, "Open, O Simsim!" he pushed in and saw the dead body of Kasim, two parts hanging to the right, and the rest to the left of the entrance. Albeit he was affrighted beyond measure of affright he wrapped the quarters in two cloths and laid them upon one of his asses, hiding them carefully with sticks and fuel that none might see them. Then he placed the bags of gold upon the two other animals and likewise covered them most carefully; and, when all was made ready he closed the cave-door with the magical words, and set him forth wending homewards with all ward and watchfulness. The asses with the load of Ashrafis he made over to his wife and bade her bury the bags with diligence; but he told her not the condition in which he had come upon his brother Kasim. Then he went with the other ass, to wit, the beast whereon was laid the corpse to the widow's house and knocked gently at the door. Now Kasim had a slave-girl shrewd and sharp-witted, Morgiana hight. She as softly undid the bolt and admitted Ali Baba and the ass into the courtyard of the house, when he let down the body from the beast's back and said, "O Morgiana, haste thee and make thee ready to perform the rites for the burial of thy lord: I now go to tell the tidings to thy mistress and I will quickly return to help thee in this matter." At that instant Kasim's widow seeing her brother-in-law, exclaimed, "O Ali Baba, what news bringest thou of my spouse? Alas, I see grief tokens written upon thy countenance. Say quickly what hath happened." Then he recounted to her how it had fared with her husband and how he had been slain by the robbers and in what wise he had brought home the dead body. Ali Baba pursued:—"O my lady, what was to happen hath happened, but it behoveth us to keep this matter secret, for that our lives depend upon privacy." She wept with sore weeping and made answer, "It hath fared with my husband according to the fiat of Fate; and now for thy safety's sake I give thee my word to keep the affair concealed." He replied, "Naught can avail when Allah hath decreed. Rest thee in patience until the days of thy widowhood be accomplisht; after which time I will take thee to wife, and thou shalt live in comfort and happiness; and fear not lest my first spouse vex thee or show aught of jealousy, for that she is kindly and tender of heart." The widow lamenting her loss noisily, cried, "Be it as e'en thou please." Then Ali Baba farewelled her, weeping and wailing for her husband; and joining Morgiana took counsel with her how to manage the burial of his brother. So, after much consultation and many warnings, he left the slave-girl and departed home driving his ass before him. As soon as Ali Baba had fared forth Morgiana went quickly to a druggist's shop; and, that she might the better dissemble with him and not make known the matter, she asked of him a drug often administered to men when diseased with dangerous distemper. He gave it saying, "Who is there in thy house that lieth so ill as to require this medicine?" and said she, "My Master Kasim is sick well nigh unto death: for many days he hath not spoken nor tasted aught of food, so that almost we despair of his life." Next day Morgiana went again and asked the druggist for more of medicine and essences such as are adhibited to the sick when at door of death, that the moribund may haply rally before the last breath. The man gave the potion and she taking it sighed aloud and wept, saying, "I fear me he may not have strength to drink this draught: methinks all will be over with him ere I return to the house." Meanwhile Ali Baba was anxiously awaiting to hear sounds of wailing and lamentation in Kasim's home that he might at such signal hasten thither and take part in the ceremonies of the funeral. Early on the second day Morgiana went with veiled face to one Baba Mustafa, a tailor well shotten in years whose craft was to make shrouds and cerecloths; and as soon as she saw him open his shop she gave him a gold piece and said, "Do thou bind a bandage over thine eyes and come along with me." Mustafa made as though he would not go, whereat Morgiana placed a second gold coin in his palm and entreated him to accompany her. The tailor presently consented for greed of gain, so tying a kerchief tightly over his eyes she led him by the hand to the house wherein lay the dead body of her master. Then, taking off the bandage in the darkened room she bade him sew together the quarters of the corpse, limb to its limb; and casting a cloth upon the body, said to the tailor, "Make haste and sew a shroud according to the size of this dead man and I will give thee therefor yet another ducat." Baba Mustafa quickly made the cerecloth of fitting length and breadth, and Morgiana paid him the promised Ashrafi; then once more bandaging his eyes led him back to the place whence she had brought him. After this she returned hurriedly home and with the help of Ali Baba washed the body in warm water and donning the shroud lay the corpse upon a clean place ready for burial. This done Morgiana went to the mosque and gave notice to an Imam that a funeral was awaiting the mourners in a certain household, and prayed that he would come to read the prayers for the dead; and the Imam went back with her. Then four neighbours took up the bier and bore it on their shoulders and fared forth with the Imam and others who were wont to give assistance at such obsequies. After the funeral prayers were ended four other men carried off the coffin; and Morgiana walked before it bare of head, striking her breast and weeping and wailing with exceeding loud lament, whilst Ali Baba and the neighbours came behind. In such order they entered the cemetery and buried him; then, leaving him to Munkar and Nakir—the Questioners of the Dead—all wended their ways. Presently the women of the quarter, according to the custom of the city, gathered together in the house of mourning and sat an hour with Kasim's widow comforting and condoling, presently leaving her somewhat resigned and cheered. Ali Baba stayed forty days at home in ceremonial lamentation of the loss of his brother; so none within the town save himself and his wife (Kasim's widow) and Morgiana knew aught the secret. And when the forty days of mourning were ended Ali Baba removed to his own quarters all the property belonging to the deceased and openly married the widow; then he appointed his nephew, his brother's eldest son, who had lived a long time with a wealthy merchant and was perfect of knowledge in all matters of trade, such as selling and buying, to take charge of the defunct's shop and to carry on the business. It so chanced one day when the robbers, as was their wont, came to the treasure-cave that they marvelled exceedingly to find nor sign nor trace of Kasim's body whilst they observed that much of gold had been carried off. Quoth the Captain, "Now it behoveth us to make enquiry in this matter; else shall we suffer much of loss and this our treasure, which we and our forefathers have amassed during the course of many years, will little by little be wasted and spoiled." Hereto all assented and with single mind agreed that he whom they had slain had knowledge of the magical words whereby the door was made to open; moreover that some one beside him had cognizance of the spell and had carried off the body, and also much of gold; wherefore they needs must make diligent research and find out who the man ever might be. They then took counsel and determined that one amongst them, who should be sagacious and deft of wit, must don the dress of some merchant from foreign parts; then, repairing to the city he must go about from quarter to quarter and from street to street, and learn if any townsman had lately died and if so where he wont to dwell, that with this clue they might be enabled to find the wight they sought. Hereat said one of the robbers, "Grant me leave that I fare and find out such tidings in the town and bring thee word anon; and if I fail of my purpose I hold my life in forfeit." Accordingly that bandit, after disguising himself by dress, pushed at night into the town and next morning early he repaired to the market-square and saw that none of the shops had yet been opened, save only that of Baba Mustafa the tailor, who thread and needle in hand sat upon his working-stool. The thief bade him good day and said, "'Tis yet dark: how canst thou see to sew?" Said the tailor, "I perceive thou art a stranger. Despite my years my eyesight is so keen that only yesterday I sewed together a dead body whilst sitting in a room quite darkened." Quoth the bandit thereupon to himself, "I shall get somewhat of my want from this snip;" and to secure a further clue he asked, "Meseemeth thou wouldst jest with me and thou meanest that a cerecloth for a corpse was stitched by thee and that thy business is to sew shrouds." Answered the tailor, "It mattereth not to thee: question me no more questions." Thereupon the robber placed an Ashrafi in his hand and continued, "I desire not to discover aught thou hidest, albeit my breast like every honest man's is the grave of secrets; and this only would I learn of thee, in what house didst thou do that job? Canst thou direct me thither, or thyself conduct me thereto?" The tailor took the gold with greed and cried, "I have not seen with my own eyes the way to that house. A certain bondswoman led me to a place which I know right well and there she bandaged my eyes and guided me to some tenement and lastly carried me into a darkened room where lay the dead body dismembered. Then she unbound the kerchief and bade me sew together first the corpse and then the shroud, which having done she again blindfolded me and led me back to the stead whence she had brought me and left me there. Thou seest then I am not able to tell thee where thou shalt find the house." Quoth the robber, "Albeit thou knowest not the dwelling whereof thou speakest, still canst thou take me to the place where thou wast blindfolded; then I will bind a kerchief over thine eyes and lead thee as thou wast led: on this wise perchance thou mayest hit upon the site. An thou wilt do this favour by me, see here another golden ducat is thine." Thereupon the bandit slipped a second Ashrafi into the tailor's palm, and Baba Mustafa thrust it with the first into his pocket; then, leaving his shop as it was, he walked to the place where Morgiana had tied the kerchief around his eyes, and with him went the robber who, after binding on the bandage, led him by the hand. Baba Mustafa, who was clever and keen-witted, presently striking the street whereby he had fared with the handmaid, walked on counting step by step; then, halting suddenly, he said, "Thus far I came with her;" and the twain stopped in front of Kasim's house wherein now dwelt his brother Ali Baba. The robber then made marks with white chalk upon the door to the end that he might readily find it at some future time, and removing the bandage from the tailor's eyes said, "O Baba Mustafa, I thank thee for this favour: and Almighty Allah guerdon thee for thy goodness. Tell me now, I pray thee, who dwelleth in yonder house?" Quoth he, "In very sooth I wot not, for I have little knowledge concerning this quarter of the city;" and the bandit, understanding that he could find no further clue from the tailor, dismissed him to his shop with abundant thanks, and hastened back to the tryst-place in the jungle where the band awaited his coming. Not long after it so fortuned that Morgiana, going out upon some errand, marvelled exceedingly at seeing the chalk-marks showing white on the door; she stood awhile deep in thought and presently divined that some enemy had made the signs that he might recognise the house and play some sleight upon her lord. She therefore chalked the doors of all her neighbours in like manner and kept the matter secret, never entrusting it or to master or to mistress. Meanwhile the robber told his comrades his tale of adventure and how he had found the clue; so the captain and with him all the band went one after other by different ways till they entered the city; and he who had placed the mark on Ali Baba's door accompanied the Chief to point out the place. He conducted him straightway to the house and shewing the sign exclaimed, "Here dwelleth he of whom we are in search!" But when the Captain looked around him he saw that all the dwellings bore chalk-marks after like fashion and he wondered saying, "By what manner of means knowest thou which house of all these houses that bear similar signs is that whereof thou spakest?" Hereat the robber-guide was confounded beyond measure of confusion, and could make no answer; then with an oath he cried, "I did assuredly set a sign upon a door, but I know not whence came all the marks upon the other entrances; nor can I say for a surety which it was I chalked." Thereupon the Captain returned to the market-place and said to his men, "We have toiled and laboured in vain, nor have we found the house we went forth to seek. Return we now to the forest our rendezvous: I also will fare thither." Then all trooped off and assembled together within the treasure-cave; and, when the robbers had all met, the Captain judged him worthy of punishment who had spoken falsely and had led them through the city to no purpose. So he imprisoned him in presence of them all; and then said he, "To him amongst you will I show special favour who shall go to town and bring me intelligence whereby we may lay hands upon the plunderer of our property." Hereat another of the company came forward and said, "I am ready to go and enquire into the case, and 'tis I who will bring thee to thy wish." The Captain after giving him presents and promises despatched him upon his errand; and by the decree of Destiny which none may gainsay, this second robber went first to the house of Baba Mustafa the tailor, as had done the thief who had foregone him. In like manner he also persuaded the snip with gifts of golden coin that he be led hoodwinked and thus too he was guided to Ali Baba's door. Here noting the work of his predecessor, he affixed to the jamb a mark with red chalk the better to distinguish it from the others whereon still showed the white. Then hied he back in stealth to his company; but Morgiana on her part also descried the red sign on the entrance and with subtle forethought marked all the others after the same fashion; nor told she any what she had done. Meanwhile the bandit rejoined his band and vauntingly said, "O our Captain, I have found the house and thereon put a mark whereby I shall distinguish it clearly from all its neighbours." But, as aforetime, when the troop repaired thither they saw each and every house marked with signs of red chalk. So they returned disappointed and the Captain, waxing displeased exceedingly and distraught, clapped also this spy into gaol. Then said the Chief to himself, "Two men have failed in their endeavour and have met their rightful meed of punishment; and I trow that none other of my band will essay to follow up their research; so I myself will go and find the house of this wight." Accordingly he fared along and aided by the tailor Baba Mustafa, who had gained much gain of golden pieces in this matter, he hit upon the house of Ali Baba; and here he made no outward show or sign, but marked it on the tablet of his heart and impressed the picture upon the page of his memory. Then returning to the jungle he said to his men, "I have full cognizance of the place and have limned it clearly in my mind; so now there will be no difficulty in finding it. Go forth straightways and buy me and bring hither nineteen mules together with one large leathern jar of mustard oil and seven and thirty vessels of the same kind clean empty. Without me and the two locked up in gaol ye number thirty-seven souls; so I will stow you away armed and accoutred each within his jar and will load two upon each mule, and upon the nineteenth mule there shall be a man in an empty jar on one side, and on the other the jar full of oil. I for my part, in guise of an oil-merchant, will drive the mules into the town, arriving at the house by night, and will ask permission of its master to tarry there until morning. After this we shall seek occasion during the dark hours to rise up and fall upon him and slay him." Furthermore the Captain spake saying, "When we have made an end of him we shall recover the gold and treasure whereof he robbed us and bring it back upon the mules." This counsel pleased the robbers who went forthwith and purchased mules and huge leathern jars, and did as the Captain had bidden them. And after a delay of three days shortly before nightfall they arose; and over-smearing all the jars with oil of mustard, each hid him inside an empty vessel. The Chief then disguised himself in trader's gear and placed the jars upon the nineteen mules; to wit, the thirty-seven vessels in each of which lay a robber armed and accoutred, and the one that was full of oil. This done, he drove the beasts before him and presently he reached Ali Baba's place at nightfall; when it chanced that the house-master was strolling after supper to and fro in front of his home. The Captain saluted him with the salam and said, "I come from such and such a village with oil; and ofttimes have I been here a-selling oil, but now to my grief I have arrived too late and I am sore troubled and perplexed as to where I shall spend the night. An thou have pity on me I pray thee grant that I tarry here in thy courtyard and ease the mules by taking down the jars and giving the beasts somewhat of fodder." Albeit Ali Baba had heard the Captain's voice when perched upon the tree and had seen him enter the cave, yet by reason of the disguise he knew him not for the leader of the thieves, and granted his request with hearty welcome and gave him full license to halt there for the night. He then pointed out an empty shed wherein to tether the mules, and bade one of the slave-boys go fetch grain and water. He also gave orders to the slave-girl Morgiana saying, "A guest hath come hither and tarrieth here to-night. Do thou busy thyself with all speed about his supper and make ready the guest-bed for him." Presently, when the Captain had let down all the jars and had fed and watered his mules, Ali Baba received him with all courtesy and kindness, and summoning Morgiana said in his presence, "See thou fail not in service of this our stranger nor suffer him to lack for aught. Tomorrow early I would fare to the Hammam and bathe; so do thou give my slave-boy Abdullah a suit of clean white clothes which I may put on after washing; moreover make thee ready a somewhat of broth overnight that I may drink it after my return home." Replied she, "I will have all in readiness as thou hast bidden." So Ali Baba retired to his rest, and the Captain, having supped, repaired to the shed and saw that all the mules had their food and drink for the night. And finding utter privacy, whispered to his men who were in ambush, "This night at midnight when ye hear my voice, do you quickly open with your sharp knives the leathern jars from top to bottom and issue forth without delay." Then passing through the

kitchen he reached the chamber wherein a bed had been dispread for
him, Morgiana showing the way with a lamp. Quoth she, "An thou
need aught beside I pray thee command this thy slave who is ever ready
to obey thy say!" He made answer, "Naught else need I;" then, putting
out the light, he lay down on the bed to sleep awhile ere the time came
to rouse his men and finish off the work. Meanwhile Morgiana did as
her master had bidden her: she first took out a suit of clean white
clothes and made it over to Abdullah who had not yet gone to rest; then
she placed the pipkin upon the hearth to boil the broth and blew the
fire till it burnt briskly. After a short delay she needs must see an the
broth be boiling, but by that time all the lamps had gone out and she
found that the oil was spent and that nowhere could she get a light. The
slave boy Abdullah observed that she was troubled and perplexed
hereat, and quoth he to her, "Why make so much ado? In yonder shed
are many jars of oil: go now and take as much soever as thou listest."
Morgiana gave thanks to him for his suggestion; and Abdullah, who
was lying at his ease in the hall, went off to sleep so that he might wake
betimes and serve Ali Baba in the bath. So the handmaiden rose and
with oil-can in hand walked to the shed where stood the leathern jars
all ragged in rows. Now, as she drew nigh unto one of the vessels, the
thief who was hidden therein hearing the tread of footsteps bethought
him that it was of his Captain whose summons he awaited; so he
whispered, "Is it now time for us to sally forth?" Morgiana started back
affrighted at the sound of human accents; but, inasmuch as she was
bold and ready of wit, she replied, "The time is not yet come," and said
to herself, "These jars are not full of oil and herein I perceive a manner
of mystery. Haply the oil merchant hatcheth some treacherous plot
against my lord; so Allah, the Compassionating, the Compassionate,
protect us from his snares!" Wherefore she answered in a voice made
like to the Captain's, "Not yet, the time is not come." Then she went
to the next jar and returned the same reply to him who was within, and
so on to all the vessels one by one. Then said she in herself, "Laud to
the Lord! My master took this fellow in believing him to be an oil-
merchant, but lo, he hath admitted a band of robbers, who only await
the signal to fall upon him and plunder the place and do him die."
Then passed she on to the furthest jar and finding it brimming with
oil, filled her can, and returning to the kitchen, trimmed the lamp and
lit the wicks; then, bringing forth a large cauldron, she set it upon the
fire, and filling it with oil from out the jar heaped wood upon the
hearth and fanned it to a fierce flame the readier to boil its contents.
When this was done she baled it out in potfuls and poured it seething
hot into the leathern vessels one by one while the thieves unable to
escape were scalded to death and every jar contained a corpse. Thus

did this slave-girl by her subtle wit make a clean end of all noiselessly and unknown even to the dwellers in the house. Now when she had satisfied herself that each and every of the men had been slain, she went back to the kitchen and shutting to the door sat brewing Ali Baba's broth. Scarce had an hour passed before the Captain woke from his sleep and, opening wide his window, saw that all was dark and silent; so he clapped his hands as a signal for his men to come forth but not a sound was heard in return. After awhile he clapped again and called aloud but got no answer; and when he cried out a third time without reply he was perplexed and went out to the shed wherein stood the jars. He thought to himself, "Perchance all are fallen asleep whenas the time for action is now at hand, so I must e'en awaken them without stay or delay." Then approaching the nearest jar he was startled by a smell of oil and seething flesh; and touching it outside he felt it reeking hot; then going to the others one by one, he found all in like condition. Hereat he knew for a surety the fate which had betided his band and, fearing for his own safety, he clomb on to the wall, and thence dropping into a garden made his escape in high dudgeon and sore disappointment. Morgiana awaited awhile to see the Captain return from the shed but he came not; whereat she knew that he had scaled the wall and had taken to flight, for that the street-door was double-locked; and the thieves being all disposed of on this wise Morgiana laid her down to sleep in perfect solace and ease of mind. When two hours of darkness yet remained, Ali Baba awoke and went to the Hammam knowing naught of the night-adventure, for the gallant slave-girl had not aroused him, nor indeed had she deemed such action expedient, because had she sought an opportunity of reporting to him her plan, she might haply have lost her chance and spoiled the project. The sun was high over the horizon when Ali Baba walked back from the Baths; and he marvelled exceedingly to see the jars still standing under the shed and said, "How cometh it that he, the oil-merchant my guest, hath not carried to the market his mules and jars of oil?" She answered, "Allah Almighty vouchsafe to thee six score years and ten of safety! I will tell thee in privacy of this merchant." So Ali Baba went apart with his slave-girl, who taking him without the house first locked the court-door; then showing him a jar she said, "Prithee look into this and see if within there be oil or aught else." Thereupon peering inside it he perceived a man at which sight he cried aloud and fain would have fled in his fright. Quoth Morgiana, "Fear him not, his man hath no longer the force to work thee harm, he lieth dead and stone-dead." Hearing such words of comfort and reassurance Ali Baba asked, "O Morgiana, what evils have we escaped and by what means hath this wretch become the quarry of Fate?" She answered "Alhamdolillah—Praise be to Almighty

Allah!—I will inform thee fully of the case; but hush thee, speak not aloud, lest haply the neighbours learn the secret and it end in our confusion. Look now into all the jars, one by one from first to last." So Ali Baba examined them severally and found in each a man fully armed and accoutred and all lay scalded to death. Hereat speechless for sheer amazement he stared at the jars, but presently recovering himself he asked, "And where is he, the oil-merchant?" Answered she, "Of him also I will inform thee. The villain was no trader but a traitorous assassin whose honied words would have ensnared thee to thy doom; and now I will tell thee what he was and what hath happened; but, meanwhile thou art fresh from the Hammam and thou shouldst first drink somewhat of this broth for thy stomach's and thy health's sake." So Ali Baba went within and Morgiana served up the mess; after which quoth her master, "I fain would hear this wondrous story: prithee tell it to me and set my heart at ease." Hereat the handmaid fell to relating whatso had betided in these words, "O my master, when thou badest me boil the broth and retiredst to rest, thy slave in obedience to thy command took out a suit of clean white clothes and gave it to the boy Abdullah; then kindled the fire and set on the broth. As soon as it was ready I had need to light a lamp so that I might see to skim it, but all the oil was spent, and, learning this I told my want to the slave-boy Abdullah, who advised me to draw somewhat from the jars which stood under the shed. Accordingly, I took a can and went to the first vessel when suddenly I heard a voice within whisper with all caution, 'Is it now time for us to sally forth?' I was amazed thereat and judged that the pretended merchant had laid some plot to slay thee; so I replied, 'The time is not yet come.' Then I went to the second jar and heard another voice to which I made the like answer, and so on with all of them. I now was certified that these men awaited only some signal from the Chief whom thou didst take to guest within thy walls supposing him to be a merchant in oil; and that after thou receivedst him hospitably the miscreant had brought these men to murther thee and to plunder thy goods and spoil thy house. But I gave him no opportunity to win his wish. The last jar I found full of oil and taking somewhat therefrom I lit the lamp; then, putting a large cauldron upon the fire, I filled it up with oil which I brought from the jar and made a fierce blaze under it; and, when the contents were seething hot, I took out sundry cansful with intent to scald them all to death, and going to each jar in due order, I poured within them one by one boiling oil. On this wise having destroyed them utterly, I returned to the kitchen and having extinguished the lamps stood by the window watching what might happen, and how that false merchant would act next. Not long after I had taken my station, the robber-captain awoke and ofttimes signalled to his thieves. Then getting no reply he came downstairs and went out to the jars, and finding that all his men were slain he fled through the darkness I know not whither. So when he had clean disappeared I was assured that, the door being double-locked, he had scaled the wall and dropped into the garden and made his escape. Then with my heart at rest I slept." And Morgiana, after telling her story to her master, presently added, "This is the whole truth I have related to thee. For some days indeed have I had inkling of such matter, but withheld it from thee deeming it inexpedient to risk the chance of its meeting the neighbours' ears; now, however, there is no help but to tell thee thereof. One day as I came to the house-door I espied thereon a white chalk-mark, and on the next day a red sign beside the white. I knew not the intent wherewith the marks were made, nevertheless I set others upon the entrances of sundry neighbours, judging that some enemy had done this deed whereby to encompass my master's destruction. Therefore I made the marks on all the other doors in such perfect conformity with those I found, that it would be hard to distinguish amongst them. Judge now and see if these signs and all this villainy be not the work of the bandits of the forest, who marked our house that on such wise they might know it again. Of these forty thieves there yet remain two others concerning whose case I know naught; so beware of them, but chiefly of the third remaining robber, their Captain, who fled hence alive. Take good heed and be thou cautious of him, for, shouldst thou fall into his hands, he will in no wise spare thee but will surely murther thee. I will do all that lieth in me to save from hurt and harm thy life and property, nor shall thy slave be found wanting in any service to my lord." Hearing these words Ali Baba rejoiced with exceeding joyance and said to her, "I am well pleased with thee for this thy conduct; and say me what wouldst thou have me do in thy behalf; I shall not fail to remember thy brave deed so long as breath in me remaineth." Quoth she, "It behoveth us before all things forthright to bury these bodies in the ground, that so the secret be not known to any one." Hereupon Ali Baba took with him his slave-boy Abdullah into the garden and there under a tree they dug for the corpses of the thieves a deep pit in size proportionate to its contents, and they dragged the bodies (having carried off their weapons) to the fosse and threw them in; then, covering up the remains of the seven and thirty robbers they made the ground appear level and clean as it wont to be. They also hid the leathern jars and the gear and arms and presently Ali Baba sent the mules by ones and twos to the bazar and sold them all with the able aid of his slave-boy Abdullah. Thus the matter was hushed up nor did it reach the ears of any; however, Ali Baba ceased not to be ill at ease lest haply the Captain or the surviving two robbers should wreak their vengeance on his head. He kept himself private with all caution and took heed that none learn a word of what had happened and of the wealth which he had carried off from the bandits' cave. Meanwhile the Captain of the thieves having escaped with his life, fled to the forest in hot wrath and sore irk of mind; and his senses were scattered and the colour of his visage vanished like ascending smoke. Then he thought the matter over again and again, and at last he firmly resolved that he needs must take the life of Ali Baba, else he would lose all the treasure which his enemy, by knowledge of the magical words, would take away and turn to his own use. Furthermore, he determined that he would undertake the business single-handed; and, that after getting rid of Ali Baba, he would gather together another band of banditti and would pursue his career of brigandage, as indeed his forebears had done for many generations. So he lay down to rest that night, and rising early in the morning donned a dress of suitable appearance; then going to the city alighted at a caravanserai, thinking to himself, "Doubtless the murther of so many men hath reached the Wali's ears, and Ali Baba hath been seized and brought to justice, and his house is levelled and his goods are confiscated. The townfolk must surely have heard tidings of these matters." So he straightway asked of the keeper of the khan, "What strange things have happened in the city during the last few days?" and the other told him all that he had seen and heard, but the Captain could not learn a whit of that which most concerned him. Hereby he understood that Ali Baba was ware and wise, and that he had not only carried away such store of treasure but he had also destroyed so many lives and withal had come off scatheless; furthermore, that he himself must needs have all his wits alert not to fall into the hands of his foe and perish. With this resolve the Captain hired a shop in the Bazar, whither he bore whole bales of the finest stuffs and goodly merchandise from his forest treasure-house; and presently he took his seat within the store and fell to doing merchant's business. By chance his place fronted the booth of the defunct Kasim where his son, Ali Baba's nephew, now traded; and the Captain, who called himself Khwajah Hasan, soon formed acquaintance and friendship with the shop keepers around about him and treated all with profuse civilities, but he was especially gracious and cordial to the son of Kasim, a handsome youth and a well-dressed, and ofttimes he would sit and chat with him for a long while. A few days after it chanced that Ali Baba, as he was sometimes wont to do, came to see his nephew, whom he found sitting in his shop. The Captain saw and recognised him at sight and one morning he asked the young man, saying, "Prithee tell me, who is he that ever and anon cometh to thee at thy place of sale?" whereto the youth made answer, "He is my uncle, the brother of my father." Whereupon the Captain showed him yet greater favour and affection the better to deceive him for his own devices, and gave him presents and made him sit at meat with him and fed him with the daintiest of dishes. Presently Ali Baba's nephew bethought him it was only right and proper that he also should invite the merchant to supper, but whereas his own house was small, and he was straitened for room and could not make a show of splendour, as did Khwajah Hasan, he took counsel with his uncle on the matter. Ali Baba replied to his nephew:—"Thou sayest well: it behoveth thee to entreat thy friend in fairest fashion even as he hath entreated thee. On the morrow, which is Friday, shut thy shop as do all merchants of repute; then, after the early meal, take Khwajah Hasan to smell the air, and as thou walkest lead him hither unawares; meanwhile I will give orders that Morgiana shall make ready for his coming the best of viands and all necessaries for a feast. Trouble not thyself on any wise, but leave the matter in my hands." Accordingly on the next day, to wit, Friday, the nephew of Ali Baba took Khwajah Hasan to walk about the garden; and, as they were returning he led him by the street wherein his uncle dwelt. When they came to the house, the youth stopped at the door and knocking said, "O my lord, this is my second home: my uncle hath heard much of thee and of thy goodness mewards and desireth with exceeding desire to see thee; so, shouldst thou consent to enter and visit him, I shall be truly glad and thankful to thee." Albeit Khwajah Hasan rejoiced in heart that he had thus found means whereby he might have access to his enemy's house and household, and although he hoped soon to attain his end by treachery, yet he hesitated to enter in and stood to make his excuses and walk away. But when the door was opened by the slave-porter, Ali Baba's nephew seized his companion's hand and after abundant persuasion led him in, whereat he entered with great show of cheerfulness as though much pleased and honoured. The house-master received him with all favour and worship and asked him of his welfare, and said to him, "O my lord, I am obliged and thankful to thee for that thou hast shewn favour to the son of my brother and I perceive that thou regardest him with an affection even fonder than my own." Khwajah Hasan replied with pleasant words and said, "Thy nephew vastly taketh my fancy and in him I am well pleased, for that although young in years yet he hath been endued by Allah with much of wisdom." Thus they twain conversed with friendly conversation and presently the guest rose to depart and said, "O my lord, thy slave must now farewell thee; but on some future day—Inshallah—he will again wait upon thee." Ali Baba, however, would not let him leave and asked, "Whither wendest thou, O my friend? I would invite thee to my table and I pray thee sit at meat with us and after hie thee home in peace. Perchance the dishes are not as delicate as those whereof thou art wont to eat, still deign grant me this request I pray thee and refresh thyself with my victual." Quoth Khwajah Hasan, "O lord, I am beholden to thee for thy gracious invitation, and with pleasure would I sit at meat with thee, but for a special reason must I needs excuse myself; suffer me therefore to depart for I may not tarry longer nor accept thy gracious offer." Hereto the host made reply, "I pray thee, O my lord, tell me what may be the reason so urgent and weighty?" And Khwajah Hasan answered, "The cause is this: I must not, by order of the physician, who cured me lately of my complaint, eat aught of food prepared with salt." Quoth Ali Baba, "An this be all, deprive me not, I pray thee, of the honour thy company will confer upon me: as the meats are not yet cooked, I will forbid the kitchener to make use of any salt. Tarry here awhile and I will return anon to thee." So saying Ali Baba went in to Morgiana and bade her not put salt into any one of the dishes; and she, while busied with her cooking, fell to marvelling greatly at such order and asked her master, "Who is he that eateth meat wherein is no salt?" He answered, "What to thee mattereth it who he may be? Only do thou my bidding." She rejoined, "'Tis well: all shall be as thou wishest;" but in mind she wondered at the man who made such strange request and desired much to look upon him. Wherefore, when all the meats were ready for serving up, she helped the slave-boy Abdullah to spread the table and set on the meal; and no sooner did she see Khwajah Hasan than she knew who he was, albeit he had disguised himself in the dress of a stranger merchant; furthermore, when she eyed him attentively she espied a dagger hidden under his robe. "So ho!" quoth she to herself, "this is the cause why the villain eateth not of salt, for that he seeketh an opportunity to slay my master whose mortal enemy he is; howbeit I will be beforehand with him and despatch him ere he find a chance to harm my lord." Now when Ali Baba and Khwajah Hasan had eaten their sufficiency, the slave-boy Abdullah brought Morgiana word to serve the dessert, and she cleared the table and set on fruit fresh and dried in salvers, then she placed by the side of Ali Baba a small tripod for three cups with a flagon of wine, and lastly she went off with the slave-boy Abdullah into another room, as though she would herself eat supper. Then Khwajah Hasan, that is, the Captain of the robbers, perceiving that the coast was clear, exulted mightily saying to himself, "The time hath come for me to take full vengeance; with one thrust of my dagger I will despatch this fellow, then escape across the garden and wend my ways. His nephew will not aventure to stay my hand, for an he do but move a finger or toe with that intent another stab will settle his earthly account. Still must I wait awhile until the slave-boy and the cook-maid shall have eaten and lain down to rest them in the kitchen." Morgiana, however, watched him wistfully and divining his purpose said in her mind, "I must not allow this villain advantage over my lord, but by some means I must make void his project and at once put an end to the life of him." Accordingly, the trusty slave-girl changed her dress with all haste and donned such clothes as dancers wear; she veiled her face with a costly kerchief; around her head she bound a fine turband, and about her middle she tied a waist-cloth worked with gold and silver wherein she stuck a dagger, whose hilt was rich in filigree and jewellery. Thus disguised she said to the slave-boy Abdullah, "Take now thy tambourine that we may play and sing and dance in honour of our master's guest." So he did her bidding and the twain went into the room, the lad playing and the lass following. Then, making a low congée, they asked leave to perform and disport and play; and Ali Baba gave permission, saying "Dance now and do your best that this our guest may be mirthful and merry." Quoth Khwajah Hasan, "O my lord, thou dost indeed provide much pleasant entertainment." Then the slave-boy Abdullah standing by began to strike the tambourine whilst Morgiana rose up and showed her perfect art and pleased them vastly with graceful steps and sportive motion; and suddenly drawing the poniard from her belt she brandished it and paced from side to side, a spectacle which pleased them most of all. At times also she stood before them, now clapping the sharp-edged dagger under her armpit and then setting it against her breast. Lastly she took the tambourine from the slave-boy Abdullah, and still holding the poniard in her right she went round for largesse as is the custom amongst merry-makers. First she stood before Ali Baba who threw a gold coin into the tambourine, and his nephew likewise put in an Ashrafi; then Khwajah Hasan, seeing her about to approach him, fell to pulling out his purse, when she heartened her heart and quick as the blinding leven she plunged the dagger into his vitals, and forthwith the miscreant fell back stone-dead. Ali Baba was dismayed and cried in his wrath, "O unhappy, what is this deed thou hast done to bring about my ruin!" But she replied, "Nay, O my lord, rather to save thee and not to cause thee harm have I slain this man: loosen his garments and see what thou wilt discover thereunder." So Ali Baba searched the dead man's dress and found concealed therein a dagger. Then said Morgiana, "This wretch was thy deadly enemy. Consider him well: he is none other than the oil-merchant, the Captain of the band of robbers. Whenas he came hither with intent to take thy life, he would not eat thy salt; and when thou toldest me that he wished not any in the meat I suspected him and at first sight I was assured that he would surely do thee die; Almighty Allah be praised 'tis even as I thought." Then Ali Baba lavished upon her thanks and expressions of gratitude, saying, "Lo, these two times hast thou saved me from his hand," and falling upon her neck he cried, "See thou art free, and as reward for this thy fealty I have wedded thee to my nephew." Then turning to the youth he said, "Do as I bid thee and thou shalt prosper. I would that thou marry Morgiana, who is a model of duty and loyalty: thou seest now yon Khwajah Hasan sought thy friendship only that he might find opportunity to take my life, but this maiden with her good sense and her wisdom hath slain him and saved us." Ali Baba's nephew straightway consented to marry Morgiana. After which the three, raising the dead body bore it forth with all heed and vigilance and privily buried it in the garden, and for many years no one knew aught thereof. In due time Ali Baba married his brother's son to Morgiana with great pomp, and spread a bride-feast in most sumptuous fashion for his friends and neighbours, and made merry with them and enjoyed singing and all manner of dancing and amusements. He prospered in every undertaking and Time smiled upon him and a new source of wealth was opened to him. For fear of the thieves he had not once visited the jungle-cave wherein lay the treasure, since the day he had carried forth the corpse of his brother Kasim. But some time after, he mounted his hackney one morning and journeyed thither, with all care and caution, till finding no signs of man or horse, and reassured in his mind he ventured to draw near the door. Then alighting from his beast he tied it up to a tree, and going to the entrance pronounced the words which he had not forgotten, "Open, O Simsim!" Hereat, as was its wont, the door flew open, and entering thereby he saw the goods and hoard of gold and silver untouched and lying as he had left them. So he felt assured that not one of all the thieves remained alive, and, that save himself there was not a soul who knew the secret of the place. At once he bound in his saddle-cloth a load of Ashrafis such as his horse could bear and brought it home; and in after days he showed the hoard to his sons and sons' sons and taught them how the door could be caused to open and shut. Thus Ali Baba and his household lived all their lives in wealth and joyance in that city where erst he had been a pauper, and by the blessing of that secret treasure he rose to high degree and dignities. Furthermore they relate a tale anent

THE FISHERMAN AND THE JINNI

IT HATH REACHED me, O auspicious King, that there was a Fisherman well stricken in years who had a wife and three children, and withal was of poor condition. Now it was his custom to cast his net every day four times, and no more. On a day he went forth about noontide to the sea-shore, where he laid down his basket; and, tucking up his shirt and plunging into the water, made a cast with his net and waited till it settled to the bottom. Then he gathered the cords together and haled away at it, but found it weighty; and however much he drew it landwards, he could not pull it up; so he carried the ends ashore and drove a stake into the ground and made the net fast to it. Then he stripped and dived into the water all about the net, and left not off working hard until he had brought it up. He rejoiced thereat and, donning his clothes, went to the net, when he found in it a dead jackass which had torn the meshes. Now when he saw it, he exclaimed in his grief, "There is no Majesty, and there is no Might save in Allah the Glorious, the Great!" Then quoth he, "This is a strange manner of daily bread;" and he began reciting in extempore verse: —

> O toiler through the glooms of night in peril and in pain
> Thy toiling stint for daily bread comes not by might and main!
> Seest thou not the fisher seek afloat upon the sea
> His bread, while glimmer stars of night as set in tangled skein.
> Anon he plungeth in despite the buffet of the waves
> The while to sight the bellying net his eager glances strain;
> Till joying at the night's success, a fish he bringeth home
> Whose gullet by the hook of Fate was caught and cut in twain.
> When buys that fish of him a man who spent the hours of night
> Reckless of cold and wet and gloom in ease and comfort fain,
> Laud to the Lord who gives to this, to that denies his wishes
> And dooms one toil and catch the prey and other eat the fishes.

Then quoth he, "Up and to it; I am sure of His beneficience, Inshallah!" So he continued: —

> When thou art seized of Evil Fate, assume
> The noble soul's long-suffering: 'tis thy best:
> Complain not to the creature; this be 'plaint
> From one most Ruthful to the ruthlessest.

The Fisherman, when he had looked at the dead ass, got it free of the toils and wrung out and spread his net; then he plunged into the sea, saying, "In Allah's name!" and made a cast and pulled at it, but it grew heavy and settled down more firmly than the first time. Now he thought that there were fish in it, and he made it fast, and doffing his clothes went into the water, and dived and haled until he drew it up upon dry land. Then found he in it a large earthen pitcher which was full of sand and mud; and seeing this he was greatly troubled. So he prayed pardon of Allah and, throwing away the jar, wrung his net and cleansed it and returned to the sea the third time to cast his net and waited till it had sunk. Then he pulled at it and found therein potsherds and broken glass. Then raising his eyes heavenwards he said, "O my God! verily Thou wottest that I cast not my net each day save four times; the third is done and as yet Thou hast vouchsafed me nothing. So this time, O my God, deign give me my daily bread." Then, having called on Allah's name, he again threw his net and waited its sinking and settling; whereupon he haled at it but could not draw it in for that it was entangled at the bottom. He cried out in his vexation "There is no Majesty and there is no Might save in Allah!" and he began reciting: —

> Fie on this wretched world, an so it be
> I must be whelmed by grief and misery:
> Tho' gladsome be man's lot when dawns the morn
> He drains the cup of woe ere eve he see:
> Yet was I one of whom the world when asked
> "Whose lot is happiest?" oft would say "'Tis he!"

Thereupon he stripped and, diving down to the net, busied himself with it till it came to land. Then he opened the meshes and found therein a cucumber-shaped jar of yellow copper, evidently full of something, whose mouth was made fast with a leaden cap, stamped with the seal-ring of our Lord Sulayman son of David (Allah accept the twain!). Seeing this the Fisherman rejoiced and said, "If I sell it in the brass-bazar 'tis worth ten golden dinars." He shook it and finding it heavy continued, "Would to Heaven I knew what is herein. But I must and will open it and look to its contents and store it in my bag and sell it in the brass-market." And taking out a knife he worked at the lead till he had loosened it from the jar; then he laid the cup on the ground and shook the vase to pour out whatever might be inside. He found nothing in it; whereat he marvelled with an exceeding marvel. But presently there came forth from the jar a smoke which spired heavenwards into ether (whereat he again marvelled with mighty marvel), and which trailed along earth's surface till presently, having reached its full height, the thick vapour condensed, and became an Ifrit, huge of bulk, whose crest touched the clouds while his feet were on the ground. His head was as a dome, his hands like pitchforks, his legs long as masts and his mouth big as a cave; his teeth were like large stones, his nostrils ewers, his eyes two lamps and his look was fierce and lowering. Now when the fisherman saw the Ifrit his side muscles quivered, his teeth chattered, his spittle dried up and he became blind about what to do. Upon this the Ifrit looked at him and cried, "There is no god but *the* God, and Sulayman is the prophet of God;" presently adding, "O Apostle of Allah, slay me not; never again will I gainsay thee in word nor sin against thee in deed." Quoth the Fisherman, "O Marid, diddest thou say, Sulayman the Apostle of Allah; and Sulayman is dead some thousand and eight hundred years ago, and we are now in the last days of the world! What is thy story, and what is thy account of thyself, and what is the cause of thy entering into this cucurbit?" Now when the Evil Spirit heard the words of the Fisherman, quoth he; "There is no god but *the* God: be of good cheer, O Fisherman!" Quoth the Fisherman, "Why biddest thou me to be of good cheer?" and he replied, "Because of thy having to die an ill death in this very hour." Said the Fisherman, "Thou deservest for thy good tidings the withdrawal of Heaven's protection, O thou distant one! Wherefore shouldest thou kill me and what thing have I done to deserve death, I who freed thee from the jar, and saved thee from the depths of the sea, and brought thee up on the dry land?" Replied the Ifrit, "Ask of me only what mode of death thou wilt die, and by what manner of slaughter shall I slay thee." Rejoined the Fisherman, "What is my crime and wherefore such retribution?" Quoth the Ifrit, "Hear my story, O Fisherman!" and he answered, "Say on, and be brief in thy saying, for of very sooth my life-breath is in my nostrils." Thereupon quoth the Jinni, "Know, that I am one among the heretical Jann and I sinned against Sulayman, David-son (on the twain be peace!) I together with the famous Sakhr al-Jinni; whereupon the Prophet sent his minister, Asaf son of Barkhiya, to seize me; and this Wazir brought me against my will and led me in bonds to him (I being downcast despite my nose) and he placed me standing before him like a suppliant. When Sulayman saw me, he took refuge with Allah and bade me embrace the True Faith and obey his behests; but I refused, so sending for this cucurbit he shut me up therein, and stopped it over with lead whereon he impressed the Most High Name, and gave his orders to the Jann who carried me off, and cast me into the midmost of the ocean. There I abode an hundred years, during which I said in my heart, "Whoso shall release me, him will I enrich for ever and ever." But the full century went by and, when no one set me free, I entered upon the second five score saying, "Whoso shall release me, for him I will open the hoards of the earth." Still no one set me free and thus four hundred years passed away. Then quoth I, "Whoso shall release me, for him will I fulfil three wishes." Yet no one set me free. Thereupon I waxed wroth with exceeding wrath and said to myself, "Whoso shall release me from this time forth, him will I slay and I will give him choice of what death he will die; and now, as thou hast released me, I give thee full choice of deaths." The Fisherman, hearing the words of the Ifrit, said, "O Allah! the wonder of it that I have not come to free thee save in these days!" adding, "Spare my life, so Allah spare thine; and slay me not, lest Allah set one to slay thee." Replied the Contumacious One, "There is no help for it; die thou must; so ask by way of boon what manner of death thou wilt die." Albeit thus certified the Fisherman again addressed the Ifrit saying, "Forgive me this my death as a generous reward for having freed thee;" and the Ifrit, "Surely I would not slay thee save on account of that same release." "O Chief of the Ifrits," said the Fisherman, "I do thee good and thou requitest me with evil! in very sooth the old saw lieth not when it saith:—

> We wrought them weal, they met our weal with ill;
> Such, by my life! is every bad man's labour:
> To him who benefits unworthy wights
> Shall hap what hapt to Ummi-Amir's neighbour.[1]

Now when the Ifrit heard these words he answered, "No more of this talk, needs must I kill thee." Upon this the Fisherman said to himself, "This is a Jinni; and I am a man to whom Allah hath given a passably cunning wit, so I will now cast about to compass his destruction by my contrivance and by mine intelligence; even as he took counsel only of his malice and his forwardness." He began by asking the Ifrit, "Hast thou indeed resolved to kill me?" and, receiving for all answer, "Even so," he cried, "Now in the Most Great Name, graven on the seal-ring of Sulayman the Son of David (peace be with the holy twain!), an I question thee on a certain matter wilt thou give me a true answer?" The Ifrit replied "Yea;" but, hearing mention of the Most Great Name, his wits were troubled and he said with trembling, "Ask and be brief." Quoth the Fisherman, "How didst thou fit into this bottle which would not hold thy hand; no, nor even thy foot and how came it to be large enough to contain the whole of thee?" Replied the Ifrit, "What! dost not believe that I was all there?" and the Fisherman rejoined, "Nay! I will never believe it until I see thee inside with my own eyes." The Evil Spirit on the instant shook and became a vapour, which condensed, and entered the jar little and little, till all was well inside when lo! the Fisherman in hot haste took the leaden cap with the seal and stoppered therewith the mouth of the jar and called out to the Ifrit, saying, "Ask me by way of boon what death thou wilt die! By Allah, I will throw thee into the sea before us and here will I build me a lodge; and whoso cometh hither I will warn him against fishing and will say:—In these waters abideth an Ifrit who giveth as a last favour a choice of deaths and fashion of slaughter to the man who saveth him!" Now when the Ifrit heard this from the Fisherman and saw himself in limbo, he was minded to escape, but this was prevented by Solomon's seal; so he

---

[1] Arab. meaning "the Mother of Amir," a nickname for the hyena, which bites the hand that feeds it.

knew that the Fisherman had cozened and outwitted him, and he waxed lowly and submissive and began humbly to say, "I did but jest with thee." But the other answered, "Thou liest, O vilest of the Ifrits, and meanest and filthiest!" and he set off with the bottle for the sea side; the Ifrit calling out "Nay! Nay!" and he calling out "Aye! Aye!" Thereupon the Evil Spirit softened his voice and smoothed his speech and abased himself, saying, "What wouldest thou do with me, O Fisherman?" "I will throw thee back into the sea," he answered; "where thou hast been housed and homed for a thousand and eight hundred years; and now I will leave thee therein till Judgment-day; did I not say to thee:—Spare me and Allah shall spare thee; and slay me not lest Allah slay thee? yet thou spurnedst my supplication and hadst no intention save to deal ungraciously by me, and Allah hath now thrown thee into my hands and I am cunninger than thou." Quoth the Ifrit, "Open for me that I may bring thee weal." Quoth the Fisherman, "Thou liest, thou accursed! Nothing would satisfy thee save my death; so now I will do thee die by hurling thee into this sea." Then the Marid roared aloud and cried, "Allah upon thee, O Fisherman, don't! Spare me, and pardon my past doings; and, as I have been tyrannous, so be thou generous, for it is said among sayings that go current:—O thou who doest good to him who hath done thee evil, suffice for the ill-doer his ill-deeds, and do not deal with me as did Umamah to 'Atikah." Asked the Fisherman, "And what was their case?" and the Ifrit answered, "This is not the time for story-telling and I in this prison; but set me free and I will tell thee the tale." Quoth the Fisherman, "Leave this language: there is no help but that thou be thrown back into the sea nor is there any way for thy getting out of it for ever and ever. Vainly I placed myself under thy protection, and I humbled myself to thee with weeping, while thou soughtest only to slay me, who had done thee no injury deserving this at thy hands; nay, so far from injuring thee by any evil act, I worked thee nought but weal in releasing thee from that jail of thine. Now I knew thee to be an evil-doer when thou diddest to me what thou didst, and know, that when I have cast thee back into this sea, I will warn whomsoever may fish thee up of what hath befallen me with thee, and I will advise him to toss thee back again; so shalt thou abide here under these waters till the End of Time shall make an end of thee." But the Ifrit cried aloud, "Set me free; this is a noble occasion for generosity and I make covenant with thee and vow never to do thee hurt and harm; nay, I will help thee to what shall put thee out of want." The Fisherman accepted his promises on both conditions, not to trouble him as before, but on the contrary to do him service; and, after making firm the plight and swearing him a solemn oath by Allah Most Highest he opened the cucurbit. Thereupon the pillar of smoke rose up till all of it was fully out; then it thickened and once more became an Ifrit of hideous presence, who forthright administered a kick to the bottle and sent it flying into the sea. The Fisherman, seeing how the cucurbit was treated and making sure of his own death, piddled in his clothes and said to himself, "This promiseth badly;" but he fortified his heart, and cried, "O Ifrit, Allah hath said:—Perform your covenant; for the performance of your covenant shall be inquired into hereafter. Thou hast made a vow to me and hast sworn an oath not to play me false lest Allah play thee false, for verily he is a jealous God who respiteth the sinner, but letteth him not escape. I say to thee as said the Sage Duban to King Yunan, "Spare me so Allah may spare thee!" The Ifrit burst into laughter and stalked away, saying to the Fisherman, "Follow me;" and the man paced after him at a safe distance (for he was not assured of escape) till they had passed round the suburbs of the city. Thence they struck into the uncultivated grounds, and crossing them descended into a broad wilderness, and lo! in the midst of it stood a mountain-tarn. The Ifrit waded in to the middle and again cried, "Follow me;" and when this was done he took his stand in the centre and bade the man cast his net and catch his fish. The Fisherman looked into the water and was much astonished to see therein vari-coloured fishes, white and red, blue and yellow; however he cast his net and, hauling it in, saw that he had netted four fishes, one of each colour. Thereat he rejoiced greatly and more when the Ifrit said to him, "Carry these to the Sultan and set them in his presence; then he will give thee what shall make thee a wealthy man; and now accept my excuse, for by Allah at this time I wot none other way of benefiting thee, inasmuch I have lain in this sea eighteen hundred years and have not seen the face of the world save within this hour. But I would not have thee fish here save once a day." The Ifrit then gave him Godspeed, saying, "Allah grant we meet again;" and struck the earth with one foot, whereupon the ground clove asunder and swallowed him up. The Fisherman, much marvelling at what had happened to him with the Ifrit, took the fish and made for the city; and as soon as he reached home he filled an earthen bowl with water and therein threw the fish which began to struggle and wriggle about. Then he bore off the bowl upon his head and, repairing to the King's palace (even as the Ifrit had bidden him) laid the fish before the presence; and the King wondered with exceeding wonder at the sight, for never in his lifetime had he seen fishes like these in quality or in conformation. So he said, "Give those fish to the stranger slave-girl who now cooketh for us," meaning the bond-maiden whom the King of Roum had sent to him only three days before, so that he had not yet made trial of her talents in the dressing of meat. Thereupon the Wazir carried the fish to the cook and bade her fry them, saying, "O damsel, the King sendeth this say to thee:—I have not treasured thee, O tear o' me! save for stress-time of me; approve, then, to us this day thy delicate handiwork and thy savoury cooking; for this dish of fish is a present sent to the Sultan and evidently a rarity." The Wazir, after he had carefully charged her, returned to the King, who commanded him to give the Fisherman four hundred dinars: he gave them accordingly, and the man took them to his bosom and ran off home stumbling and falling and rising again and deeming the whole thing to be a dream. However, he bought for his family all they wanted and lastly he went to his wife in huge joy and gladness. So far concerning him; but as regards the cookmaid, she took the fish and cleansed them and set them in the frying-pan, basting them with oil till one side was dressed. Then she turned them over and, behold, the kitchen wall clave asunder, and therefrom came a young lady, fair of form, oval of face, perfect in grace, with eyelids which Kohl-lines enchase.[1] Her dress was a silken head-kerchief fringed and tasseled with blue: a large ring hung from either ear; a pair of bracelets adorned her wrists; rings with bezels of priceless gems were on her fingers; and she hent in hand a long rod of rattan-cane which she thrust into the frying-pan, saying, "O fish! O fish! be ye constant to your covenant?" When the cookmaiden saw this apparition she swooned away. The young lady repeated her words a second time and a third time, and at last the fishes raised their heads from the pan, and saying in articulate speech "Yes! Yes!" began with one voice to recite:—

> Come back and so will I! Keep faith and so will I!
> And if ye fain forsake, I'll requite till quits we cry!

After this the young lady upset the frying-pan and went forth by the way she came in and the kitchen wall closed upon her. When the cook-maiden recovered from her fainting-fit, she saw the four fishes charred black as charcoal, and crying out, "His staff brake in his first bout," she again fell swooning to the ground. Whilst she was in this case the Wazir came for the fish, and looking upon her as insensible she lay, not knowing Sunday from Thursday, shoved her with his foot and said, "Bring the fish for the Sultan!" Thereupon recovering from her fainting-fit she wept and informed him of her case and all that had befallen her. The Wazir marvelled greatly and exclaiming, "This is none other than a right strange matter!" he sent after the Fisherman and said to him,

---

[1] Arab. "Kahilat al-taraf" = lit. eyelids lined with Kohl; and figuratively "with black lashes and languorous look."

"Thou, O Fisherman, must needs fetch us four fishes like those thou broughtest before." Thereupon the man repaired to the tarn and cast his net; and when he landed it, lo! four fishes were therein exactly like the first. These he at once carried to the Wazir, who went in with them to the cookmaiden and said, "Up with thee and fry these in my presence, that I may see this business." The damsel arose and cleansed the fish, and set them in the frying-pan over the fire; however they remained there but a little while ere the wall clave asunder and the young lady appeared, clad as before and holding in hand the wand which she again thrust into the frying-pan, saying, "O fish! O fish! be ye constant to your olden covenant?" And behold, the fish lifted their heads, and repeated "Yes! Yes!" and recited this couplet:

> Come back and so will I! Keep faith and so will I!
> But if ye fain forsake, I'll requite till quits we cry!

When the fishes spoke, and the young lady upset the frying-pan with her rod, and went forth by the way she came and the wall closed up, the Wazir cried out, "This is a thing not to be hidden from the King." So he went and told him what had happened, whereupon quoth the King, "There is no help for it but that I see this with mine own eyes." Then he sent for the Fisherman and commanded him to bring four other fish like the first and to take with him three men as witnesses. The Fisherman at once brought the fish: and the King, after ordering them to give him four hundred gold pieces, turned to the Wazir and said, "Up and fry me the fishes here before me!" The Minister, replying "To hear is to obey," bade bring the frying-pan, threw therein the cleansed fish and set it over the fire; when lo! the wall clave asunder, and out burst a black slave like a huge rock or a remnant of the tribe Ad bearing in hand a branch of a green tree; and he cried in loud and terrible tones, "O fish! O fish! be ye all constant to your antique covenant?" whereupon the fishes lifted their heads from the frying-pan and said, "Yes! Yes! we be true to our vow;" and they again recited the couplet:

> Come back and so will I! Keep faith and so will I!
> But if ye fain forsake, I'll requite till quits we cry!

Then the huge blackamoor approached the frying-pan and upset it with the branch and went forth by the way he came in. When he vanished from their sight the King inspected the fish; and, finding them all charred black as charcoal, was utterly bewildered and said to the Wazir, "Verily this is a matter whereanent silence cannot be kept, and as for the fishes, assuredly some marvellous adventure connects with them." So he bade bring the Fisherman and asked him, saying "Fie on thee, fellow! whence come these fishes?" and he answered, "From a tarn between four heights lying behind this mountain which is in sight of thy city." Quoth the King, "How many days' march?" Quoth he, "O our lord the Sultan, a walk of half hour." The King wondered and, straightway ordering his men to march and horsemen to mount, led off the Fisherman who went before as guide, privily damning the Ifrit. They fared on till they had climbed the mountain and descended unto a great desert which they had never seen during all their lives; and the Sultan and his merry men marvelled much at the wold set in the midst of four mountains, and the tarn and its fishes of four colours, red and white, yellow and blue. The King stood fixed to the spot in wonderment and asked his troops and all present, "Hath any one among you ever seen this piece of water before now?" and all made answer, "O King of the age, never did we set eyes upon it during all our days." They also questioned the oldest inhabitants they met, men well stricken in years, but they replied, each and every, "A lakelet like this we never saw in this place." Thereupon quoth the King, "By Allah I will neither return to my capital nor sit upon the throne of my forebears till I learn the truth about this tarn and the fish therein." He then ordered his men to dismount and bivouac all around the mountain; which they did; and summoning his Wazir, a Minister of much experience, sagacious, of penetrating wit and well versed in affairs, said to him, "'Tis in my mind to do a certain thing, whereof I will inform thee; my heart telleth me to fare forth alone this night and root out the mystery of this tarn and its fishes. Do thou take thy seat at my tent-door, and say to the Emirs and Wazirs, the Nabobs and the Chamberlains, in fine to all who ask thee:—The Sultan is ill at ease, and he hath ordered me to refuse all admittance; and be careful thou let none know my design." And the Wazir could not oppose him. Then the King changed his dress and ornaments and, slinging his sword over his shoulder, took a path which led up one of the mountains and marched for the rest of the night till morning dawned; nor did he cease wayfaring till the heat was too much for him. After his long walk he rested for a while, and then resumed his march and fared on through the second night till dawn, when suddenly there appeared a black point in the far distance. Hereat he rejoiced and said to himself, "Haply some one here shall acquaint me with the mystery of the tarn and its fishes." Presently, drawing near the dark object he found it a palace built of swart stone plated with iron; and, while one leaf of the gate stood wide open, the other was shut. The King's spirits rose high as he stood before the gate and rapped a light rap; but hearing no answer he knocked a second knock and a third; yet there came no sign. Then he knocked his loudest but still no answer, so he said, "Doubtless 'tis empty." Thereupon he mustered up resolution, and boldly walked through the main gate into the great hall and there cried out aloud, "Holla, ye people of the palace! I am a stranger and a wayfarer; have you aught here of victual?" He repeated his cry a second time and a third but still there came no reply; so strengthening his heart and making up his mind he stalked through the vestibule into the very middle of the palace and found no man in it. Yet it was furnished with silken stuffs gold-starred; and the hangings were let down over the doorways. In the midst was a spacious court off which set four open saloons each with its raised daïs, saloon facing saloon; a canopy shaded the court and in the centre was a jetting fount with four figures of lions made of red gold, spouting from their mouths water clear as pearls and diaphanous gems. Round about the palace birds were let loose and over it stretched a net of golden wire, hindering them from flying off; in brief there was everything but human beings. The King marvelled mightily thereat, yet felt he sad at heart for that he saw no one to give him an account of the waste and its tarn, the fishes, the mountains and the palace itself. Presently as he sat between the doors in deep thought behold, there came a voice of lament, as from a heart grief-spent and he heard the voice chanting these verses:—

> I hid what I endured of him and yet it came to light,
> And nightly sleep mine eyelids fled and changed to sleepless night:
> Oh world! Oh Fate! withhold thy hand and cease thy hurt and harm
> Look and behold my hapless sprite in dolour and affright:
> Wilt ne'er show ruth to highborn youth who lost him on the way
> Of Love, and fell from wealth and fame to lowest basest wight.
> Jealous of Zephyr's breath was I as on your form he breathed
> But whenas Destiny descends she blindeth human sight,
> What shall the hapless archer do who when he fronts his foe
> And bends his bow to shoot the shaft shall find his string undight?
> When cark and care so heavy bear on youth of generous soul
> How shall he 'scape his lot and where from Fate his place of flight?

Now when the Sultan heard the mournful voice he sprang to his feet; and, following the sound, found a curtain let down over a chamber-door. He raised it and saw behind it a young man sitting upon a couch about a cubit above the ground; and he fair to the sight, a well shaped wight, with eloquence dight; his forehead was flower-white, his cheek rosy bright, and a mole on his cheek-breadth like an ambergris-mite; even as the poet doth indite:—

A youth slim-waisted from whose locks and brow
The world in blackness and in light is set.
Throughout Creation's round no fairer show
No rarer sight thine eye hath ever met:
A nut-brown mole sits throned upon a cheek
Of rosiest red beneath an eye of jet.

The King rejoiced and saluted him, but he remained sitting in his caftan of silken stuff purfled with Egyptian gold and his crown studded with gems of sorts; but his face was sad with the traces of sorrow. He returned the royal salute in most courteous wise adding, "O my lord, thy dignity demandeth my rising to thee; and my sole excuse is to crave thy pardon." Quoth the King, "Thou art excused, O youth; so look upon me as thy guest come hither on an especial object. I would thou acquaint me with the secrets of this tarn and its fishes and of this palace and thy loneliness therein and the cause of thy groaning and wailing." When the young man heard these words he wept with sore weeping till his bosom was drenched with tears. The King marvelled and asked him, "What maketh thee weep, O young man?" and he answered, "How should I not weep, when this is my case!" Thereupon he put out his hand and raised the skirt of his garment, when lo! the lower half of him appeared stone down to his feet while from his navel to the hair of his head he was a man. The King, seeing this his plight, grieved with sore grief and of his compassion cried, "Alack and well-away! in very sooth, O youth, thou heapest sorrow upon my sorrow. I was minded to ask thee the mystery of the fishes only: whereas now I am concerned to learn thy story as well as theirs. But there is no Majesty and there is no Might save in Allah, the Glorious, the Great! Lose no time, O youth, but tell me forthright thy whole tale." Quoth he, "Lend me thine ears, thy sight and thine insight;" and quoth the King, "All are at thy service!" Thereupon the youth began, "Right wondrous and marvellous is my case and that of these fishes; and were it graven with gravers upon the eye-corners it were a warner to whoso would be warned." "How is that?" asked the King, and the young man began to tell

The Tale of the Ensorcelled Prince

Know then, O my lord, that whilome my sire was King of this city, and his name was Mahmud, entitled Lord of the Black Islands, and owner of what are now these four mountains. He ruled threescore and ten years, after which he went to the mercy of the Lord and I reigned as Sultan in his stead. I took to wife my cousin, the daughter of my paternal uncle, and she loved me with such abounding love that whenever I was absent she ate not and she drank not until she saw me again.

She cohabited with me for five years till a certain day when she went forth to the Hammam-bath; and I bade the cook hasten to get ready all requisites for our supper. And I entered this palace and lay down on the bed where I was wont to sleep and bade two damsels to fan my face, one sitting by my head and the other at my feet. But I was troubled and made restless by my wife's absence and could not sleep; for although my eyes were closed my mind and thoughts were wide awake. Presently I heard the slave-girl at my head say to her at my feet, "O Mas'udah, how miserable is our master and how wasted in his youth and oh! the pity of his being so betrayed by our mistress, the accursed whore!" The other replied, "Yes indeed: Allah curse all faithless women and adulterous; but the like of our master, with his fair gifts, deserveth something better than this harlot who lieth abroad every night." Then quoth she who sat by my head, "Is our lord dumb or fit only for bubbling that he questioneth her not!" and quoth the other, "Fie on thee! doth our lord know her ways or doth she allow him his choice? Nay, more, doth she not drug every night the cup she giveth him to drink before sleep-time, and put Bhang into it? So he sleepeth and wotteth not whither she goeth, nor what she doeth; but we know that, after giving him the drugged wine, she donneth her richest raiment and perfumeth herself and then she fareth out from him to be away till break of day; then she cometh to him, and burneth a pastile under his nose and he awaketh from his death-like sleep." When I heard the slave-girls' words, the light became black before my sight and I thought night would never fall. Presently the daughter of my uncle came from the baths; and they set the table for us and we ate and sat together a fair half-hour quaffing our wine as was ever our wont. Then she called for the particular wine I used to drink before sleeping and reached me the cup; but, seeming to drink it according to my wont, I poured the contents into my bosom; and, lying down, let her hear that I was asleep. Then, behold, she cried, "Sleep out the night, and never awake again; by Allah, I loathe thee and I loathe thy whole body, and my soul turneth in disgust from cohabiting with thee; and I see not the moment when Allah shall snatch away thy life!" Then she rose and donned her fairest dress and perfumed her person and slung my sword over her shoulder; and, opening the gates of the palace, went her ill way. I rose and followed her as she left the palace and she threaded the streets until she came to the city gate, where she spoke words I understood not, and the padlocks dropped of themselves as if broken and the gate-leaves opened. She went forth (and I after her without her noticing aught) till she came at last to the out-lying mounds and a reed fence built about a round-roofed hut of mud-bricks. As she entered the door, I climbed upon the roof which commanded a view of the interior, And lo! my fair cousin had gone in to a hideous negro slave with his upper lip like the cover of a pot, and his lower like an open pot; lips which might sweep up sand from the gravel-floor of the cot. He was to boot a leper and a paralytic, lying upon a strew of sugar-cane trash and wrapped in an old blanket and the foulest rags and tatters. She kissed the earth before him, and he raised his head so as to see her and said, "Woe to thee! what call hadst thou to stay away all this time? Here have been with me sundry of the black brethren, who drank their wine and each had his young lady, and I was not content to drink because of thine absence." Then she, "O my lord, my heart's love and coolth of my eyes, knowest thou not that I am married to my cousin whose very look I loathe, and hate myself when in his company? And did not I fear for thy sake, I would not let a single sun arise before making his city a ruined heap wherein raven should croak and howlet hoot, and jackal and wolf harbour and loot; nay I had removed its very stones to the back side of Mount Kaf." Rejoined the slave, "Thou liest, damn thee! Now I swear an oath by the valour and honour of blackamoor men (and deem not our manliness to be the poor manliness of white men), from to-day forth if thou stay away till this hour, I will not keep company with thee nor will I glue my body with thy body. Dost play fast and loose with us, thou cracked pot, that we may satisfy thy dirty lusts, O vilest of the vile whites?" When I heard his words, and saw with my own eyes what passed between these two wretches, the world waxed dark before my face and my soul knew not in what place it was. But my wife humbly stood up weeping before and wheedling the slave, and saying, "O my beloved, and very fruit of my heart, there is none left to cheer me but thy dear self; and, if thou cast me off who shall take me in, O my beloved, O light of my eyes?" And she ceased not weeping and abasing herself to him until he deigned be reconciled with her. Then was she right glad and stood up and doffed her clothes, even to her petticoat-trousers, and said, "O my master what hast thou here for thy handmaiden to eat?" "Uncover the basin," he grumbled, "and thou shalt find at the bottom the broiled bones of some rats we dined on; pick at them, and then go to that slop-pot where thou shalt find some leavings of beer which thou mayest drink." So she ate and drank and washed her hands, and went and lay down by the side of the slave, upon the cane-trash, and crept in with him under his foul coverlet and his rags and tatters. When I saw my wife, my cousin, the daughter of my uncle, do this deed I clean lost my wits, and climbing down from the roof, I entered and took the sword which she had with her and drew it, determined to cut down the twain. I first struck at the slave's neck and thought that the death decree had fallen on him for he groaned a loud hissing groan, but I had cut only the skin and flesh of the gullet and the two arteries! It awoke the daughter of my uncle, so I sheathed the sword and fared forth for the city; and, entering the palace, lay upon my bed and slept till morning when my wife aroused me and I saw that she had cut off her hair and had donned mourning garments. Quoth she:—O son of my uncle, blame me not for what I do; it hath just reached me that my mother is dead, and my father hath been killed in holy war, and of my brothers one hath lost his life by a snake-sting and the other by falling down some precipice; and I can and should do naught save weep and lament. When I heard her words I refrained from all reproach and said only:—Do as thou list; I certainly will not thwart thee. She continued sorrowing, weeping and wailing one whole year from the beginning of its circle to the end, and when it was finished she said to me:—I wish to build me in thy palace a tomb with a cupola, which I will set apart for my mourning and will name the House of Lamentations. Quoth I again:—Do as thou list! Then she builded for herself a cenotaph wherein to mourn, and set on its centre a dome under which showed a tomb like a Santon's sepulchre. Thither she carried the slave and lodged him; but he was exceeding weak by reason of his wound, and unable to do her love-service; he could only drink wine and from the day of his hurt he spake not a word, yet he lived on because his appointed hour was not come. Every day, morning and evening, my wife went to him and wept and wailed over him and gave him wine and strong soups, and left not off doing after this manner a second year; and I bore with her patiently and paid no heed to her. One day, however, I went in to her unawares; and I found her weeping and beating her face and crying:—Why art thou absent from my sight, O my heart's delight? Speak to me, O my life; talk with me, O my love? When she had ended for a time her words and her weeping I said to her:—O my cousin, let this thy mourning suffice, for in pouring forth tears there is little profit! Thwart me not, answered she, in aught I do, or I will lay violent hands on myself! So I held my peace and left her to go her own way; and she ceased not to cry and keen and indulge her affliction for yet another year. At the end of the third year I waxed aweary of this longsome mourning, and one day I happened to enter the cenotaph when vexed and angry with some matter which had thwarted me, and suddenly I heard her say:—O my lord, I never hear thee vouchsafe a single word to me! Why dost thou not answer me, O my master? and she began reciting:—

> O thou tomb! O thou tomb! be his beauty set in shade?
> Hast thou darkened that countenance all-sheeny as the noon?
> O thou tomb! neither earth nor yet heaven art to me
> Then how cometh it in thee are conjoined my sun and moon?

When I heard such verses as these rage was heaped upon my rage; I cried out:—Well-away! how long is this sorrow to last? and I began repeating:

O thou tomb! O thou tomb! be his horrors set in blight?
Hast thou darkened his countenance that sickeneth the soul?
O thou tomb! neither cess-pool nor pipkin art to me
Then how cometh it in thee are conjoined soil and coal?

When she heard my words she sprang to her feet crying:—Fie upon thee, thou cur! all this is of thy doings; thou hast wounded my heart's darling and thereby worked me sore woe and thou hast wasted his youth so that these three years he hath lain abed more dead than alive! In my wrath I cried:—O thou foulest of harlots and filthiest of whores ever futtered by negro slaves who are hired to have at thee! Yes indeed it was I who did this good deed; and snatching up my sword I drew it and made at her to cut her down. But she laughed my words and mine intent to scorn crying: To heel, hound that thou art! Alas for the past which shall no more come to pass nor shall any one avail the dead to raise. Allah hath indeed now given into my hand him who did to me this thing, a deed that hath burned my heart with a fire which died not and a flame which might not be quenched! Then she stood up; and, pronouncing some words to me unintelligible, she said:—By virtue of my egromancy become thou half stone and half man; whereupon I became what thou seest, unable to rise or to sit, and neither dead nor alive. Moreover she ensorcelled the city with all its streets and garths, and she turned by her gramarye the four islands into four mountains around the tarn whereof thou questionest me; and the citizens, who were of four different faiths, Moslem, Nazarene, Jew and Magian, she transformed by her enchantments into fishes; the Moslems are the white, the Magians red, the Christians blue and the Jews yellow. And every day she tortureth me and scourgeth me with an hundred stripes, each of which draweth floods of blood and cutteth the skin of my shoulders to strips; and lastly she clotheth my upper half with a hair-cloth and then throweth over them these robes.—Hereupon the young man again shed tears and began reciting:—

In patience, O my God, I endure my lot and fate;
I will bear at will of Thee whatsoever be my state:
They oppress me; they torture me; they make my life a woe
Yet haply Heaven's happiness shall compensate my strait;
Yea, straitened is my life by the bane and hate o' foes
But Mustafa and Murtaza shall ope me Heaven's gate.

After this the Sultan turned towards the young Prince and said, "O youth, thou hast removed one grief only to add another grief; but now, O my friend, where is she; and where is the mausoleum wherein lieth the wounded slave?" "The slave lieth under yon dome," quoth the young man, "and she sitteth in the chamber fronting yonder door. And every day at sunrise she cometh forth, and first strippeth me, and whippeth me with an hundred strokes of the leathern scourge, and I weep and shriek; but there is no power of motion in my lower limbs to keep her off me. After ending her tormenting me she visiteth the slave, bringing him wine and boiled meats. And to-morrow at an early hour she will be here." Quoth the King, "By Allah, O youth, I will assuredly do thee a good deed which the world shall not willingly let die, and an act of derring-do which shall be chronicled long after I am dead and gone by." Then the King sat him by the side of the young Prince and talked till nightfall, when he lay down and slept; but, as soon as the false dawn showed, he arose and doffing his outer garments bared his blade and hastened to the place wherein lay the slave. Then was he ware of lighted candles and lamps, and the perfume of incenses and unguents; and, directed by these, he made for the slave and struck him one stroke killing him on the spot: after which he lifted him on his back and threw him into a well that was in the palace. Presently he returned and, donning the slave's gear, lay down at length within the mausoleum with the drawn sword laid close to and along his side. After an hour or so the accursed witch came; and, first going to her husband, she stripped off his clothes and, taking a whip, flogged him cruelly while he cried out, "Ah! enough for me the case I am in! take pity on me, O my cousin!" But she replied, "Didst thou take pity on me and spare the life of my true love on whom I doated?" Then she drew the cilice over his raw and bleeding skin and threw the robe upon all and went down to the slave with a goblet of wine and a bowl of meat-broth in her hands. She entered under the dome weeping and wailing, "Wellaway!" and crying, "O my lord! speak a word to me! O my master! talk awhile with me!" and began to recite these couplets:—

> How long this harshness, this unlove, shall bide?
> Suffice thee not tear-floods thou hast espied?
> Thou dost prolong our parting purposely
> And if wouldst please my foe, thou'rt satisfied!

Then she wept again and said, "O my lord! speak to me, talk with me!" The King lowered his voice and, twisting his tongue, spoke after the fashion of the blackamoors and said "'lack! 'lack! thee be no Ma'esty and there be no Might save in Allauh, the Gloriose, the Great!" Now when she heard these words she shouted for joy, and fell to the ground fainting; and when her senses returned she asked, "O my lord can it be true that thou hast power of speech?" and the King making his voice

small and faint answered, "O my cuss! dost thou deserve that I talk to
thee and speak with thee?" "Why and wherefore?" rejoined she; and he
replied "The why is that all the livelong day thou tormentest thy hubby;
and he keeps calling on 'eaven for aid until sleep is strange to me even
from evenin' till mawnin', and he prays and damns, cussing us two, me
and thee, causing me disquiet and much bother: were this not so, I
should long ago have got my health; and it is this which prevents my
answering thee." Quoth she, "With thy leave I will release him from
what spell is on him;" and quoth the King, "Release him and let's have
some rest!" She cried, "To hear is to obey;" and, going from the cenotaph to the palace, she took a metal bowl and filled it with water and
spake over it certain words which made the contents bubble and boil
as a cauldron seetheth over the fire. With this she sprinkled her husband saying, "By virtue of the dread words I have spoken, if thou
becamest thus by my spells, come forth out of that form into thine own
former form." And lo and behold! the young man shook and trembled;
then he rose to his feet and, rejoicing at his deliverance, cried aloud, "I
testify that there is no god but *the* God, and in very truth Mohammed
is His Apostle, whom Allah bless and keep!" Then she said to him, "Go
forth and return not hither, for if thou do I will surely slay thee;"
screaming these words in his face. So he went from between her hands;
and she returned to the dome and, going down to the sepulchre, she
said, "O my lord, come forth to me that I may look upon thee and thy
goodliness!" The King replied in faint low words, "What thing hast
thou done? Thou hast rid me of the branch but not of the root." She
asked, "O my darling! O my negroling! what is the root?" And he
answered, "Fie on thee, O my cuss! The people of this city and of the
four islands every night when it's half passed lift their heads from the
tank in which thou hast turned them to fishes and cry to Heaven and
call down its anger on me and thee; and this is the reason why my
body's baulked from health. Go at once and set them free; then come
to me and take my hand, and raise me up, for a little strength is already
back in me." When she heard the King's words (and she still supposed
him to be the slave) she cried joyously, "O my master, on my head and
on my eyes be thy command, Bismillah!" So she sprang to her feet and,
full of joy and gladness, ran down to the tarn and took a little of its
water in the palm of her hand and spake over it words not to be understood, and the fishes lifted their heads and stood up on the instant like
men, the spell on the people of the city having been removed. What
was the lake again became a crowded capital; the bazars were thronged
with folk who bought and sold; each citizen was occupied with his own
calling and the four hills became islands as they were whilome. Then
the young woman, that wicked sorceress, returned to the King and (still

thinking he was the negro) said to him, "O my love! stretch forth thy honoured hand that I may assist thee to rise." "Nearer to me," quoth the King in a faint and feigned tone. She came close as to embrace him when he took up the sword lying hid by his side and smote her across the breast, so that the point showed gleaming behind her back. Then he smote her a second time and cut her in twain and cast her to the ground in two halves. After which he fared forth and found the young man, now freed from the spell, awaiting him and gave him joy of his happy release while the Prince kissed his hand with abundant thanks. Quoth the King, 'Wilt thou abide in this city or go with me to my capital?" Quoth the youth, "O King of the age, wottest thou not what journey is between thee and thy city?" "Two days and a half," answered he; whereupon said the other, "An thou be sleeping, O King, awake! Between thee and thy city is a year's march for a well-girt walker, and thou haddest not come hither in two days and a half save that the city was under enchantment. And I, O King, will never part from thee; no, not even for the twinkling of an eye." The King rejoiced at his words and said, "Thanks be to Allah who hath bestowed thee upon me! From this hour thou art my son and my only son, for that in all my life I have never been blessed with issue." Thereupon they embraced and joyed with exceeding great joy; and, reaching the palace, the Prince who had been spell-bound informed his lords and his grandees that he was about to visit the Holy Places as a pilgrim, and bade them get ready all things necessary for the occasion. The preparations lasted ten days, after which he set out with the Sultan, whose heart burned in yearning for his city whence he had been absent a whole twelve-month. They journeyed with an escort of Mamelukes carrying all manners of precious gifts and rarities, nor stinted they wayfaring day and night for a full year until they approached the Sultan's capital, and sent on messengers to announce their coming. Then the Wazir and the whole army came out to meet him in joy and gladness, for they had given up all hope of ever seeing their King; and the troops kissed the ground before him and wished him joy of his safety. He entered and took seat upon his throne and the Minister came before him and, when acquainted with all that had befallen the young Prince, he congratulated him on his narrow escape. When order was restored throughout the land the King gave largesse to many of his people, and said to the Wazir, "Hither the Fisherman who brought us the fishes!" So he sent for the man who had been the first cause of the city and the citizens being delivered from enchantment and, when he came into the presence, the Sultan bestowed upon him a dress of honour, and questioned him of his condition and whether he had children. The Fisherman gave him to know that he had two daughters and a son, so the King sent for them and, taking one daughter to wife, gave the other to the young Prince and made the son his head-treasurer. Furthermore he invested his Wazir with the Sultanate of the City in the Black Islands whilome belonging to the young Prince, and dispatched with him the escort of fifty armed slaves together with dresses of honour for all the Emirs and Grandees. The Wazir kissed hands and fared forth on his way; while the Sultan and the Prince abode at home in all the solace and the delight of life; and the Fisherman became the richest man of his age, and his daughters wived with the Kings, until death came to them. And yet, O King! this is not more wondrous than the story of

JUDAR AND HIS BRETHREN

THERE WAS ONCE a man and a merchant named Omar and he had for issue three sons, the eldest called Sálim, the youngest Judar, and the cadet Salím. He reared them all till they came to man's estate, but the youngest he loved more than his brothers, who, seeing this, waxed jealous of Judar and hated him. Now when their father, who was a man shotten in years, saw that his two eldest sons hated their brother, he feared lest after his death trouble should befal him from them. So he assembled a company of his kinsfolk, together with divers men of learning and property-distributors of the Kazi's court, and bidding bring all his monies and cloth, said to them, "O folk, divide ye this money and stuff into four portions according to the law." They did so, and he gave one part to each of his sons and kept the fourth himself, saying, "This was my good and I have divided it among them in my lifetime; and this that I have kept shall be for my wife, their mother, wherewithal to provide for her subsistence whenas she shall be a widow." A little while after this he died, and neither of the two elder brothers was content with his share, but sought more of Judar, saying, "Our father's wealth is in thy hands." So he appealed to the judges; and the Moslems who had been present at the partition came and bore witness of that which they knew, wherefore the judge forbade them from one another; but Judar and his brothers wasted much money in bribes to him. After this, the twain left him awhile; presently, however, they began again to plot against him and he appealed a second time to the magistrate, who once more decided in his favour; but all three lost much money which went to the judges. Nevertheless Sálim and Salím forebore not to seek his hurt and to carry the case from court to court, he and they losing till they had given all their good for food to the oppressors and they became poor, all three. Then the two elder brothers went to their mother and flouted her and beat her, and seizing her money drave her away. So she betook herself to her son Judar and told him how his brothers had dealt with her and fell to cursing the twain. Said he, "O my mother, do not curse them, for Allah will requite each of them according to his deed. But, O mother mine, see, I am become poor, and so are my brethren, for strife occasioneth loss ruin-rife, and we have striven amain, and fought, I and they, before the judges, and it hath profited us naught: nay, we have wasted all our father left us and are disgraced among the folk by reason of our testimony one against other. Shall I then contend with them anew on thine account and shall we appeal to the judges? This may not be! Rather do thou take up thine abode with me, and the scone I eat I will share with thee. Do thou pray for me and Allah will give me the means of thine alimony. Leave them to receive of the Almighty the recompense of their deed, and console thyself with the saying of the poet who said: —

> If a fool oppress thee bear patiently;
> And from Time expect thy revenge to see:
> Shun tyranny; for if mount oppressed
> A mount, 'twould be shattered by tyranny."

And he soothed and comforted her till she consented and took up her dwelling with him. Then he gat him a net and went a-fishing every day in the river or the banks about Bulak and old Cairo or some other place in which there was water; and one day he would earn ten coppers, another twenty and another thirty, which he spent upon his mother and himself, and they ate well and drank well. But, as for his brothers, they plied no craft and neither sold nor bought; misery and ruin and overwhelming calamity entered their houses and they wasted that which they had taken from their mother and became of the wretched naked beggars. So at times they would come to their mother, humbling themselves before her exceedingly and complaining to her of hunger; and she (a mother's heart being pitiful) would give them some mouldy, sour-smelling bread or, if there were any meat cooked the day before, she would say to them, "Eat it quick and go ere your brother come; for 'twould be grievous to him and he would harden his heart against me, and ye would disgrace me with him." So they would eat in haste and go. One day among days they came in to their mother, and she set cooked meat and bread before them. As they were eating, behold, in came their brother Judar, at whose sight the parent was put to shame and confusion, fearing lest he should be wroth with her; and she bowed her face earthwards abashed before her son. But he smiled in their faces, saying, "Welcome, O my brothers! A blessed day! How comes it that ye visit me this blessed day?" Then he embraced them both and entreated them lovingly, saying to them, "I thought not that ye would have left me desolate by your absence nor that ye would have forborne to come and visit me and your mother." Said they, "By Allah, O our brother, we longed sore for thee and naught withheld us but abashment because of what befel between us and thee; but indeed we have repented much. 'Twas Satan's doing, the curse of Allah the Most High be upon him! And now we have no blessing but thyself and our mother." And his mother exclaimed, "Allah whiten thy face, and increase thy prosperity, for thou art the most generous of us all, O my son!" Then he said "Welcome to you both! Abide with me; for the Lord is bountiful and good aboundeth with me." So he made peace with them, and they supped and nighted with him; and next morning, after they had broken their fast, Judar shouldered his net and went out, trusting in The Opener whilst the two others also went forth and were absent till midday, when they returned and their mother set the noon-meal before them. At nightfall Judar came home, bearing meat and greens, and they abode on this wise a month's space, Judar catching fish and selling it and spending their price on his mother and his brothers, and these eating and frolicking till, one day, it chanced he went down to the riverbank and throwing his net, brought it up empty. He cast it a second time, but again it came up empty and he said to himself, "No fish in this place!" So he removed to another and threw the net there, but without avail. And he ceased not to remove from place to place till nightfall, but caught not a single sprat and said to himself, "Wonderful! Hath the fish fled the river or what?" Then he shouldered the net and made for home, chagrined, concerned, feeling for his mother and brothers and knowing not how he should feed them that night. Presently, he came to a baker's oven and saw the folk crowding for bread, with silver in their hands, whilst the baker took no note of them. So he stood there sighing, and the baker said to him, "Welcome to thee, O Judar! Dost thou want bread?" But he was silent and the baker continued, "An thou have no dirhams, take thy sufficiency and thou shalt get credit." So Judar said, "Give me ten coppers' worth of bread and take this net in pledge." Rejoined the baker, "Nay, my poor fellow, the net is thy gate of earning thy livelihood, and if I take it from thee, I shall close up against thee the door of thy subsistence. Take thee ten Nusfs' worth of bread and take these other ten, and to-morrow bring me fish for the twenty." "On my head and eyes be it!" quoth Judar and took the bread and money saying, "To-morrow the Lord will dispel the trouble of my case and will provide me the means of acquittance." Then he bought meat and vegetables and carried them home to his mother, who cooked them and they supped and went to bed. Next morning he arose at daybreak and took the net, and his mother said to

him, "Sit down and break thy fast." But he said, "Do thou and my
brothers breakfast," and went down to the river about Bulak where he
ceased not to cast once, twice, thrice; and to shift about all day, without aught falling to him, till the hour of mid-afternoon prayer, when he
shouldered his net and went away sore dejected. His way led him perforce by the booth of the baker who when he saw him, counted out to
him the loaves and the money, saying, "Come, take it and go; an it be
not today, 'twill be to-morrow." Judar would have excused himself, but
the baker said to him, "Go! There needeth no excuse; an thou had netted aught, it would be with thee; so seeing thee empty-handed, I knew
thou hadst gotten naught; and if to-morrow thou have no better luck,
come and take bread and be not abashed, for I will give thee credit." So
Judar took the bread and money and went home. On the third day also
he sallied forth and fished from tank to tank until the time of after-
noon-prayer, but caught nothing; so he went to the baker and took the
bread and silver as usual. On this wise he did seven days running, till
he became disheartened and said in himself, "To-day I go to the Lake
Karun." So he went thither and was about to cast his net, when there
came up to him unawares a Maghribi, a Moor, clad in splendid attire
and riding a she-mule with a pair of gold-embroidered saddle-bags on
her back and all her trappings also orfrayed. The Moor alighted and
said to him, "Peace be upon thee, O Judar, O son of Omar!" "And on
thee likewise be peace, O my lord the pilgrim!" replied the fisherman.
Quoth the Maghribi, "O Judar, I have need of thee and, given thou
obey me, thou shalt get great good and shalt be my companion and
manage my affairs for me." Quoth Judar, "O my lord, tell me what is in
thy mind and I will obey thee, without demur." Said the Moor, "Repeat
the Fatihah, the Opening Chapter of the Koran." So he recited it with
him and the Moor bringing out a silken cord, said to Judar, "Pinion my
elbows behind me with his cord, as fast as fast can be, and cast me into
the lake; then wait a little while; and, if thou see me put forth my hands
above the water, raising them high ere my body show, cast thy net over
me and drag me out in haste; but if thou see me come up feet foremost,
then know that I am dead; in which case do thou leave me and take the
mule and saddle-bags and carry them to the merchants' bazar, where
thou wilt find a Jew by name Shamayah. Give him the mule and he
will give thee an hundred dinars, which do thou take and go thy ways
and keep the matter secret with all secrecy." So Judar tied his arms
tightly behind his back and he kept saying, "Tie tighter." Then said he,
"Push me till I fall into the lake:" so he pushed him in and he sank.
Judar stood waiting some time till, behold, the Moor's feet appeared
above the water, whereupon he knew that he was dead. So he left him
and drove the mule to the bazar, where seated on a stool at the door of

his storehouse he saw the Jew who spying the mule, cried, "In very sooth the man hath perished," adding, "and naught undid him but covetise." Then he took the mule from Judar and gave him an hundred dinars, charging him to keep the matter secret. So Judar went and bought what bread he needed, saying to the baker, "Take this gold piece!"; and the man summed up what was due to him and said, "I still owe thee two days bread." Judar replied, "Good," and went on to the butcher, to whom he gave a gold piece and took meat, saying, "Keep the rest of the dinar on account." Then he bought vegetables and going home, found his brothers importuning their mother for victual, whilst she cried, "Have patience till your brother come home, for I have naught." So he went in to them and said, "Take and eat;" and they fell on the food like cannibals. Then he gave his mother the rest of his gold saying, "If my brothers come to thee, give them wherewithal to buy food and eat in my absence." He slept well that night and next morning he took his net and going down to Lake Karun stood there and was about to cast his net, when behold, there came up to him a second Maghribi, riding on a she-mule more handsomely accoutred than he of the day before and having with him a pair of saddle-bags of which each pocket contained a casket. "Peace be with thee, O Judar!" said the Moor: "And with thee be peace, O my lord the pilgrim!" replied Judar. Asked the Moor, "Did there come to thee yesterday a Moor riding on a mule like this of mine?" Hereat Judar was alarmed and answered, "I saw none," fearing lest the other say, "Whither went he?" and if he replied, "He was drowned in the lake," that haply he should charge him with having drowned him; wherefore he could not but deny. Rejoined the Moor, "Hark-ye, O unhappy! this was my brother, who is gone before me." Judar persisted, "I know naught of him." Then the Moor enquired, "Didst thou not bind his arms behind him and throw him into the lake, and did he not say to thee:—If my hands appear above the water first, cast thy net over me and drag me out in haste; but, if my feet show first, know that I am dead and carry the mule to the Jew Shamayah, who shall give thee an hundred dinars." Quoth Judar, "Since thou knowest all this why and wherefore dost thou question me?"; and quoth the Moor, "I would have thee do with me as thou didst with my brother." Then he gave him a silken cord, saying, "Bind my hands behind me and throw me in, and if I fare as did my brother, take the mule to the Jew and he will give thee other hundred dinars." Said Judar, "Come on;" so he came and he bound him and pushed him into the lake, where he sank. Then Judar sat watching and after a while, his feet appeared above the water and the fisher said, "He is dead and damned! Inshallah, may Maghribis come to me every day, and I will pinion them and push them in and they shall die; and I will

content me with an hundred dinars for each dead man." Then he took
the mule to the Jew, who seeing him asked, "The other is dead?"
Answered Judar, "May thy head live!"; and the Jew said, "This is the
reward of the covetous!" Then he took the mule and gave Judar an
hundred dinars, with which he returned to his mother. "O my son,"
said she, "whence hast thou this?" So he told her, and she said, "Go not
again to Lake Karun, indeed I fear for thee from the Moors." Said he,
"O my mother, I do but cast them in by their own wish, and what am
I to do? This craft bringeth me an hundred dinars a day and I return
speedily; wherefore, by Allah, I will not leave going to Lake Karun, till
the trace of the Magharibah is cut off and not one of them is left." So,
on the morrow which was the third day, he went down to the lake and
stood there, till there came up a third Moor, riding on a mule with saddle-bags and still more richly accoutred than the first two, who said to
him, "Peace be with thee, O Judar, O son of Omar!" And the fisherman
saying in himself, "How comes it that they all know me?" returned his
salute. Asked the Maghribi, "Have any Moors passed by here?" "Two,"
answered Judar. "Whither went they?" enquired the Moor, and Judar
replied, "I pinioned their hands behind them and cast them into the
lake, where they were drowned, and the same fate is in store for thee."
The Moor laughed and rejoined, saying, "O unhappy! every life hath
its term appointed." Then he alighted and gave the fisherman the
silken cord, saying, "Do with me, O Judar, as thou didst with them."
Said Judar, "Put thy hands behind thy back, that I may pinion thee, for
I am in haste, and time flies." So he put his hands behind him and
Judar tied him up and cast him in. Then he waited awhile; presently
the Moor thrust both hands forth of the water and called out to him,
saying, "Ho, good fellow, cast out thy net!" So Judar threw the net over
him and drew him ashore, and lo! in each hand he held a fish as red as
coral. Quoth the Moor, "Bring me the two caskets that are in the saddle-
bags." So Judar brought them and opened them to him, and he laid in
each casket a fish and shut them up. Then he pressed Judar to his
bosom and kissed him on the right cheek and the left, saying, "Allah
save thee from all stress! By the Almighty, hadst thou not cast the net
over me and pulled me out, I should have kept hold of these two fishes
till I sank and was drowned, for I could not get ashore of myself." Quoth
Judar, "O my lord the pilgrim, Allah upon thee, tell me the true history
of the two drowned men and the truth anent these two fishes and the
Jew." The Maghribi answered:—Know, O Judar, that these drowned
men were my two brothers, by name Abd al-Salam and Abd al-Ahad.
My own name is Abd al-Samad, and the Jew also is our brother; his
name is Abd al-Rahim and he is no Jew, but a true believer of the
Maliki school. Our father, whose name was Abd al-Wadud, taught us

magic and the art of solving mysteries and bringing hoards to light, and we applied ourselves thereto, till we compelled the Ifrits and Marids of the Jinn to do us service. By-and-by, our sire died and left us much wealth, and we divided amongst us his treasures and talismans, till we came to the books, when we fell out over a volume called "The Fables of the Ancients," whose like is not in the world, nor can its price be paid of any, nor is its value to be evened with gold and jewels; for in it are particulars of all the hidden hoards of the earth and the solution of every secret. Our father was wont to make use of this book, of which we had some small matter by heart, and each of us desired to possess it, that he might acquaint himself with what was therein. Now when we fell out there was in our company an old man by name Cohen Al-Abtan, who had reared our sire and taught him divination and gramarye, and he said to us, "Bring me the book." So we gave it to him and he continued:—Ye are my son's sons, and it may not be that I should wrong any of you. So whoso is minded to have the volume, let him address himself to achieve the treasure of Al-Shamardal and bring me the celestial planisphere and the Kohl-phial and the seal-ring and the sword. For the ring hath a Marid that serveth it called Al-Ra'ad al-Kasif; and whoso hath possession thereof, neither King nor Sultan may prevail against him; and if he will, he may therewith make himself master of the earth, in all the length and breadth thereof. As for the brand, if its bearer draw it and brandish it against an army, the army will be put to the rout; and if he say the while, "Slay yonder host," there will come forth of that sword lightning and fire, that will kill the whole many. As for the planisphere, its possessor hath only to turn its face toward any country, east or west, with whose sight he hath a mind to solace himself, and therein he will see that country and its people, as they were between his hands and he sitting in his place; and if he be wroth with a city and have a mind to burn it, he hath but to face the planisphere towards the sun's disc, saying, "Let such a city be burnt," and that city will be consumed with fire. As for the Kohl-phial, whoso pencilleth his eyes therefrom, he shall espy all the treasures of the earth. And I make this condition with you which is that whoso faileth to hit upon the hoards shall forfeit his right; and that none save he who shall achieve the treasure and bring me the four precious things which be therein shall have any claim to take this book. So we all agreed to this condition, and he continued, "O my sons, know that the treasure of Al-Shamardal is under the commandment of the sons of the Red King, and your father told me that he had himself essayed to open the treasure, but could not; for the sons of the Red King fled from him into the land of Egypt and took refuge in a lake there, called Lake Karun, whither he pursued them, but could not prevail over them, by reason of their stealing into that lake, which was guarded by a spell. So your father returned empty-handed and unable to win to his wish; and after failing he complained to me of his ill-success, whereupon I drew him an astrological figure and found that the treasure could be achieved only by means of a young fisherman of Cairo, hight Judar bin Omar, the place of foregathering with whom was at Lake Karun, for that he should be the means of capturing the sons of the Red King and that the charm would not be dissolved, save if he should bind the hands of the treasure-seeker behind him and cast him into the lake, there to do battle with the sons of the Red King. And he whose lot it was to succeed would lay hands upon them; but, if it were not destined to him he should perish and his feet appear above water. As for him who was successful, his hands would show first, whereupon it behoved that Judar should cast the net over him and draw him ashore." Now quoth my brothers Abd al-Salam and Abd al-Ahad, "We will wend and make trial, although we perish;" and quoth I, "And I also will go;" but my brother Abd al-Rahim (he whom thou sawest in the habit of a Jew) said, "I have no mind to this." Thereupon we agreed with him that he should repair to Cairo in the disguise of a Jewish merchant, so that if one of us perished in the lake, he might take his mule and saddle-bags and give the bearer an hundred dinars. The first that came to thee the sons of the Red King slew, and so did they with my second brother; but against me they could not prevail and I laid hands on them. Cried Judar, "And where is thy catch?" Asked the Moor, "Didst thou not see me shut them in the caskets?" "Those were fishes," said Judar. "Nay," answered the Maghribi, "they are Ifrits in the guise of fish. But, O Judar," continued he, "thou must know that the treasure can be opened only by thy means: so say, wilt thou do my bidding and go with me to the city Fez and Mequinez where we will open the treasure?; and after I will give thee what thou wilt and thou shalt ever be my brother in the bond of Allah and return to thy family with a joyful heart." Said Judar, "O my lord the pilgrim, I have on my neck a mother and two brothers, whose provider I am; and if I go with thee, who shall give them bread to eat?" Replied the Moor, "This is an idle excuse! if it be but a matter of expenditure, I will give thee a thousand ducats for thy mother, wherewith she may provide herself till thou come back; and indeed thou shalt return before the end of four months." So when Judar heard mention of the thousand dinars, he said, "Here with them, O Pilgrim, and I am thy man," and the Moor, pulling out the money, gave it to him, whereupon he carried it to his mother and told her what had passed between them, saying, "Take these thousand dinars and expend of them upon thyself and my brothers, whilst I journey to Marocco with the Moor, for I shall be absent four months, and great good will betide me; so bless me, O

my mother!" Answered she, "O my son, thou desolatest me and I fear
for thee." "O my mother," rejoined he, "no harm can befal him who is
in Allah's keeping, and the Maghribi is a man of worth;" and he went
on to praise his condition to her. Quoth she, "Allah incline his heart to
thee! Go with him, O my son; peradventure, he will give thee somewhat." So he took leave of his mother and rejoined the Moor Abd al-
Samad, who asked him, "Hast thou consulted thy mother?" "Yes,"
answered Judar; "and she blessed me." "Then mount behind me," said
the Maghribi. So Judar mounted the mule's crupper and they rode on
from noon till the time of mid-afternoon prayer, when the fisherman
was anhungered; but seeing no victual with the Moor, said to him, "O
my lord the pilgrim, belike thou hast forgotten to bring us aught to eat
by the way?" Asked the Moor, "Art thou hungry?" and Judar answered,
"Yes." So Abd al-Samad alighted and made Judar alight and take down
the saddle-bags; then he said to him, "What wilt thou have, O my
brother?" "Anything." "Allah upon thee, tell me what thou hast a mind
to." "Bread and cheese." "O my poor fellow! bread and cheese besit
thee not; wish for something good." "Just now everything is good to
me." "Dost thou like nice browned chicken?" "Yes!" "Dost thou like
rice and honey?" "Yes!" And the Moor went on to ask him if he liked
this dish and that dish till he had named four-and-twenty kinds of
meats; and Judar thought to himself, "He must be daft! Where are all
these dainties to come from, seeing he hath neither cook nor kitchen?
But I'll say to him, 'Tis enough!" So he cried, "That will do: thou makest me long for all these meats, and I see nothing." Quoth the Moor,
"Thou art welcome, O Judar!" and, putting his hand into the saddle-
bags, pulled out a golden dish containing two hot browned chickens.
Then he thrust his hand a second time and drew out a golden dish, full
of kabobs; nor did he stint taking out dishes from saddle-bags, till he
had brought forth the whole of the four-and-twenty kinds he had
named, whilst Judar looked on. Then said the Moor, "Fall to, poor
fellow!", and Judar said to him, "O my lord, thou carriest in yonder
saddle-bags kitchen and kitcheners!" The Moor laughed and replied,
"These are magical saddle-bags and have a servant, who would bring us
a thousand dishes an hour, if we called for them," Quoth Judar, "By
Allah, a meet thing in saddle-bags!" Then they ate their fill and threw
away what was left; after which the Moor replaced the empty dishes in
the saddle-bags and putting in his hand, drew out an ewer. They drank
and making the Wuzu-ablution, prayed the mid-afternoon prayer; after
which Abd al-Samad replaced the ewer and the two caskets in the saddle-
bags and throwing them over the mule's back, mounted and cried, "Up
with thee and let us be off," presently adding, "O Judar, knowest thou
how far we have come since we left Cairo?" "Not I, by Allah," replied

he, and Abd al-Samad, "We have come a whole month's journey."
Asked Judar, "And how is that?"; and the Moor answered, "Know, O
Judar, that this mule under us is a Marid of the Jinn who every day per-
formeth a year's journey; but, for thy sake, she hath gone an easier
pace." Then they set out again and fared on westwards till nightfall,
when they halted and the Maghribi brought out supper from the
saddle-bags, and in like manner, in the morning, he took forth wherewithal to break their fast. So they rode on four days, journeying till
midnight and then alighting and sleeping until morning, when they
fared on again; and all that Judar had a mind to, he sought of the Moor,
who brought it out of the saddle-bags. On the fifth day, they arrived at
Fez and Mequinez and entered the city, where all who met the
Maghribi saluted him and kissed his hands; and he continued riding
through the streets, till he came to a certain door, at which he knocked,
whereupon it opened and out came a girl like the moon, to whom said
he, "O my daughter, O Rahmah, open us the upper chamber." "On my
head and eyes, O my papa!" replied she and went in, swaying her hips
to and fro with a graceful and swimming gait like a thirsting gazelle,
movements that ravished Judar's reason, and he said, "This is none
other than a King's daughter." So she opened the upper chamber, and
the Moor, taking the saddle-bags from the mule's back, said, "Go, and
God bless thee!" when lo! the earth clove asunder and swallowing the
mule, closed up again as before. And Judar said, "O Protector! praised
be Allah, who hath kept us in safety on her back!" Quoth the Maghribi,
"Marvel not, O Judar. I told thee that the mule was an Ifrit; but come
with us into the upper chamber." So they went up into it, and Judar was
amazed at the profusion of rich furniture and pendants of gold and silver and jewels and other rare and precious things which he saw there.
As soon as they were seated, the Moor bade Rahmah bring him a certain bundle and opening it, drew out a dress worth a thousand dinars,
which he gave to Judar, saying, "Don this dress, O Judar, and welcome
to thee!" So Judar put it on and became a fair ensample of the Kings of
the West. Then the Maghribi laid the saddle-bags before him, and,
putting in his hand, pulled out dish after dish, till they had before them
a tray of forty kinds of meat, when he said to Judar, "Come near, O my
master! eat and excuse us for that we know not what meats thou
desirest; but tell us what thou hast a mind to, and we will set it before
thee without delay." Replied Judar, "By Allah, O my lord the pilgrim, I
love all kinds of meat and unlove none; so ask me not of aught, but
bring all that cometh to thy thought, for save eating to do I have
nought." After this he tarried twenty days with the Moor, who clad him
in new clothes every day, and all this time they ate from the saddle-
bags; for the Maghribi bought neither meat nor bread nor aught else,

nor cooked, but brought everything out of the bags, even to various sorts of fruit. On the twenty-first day, he said, "O Judar, up with thee; this is the day appointed for opening the hoard of Al-Shamardal." So he rose and they went afoot without the city, where they found two slaves, each holding a she-mule. The Moor mounted one beast and Judar the other, and they ceased not riding till noon, when they came to a stream of running water, on whose banks Abd al-Samad alighted saying, "Dismount, O Judar!" Then he signed with his hand to the slaves and said, "To it!" So they took the mules and going each his own way, were absent awhile, after which they returned, one bearing a tent, which he pitched, and the other carpets, which he spread in the tent and laid mattresses, pillows and cushions therearound. Then one of them brought the caskets containing the two fishes; and another fetched the saddle-bags; whereupon the Maghribi arose and said, "Come, O Judar!" So Judar followed him into the tent and sat down beside him; and he brought out dishes of meat from the saddle-bags and they ate the undurn meal. Then the Moor took the two caskets and conjured over them both, whereupon there came from within voices that said, "Adsumus, at thy service, O diviner of the world! Have mercy upon us!" and called aloud for aid. But he ceased not to repeat conjurations and they to call for help, till the two caskets flew in sunder, the fragments flying about, and there came forth two men, with pinioned hands saying, "Quarter, O diviner of the world! What will thou with us?" Quoth he, "My will is to burn you both with fire, except ye make a covenant with me, to open to me the treasure of Al-Shamardal." Quoth they, "We promise this to thee, and we will open the treasure to thee, so thou produce to us Judar bin Omar, the fisherman, for the hoard may not be opened but by his means, nor can any enter therein save Judar." Cried the Maghribi, "Him of whom ye speak, I have brought, and he is here, listening to you and looking at you." Thereupon they covenanted with him to open the treasure to him, and he released them. Then he brought out a hollow wand and tablets of red carnelian which he laid on the rod; and after this he took a chafing-dish and setting charcoal thereon, blew one breath into it and it kindled forthwith. Presently he brought incense and said, "O Judar, I am now about to begin the necessary conjurations and fumigations, and when I have once begun, I may not speak, or the charm will be naught; so I will teach thee first what thou must do to win thy wish." "Teach me," quoth Judar. "Know," quoth the Moor, "that when I have recited the spell and thrown on the incense, the water will dry up from the river's bed and discover to thee, a golden door, the bigness of the city-gate, with two rings of metal thereon; whereupon do thou go down to the door and knock a light knock and wait awhile; then knock a second time a knock louder than the first and wait another while; after which give three knocks in rapid succession, and thou wilt hear a voice ask:—Who knocketh at the door of the treasure, unknowing how to solve the secrets? Do thou answer:— I am Judar the fisherman son of Omar; and the door will open and there will come forth a figure with a brand in hand who will say to thee: If thou be that man, stretch forth thy neck, that I may strike off thy head. Then do thou stretch forth thy neck and fear not; for, when he lifts his hand and smites thee with the sword, he will fall down before thee, and in a little thou wilt see him a body sans soul; and the stroke shall not hurt thee nor shall any harm befal thee; but, if thou gainsay him, he will slay thee. When thou hast undone his enchantment by obedience, enter and go on till thou see another door, at which do thou knock, and there will come forth to thee a horseman riding a mare with a lance on his shoulder and say to thee:—What bringeth thee hither, where none may enter ne man ne Jinni? And he will shake his lance at thee. Bare thy breast to him and he will smite thee and fall down forth-right and thou shalt see him a body without a soul; but if thou cross him he will kill thee. Then go on to the third door, whence there will come forth to thee a man with a bow and arrows in his hand and take aim at thee. Bare thy breast to him and he will shoot at thee and fall down before thee, a body without a soul; but if thou oppose him, he will kill thee. Then go on to the fourth door and knock and it shall be opened to thee, when there will come forth to thee a lion huge of bulk which will rush upon thee, opening his mouth and showing he hath a mind to devour thee. Have no fear of him, neither flee from him: but when he cometh to thee, give him thy hand and he will bite at it and fall straightway, nor shall aught of hurt betide thee. Then enter the fifth door, where thou shalt find a black slave, who will say to thee, Who art thou? Say, I am Judar! and he will answer, If thou be that man, open the sixth door. Then do thou go up to the door and say, O Isa, tell Musa to open the door; whereupon the door will fly open and thou wilt see two dragons, one on the left hand and another on the right, which will open their mouths and fly at thee, both at once. Do thou put forth to them both hands and they will bite each a hand and fall down dead; but an thou resist them, they will slay thee. Then go on to the seventh door and knock, whereupon there will come forth to thee thy mother and say:—Welcome, O my son! Come, that I may greet thee! But do thou reply, Hold off from me and doff thy dress. And she will make answer:—O my son, I am thy mother and I have claim upon thee for suckling thee and for rearing thee: how then wouldst thou strip me naked? Then do thou say, Except thou put off thy clothes, I will kill thee! and look to thy right where thou wilt see a sword hanging up. Take it and draw it upon her, saying, Strip! whereupon she will wheedle thee and humble herself to thee; but have thou no ruth on her nor be beguiled, and as often as she putteth off aught, say to her, Off with the lave; nor do thou cease to threaten her with death, till she doff all that is upon her and fall down, whereupon the enchantment will be dissolved and the charms undone, and thou wilt be safe as to thy life. Then enter the hall of the treasure, where thou wilt see the gold lying in heaps; but pay no heed to aught thereof, but look to a closet at the upper end of the hall, where thou wilt see a curtain drawn. Draw back the curtain and thou wilt descry the enchanter, Al-Shamardal, lying upon a couch of gold, with something at his head round and shining like the moon, which is the celestial planisphere. He is baldrick'd with the sword; on his finger is the ring and about his neck hangs a chain, to which hangs the Kohl-phial. Bring me the four talismans, and beware lest thou forget aught of that which I have told thee, or thou wilt repent and there will be fear for thee." And he repeated his directions a second and a third and a fourth time, till Judar said, "I have them by heart: but who may face all these enchantments that thou namest and endure against these mighty terrors?" Replied the Moor, "O Judar, fear not, for they are semblances without life;" and he went on to hearten him, till he said, "I put my trust in Allah." Then Abd al-Samad threw perfumes on the chafing-dish, and addressed himself to reciting conjurations for a time when, behold, the water disappeared and uncovered the river-bed and discovered the door of the treasure, whereupon Judar went down to the door and knocked. Therewith he heard a voice saying, "Who knocketh at the door of the treasure, unknowing how to solve the secrets?" Quoth he, "I am Judar son of Omar;" whereupon the door opened and there came forth a figure with a drawn sword, who said to him, "Stretch forth thy neck." So he stretched forth his neck and the species smote him and fell down, lifeless. Then he went on to the second door and did the like, nor did he cease to do thus, till he had undone the enchantments of the first six doors and came to the seventh door, whence there issued forth to him his mother, saying, "I salute thee, O my son!" He asked, "What art thou?", and she answered, "O my son, I am thy mother who bare thee nine months and suckled thee and reared thee." Quoth he, "Put off thy clothes." Quoth she, "Thou art my son, how wouldst thou strip me naked?" But he said "Strip, or I will strike off thy head with this sword;" and he stretched out his hand to the brand and drew it upon her saying, "Except thou strip, I will slay thee." Then the strife became long between them and as often as he redoubled on her his threats, she put off somewhat of her clothes and he said to her, "Doff the rest," with many menaces; while she removed each article slowly and kept saying, "O my son, thou hast disappointed my fosterage of thee," till she had nothing left but her petticoat-trousers. Then said she, "O my son, is thy heart stone? Wilt thou dishonour me by discovering my shame? Indeed, this is unlawful, O my son!" And he answered, "Thou sayest sooth; put not off thy trousers." At once, as he uttered these words, she cried out, "He hath made default; beat him!" Whereupon there fell upon him blows like rain-drops and the servants of the treasure flocked to him and dealt him a tunding which he forgot not in all his days; after which they thrust him forth and threw him down without the treasure and the hoard-doors closed of themselves, whilst the waters of the river returned to their bed. Abd al-Samad the Maghribi took Judar up in haste and repeated conjurations over him, till he came to his senses but still dazed as with drink, when he asked him, "What hast thou done, O wretch?" Answered Judar, "O my brother, I undid all the opposing enchantments, till I came to my mother and there befel between her and myself a long contention. But I made her doff her clothes, O my brother, till but her trousers remained upon her and she said to me, Do not dishonour me; for to discover one's shame is forbidden. So I left her her trousers out of pity, and behold, she cried out and said, He hath made default; beat him! Whereupon there came out upon me folk, whence I know not, and tunding me with a belabouring which was a Sister of Death, thrust me forth; nor do I know what befel me after this." Quoth the Moor, "Did I not warn thee not to swerve from my directions? Verily, thou hast injured me and hast injured thyself: for if thou hadst made her take off her petticoat-trousers, we had won to our wish; but now thou must abide with me till this day next year." Then he cried out to the two slaves, who struck the tent forthright and loaded it on the beasts; then they were absent awhile and presently returned with the two mules; and the twain mounted and rode back to the city of Fez, where Judar tarried with the Maghribi, eating well and drinking well and donning a grand dress every day, till the year was ended and the anniversary day dawned. Then the Moor said to him, "Come with me, for this is the appointed day." And Judar said, "'Tis well." So the Maghribi carried him without the city, where they found the two slaves with the mules, and rode on till they reached the river. Here the slaves pitched the tent and furnished it; and the Moor brought forth the tray of food and they ate the morning meal; after which Abd al-Samad brought out the wand and the tablets as before and, kindling the fire in the chafing-dish, made ready the incense. Then said he, "O Judar, I wish to renew my charge to thee." "O my lord the pilgrim," replied he, "if I have forgotten the bastinado, I have forgotten the injunctions." Asked the Moor, "Dost thou indeed remember them?" and he answered, "Yes." Quoth the Moor, "Keep thy wits, and think not that the woman is thy very mother; nay, she is but an enchantment in her semblance, whose purpose is to find thee defaulting. Thou camest off alive the first time; but, an thou trip this time, they will slay thee." Quoth Judar, "If I slip this time, I deserve to be burnt of them." Then Abd al-Samad cast the perfumes into the fire and recited the conjurations, till the river dried up; whereupon Judar descended and knocked. The door opened and he entered and undid the several enchantments, till he came to the seventh door and the semblance of his mother appeared before him, saying, "Welcome, O my son!" But he said to her, "How am I thy son, O accursed? Strip!" And she began to wheedle him and put off garment after garment, till only her trousers remained; and he said to her, "Strip, O accursed!" So she put off her trousers and became a body without a soul. Then he entered the hall of the treasures, where he saw gold lying in heaps, but paid no heed to it and passed on to the closet at the upper end, where he saw the enchanter Al-Shamardal lying on a couch of gold, baldrick'd with the sword, with the ring on his finger, the Kohl-phial on his breast and the celestial planisphere hanging over his head. So he loosed the sword and taking the ring, the Kohl-phial and the planisphere, went forth, when behold, a band of music sounded for him and the servants of the treasure cried out, saying, "Mayest thou be assained with that thou hast gained, O Judar!" Nor did the music leave sounding, till he came forth of the treasure to the Maghribi, who gave up his conjurations and fumigations and rose up and embraced him and saluted him. Then Judar made over to him the four hoarded talismans, and he took them and cried out to the slaves, who carried away the tent and brought the mules. So they mounted and returned to Fez-city, where the Moor fetched the saddle-bags and brought forth dish after dish of meat, till the tray was full, and said, "O my brother, O Judar, eat!" So he ate till he was satisfied, when the Moor emptied what remained of the meats and other dishes and returned the empty platters to the saddle-bags. Then quoth he, "O Judar, thou hast left home and native land on our account and thou hast accomplished our dearest desire; wherefore thou hast a right to require a reward of us. Ask, therefore, what thou wilt, it is Almighty Allah who giveth unto thee by our means. Ask thy will and be not ashamed, for thou art deserving." "O my lord," quoth Judar, "I ask first of Allah the Most High and then of thee, that thou give me yonder saddle-bags." So the Maghribi called for them and gave them to him, saying, "Take them, for they are thy due; and, if thou hadst asked of me aught else instead, I had given it to thee. Eat from them, thou and thy family; but, my poor fellow, these will not profit thee, save by way of provaunt, and thou hast wearied thyself with us and we promised to send thee home rejoicing. So we join to these other saddle-bags, full of gold and gems, and forward thee back to thy native land, where thou shalt become a gentleman and a merchant and clothe thyself and thy family; nor shalt thou want ready money for thine expenditure. And know that the manner of using our gift is on this wise. Put thy hand therein and say: — O servant of these saddle-bags, I conjure thee by the virtue of the Mighty Names which have power over thee, bring me such a dish! And he will bring thee whatsoever thou askest, though thou shouldst call for a thousand different dishes a day." So saying, he filled him a second pair of saddle-bags half with gold and half with gems and precious stones; and, sending for a slave and a mule, said to him, "Mount this mule, and the slave shall go before thee and show thee the way, till thou come to the door of thy house, where do thou take the two pairs of saddle-bags and give him the mule, that he may bring it back. But admit none into thy secret; and so we commend thee to Allah!" "May the Almighty increase thy good!" replied Judar and, laying the two pairs of saddle-bags on the mule's back, mounted and set forth. The slave went on before him and the mule followed him all that day and night, and on the morrow he entered Cairo by the Gate of Victory, where he saw his mother seated, saying, "Alms, for the love of Allah!" At this sight he well-nigh lost his wits and alighting, threw himself upon her: and when she saw him she wept. Then he mounted her on the mule and walked by her stirrup, till they came to the house, where he set her down and, taking the saddle-bags, left the she-mule to the slave, who led her away and returned with her to his master, for that both slave and mule were devils. As for Judar, it was grievous to him that his mother should beg; so, when they were in the house, he asked her, "O my mother, are my brothers well?"; and she answered, "Thy are both well." Quoth he, "Why dost thou beg by the wayside?" Quoth she, "Because I am hungry, O my son," and he, "Before I went away, I gave thee an hundred dinars one day, the like the next and a thousand on the day of my departure." "O my son, they cheated me and took the money from me, saying: — We will buy goods with it. Then they drove me away, and I fell to begging by the wayside, for stress of hunger." "O my mother, no harm shall befal thee, now I am come; so have no concern, for these saddle-bags are full of gold and gems, and good aboundeth with me." "Verily, thou art blessed, O my son! Allah accept of thee and increase thee of His bounties! Go, O my son, fetch us some victual, for I slept not last night for excess of hunger, having gone to bed supperless." "Welcome to thee, O my mother! Call for what thou wilt to eat, and I will set it before thee this moment; for I have no occasion to buy from the market, nor need I any to cook." "O my son, I see naught with thee." "I have with me in these saddle-bags all manner of meats." "O my son, whatever is ready will serve to stay hunger." "True, when there is no choice, men are content with the smallest thing; but where there is plenty, they like to eat what is good: and I have abundance; so call for what thou hast a mind to." "O my son, give me some hot bread and a slice of cheese." "O my mother, this befitteth not thy condition." "Then give me to eat of that which besitteth my case, for thou knowest it." "O my mother," rejoined he, "what suit thine estate are browned meat and roast chicken and peppered rice and it becometh thy rank to eat of sausages and stuffed cucumbers and stuffed lamb and stuffed ribs of mutton and vermicelli with broken almonds and nuts and honey and sugar and fritters and almond cakes." But she thought he was laughing at her and making mock of her; so she said to him, "Yauh Yauh! what is come to thee? Dost thou dream or art thou daft?" Asked he, "Why deemest thou that I am mad?" and she answered, "Because thou namest to me all manner rich dishes. Who can avail unto their price, and who knoweth how to dress them?" Quoth he, "By my life! thou shalt eat of all that I have named to thee, and that at once;" and quoth she, "I see nothing;" and he, "Bring me the saddle-bags." So she fetched them and feeling them, found them empty. However, she laid them before him and he thrust in his hand and pulled out dish after dish, till he had set before her all he had named. Whereupon asked she, "O my son, the saddle-bags are small and moreover they were empty; yet hast thou taken thereout all these dishes. Where then were they all?"; and he answered, "O my mother, know that these saddle-bags, which the Moors gave me, are enchanted and they have a servant whom, if one desire aught, he hath but to adjure by the Names which command him, saying, O servant of these saddle-bags, bring me such a dish! and he will bring it." Quoth his mother, "And may I put out my hand and ask of him?" Quoth he, "Do so." So she stretched out her hand and said, "O servant of the saddle-bags, by the virtue of the Names which command thee, bring me stuffed ribs." Then she thrust in her hand and found a dish containing delicate stuffed ribs of lamb. So she took it out, and called for bread and what else she had a mind to: after which Judar said to her, "O my mother, when thou hast made an end of eating, empty what is left of the food into dishes other than these, and restore the empty platters to the saddle-bags carefully." So she arose and laid them up in a safe place. "And look, O mother mine, that thou keep this secret," added he; "and whenever thou hast a mind to aught, take it forth of the saddle-bags and give alms and feed my brothers, whether I be present or absent." Then he fell to eating with her and behold, while they were thus occupied, in came his two brothers, whom a son of the quarter had apprised of his return, saying, "Your brother is come back, riding on a she-mule, with a slave before him, and wearing a dress that hath not its like." So they said to each other, "Would to Heaven we had not

evilly entreated our mother! There is no hope but that she will surely
tell him how we did by her, and then, oh our disgrace with him!" But
one of the twain said, "Our mother is soft-hearted, and if she tell him,
our brother is yet tenderer over us than she; and, given we excuse ourselves to him, he will accept our excuse." So they went in to him and
he rose to them and saluting them with the friendliest salutation, bade
them sit down and eat. So they ate till they were satisfied, for they were
weak with hunger; after which Judar said to them, "O my brothers, take
what is left and distribute it to the poor and needy." "O brother," replied
they, "let us keep it to sup withal." But he answered, "When suppertime cometh, ye shall have more than this." So they took the rest of the
victual and going out, gave it to every poor man who passed by them,
saying, "Take and eat," till nothing was left. Then they brought back
the dishes and Judar said to his mother, "Put them in the saddle-bags."
And when it was eventide, he entered the saloon and took forth of the
saddle-bags a table of forty dishes; after which he went up to the upper
room and, sitting down between his brothers, said to his mother, "Bring
the supper." So she went down to the saloon and, finding there the
dishes ready, laid the tray and brought up the forty dishes, one after
nother. Then they ate the evening meal, and when they had done,
Judar said to his brothers, "Take and feed the poor and needy." So they
took what was left and gave alms thereof, and presently he brought
forth to them sweetmeats, whereof they ate, and what was left he bade
them give to the neighbours. On the morrow, they brake their fast after
the same fashion, and thus they fared ten days, at the end of which time
quoth Sálim to Salím, "How cometh it that our brother setteth before
us a banquet in the morning, a banquet at noon, and a banquet at sundown, besides sweetmeats late at night, and all that is left he giveth to
the poor? Verily, this is the fashion of Sultans. Yet we never see him buy
aught, and he hath neither kitchener nor kitchen, nor doth he light a
fire. Whence hath he this great plenty? Hast thou not a mind to discover the cause of all this?" Quoth Salím, "By Allah, I know not: but
knowest thou any who will tell us the truth of the case?" Quoth Sálim,
"None will tell us save our mother." So they laid a plot and repairing to
their mother one day, in their brother's absence, said to her, "O our
mother, we are hungry." Replied she, "Rejoice, for ye shall presently be
satisfied;" and going into the saloon, sought of the servant of the saddle-
bags hot meats, which she took out and set before her sons. "O our
mother," cried they, "this meat is hot; yet hast thou not cooked, neither
kindled a fire." Quoth she, "It cometh from the saddle-bags;" and quoth
they, "What manner of thing be these saddle-bags?" She answered,
"They are enchanted; and the required is produced by the charm:" she
then told her sons their virtue, enjoining them to secrecy. Said they,

"The secret shall be kept, O our mother, but teach us the manner of this." So she taught them the fashion thereof and they fell to putting their hands into the saddle-bags and taking forth whatever they had a mind to. But Judar knew naught of this. Then quoth Sálim privily to Salím, "O my brother, how long shall we abide with Judar servant-wise and eat of his alms? Shall we not contrive to get the saddle-bags from him and make off with them?" "And how shall we make shift to do this?" "We will sell him to the galleys." "How shall we do that?" "We two will go to the Rais, the Chief Captain of the Sea of Suez and bid him to an entertainment, with two of his company. What I say to Judar do thou confirm, and at the end of the night I will show thee what I will do." So they agreed upon the sale of their brother and going to the Captain's quarters said to him, "O Rais, we have come to thee on an errand that will please thee." "Good," answered he; and they continued, "We are two brethren, and we have a third brother, a lewd fellow and good-for-nothing. When our father died, he left us some money, which we shared amongst us, and he took his part of the inheritance and wasted it in frowardness and debauchery, till he was reduced to poverty, when he came upon us and cited us before the magistrates, avouching that we had taken his good and that of his father, and we disputed the matter before the judges and lost the money. Then he waited awhile and attacked us a second time, until he brought us to beggary; nor will he desist from us, and we are utterly weary of him; wherefore we would have thee buy him of us." Quoth the Captain, "Can ye cast about with him and bring him to me here? If so, I will pack him off to sea forthright." Quoth they, "We cannot manage to bring him here; but be thou our guest this night and bring with thee two of thy men, not one more; and when he is asleep, we will aid one another to fall upon him, we five, and seize and gag him. Then shalt thou carry him forth the house, under cover of the night, and after do thou with him as thou wilt." Rejoined the Captain, "With all my heart! Will ye sell him for forty dinars?" and they, "Yes, come after nightfall to such a street, by such a mosque, and thou shalt find one of us awaiting thee." And he replied, "Now be off." Then they repaired to Judar and waited awhile, after which Sálim went up to him and kissed his hand. Quoth Judar, "What ails thee, O my brother?" And he made answer, saying, "Know that I have a friend, who hath many a time bidden me to his house in thine absence and hath ever hospitably entreated me, and I owe him a thousand kindnesses, as my brother here wotteth. I met him to-day and he invited me to his house, but I said to him:—I cannot leave my brother Judar. Quoth he, Bring him with thee; and quoth I:—He will not consent to that; but if ye will be my guests, thou and thy brothers (for his brothers were sitting with him); and I invited them thinking that they would refuse. But he accepted my invitation for all of them, saying, Look for me at the gate of the little mosque, and I will come to thee, I and my brothers. And now I fear they will come and am ashamed before thee. So wilt thou hearten my heart and entertain them this night, for thy good is abundant, O my brother? Or if thou consent not, give me leave to take them into the neighbours' houses." Replied Judar, "Why shouldst thou carry them into the neighbours' houses? Is our house then so strait or have we not wherewith to give them supper? Shame on thee to consult me! Thou hast but to call for what thou needest and have rich viands and sweetmeats and to spare. Whenever thou bringest home folk in my absence, ask thy mother, and she will set before thee victual more than enough. Go and fetch them; blessings have descended upon us through such guests." So Sálim kissed his hand and going forth, sat at the gate of the little mosque till after sundown, when the Captain and his men came up to him, and he carried them to the house. When Judar saw them he bade them welcome and seated them and made friends of them, knowing not what the future had in store for him at their hands. Then he called to his mother for supper, and she fell to taking dishes out of the saddlebags, whilst he said, "Bring such and such meats," till she had set forty different dishes before them. They ate their sufficiency and the tray was taken away, the sailors thinking the while that this liberal entertainment came from Sálim. When a third part of the night was past, Judar set sweetmeats before them and Sálim served them, whilst his two brothers sat with the guests, till they sought to sleep. Accordingly Judar lay down and the others with him, who waited till he was asleep, when they fell upon him together and gagging and pinioning him, before he was awake, carried him forth of the house, under cover of the night, and at once packed him off to Suez, where they shackled him and set him to work as a galley-slave; and he ceased not to serve thus in silence a whole year. So far concerning Judar; but as for his brothers, they went in next morning to his mother and said to her, "O our mother, our brother Judar is not awake." Said she, "Do ye wake him." Asked they, "Where lieth he?" and she answered, "With the guests." They rejoined, "Haply he went away with them whilst we slept, O mother. It would seem that he had tasted of strangerhood and yearned to get at hidden hoards; for we heard him at talk with the Moors, and they said to him, We will take thee with us and open the treasure to thee." She enquired, "Hath he then been in company with Moors?"; and they replied, saying, "Were they not our guests yesternight?" And she, "Most like he hath gone with them, but Allah will direct him on the right way; for there is a blessing upon him and he will surely come back with great good." But she wept, for it was grievous to her to be parted from her son. Then said they to her, "O accursed woman, dost thou love Judar with all this love, whilst as for us, whether we be absent or present, thou neither joyest in us nor sorrowest for us? Are we not thy sons, even as Judar is thy son?" She said, "Ye are indeed my sons: but ye are reprobates who deserve no favour of me, for since your father's death I have never seen any good in you; whilst as for Judar, I have had abundant good of him and he hath heartened my heart and entreated me with honour; wherefore it behoveth me to weep for him, because of his kindness to me and to you." When they heard this, they abused her and beat her; after which they sought for the saddle-bags, till they found the two pairs and took the enchanted one and all the gold from one pouch and jewels from the other of the unenchanted, saying, "This was our father's good." Said their mother, "Not so, by Allah!; it belongeth to your brother Judar, who brought it from the land of the Magharibah." Said they, "Thou liest, it was our father's property; and we will dispose of it, as we please." Then they divided the gold and jewels between them; but a brabble arose between them concerning the enchanted saddle-bags, Sálim saying, "I will have them;" and Salím, saying, "I will take them;" and they came to high words. Then said she, "O my sons, ye have divided the gold and the jewels, but this may not be divided, nor can its value be made up in money; and if it be cut in twain, its spell will be voided; so leave it with me and I will give you to eat from it at all times and be content to take a morsel with you. If ye allow me aught to clothe me, 'twill be of your bounty, and each of you shall traffic with the folk for himself. Ye are my sons and I am your mother; wherefore let us abide as we are, lest your brother come back and we be disgraced." But they accepted not her words and passed the night, wrangling with each other. Now it chanced that a Janissary of the King's guards was a guest in the house adjoining Judar's and heard them through the open window. So he looked out and listening, heard all the angry words that passed between them and saw the division of the spoil. Next morning he presented himself before the King of Egypt, whose name was Shams al-Daulah, and told him all he had heard, whereupon he sent for Judar's brothers and put them to the question, till they confessed; and he took the two pairs of saddle-bags from them and clapped them in prison, appointing a sufficient daily allowance to their mother. Now as regards Judar, he abode a whole year in service at Suez, till one day, being in a ship bound on a voyage over the sea, a wind arose against them and cast the vessel upon a rock projecting from a mountain, where she broke up and all on board were drowned and none gat ashore save Judar. As soon as he landed he fared on inland, till he reached an encampment of Badawi, who questioned him of his case, and he told them he had been a sailor. Now there was in camp a merchant, a native of Jiddah, who took pity on him and said to him, "Wilt thou take service with me, O Egyptian, and I will clothe thee and carry thee with me to Jiddah?" So Judar took service with him and companied him to Jiddah, where he showed him much favour. After awhile, his master the merchant set out on a pilgrimage to Meccah, taking Judar with him, and when they reached the city, the Cairene repaired to the Haram temple, to circumambulate the Ka'abah. As he was making the prescribed circuits, he suddenly saw his friend Abd al-Samad the Moor doing the like; and when the Maghribi caught sight of him, he saluted him and asked him of his state; whereupon Judar wept and told him all that had befallen him. So the Moor carried him to his lodging and entreated him with honour, clothing him in a dress of which the like was not, and saying to him, "Thou hast seen the end of thine ills, O Judar." Then he drew out for him a geomantic figure, which showed what had befallen Sálim and Salím and said to Judar, "Such and such things have befallen thy brothers and they are now in the King of Egypt's prison; but thou art right welcome to abide with me and accomplish thine ordinances of pilgrimage and all shall be well." Replied Judar, "O my lord, let me go and take leave of the merchant with whom I am and after I will come back to thee." "Dost thou owe money?" asked the Moor, and he answered, "No." Said Abd al-Samad, "Go thou and take leave of him and come back forthright, for bread hath claims of its own from the ingenuous." So Judar returned to the merchant and farewelled him, saying, "I have fallen in with my brother." "Go bring him here," said the merchant, "and we will make him an entertainment." But Judar answered, saying, "He hath no need of that; for he is a man of wealth and hath many servants." Then the merchant gave Judar twenty dinars, saying, "Acquit me of responsibility;" and he bade him adieu and went forth from him. Presently, he saw a poor man, so he gave him the twenty ducats and returned to the Moor, with whom he abode till they had accomplished the pilgrimage-rites when Abd al-Samad gave him the seal-ring, that he had taken from the treasure of Al-Shamardal, saying, "This ring will win thee thy wish, for it enchanteth and hath a servant, by name Al-Ra'ad al-Kasif; so whatever thou hast a mind to of the wants of this world, rub this ring and its servant will appear and do all thou biddest him." Then he rubbed the ring before him, whereupon the Jinni appeared, saying, "Adsum, O my lord! Ask what thou wilt and it shall be given thee. Hast thou a mind to people a ruined city or ruin a populous one? to slay a king or to rout a host?" "O Ra'ad," said Abd al-Samad, "this is become thy lord; do thou serve him faithfully." Then he dismissed him and said to Judar, "Rub the ring and the servant will appear; and do thou command him to do whatever thou desirest, for he

will not gainsay thee. Now go to thine own country and take care of the
ring, for by means of it thou wilt battle thine enemies; and be not ignorant of its puissance." "O my lord," quoth Judar, "with thy leave, I will
set out homewards." Quoth the Maghribi, "Summon the Jinni and
mount upon his back; and if thou say to him:—Bring me to my native
city this very day, he will not disobey thy commandment." So he took
leave of Moor Abd al-Samad and rubbed the ring, whereupon Al-Ra'ad
presented himself, saying, "Adsum; ask and it shall be given to thee."
Said Judar, "Carry me to Cairo this day"; and he replied, "Thy will be
done;" and, taking him on his back, flew with him from noon till midnight, when he set him down in the courtyard of his mother's house
and disappeared. Judar went in to his mother, who rose weeping, and
greeted him fondly, and told him how the King had beaten his brothers and cast them into gaol and taken the two pairs of saddle-bags;
which when he heard, it was no light matter to him and he said to her,
"Grieve not for the past; I will show thee what I can do and bring my
brothers hither forthright." So he rubbed the ring, whereupon its servant appeared, saying, "Here am I! Ask and thou shalt have." Quoth
Judar, "I bid thee bring me my two brothers from the prison of the
King." So the Jinni sank into the earth and came not up but in the
midst of the gaol where Sálim and Salím lay in piteous plight and sore
sorrow for the plagues of prison,[1] so that they wished for death, and one
of them said to the other, "By Allah, O my brother, affliction is longsome upon us! How long shall we abide in this prison? Death would be
relief." As he spoke, behold, the earth clove in sunder and out came Al-
Ra'ad, who took both up and plunged with them into the earth. They
swooned away for excess of fear, and when they recovered, they found
themselves in their mother's house and saw Judar seated by her side.
Quoth he, "I salute you, O my brothers! you have cheered me by your
presence." And they bowed their heads and burst into tears. Then said
he, "Weep not, for it was Satan and covetise that led you to do thus.
How could you sell me? But I comfort myself with the thought of
Joseph, whose brothers did with him even more than ye did with me,
because they cast him into the pit. Repent unto Allah and crave pardon
of Him, and He will forgive you both, for He is the Most Forgiving, the

---

[1] A Moslem prison is like those of Europe a century ago, to think of it gives
gooseflesh. Easterns laugh at our idea of penitentiary and the Arabs of
Bombay call it "Al-Bistan" (the Garden) because the court contains a few
trees and shrubs. And with them a garden always suggests an idea of Paradise.
There are indeed only two efficacious forms of punishment all the world
over, corporal for the poor and fines for the rich, the latter being the severer
form.

Merciful. As for me, I pardon you and welcome you: no harm shall befal you." Then he comforted them and set their hearts at ease and related to them all he had suffered, till he fell in with Shaykh Abd al-Samad, and told them also of the seal-ring. They replied, "O our brother, forgive us this time; and, if we return to our old ways, do with us as thou wilt." Quoth he, "No harm shall befal you; but tell me what the King did with you." Quoth they, "He beat us and threatened us with death and took the two pairs of saddle-bags from us." "Will he not care?" said Judar, and rubbed the ring, whereupon Al-Ra'ad appeared. When his brothers saw him, they were affrighted and thought Judar would bid him slay them; so they fled to their mother, crying, "O our mother, we throw ourselves on thy generosity; do thou intercede for us, O our mother!" And she said to them, "O my sons, fear nothing!" Then said Judar to the servant, "I command thee to bring me all that is in the King's treasury of goods and such; let nothing remain and fetch the two pairs of saddle-bags he took from my brothers." "I hear and I obey," replied Al-Ra'ad; and, disappearing straightway gathered together all he found in the treasury and returned with the two pairs of saddle-bags and the deposits therein and laid them before Judar, saying, "O my lord, I have left nothing in the treasury." Judar gave the treasure to his mother bidding her keep it and laying the enchanted saddle-bags before him, said to the Jinni, "I command thee to build me this night a lofty palace and overlay it with liquid gold and furnish it with magnificent furniture: and let not the day dawn, ere thou be quit of the whole work." Replied he, "Thy bidding shall be obeyed;" and sank into the earth. Then Judar brought forth food and they ate and took their ease and lay down to sleep. Meanwhile, Al-Ra'ad summoned his attendant Jinn and bade them build the palace. So some of them fell to hewing stones and some to building, whilst others plastered and painted and furnished; nor did the day dawn ere the ordinance of the palace was complete; whereupon Al-Ra'ad came to Judar and said to him, "O my lord, the palace is finished and in best order, an it please thee to come and look on it." So Judar went forth with his mother and brothers and saw a palace, whose like there was not in the whole world; and it confounded all minds with the goodliness of its ordinance. Judar was delighted with it while he was passing along the highway and withal it had cost him nothing. Then he asked his mother, "Say me, wilt thou take up thine abode in this palace?" and she answered, "I will, O my son," and called down blessings upon him. Then he rubbed the ring and bade the Jinni fetch him forty handsome white hand-maids and forty black damsels and as many Mamelukes and negro slaves. "Thy will be done," answered Al-Ra'ad and betaking himself, with forty of his attendant Jinni to Hind and Sind and Persia, snatched up every beautiful girl and boy they saw, till they had made up the required number. Moreover, he sent other fourscore, who fetched comely black girls, and forty others brought male chattels and carried them all to Judar's house, which they filled. Then he showed them to Judar, who was pleased with them and said, "Bring for each a dress of the finest." "Ready!" replied the servant. Then quoth he, "Bring a dress for my mother and another for myself, and also for my brothers." So the Jinni fetched all that was needed and clad the female slaves, saying to them, "This is your mistress: kiss her hands and cross her not, but serve her, white and black." The Mamelukes also dressed themselves and kissed Judar's hands; and he and his brothers arrayed themselves in the robes the Jinni had brought them and Judar became like unto a King and his brothers as Wazirs. Now his house was spacious; so he lodged Sálim and his slave-girls in one part thereof and Salím and his slave-girls in another, whilst he and his mother took up their abode in the new palace; and each in his own palace was like a Sultan. So far concerning them; but as regards the King's Treasurer, thinking to take something from the treasury, he went in and found it altogether empty, even as saith the poet:—

> 'Twas as a hive of bees that greatly thrived;
> But, when the bee-swarm fled, 'twas clean unhived.

So he gave a great cry and fell down in a fit. When he came to himself, he left the door open and going in to King Shams al-Daulah, said to him, "O Commander of the Faithful, I have to inform thee that the treasury hath become empty during the night." Quoth the King, "What hast thou done with my monies which were therein?" Quoth he, "By Allah, I have not done aught with them nor know I what is come of them! I visited the place yesterday and saw it full; but to-day when I went in, I found it clean empty, albeit the doors were locked, the walls were unpierced and the bolts are unbroken; nor hath a thief entered it." Asked the King, "Are the two pairs of saddle-bags gone?" "Yes," replied the Treasurer; whereupon the King's reason flew from his head and he rose to his feet, saying, "Go thou before me." Then he followed the Treasurer to the treasury and he found nothing there, whereat he was wroth with him; and he said to them, "O soldiers! know that my treasury hath been plundered during the night, and I know not who did this deed and dared thus to outrage me, without fear of me." Said they, "How so?"; and he replied, "Ask the Treasurer." So they questioned him, and he answered, saying, "Yesterday I visited the treasury and it was full, but this morning when I entered it I found it empty, though the walls were unpierced and the doors unbroken." They all marvelled at this and could make the King no answer, when in came the Janissary, who had denounced Sálim and Salím, and said to Shams al-Daulah, "O King of the age, all this night I have not slept for that which I saw." And the King asked, "And what didst thou see?" "Know, O King of the age," answered the Kawwas, "that all night long I have been amusing myself with watching builders at work; and, when it was day, I saw a palace ready edified, whose like is not in the world. So I asked about it and was told that Judar had come back with great wealth and Mamelukes and slaves and that he had freed his two brothers from prison, and built this palace, wherein he is as a Sultan." Quoth the King, "Go, look in the prison." So they went thither and not finding Sálim and Salím, returned and told the King, who said, "It is plain now who be the thief; he who took Sálim and Salím out of prison it is who hath stolen my monies." Quoth the Wazir, "O my lord, and who is he?"; and quoth the King, "Their brother Judar, and he hath taken the two pairs of saddle-bags; but, O Wazir, do thou send him an Emir with fifty men to seal up his goods and lay hands on him and his brothers and bring them to me, that I may hang them." And he was sore enraged and said, "Ho, off with the Emir at once, and fetch them, that I may put them to death." But the Wazir said to him, "Be thou merciful, for Allah is merciful and hasteth not to punish His servants, whenas they sin against Him. Moreover, he who can build a palace in a single night, as these say, none in the world can vie with him; and verily I fear lest the Emir fall into difficulty for Judar. Have patience, therefore, whilst I devise for thee some device of getting at the truth of the case, and so shalt thou win thy wish, O King of the age." Quoth the King, "Counsel me how I shall do, O Wazir." And the Minister said, "Send him an Emir with an invitation; and I will make much of him for thee and make a show of love for him and ask him of his estate; after which we will see. If we find him stout of heart, we will use sleight with him, and if weak of will, then do thou seize him and do with him thy desire." The King agreed to this and despatched one of his Emirs, Othman hight, to go and invite Judar and say to him, "The King biddeth thee to a banquet;" and the King said to him, "Return not, except with him." Now this Othman was a fool, proud and conceited; so he went forth upon his errand, and when he came to the gate of Judar's palace, he saw before the door an eunuch seated upon a chair of gold, who at his approach rose not, but sat as if none came near, though there were with the Emir fifty footmen. Now this eunuch was none other than Al-Ra'ad al-Kasif, the servant of the ring, whom Judar had commanded to put on the guise of an eunuch and sit at the palace-gate. So the Emir rode up to him and asked him, "O slave, where is thy lord?"; whereto he answered, "In the palace;" but he stirred not from his leaning posture; whereupon the Emir Othman waxed wroth and said to him, "O pestilent slave, art thou not ashamed, when I speak to thee, to answer me, sprawl-ing at thy length, like a gallows-bird?" Replied the eunuch, "Off and multiply not words." Hardly had Othman heard this, when he was filled with rage and drawing his mace would have smitten the eunuch, knowing not that he was a devil; but Al-Ra'ad leapt upon him and tak-ing the mace from him, dealt him four blows with it. Now when the fifty men saw their lord beaten, it was grievous to them; so they drew their swords and ran to slay the slave; but he said, "Do ye draw on us, O dogs?" and rose at them with the mace, and every one whom he smote, he broke his bones and drowned him in his blood. So they fell back before him and fled, whilst he followed them, beating them, till he had driven them far from the palace-gate; after which he returned and sat down on his chair at the door, caring for none. But as for the Emir and his company, they returned, discomfited and tunded, to King Shams al-Daulah, and Othman said, "O King of the age, when I came to the palace-gate, I espied an eunuch seated there in a chair of gold and he was passing proud for, when he saw me approach, he stretched himself at full length albeit he had been sitting in his chair and entreated me contumeliously, neither offered to rise to me. So I began to speak to him and he answered without stirring, whereat wrath got hold of me and I drew the mace upon him, thinking to smite him. But he snatched it from me and beat me and my men therewith and over-threw us. So we fled from before him and could not prevail against him." At this, the King was wroth and said, "Let an hundred men go down to him." Accordingly, the hundred men went down to attack him; but he arose and fell upon them with the mace and ceased not smiting them till he had put them to the rout; when he regained his chair; upon which they returned to the King and told him what had passed, saying, "O King of the age, he beat us and we fled for fear of him." Then the King sent two hundred men against him, but these also he put to the rout, and Shams al-Daulah said to his Minister, "I charge thee, O Wazir, take five hundred men and bring this eunuch in haste, and with him his master Judar and his brothers." Replied the Wazir, "O King of the age, I need no soldiers, but will go down to him alone and unarmed." "Go," quoth the King, "and do as thou seest suitable." So the Wazir laid down his arms and donning a white habit, took a rosary in his hand and set out afoot alone and unattended. When he came to Judar's gate, he saw the slave sitting there; so he went up to him and seating himself by his side courteously, said to him, "Peace be with thee!"; whereto he replied, "And on thee be peace, O mortal! What wilt thou?" When the Wazir heard him say "O mortal," he knew him to be of the Jinn and quaked for fear; then he asked him, "O my lord, tell me, is thy master Judar here?" Answered the eunuch, "Yes, he is in the palace." Quoth the Minister, "O my lord, go thou to him and say to him: — King Shams al-Daulah saluteth thee and biddeth thee honour his dwelling with thy presence and eat of a banquet he hath made for thee." Quoth the eunuch, "Tarry thou here, whilst I consult him." So the Wazir stood in a respectful attitude, whilst the Marid went up to the palace and said to Judar, "Know, O my lord, that the King sent to thee an Emir and fifty men, and I beat them and drove them away. Then he sent an hundred men and I beat them also; then two hundred, and these also I put to the rout. And now he hath sent thee his Wazir unarmed, bidding thee visit him and eat of his banquet. What sayst thou?" Said Judar, "Go bring the Wazir hither." So the Marid went down and said to him, "O Wazir, come speak with my lord." "On my head be it," replied he and going in to Judar, found him seated, in greater state than the King, upon a carpet, whose like the King could not spread, and was dazed and amazed at the goodliness of the palace and its decoration and appointments, which made him seem as he were a beggar in comparison. So he kissed the ground before Judar and called down blessings on him; and Judar said to him, "What is thy business, O Wazir?" Replied he, "O my lord, thy friend King Shams al-Daulah saluteth thee with the salam and longeth to look upon thy face; wherefore he hath made thee an entertainment. So say, wilt thou heal his heart and eat of his banquet?" Quoth Judar, "If he be indeed my friend, salute him and bid him come to me." "On my head be it," quoth the Minister. Then Judar bringing out the ring rubbed it and bade the Jinni fetch him a dress of the best, which he gave to the Wazir, saying, "Don this dress and go tell the King what I say." So the Wazir donned the dress, the like whereof he had never donned, and returning to the King told him what had passed and praised the palace and that which was therein, saying, "Judar biddeth thee to him." So the King called out, "Up, ye men; mount your horses and bring me my steed, that we may go to Judar!" Then he and his suite rode off for the Cairene palace. Meanwhile Judar summoned the Marid and said to him, "It is my will that thou bring me some of the Ifrits at thy command in the guise of guards and station them in the open square before the palace, that the King may see them and be awed by them; so shall his heart tremble and he shall know that my power and majesty be greater than his." Thereupon Al-Ra'ad brought him two hundred Ifrits of great stature and strength, in the guise of guards, magnificently armed and equipped, and when the King came and saw these tall burly fellows his heart feared them. Then he entered the palace, and found Judar sitting in such state as nor King nor Sultan could even. So he saluted him and made his obeisance to him; yet Judar rose not to him nor did him honour nor said "Be seated," but left him standing, so that fear entered into him and he could neither sit nor go away and said to himself, "If he feared me, he would not leave me thus unheeded; peradventure he will do me a mischief, because of that which I did with his brothers." Then said Judar, "O King of the age, it beseemeth not the like of thee to wrong the folk and take away their good." Replied the King, "O my lord, deign excuse me, for greed impelled me to this and fate was thereby fulfilled; and, were there no offending, there would be no forgiving." And he went on to excuse himself for the past and pray to him for pardon and indulgence. And he ceased not to humble himself before him, till he said, "Allah pardon thee!" and bade him be seated. So he sat down and Judar invested him with garments of pardon and immunity and ordered his brothers spread the table. When they had eaten, he clad the whole of the King's company in robes of honour and gave them largesse; after which he bade the King depart. So he went forth and thereafter came every day to visit Judar and held not his Divan save in his house: wherefore friendship and familiarity waxed great between them, and they abode thus awhile, till one day the King, being alone with his Minister, said to him, "O Wazir, I fear lest Judar slay me and take the kingdom away from me." Replied the Wazir, "O King of the age, as for his taking the kingdom from thee, have no fear that, for Judar's present estate is greater than that of the King, and to take the kingdom would be a lowering of his dignity; but, if thou fear of that he kill thee, thou hast a daughter: give her to him to wife and thou and he will be of one condition." Quoth the King, "O Wazir, be thou intermediary between us and him"; and quoth the Minister, "Do thou invite him to an entertainment and pass the night with him in one of thy saloons. Then bid thy daughter don her richest dress and ornaments and pass by the door of the saloon. When he seeth her, he will assuredly fall in love with her, and when we know this, I will turn to him and tell him that she is thy daughter and engage him in converse and lead him on, so that thou shalt seem to know nothing of the matter, till he ask her of thee to wife. When thou hast married him to the Princess, thou and he will be as one thing and thou wilt be safe from him; and if he die, thou wilt inherit all he hath, both great and small." Replied the King, "Thou sayst sooth, O my Wazir," and made a banquet and invited thereto Judar who came to the Sultan's palace and they sat in the saloon in great good cheer till the end of the day. Now the King had commanded his wife to array the maiden in her richest raiment and ornaments and carry her by the door of the saloon. She did as he told her, and when Judar saw the Princess, who had not her match for beauty and grace, he looked fixedly at her and said, "Ah!"; and his limbs were loosened; for love and longing and passion and pine were sore upon him; desire and transport gat hold upon him and he

turned pale. Quoth the Wazir, "May no harm befal thee, O my lord!
Why do I see thee change colour and in suffering?" Asked Judar, "O
Wazir, whose daughter is this damsel? Verily she hath enthralled me
and ravished my reason." Replied the Wazir, "She is the daughter of thy
friend the King; and if she please thee, I will speak to him that he marry
thee to her." Quoth Judar, "Do so, O Wazir, and as I live, I will bestow
on thee what thou wilt and will give the King whatsoever he shall ask
to her dowry; and we will become friends and kinsfolk." Quoth the
Minister, "It shall go hard but thy desire be accomplished." Then he
turned to the King and said in his ear, "O King of the age, thy friend
Judar seeketh alliance with thee and will have me ask of thee for him
the hand of thy daughter, the Princess Asiyah; so disappoint me not, but
accept my intercession, and what dowry soever thou askest he will give
thee." Said the King, "The dowry I have already received, and as for the
girl, she is his handmaid; I give her to him to wife and he will do me
honour by accepting her." So they spent the rest of that night together
and on the morrow the King held a court, to which he summoned great
and small, together with the Shaykh al-Islam. Then Judar demanded
the Princess in marriage and the King said, "The dowry I have
received." Thereupon they drew up the marriage-contract and Judar
sent for the saddle-bags containing the jewels and gave them to the
King as settlement upon his daughter. The drums beat and the pipes
sounded and they held high festival, whilst Judar went in unto the girl.
Thenceforward he and the King were as one flesh and they abode thus
for many days, till Shams al-Daulah died; whereupon the troops proclaimed Judar Sultan, and he refused; but they importuned him, till he
consented and they made him King in his father-in-law's stead. Then
he bade build a cathedral-mosque over the late King's tomb in the
Bundukaniyah quarter and endowed it. Now the quarter of Judar's
house was called Yamaniyah; but, when he became Sultan he built
therein a congregational mosque and other buildings, wherefore the
quarter was named after him and was called the Judariyah quarter.
Moreover, he made his brother Sálim his Wazir of the right and his
brother Salím his Wazir of the left hand; and thus they abode a year
and no more; for, at the end of that time, Sálim said to Salím, "O my
brother, how long is this state to last? Shall we pass our whole lives in
slavery to our brother Judar? We shall never enjoy luck or lordship
whilst he lives," adding, "so how shall we do to kill him and take the
ring and the saddle-bags?" Replied Salím, "Thou art craftier than I; do
thou device, whereby we may kill him." "If I effect this," asked Sálim,
"wilt thou agree that I be Sultan and keep the ring and that thou be my
right-hand Wazir and have the saddle-bags?" Salím answered, "I consent to this;" and they agreed to slay Judar their brother for love of the

world and of dominion. So they laid a snare for Judar and said to him, "O our brother, verily we have a mind to glory in thee and would fain have thee enter our houses and eat of our entertainment and solace our hearts." Replied Judar, "So be it, in whose house shall the banquet be?" "In mine," said Sálim "and after thou hast eaten of my victual, thou shalt be the guest of my brother." Said Judar, "'Tis well," and went with him to his house, where he set before him poisoned food, of which when he had eaten, his flesh rotted from his bones and he died.[1] Then Sálim came up to him and would have drawn the ring from his finger, but it resisted him; so he cut off the finger with a knife. Then he rubbed the ring and the Marid presented himself, saying, "Adsum! Ask what thou wilt." Quoth Sálim, "Take my brother Salím and put him to death and carry forth the two bodies, the poisoned and the slaughtered, and cast them down before the troops." So the Marid took Salím and slew him; then, carrying the two corpses forth, he cast them down before the chief officers of the army, who were sitting at table in the parlour of the house. When they saw Judar and Salím slain, they raised their hands from the food and fear gat hold of them and they said to the Marid, "Who hath dealt thus with the Sultan and the Wazir?" Replied the Jinni, "Their brother Sálim." And behold, Sálim came up to them and said, "O soldiers, eat and make merry, for Judar is dead and I have taken to me the seal-ring, whereof the Marid before you is the servant; and I bade him slay my brother Salím lest he dispute the kingdom with me, for he was a traitor and I feared lest he should betray me. So now I am become Sultan over you; will ye accept of me? If not, I will rub the ring and bid the Marid slay you all, great and small." They replied, "We accept thee to King and Sultan." Then he bade bury his brothers and summoned the Divan; and some of the folk followed the funeral, whilst others forewent him in state procession to the audience-hall of the palace, where he sat down on the throne and they did homage to him as King; after which he said, "It is my will to marry my brother Judar's wife." Quoth they, "Wait till the days of widowhood are accomplished." Quoth he, "I know not days of widowhood nor aught else. As my head liveth, I needs must go in unto her this very night." So they drew up the marriage-contract and sent to tell the Princess Asiyah, who replied, "Bid him enter." Accordingly, he went in to her and she received him with a show of joy and welcome; but by and by she gave him poison in water and made an end of him. Then she took the ring and broke it,

---

[1] I have noted that as a rule in The Nights poetical justice is administered with much rigour and exactitude. Here, however, the tale-teller allows the good brother to be slain by the two wicked brothers.

that none might possess it thenceforward, and tore up the saddle-bags;
after which she sent to the Shaykh al-Islam and other great Officers of
state, telling them what had passed and saying to them, "Choose you
out a King to rule over you." And this is all that hath come down to us
of the story of Judar and his brethren. But there is also told, O King, the
tale of

KHALIFAH THE FISHERMAN OF BAGHDAD

THERE WAS ONCE in tides of yore and in ages and times long gone
before in the city of Baghdad a fisherman, Khalifah hight, a pauper
wight, who had never once been married in all his days. It chanced one
morning, that he took his net and went with it to the river, as was his
wont with the view of fishing before the others came. When he reached
the bank, he girt himself and tucked up his skirts; then stepping into
the water, he spread his net and cast it a first cast and a second but it
brought up naught. He ceased not to throw it, till he had made ten
casts, and still naught came up therein; wherefore his breast was straitened and his mind perplexed concerning his case and he said, "I crave
pardon of God the Great, there is no god but He, the Living, the
Eternal, and unto Him I repent. There is no Majesty and there is no
Might save in Allah, the Glorious, the Great! Whatso He willeth is and
whatso He nilleth is not! Upon Allah (to whom belong Honour and
Glory!) dependeth daily bread! Whenas He giveth to His servant, none
denieth him; and whenas He denieth a servant, none giveth to him."
And of the excess of his distress, he recited these two couplets: —

> An Fate afflict thee, with grief manifest,
> Prepare thy patience and make broad thy breast;
> For of His grace the Lord of all the worlds
> Shall send to wait upon unrest sweet Rest.

Then he said in his mind, "I will make this one more cast, trusting in
Allah, so haply He may not disappoint my hope;" and he rose and casting into the river the net as far as his arm availed, gathered the cords in
his hands and waited a full hour, after which he pulled at it and, finding it heavy, handled it gently and drew it in, little by little, till he got it
ashore, when lo and behold! he saw in it a one-eyed, lame-legged ape.
Seeing this quoth Khalifah, "There is no Majesty and there is no Might
save in Allah! Verily, we are Allah's and to Him we are returning! What
meaneth this heart-breaking, miserable ill-luck and hapless fortune?
What is come to me this blessed day? But all this is of the destinies of
Almighty Allah!" Then he took the ape and tied him with a cord to a

tree which grew on the river-bank, and grasping a whip he had with him, raised his arm in the air, thinking to bring down the scourge upon the quarry, when Allah made the ape speak with a fluent tongue, saying, "O Khalifah, hold thy hand and beat me not, but leave me bounden to this tree and go down to the river and cast thy net, confiding in Allah; for He will give thee thy daily bread." Hearing this Khalifah went down to the river and casting his net, let the cords run out. Then he pulled it in and found it heavier than before; so he ceased not to tug at it, till he brought it to land, when, behold, there was another ape in it, with front teeth wide apart, Kohl-darkened eyes and hands stained with Henna-dyes; and he was laughing and wore a tattered waistcloth about his middle. Quoth Khalifah, "Praised be Allah who hath changed the fish of the river into apes!" Then, going up to the first ape, who was still tied to the tree, he said to him, "See, O unlucky, how fulsome was the counsel thou gavest me! None but thou made me light on this second ape: and for that thou gavest me goodmorrow with thy one eye and thy lameness, I am become distressed and weary, without dirham or dinar." So saying, he hent in hand a stick and flourishing it thrice in the air, was about to come down with it upon the lame ape, when the creature cried out for mercy and said to him, "I conjure thee, by Allah, spare me for the sake of this my fellow and seek of him thy need; for he will guide thee to thy desire!" So he held his hand from him and throwing down the stick, went up to and stood by the second ape, who said to him, "O Khalifah, this my speech will profit thee naught, except thou hearken to what I say to thee; but, an thou do my bidding and cross me not, I will be the cause of thine enrichment." Asked Khalifah, "And what hast thou to say to me that I may obey thee therein?" The Ape answered, "Leave me bound on the bank and hie thee down to the river; then cast thy net a third time, and after I will tell thee what to do." So he took his net and going down to the river, cast it once more and waited awhile. Then he drew it in and finding it heavy, laboured at it and ceased not his travail till he got it ashore, when he found in it yet another ape; but this one was red, with a blue waistcloth about his middle; his hands and feet were stained with Henna and his eyes blackened with Kohl. When Khalifah saw this, he exclaimed, "Glory to God the Great! Extolled be the perfection of the Lord of Dominion! Verily, this is a blessed day from first to last: its ascendant was fortunate in the countenance of the first ape, and the scroll is known by its superscription! Verily, to-day is a day of apes: there is not a single fish left in the river, and we are come out to-day but to catch monkeys!" Then he turned to the third ape and said, "And what thing art thou also, O unlucky?" Quoth the ape, "Dost not thou know me, O Khalifah!"; and quoth he, "Not I!" The ape cried, "I am the ape

of Abu al-Sa'adat the Jew, the shroff." Asked Khalifah, "And what dost
thou for him?"; and the ape answered, "I give him good-morrow at the
first of the day, and he gaineth five ducats; and again at the end of the
day, I give him good-even and he gaineth other five ducats."
Whereupon Khalifah turned to the first ape and said to him, "See, O
unlucky, what fine apes other folk have! As for thee, thou givest me
good-morrow with thy one eye and thy lameness and thy ill-omened
phiz and I become poor and bankrupt and hungry!" So saying, he took
the cattlestick and flourishing it thrice in the air, was about to come
down with it on the first ape, when Abu al-Sa'adat's ape said to him,
"Let him be, O Khalifah, hold thy hand and come hither to me, that I
may tell thee what to do." So Khalifah threw down the stick and walking up to him cried, "And what hast thou to say to me, O monarch of
all monkeys?" Replied the ape, "Leave me and the other two apes here,
and take thy net and cast it into the river; and whatever cometh up,
bring it to me, and I will tell thee what shall gladden thee." He replied,
"I hear and obey," and took the net and gathered it on his shoulder,
reciting these couplets:—

> When straitened is my breast I will of my Creator pray,
> Who may and can the heaviest weight lighten in easiest way;
> For ere man's glance can turn or close his eye by God His grace
> Waxeth the broken whole and yieldeth gaol its prison-prey.
> Therefore with Allah one and all of thy concerns commit
> Whose grace and favour men of wit shall nevermore gainsay.

Now when Khalifah had made an end of his verse, he went down to the
river and casting his net, waited awhile; after which he drew it up and
found therein a fine young fish, with a big head, a tail like a ladle and
eyes like two gold pieces. When Khalifah saw this fish, he rejoiced, for
he had never in his life caught its like, so he took it, marvelling, and
carried it to the ape of Abu al-Sa'adat the Jew, as 'twere he had gotten
possession of the universal world. Quoth the ape, "O Khalifah, what
wilt thou do with this and with thine ape?"; and quoth the Fisherman,
"I will tell thee, O monarch of monkeys, all I am about to do. Know
then that first, I will cast about to make away with yonder accursed, my
ape, and take thee in his stead and give thee every day to eat of whatso
thou wilt." Rejoined the ape, "Since thou hast made choice of me, I
will tell thee how thou shalt do wherein, if it please Allah Almighty,
shall be the mending of thy fortune. Lend thy mind, then, to what I say
to thee and 'tis this! Take another cord and tie me also to a tree, where
leave me and go to the midst of The Dyke and cast thy net into the
Tigris. Then after waiting awhile, draw it up and thou shalt find therein

a fish, than which thou never sawest a finer in thy whole life. Bring it to me and I will tell thee how thou shalt do after this." So Khalifah rose forthright and casting his net into the Tigris, drew up a great cat-fish the bigness of a lamb; never had he set eyes on its like, for it was larger than the first fish. He carried it to the ape, who said to him, "Gather thee some green grass and set half of it in a basket; lay the fish therein and cover it with the other moiety. Then, leaving us here tied, shoulder the basket and betake thee to Baghdad. If any bespeak thee or question thee by the way, answer him not, but fare on till thou comest to the market-street of the money-changers, at the upper end whereof thou wilt find the shop of Master Abu al-Sa'adat the Jew, Shaykh of the shroffs, and wilt see him sitting on a mattress, with a cushion behind him and two coffers, one for gold and one for silver, before him, while around him stand his Mamelukes and negro-slaves and servant-lads. Go up to him and set the basket before him, saying:—O Abu al-Sa'adat, verily I went out to-day to fish and cast my net in thy name, and Allah Almighty sent me this fish. He will ask, Hast thou shown it to any but me?; and do thou answer, No, by Allah! Then will he take it of thee and give thee a dinar. Give it him back and he will give thee two dinars; but do thou return them also and so do with everything he may offer thee; and take naught from him, though he give thee the fish's weight in gold. Then will he say to thee, Tell me what thou wouldst have; and do thou reply, By Allah, I will not sell the fish save for two words! He will ask, What are they? And do thou answer, Stand up and say, Bear witness, O ye who are present in the market, that I give Khalifah the fisherman my ape in exchange for his ape, and that I barter for his lot my lot and luck for his luck. This is the price of the fish, and I have no need of gold. If he do this, I will every day give thee good-morrow and good-even, and every day thou shalt gain ten dinars of good gold; whilst this one-eyed, lame-legged ape shall daily give the Jew good-morrow, and Allah shall afflict him every day with an avanie which he must needs pay, nor will he cease to be thus afflicted till he is reduced to beggary and hath naught. Hearken then to my words; so shalt thou prosper and be guided aright." Quoth Khalifah, "I accept thy counsel, O monarch of all the monkeys! But, as for this unlucky, may Allah never bless him! I know not what to do with him." Quoth the ape, "Let him go into the water, and let me go also." "I hear and obey," answered Khalifah and unbound the three apes, and they went down into the river. Then he took up the cat-fish which he washed, then laid it in the basket upon some green grass, and covered it with other; and lastly shouldering his load, set out with the basket upon his shoulder and ceased not faring till he entered the city of Baghdad. And as he threaded the streets the folk knew him and cried out to him, saying,

"What hast thou there, O Khalifah?" But he paid no heed to them and passed on till he came to the market-street of the money-changers and fared between the shops, as the ape had charged him, till he found the Jew seated at the upper end, with his servants in attendance upon him, as he were a King of the Kings of Khorasan. He knew him at first sight; so he went up to him and stood before him, whereupon Abu al-Sa'adat raised his eyes and recognising him, said, "Welcome, O Khalifah! What wantest thou and what is thy need? If any have missaid thee or spited thee, tell me and I will go with thee to the Chief of Police, who shall do thee justice on him." Replied Khalifah, "Nay, as thy head liveth, O chief of the Jews, none hath missaid me. But I went forth this morning to the river and, casting my net into the Tigris on thy luck, brought up this fish." Therewith he opened the basket and threw the fish before the Jew who admired it and said, "By the Pentateuch and the Ten Commandments, I dreamt last night that the Virgin came to me and said:—Know, O Abu al-Sa'adat, that I have sent thee a pretty present! And doubtless 'tis this fish." Then he turned to Khalifah and said to him, "By thy faith, hath any seen it but I?" Khalifah replied, "No, by Allah, and by Abu Bakr the Viridical, none hath seen it save thou, O chief of the Jews!" Whereupon the Jew turned to one of his lads and said to him, "Come, carry this fish to my house and bid Sa'adah dress it and fry and broil it, against I make an end of my business and hie me home." And Khalifah said, "Go, O my lad; let the master's wife fry some of it and broil the rest." Answered the boy, "I hear and I obey, O my lord" and, taking the fish, went away with it to the house. Then the Jew put out his hand and gave Khalifah the fisherman a dinar, saying, "Take this for thyself, O Khalifah, and spend it on thy family." When Khalifah saw the dinar on his palm, he took it, saying, "Laud to the Lord of Dominion!" as if he had never seen aught of gold in his life, and went somewhat away; but, before he had gone far, he was minded of the ape's charge and turning back threw down the ducat, saying, "Take thy gold and give folk back their fish! Dost thou make a laughing stock of folk?" The Jew hearing this thought he was jesting and offered him two dinars upon the other, but Khalifah said, "Give me the fish and no nonsense. How knewest thou I would sell it at this price?" Whereupon the Jew gave him two more dinars and said, "Take these five ducats for thy fish and leave greed." So Khalifah hent the five dinars in hand and went away, rejoicing, and gazing and marvelling at the gold and saying, "Glory be to God! There is not with the Caliph of Baghdad what is with me this day!" Then he ceased not faring on till he came to the end of the market-street, when he remembered the words of the ape and his charge and returning to the Jew, threw him back the gold. Quoth he, "What aileth thee, O Khalifah?

Dost thou want silver in exchange for gold?" Khalifah replied, "I want nor dirhams nor dinars. I only want thee to give me back folk's fish." With this the Jew waxed wroth and shouted out at him, saying, "O fisherman, thou bringest me a fish not worth a sequin and I give thee five for it; yet art thou not content! Art thou Jinn-mad? Tell me for how much thou wilt sell it." Answered Khalifah, "I will not sell it for silver nor for gold, only for two sayings thou shalt say me." When the Jew heard speak of the "Two Sayings," his eyes sank into his head, he breathed hard and ground his teeth for rage and said to him, "O nail-pairing of the Moslems, wilt thou have me throw off my faith for the sake of thy fish, and wilt thou debauch me from my religion and stultify my belief and my conviction which I inherited of old from my forebears?" Then he cried out to the servants who were in waiting and said, "Out on you! Bash me this unlucky rogue's neck and bastinado him soundly!" So they came down upon him with blows and ceased not beating him till he fell beneath the shop, and the Jew said to them, "Leave him and let him rise." Whereupon Khalifah jumped up, as if naught ailed him, and the Jew said to him, "Tell me what price thou asketh for this fish and I will give it thee: for thou hast gotten but scant good of us this day." Answered the Fisherman, "Have no fear for me, O master, because of the beating; for I can eat ten donkeys' rations of stick." The Jew laughed at his words and said, "Allah upon thee, tell me what thou wilt have and by the right of my Faith, I will give it thee!" The Fisherman replied, "Naught from thee will remunerate me for this fish save the two words whereof I spake." And the Jew said, "Meseemeth thou wouldst have me become a Moslem?" Khalifah rejoined, "By Allah, O Jew, an thou islamise 'twill nor advantage the Moslems nor damage the Jews; and in like manner, an thou hold to thy misbelief 'twill nor damage the Moslems nor advantage the Jews. But what I desire of thee is that thou rise to thy feet and say:—Bear witness against me, O people of the market, that I barter my ape for the ape of Khalifah the Fisherman and my lot in the world for his lot and my luck for his luck." Quoth the Jew, "If this be all thou desirest 'twill sit lightly upon me." So he rose without stay or delay and standing on his feet, repeated the required words; after which he turned to the Fisherman and asked him, "Hast thou aught else to ask of me?" "No," answered he, and the Jew said, "Go in peace!" Hearing this Khalifah sprung to his feet forthright; took up his basket and net and returned straight to the Tigris, where he threw his net and pulled it in. He found it heavy and brought it not ashore but with travail, when he found it full of fish of all kinds. Presently, up came a woman with a dish, who gave him a dinar, and he gave her fish for it; and after her an eunuch, who also bought a dinar's worth of fish, and so forth till he had sold ten dinars' worth. And he continued to sell ten dinars' worth of fish daily for ten days, till he had gotten an hundred dinars. Now Khalifah the Fisherman had quarters in the Passage of the Merchants, and, as he lay one night in his lodging much bemused with Hashish, he said to himself, "O Khalifah, the folk all know thee for a poor fisherman, and now thou hast gotten an hundred golden dinars. Needs must the Commander of the Faithful, Harun al-Rashid, hear of this from some one, and haply he will be wanting money and will send for thee and say to thee:—I need a sum of money and it hath reached me that thou hast an hundred dinars: so do thou lend them to me those same." I shall answer, "O Commander of the Faithful, I am a poor man, and whoso told thee that I had an hundred dinars lied against me; for I have naught of this." Thereupon he will commit me to the Chief of Police, saying:—Strip him of his clothes and torment him with the bastinado till he confess and give up the hundred dinars in his possession. Wherefore, meseemeth to provide against this predicament, the best thing I can do, is to rise forthright and bash myself with the whip, so to use myself to beating." And his Hashish said to him, "Rise, doff thy dress." So he stood up and putting off his clothes, took a whip he had by him and set handy a leather pillow; then he fell to lashing himself, laying every other blow upon the pillow and roaring out the while, "Alas! Alas! By Allah, 'tis a false saying, O my lord, and they have lied against me; for I am a poor fisherman and have naught of the goods of the world!" The noise of the whip falling on the pillow and on his person resounded in the still of night and the folk heard it, and amongst others the merchants, and they said, "Whatever can ail the poor fellow, that he crieth and we hear the noise of blows falling on him? 'Twould seem robbers have broken in upon him and are tormenting him." Presently they all came forth of their lodgings, at the noise of the blows and the crying, and repaired to Khalifah's room, but they found the door locked and said one to other, "Belike the robbers have come in upon him from the back of the adjoining saloon. It behoveth us to climb over by the roofs." So they clomb over the roofs and coming down through the sky-light, saw him naked and flogging himself and asked him, "What aileth thee, O Khalifah?" He answered, "Know, O folk, that I have gained some dinars and fear lest my case be carried up to the Prince of True Believers, Harun al-Rashid, and he send for me and demand of me those same gold pieces; whereupon I should deny, and I fear that, if I deny, he will torture me, so I am torturing myself, by way of accustoming me to what may come." The merchants laughed at him and said, "Leave this fooling, may Allah not bless thee and the dinars thou hast gotten! Verily thou hast disturbed us this night and hast troubled our hearts." So Khalifah left flogging himself and slept till the morning, when he rose and would have gone about his business, but bethought him of his hundred dinars and said in his mind, "An I leave them at home, thieves will steal them, and if I put them in a belt about my waist, peradventure some one will see me and lay in wait for me till he come upon me in some lonely place and slay me and take the money: but I have a device that should serve me well, right well." So he jumped up forthright and made him a pocket in the collar of his gaberdine and tying the hundred dinars up in a purse, laid them in the collar-pocket. Then he took his net and basket and staff and went down to the Tigris, where he made a cast but brought up naught. So he removed from that place to another and threw again, but once more the net came up empty; and he went on removing from place to place till he had gone half a day's journey from the city, ever casting the net which kept bringing up naught. So he said to himself, "By Allah, I will throw my net a-stream but this once more, whether ill come of it or weal!" Then he hurled the net with all his force, of the excess of his wrath and the purse with the hundred dinars flew out of his collar-pocket and, lighting in mid-stream, was carried away by the strong current; whereupon he threw down the net and doffing his clothes, left them on the bank and plunged into the water after the purse. He dived for it nigh a hundred times, till his strength was exhausted and he came up for sheer fatigue without chancing on it. When he despaired of finding the purse, he returned to the shore, where he saw nothing but staff, net and basket and sought for his clothes, but could light on no trace of them: so he said in himself, "O vilest of those wherefor was made the byword:—The pilgrimage is not perfected save by copulation with the camel!" Then he wrapped the net about him and taking staff in one hand and basket in other, went trotting about like a camel in rut, running right and left and backwards and forwards, dishevelled and dusty, as he were a rebel Marid let loose from Solomon's prison. So far for what concerns the Fisherman Khalifah; but as regards the Caliph Harun al-Rashid, he had a friend, a jeweller called Ibn al-Kirnas, and all the traders, brokers and middle-men knew him for the Caliph's merchant; wherefore there was naught sold in Baghdad, by way of rarities and things of price or Mamelukes or handmaidens, but was first shown to him. As he sat one day in his shop, behold, there came up to him the Shaykh of the brokers, with a slave-girl, whose like seers never saw, for she was of passing beauty and loveliness, symmetry and perfect grace, and among her gifts was that she knew all arts and sciences and could make verses and play upon all manner musical instruments. So Ibn al-Kirnas bought her for five thousand golden dinars and clothed her with other thousand; after which he carried her to the Prince of True Believers, with whom she lay the night and who made trial of her in

every kind of knowledge and accomplishment and found her versed in
all sorts of arts and sciences, having no equal in her time. Her name
was Kut al-Kulub and she was even as saith the poet: —

> I fix my glance on her, whene'er she wends;
> And non-acceptance of my glance breeds pain:
> She favours graceful-necked gazelle at gaze;
> And "Graceful as gazelle" to say we're fain.

On the morrow the Caliph sent for Ibn al-Kirnas the Jeweller, and bade
him receive ten thousand dinars to her price. And his heart was taken
up with the slave-girl Kut al-Kulub and he forsook the Lady Zubaydah
bint al-Kasim, for all she was the daughter of his father's brother and
he abandoned all his favourite concubines and abode a whole
month without stirring from Kut al-Kulub's side save to go to the
Friday prayers and return to her all in haste. This was grievous to the
Lords of the Realm and they complained thereof to the Wazir Ja'afar
the Barmecide, who bore with the Commander of the Faithful and
waited till the next Friday, when he entered the cathedral-mosque and,
foregathering with the Caliph, related to him all that occurred to him
of extraordinary stories anent seld-seen love and lovers with intent to
draw out what was in his mind. Quoth the Caliph, "By Allah, O Ja'afar,
this is not of my choice; but my heart is caught in the snare of love
and wot I not what is to be done!" The Wazir Ja'afar replied, "O
Commander of the Faithful, thou knowest how this girl Kut al-Kulub
is become at thy disposal and of the number of thy servants, and that
which hand possesseth soul coveteth not. Moreover, I will tell thee
another thing which is that the highest boast of Kings and Princes is in
hunting and the pursuit of sport and victory; and if thou apply thyself
to this, perchance it will divert thee from her, and it may be thou wilt
forget her." Rejoined the Caliph, "Thou sayest well, O Ja'afar; come let
us go a-hunting forthright, without stay or delay." So soon as Friday
prayers were prayed, they left the mosque and at once mounting their
she-mules rode forth to the chase, occupied with talk, and their attendants out-went them. Presently the heat became overhot and Al-Rashid
said to his Wazir, "O Ja'afar, I am sore athirst." Then he looked around
and espying a figure in the distance on a high mound, asked Ja'afar,
"Seest thou what I see?" Answered the Wazir, "Yes, O Commander of
the Faithful; I see a dim figure on a high mound; belike he is the
keeper of a garden or of a cucumber-plot, and in whatso wise water will
not be lacking in his neighbourhood;" presently adding, "I will go to
him and fetch thee some." But Al-Rashid said, "My mule is swifter than
thy mule; so do thou abide here, on account of the troops, whilst I go

myself to him and get of this person drink and return." So saying, he urged his she-mule, which started off like racing wind or railing-water and, in the twinkling of an eye, made the mound, where he found the figure he had seen to be none other than Khalifah the Fisherman, naked and wrapped in the net; and indeed he was horrible to behold, as to and fro he rolled with eyes for very redness like cresset-gleam and dusty hair in dishevelled trim, as he were an Ifrit or a lion grim. Al-Rashid saluted him and he returned his salutation; but he was wroth and fires might have been lit at his breath. Quoth the Caliph, "O man, hast thou any water?"; and quoth Khalifah, "Ho thou, art thou blind, or Jinn-mad? Get thee to the river Tigris, for 'tis behind this mound." So Al-Rashid went around the mound and going down to the river, drank and watered his mule: then without a moment's delay he returned to Khalifah and said to him, "What aileth thee, O man, to stand here, and what is thy calling?" The Fisherman cried, "This is a stranger and sillier question than that about the water! Seest thou not the gear of my craft on my shoulder?" Said the Caliph, "Belike thou art a fisherman?"; and he replied, "Yes." Asked Al-Rashid, "Where is thy gaberdine, and where are thy waistcloth and girdle and where be the rest of thy raiment?" Now these were the very things which had been taken from Khalifah, like for like; so, when he heard the Caliph name them, he got into his head that it was he who had stolen his clothes from the river-bank and coming down from the top of the mound, swiftlier than the blinding leven, laid hold of the mule's bridle, saying, "Hark-ye, man, bring me back my things and leave jesting and joking." Al-Rashid replied, "By Allah, I have not seen thy clothes, nor know aught of them!" Now the Caliph had large cheeks and a small mouth; so Khalifah said to him, "Belike, thou art by trade a singer or a piper on pipes? But bring me back my clothes fairly and without more ado, or I will bash thee with this my staff till thou bepiss thyself and befoul thy clothes." When Al-Rashid saw the staff in the Fisherman's hand and that he had the vantage of him, he said to himself, "By Allah, I cannot brook from this mad beggar half a blow of that staff!" Now he had on a satin gown; so he pulled it off and gave it to Khalifah, saying, "O man, take this in place of thy clothes." The Fisherman took it and turned it about and said, "My clothes are worth ten of this painted 'Aba-cloak;" and rejoined the Caliph, "Put it on till I bring thee thy gear." So Khalifah donned the gown, but finding it too long for him, took a knife he had with him, tied to the handle of his basket, and cut off nigh a third of the skirt, so that it fell only beneath his knees. Then he turned to Al-Rashid and said to him, "Allah upon thee, O piper, tell me what wage thou gettest every month from thy master, for thy craft of piping."

Replied the Caliph, "My wage is ten dinars a month," and Khalifah continued, "By Allah, my poor fellow, thou makest me sorry for thee! Why, I make thy ten dinars every day! Hast thou a mind to take service with me and I will teach thee the art of fishing and share my gain with thee? So shalt thou make five dinars a day and be my slavey and I will protect thee against thy master with this staff." Quoth Al-Rashid, "I will well"; and quoth Khalifah, "Then get off thy she-ass and tie her up, so she may serve us to carry the fish hereafter, and come hither, that I may teach thee to fish forthright." So Al-Rashid alighted and hobbling his mule, tucked his skirts into his girdle, and Khalifah said to him, "O piper, lay hold of the net thus and put it over thy forearm thus and cast it into the Tigris thus." Accordingly, the Caliph took heart of grace and, doing as the fisherman showed him, threw the net and pulled at it, but could not draw it up. So Khalifah came to his aid and tugged at it with him; but the two together could not hale it up: whereupon said the fisherman, "O piper of ill-omen, for the first time I took thy gown in place of my clothes; but this second time I will have thine ass and will beat thee to boot, till thou bepiss and beskite thyself! An I find my net torn." Quoth Al-Rashid, "Let the twain of us pull at once." So they both pulled together and succeeded with difficulty in hauling that net ashore, when they found it full of fish of all kinds and colours; and Khalifah said to Al-Rashid, "By Allah, O piper, thou art foul of favour but, an thou apply thyself to fishing, thou wilt make a mighty fine fisherman. But now 'twere best thou bestraddle thine ass and make for the market and fetch me a pair of frails, and I will look after the fish till thou return, when I and thou will load it on thine ass's back. I have scales and weights and all we want, so we can take them with us and thou wilt have nothing to do but to hold the scales and pouch the price; for here we have fish worth twenty dinars. So be fast with the frails and loiter not." Answered the Caliph, "I hear and obey" and mounting, left him with his fish, and spurred his mule, in high good humour, and ceased not laughing over his adventure with the Fisherman, till he came up to Ja'afar, who said to him, "O Commander of the Faithful, belike, when thou wentest down to drink, thou foundest a pleasant flower-garden and enteredst and tookest thy pleasure therein alone?" At this Al-Rashid fell a laughing again and all the Barmecides rose and kissed the ground before him, saying, "O Commander of the Faithful, Allah make joy to endure for thee and do away annoy from thee! What was the cause of thy delaying when thou faredst to drink and what hath befallen thee?" Quoth the Caliph, "Verily, a right wondrous tale and a joyous adventure and a wondrous hath befallen me." And he repeated to them what had passed between himself and the Fisherman and his words, "Thou stolest my clothes!" and how he had given him his gown and how he had cut off a part of it, finding it too long for him. Said Ja'afar, "By Allah, O Commander of the Faithful, I had it in mind to beg the gown of thee: but now I will go straight to the Fisherman and buy it of him." The Caliph replied, "By Allah, he hath cut off a third part of the skirt and spoilt it! But, O Ja'afar, I am tired with fishing in the river, for I have caught great store of fish which I left on the bank with my master Khalifah, and he is watching them and waiting for me to return to him with a couple of frails and a matchet. Then we are to go, I and he, to the market and sell the fish and share the price." Ja'afar rejoined, "O Commander of the Faithful, I will bring you a purchaser for your fish." And Al-Rashid retorted, "O Ja'afar, by the virtue of my holy forefathers, whoso bringeth me one of the fish that are before Khalifah, who taught me angling, I will give him for it a gold dinar!" So the crier proclaimed among the troops that they should go forth and buy fish for the Caliph, and they all arose and made for the river-side. Now, while Khalifah was expecting the Caliph's return with the two frails, behold, the Mamelukes swooped down upon him like vultures and took the fish and wrapped them in gold-embroidered kerchiefs, beating one another in their eagerness to get at the Fisherman. Whereupon quoth Khalifah, "Doubtless these are of the fish of Paradise!" and hending two fish in right hand and left, plunged into the water up to his neck and fell a-saying, "O Allah, by the virtue of these fish, let Thy servant the piper, my partner, come to me at this very moment." And suddenly up to him came a black slave which was the chief of the Caliph's negro eunuchs. He had tarried behind the rest, by reason of his horse having stopped to make water by the way, and finding that naught remained of the fish, little or much, looked right and left, till he espied Khalifah standing in the stream, with a fish in either hand, and said to him, "Come hither, O Fisherman!" But Khalifah replied, "Begone and none of your impudence!" So the eunuch went up to him and said, "Give me the fish and I will pay thee their price." Replied the Fisherman, "Art thou little of wit? I will not sell them." Therewith the eunuch drew his mace upon him, and Khalifah cried out, saying, "Strike not, O loon! Better largesse than the mace." So saying, he threw the two fishes to the eunuch, who took them and laid them in his kerchief. Then he put hand in pouch, but found not a single dirham and said to Khalifah, "O Fisherman, verily thou art out of luck for, by Allah, I have not a silver about me! But come to-morrow to the Palace of the Caliphate and ask for the eunuch Sandal; whereupon the castratos will direct thee to me and by coming thither thou shalt get what falleth to thy lot and therewith wend thy ways." Quoth Khalifah,

"Indeed, this is a blessed day and its blessedness was manifest from the first of it!" Then he shouldered his net and returned to Baghdad; and as he passed through the streets, the folk saw the Caliph's gown on him and stared at him till he came to the gate of his quarter, by which was the shop of the Caliph's tailor. When the man saw him wearing a dress of the apparel of the Caliph, worth a thousand dinars, he said to him, "O Khalifah, whence hadst thou that gown?" Replied the Fisherman, "What aileth thee to be impudent? I had it of one whom I taught to fish and who is become my apprentice. I forgave him the cutting off of his hand[1] for that he stole my clothes and gave me this cape in their place." So the tailor knew that the Caliph had come upon him as he was fishing and jested with him and given him the gown. Such was his case; but as regards Harun al-Rashid, he had gone out a-hunting and a-fishing only to divert his thoughts from the damsel, Kut al-Kulub. But when Zubaydah heard of her and of the Caliph's devotion to her, the Lady was fired with the jealousy which the more especially fireth women, so that she refused meat and drink and rejected the delights of sleep and awaited the Caliph's going forth on a journey or what not, that she might set a snare for the damsel. So when she learnt that he was gone hunting and fishing, she bade her woman furnish the Palace fairly and decorate it splendidly and serve up viands and confections; and amongst the rest she made a China dish of the daintiest sweetmeats that can be made wherein she had put Bhang. Then she ordered one of her eunuchs go to the damsel Kut al-Kulub and bid her to the banquet, saying, "The Lady Zubaydah bint Al-Kasim, the wife of the Commander of the Faithful, hath drunken medicine to-day and, having heard tell of the sweetness of thy singing, longeth to divert herself with somewhat of thine art." Kut al-Kulub replied, "Hearing and obedience are due to Allah and the Lady Zubaydah," and rose without stay or delay, unknowing what was hidden for her in the Secret Purpose. Then she took with her what instruments she needed and, accompanying the eunuch, ceased not faring till she stood in the presence of the Princess. When she entered she kissed the ground before her again and again, then rising to her feet, said, "Peace be on the Lady of the exalted seat and the presence whereto none may avail, daughter of the house Abbasi and scion of the Prophet's family! May Allah fulfil thee of peace and prosperity in the days and the years!" Then she stood with the rest of the women and eunuchs, and presently the Lady Zubaydah raised her eyes and considered her beauty and loveliness. She saw a damsel

---

[1] The penalty of Theft.

with cheeks smooth as rose and breasts like granado, a face moon-bright, a brow flower-white and great eyes black as night; her eyelids were languor-dight and her face beamed with light, as if the sun from her forehead arose and the murks of the night from the locks of her brow; and the fragrance of musk from her breath strayed and flowers bloomed in her lovely face inlaid; the moon beamed from her forehead and in her slender shape the branches swayed. She was like the full moon shining in the nightly shade; her eyes wantoned, her eyebrows were like a bow arched and her lips of coral moulded. Her beauty amazed all who espied her and her glances amated all who eyed her. Glory be to Him who formed her and fashioned her and perfected her! Quoth the Lady Zubaydah, "Well come, and welcome and fair cheer to thee, O Kut al-Kulub! Sit and divert us with thine art and the good-liness of thine accomplishments." Quoth the damsel, "I hear and I obey"; and rose and exhibited tricks of sleight of hand and legerdemain and all manner pleasing arts, till the Princess came near to fall in love with her and said to herself, "Verily, my cousin Al-Rashid is not to blame for loving her!" Then the damsel kissed ground before Zubaydah and sat down, whereupon they set food before her. Presently they brought her the drugged dish of sweetmeats and she ate thereof; and hardly had it settled in her stomach when her head fell backward and she sank on the ground sleeping. With this, the Lady said to her women, "Carry her up to one of the chambers, till I summon her"; and they replied, "We hear and we obey." Then said she to one of her eunuchs, "Fashion me a chest and bring it hitherto to me!", and shortly afterwards she bade make the semblance of a tomb and spread the report that Kut al-Kulub had choked and died, threatening her famil-iars that she would smite the neck of whoever should say, "She is alive." Now, behold, the Caliph suddenly returned from the chase, and the first enquiry he made was for the damsel. So there came to him one of his eunuchs, whom the Lady Zubaydah had charged to declare she was dead, if the Caliph should ask for her and, kissing ground before him, said, "May thy head live, O my lord! Be certified that Kut al-Kulub choked in eating and is dead." Whereupon cried Al-Rashid, "God never gladden thee with good news, O thou bad slave!" and entered the Palace, where he heard of her death from every one and asked, "Where is her tomb?" So they brought him to the sepulchre and showed him the pretended tomb, saying, "This is her burial-place." The Caliph, weeping sore for her, abode by the tomb a full hour, after which he arose and went away, in the utmost distress and the deepest melan-choly. So the Lady Zubaydah saw that her plot had succeeded and forthright sent for the eunuch and said, "Hither with the chest!" He set it before her when she bade bring the damsel and locking her up therein, said to the Eunuch, "Take all pains to sell this chest and make it a condition with the purchaser that he buy it locked; then give alms with its price." So he took it and went forth, to do her bidding. Thus fare it with these; but as for Khalifah the Fisherman, when morning morrowed and shone with its light and sheen, he said to himself, "I cannot do aught better to-day than visit the Eunuch who bought the fish of me, for he appointed me to come to him in the Palace of the Caliphate." So he went forth of his lodging, intending for the palace, and when he came thither, he found Mamelukes, negro-slaves and eunuchs standing and sitting; and looking at them, behold, seated amongst them was the Eunuch who had taken the fish of him, with the white slaves waiting on him. Presently, one of the Mameluke-lads called out to him; whereupon the Eunuch turned to see who he was and lo! it was the Fisherman. Now when Khalifah was ware that he saw him and recognised him, he said to him, "I have not failed thee, O my little Tulip! On this wise are men of their word." Hearing his address Sandal the Eunuch laughed and replied, "By Allah, thou art right, O Fisherman," and put his hand to his pouch, to give him somewhat; but at that moment there arose a great clamour. So he raised his head to see what was to do and finding that it was the Wazir Ja'afar the Barmecide coming forth from the Caliph's presence, he rose to him and forewent him, and they walked about, conversing for a longsome time. Khalifah the Fisherman waited awhile; then, growing weary of standing and finding that the Eunuch took no heed of him, he set himself in his way and beckoned to him from afar, saying, "O my lord Tulip, give me my due and let me go!" The Eunuch heard him, but was ashamed to answer him because of the Minister's presence; so he went on talking with Ja'afar and took no notice whatever of the Fisherman. Whereupon quoth Khalifah, "O Slow o' Pay! May Allah put to shame all churls and all who take folk's goods and are niggardly with them! I put myself under thy protection, O my lord Bran-belly, to give me my due and let me go!" The Eunuch heard him, but was ashamed to answer him before Ja'afar; and the Minister saw the Fisherman beckoning and talking to him, though he knew not what he was saying; so he said to Sandal, misliking his behaviour, 'O Eunuch, what would yonder beggar with thee?" Sandal replied, "Dost thou not know him, O my lord the Wazir?"; and Ja'afar answered, "By Allah, I know him not! How should I know a man I have never seen but at this moment?" Rejoined the Eunuch, "O my lord, this is the

Fisherman whose fish we seized on the banks of the Tigris. I came too late to get any and was ashamed to return to the Prince of True Believers, empty-handed, when all the Mamelukes had some. Presently I espied the Fisherman standing in mid-stream, calling on Allah, with four fishes in his hands, and said to him:—Give me what thou hast there and take their worth. He handed me the fish and I put my hand into my pocket, purposing to gift him with somewhat, but found naught therein and said:—Come to me in the Palace, and I will give thee wherewithal to aid thee in thy poverty. So he came to me to-day and I was putting hand to pouch, that I might give him somewhat, when thou camest forth and I rose to wait on thee and was diverted with thee from him, till he grew tired of waiting; and this is the whole story, how he cometh to be standing here." The Wazir, hearing this account, smiled and said, "O Eunuch, how is it that this Fisherman cometh in his hour of need and thou satisfiest him not? Dost thou not know him, O Chief of the Eunuchs?" "No," answered Sandal and Ja'afar said, "This is the Master of the Commander of the Faithful, and his partner and our lord the Caliph hath arisen this morning, strait of breast, heavy of heart and troubled in thought, nor is there aught will broaden his breast save this fisherman. So let him not go, till I crave the Caliph's pleasure concerning him and bring him before him; perchance Allah will relieve him of his oppression and console him for the loss of Kut al-Kulub, by means of the Fisherman's presence, and he will give him wherewithal to better himself; and thou wilt be the cause of this." Replied Sandal, "O my lord, do as thou wilt and may Allah Almighty long continue thee a pillar of the dynasty of the Commander of the Faithful, whose shadow Allah perpetuate and prosper it, root and branch!" Then the Wazir Ja'afar rose up and went in to the Caliph and Sandal ordered the Mamelukes not to leave the Fisherman; whereupon Khalifah cried, "How goodly is thy bounty, O Tulip! The seeker is become the sought. I come to seek my due, and they imprison me for debts in arrears!" When Ja'afar came in to the presence of the Caliph, he found him sitting with his head bowed earthwards, breast straitened and mind melancholy, humming the verses of the poet:—

My blamers instant bid that I for her become consoled;
But I, what can I do, whose heart declines to be controlled?
And how can I in patience bear the loss of lovely maid,
When fails me patience for a love that holds with firmest hold!
Ne'er I'll forget her nor the bowl that 'twixt us both went round
And wine of glances maddened me with drunkenness ensoul'd.

Whenas Ja'afar stood in the presence, he said, "Peace be upon thee, O Commander of the Faithful, Defender of the honour of the Faith and descendant of the uncle of the Prince of Apostles, Allah assain him and save him and his family one and all!" The Caliph raised his head and answered, "And on thee be peace and the mercy of Allah and His blessings!" Quoth Ja'afar; "With leave of the Prince of True Believers, his servant would speak without restraint." Asked the Caliph, "And when was restraint put upon thee in speech and thou the Prince of Wazirs? Say what thou wilt." Answered Ja'afar, "When I went out, O my lord, from before thee, intending for my house, I saw standing at the door thy master and teacher and partner, Khalifah the Fisherman, who was aggrieved at thee and complained of thee saying:—Glory be to God! I taught him to fish and he went away to fetch me a pair of frails, but never came back: and this is not the way of a good partner or of a good apprentice. So, if thou hast a mind to partnership, well and good; and if not, tell him, that he may take to partner another." Now when the Caliph heard these words he smiled and his straitness of breast was done away with and he said, "My life on thee, is this the truth thou sayest, that the Fisherman standeth at the door?" and Ja'afar replied, "By thy life, O Commander of the Faithful, he standeth at the door." Quoth the Caliph, "O Ja'afar, by Allah, I will assuredly do my best to give him his due! If Allah at my hands send him misery, he shall have it; and if prosperity he shall have it." Then he took a piece of paper and cutting it in pieces, said to the Wazir, "O Ja'afar, write down with thine own hand twenty sums of money, from one dinar to a thousand, and the names of all kinds of offices and dignities from the least appointment to the Caliphate; also twenty kinds of punishment from the lightest beating to death." "I hear and I obey, O Commander of the Faithful," answered Ja'afar, and did as he was bidden. Then said the Caliph, "O Ja'afar, I swear by my holy forefathers and by my kinship to Hamzah and Akil, that I mean to summon the fisherman and bid him take one of these papers, whose contents none knoweth save thou and I; and whatsoever is written in the paper which he shall choose, I will give it to him; though it be the Caliphate I will divest myself thereof and invest him therewith and grudge it not to him; and, on the other hand, if there be written therein hanging or mutilation or death, I will execute it upon him. Now go and fetch him to me." When Ja'afar heard this, he said to himself, "There is no Majesty and there is no Might save in Allah, the Glorious, the Great! It may be somewhat will fall to this poor wretch's lot that will bring about his destruction, and I shall be the cause. But the Caliph hath sworn; so nothing remains now but to bring him in, and naught will happen save whatso Allah willeth."

Accordingly he went out to Khalifah the Fisherman and laid hold of his hand, to carry him in to the Caliph, whereupon his reason fled and he said in himself, "What a stupid I was to come after yonder ill-omened slave, Tulip, whereby he hath brought me in company with Bran-belly!" Ja'afar fared on with him, with Mamelukes before and behind, whilst he said, "Doth not arrest suffice, but these must go behind and before me, to hinder my making off?" till they had traversed seven vestibules, when the Wazir said to him, "Mark my words, O Fisherman! Thou standest before the Commander of the Faithful and Defender of the Faith!" Then he raised the great curtain and Khalifah's eyes fell on the Caliph, who was seated on his couch, with the Lords of the realm standing in attendance upon him. As soon as he knew him, he went up to him and said, "Well come, and welcome to thee, O piper! 'Twas not right of thee to make thyself a Fisherman and go away, leaving me sitting to guard the fish, and never to return! For, before I was aware, there came up Mamelukes on beasts of all manner colours, and snatched away the fish from me, I standing alone, and this was all of thy fault; for, hadst thou returned with the frails forthright, we had sold an hundred dinars' worth of fish. And now I come to seek my due, and they have arrested me. But thou, who hath imprisoned thee also in this place?" The Caliph smiled and raising a corner of the curtain, put forth his head and said to the Fisherman, "Come hither and take thee one of these papers." Quoth Khalifah the Fisherman, "Yesterday thou wast a fisherman, and to-day thou hast become an astrologer; but the more trades a man hath, the poorer he waxeth." Thereupon Ja'afar said, "Take the paper at once, and do as the Commander of the Faithful biddeth thee without prating." So he came forward and put forth his hand saying, "Far be it from me that this piper should ever again be my knave and fish with me!" Then taking the paper he handed it to the Caliph, saying, "O piper, what hath come out for me therein? Hide naught thereof." So Al-Rashid received it and passed it on to Ja'afar and said to him, "Read what is therein." He looked at it and said, "There is no Majesty and there is no Might save in Allah, the Glorious, the Great!" Said the Caliph, "Good news, O Ja'afar? What seest thou therein?" Answered the Wazir, "O Commander of the Faithful, there came up from the paper:—Let the Fisherman receive an hundred blows with a stick." So the Caliph commanded to beat the Fisherman and they gave him an hundred sticks: after which he rose, saying, "Allah damn this, O Bran-belly! Are gaol and sticks part of the game?" Then said Ja'afar, "O Commander of the Faithful, this poor devil is come to the river, and how shall he go away thirsting? We hope that among the alms-deeds of the Commander of the Faithful, he may have leave to take another paper, so haply somewhat may come out wherewithal he may succour his poverty." Said the Caliph, "By Allah, O Ja'afar, if he take another paper and death be written therein, I will assuredly kill him, and thou wilt be the cause." Answered Ja'afar, "If he die he will be at rest." But Khalifah the Fisherman said to him, "Allah ne'er gladden thee with good news! Have I made Baghdad strait upon you, that ye seek to slay me?" Quoth Ja'afar, "Take thee a paper and crave the blessing of Allah Almighty!" So he put out his hand and taking a paper, gave it to Ja'afar, who read it and was silent. The Caliph asked, "Why art thou silent, O son of Yahya?"; and he answered, "O Commander of the Faithful, there hath come out on this paper:—Naught shall be given to the Fisherman." Then said the Caliph, "His daily bread will not come from us: bid him fare forth from before our face." Quoth Ja'afar, "By the claims of thy pious forefathers, let him take a third paper, it may be it will bring him alimony;" and quoth the Caliph, "Let him take one and no more." So he put out his hand and took a third paper, and behold, therein was written, "Let the Fisherman be given one dinar." Ja'afar cried to him, "I sought good fortune for thee, but Allah willed not to thee aught save this dinar." And Khalifah answered, "Verily, a dinar for every hundred sticks were rare good luck, may Allah not send thy body health!" The Caliph laughed at him and Ja'afar took him by the hand and led him out. When he reached the door, Sandal the eunuch saw him and said to him, "Hither, O Fisherman! Give us portion of that which the Commander of the Faithful hath bestowed on thee, whilst jesting with thee." Replied Khalifah, "By Allah, O Tulip, thou art right! Wilt thou share with me, O nigger? Indeed, I have eaten stick to the tune of an hundred blows and have earned one dinar, and thou art but too welcome to it." So saying, he threw him the dinar and went out, with the tears flowing down the plain of his cheeks. When the Eunuch saw him in this plight, he knew that he had spoken sooth and called to the lads to fetch him back: so they brought him back and Sandal, putting his hand to his pouch, pulled out a red purse, whence he emptied an hundred golden dinars into the Fisherman's hand, saying, "Take this gold in payment of thy fish and wend thy ways." So Khalifah, in high good humour, took the hundred ducats and the Caliph's one dinar and went his way, and forgot the beating. Now, as Allah willed it for the furthering of that which He had decreed, he passed by the mart of the hand-maidens and seeing there a mighty ring where many folks were foregathering, said to himself, "What is this crowd?" So he brake through the merchants and others, who said,

"Make wide the way for Skipper Rapscallion, and let him pass." Then he looked and behold, he saw a chest, with an eunuch seated thereon and an old man standing by it, and the Shaykh was crying, "O merchants, O men of money, who will hasten and hazard his coin for this chest of unknown contents from the Palace of the Lady Zubaydah bint al-Kasim, wife of the Commander of the Faithful? How much shall I say for you, Allah bless you all!" Quoth one of the merchants, "By Allah, this is a risk! But I will say one word and no blame to me. Be it mine for twenty dinars." Quoth another, "Fifty," and they went on bidding, one against other, till the price reached an hundred ducats. Then said the crier, "Will any of you bid more, O merchants?" And Khalifah the Fisherman said, "Be it mine for an hundred dinars and one dinar." The merchants, hearing these words, thought he was jesting and laughed at him, saying, "O eunuch, sell it to Khalifah for an hundred dinars and one dinar!" Quoth the eunuch, "By Allah, I will sell it to none but him! Take it, O Fisherman, the Lord bless thee in it, and here with thy gold." So Khalifah pulled out the ducats and gave them to the eunuch, who, the bargain being duly made, delivered to him the chest and bestowed the price in alms on the spot; after which he returned to the Palace and acquainted the Lady Zubaydah with what he had done, whereat she rejoiced. Meanwhile the Fisherman hove the chest on shoulder, but could not carry it on this wise for the excess of its weight; so he lifted it on to his head and thus bore it to the quarter where he lived. Here he set it down and being weary, sat awhile, bemusing what had befallen him and saying in himself, "Would Heaven I knew what is in this chest!" Then he opened the door of his lodging and haled the chest till he got it into his closet; after which he strove to open it, but failed. Quoth he, "What folly possessed me to buy this chest? There is no help for it but to break it open and see what is herein." So he applied himself to the lock, but could not open it, and said to himself, "I will leave it till to-morrow." Then he would have stretched him out to sleep, but could find no room; for the chest filled the whole closet. So he got upon it and lay him down; but, when he had lain awhile, behold, he felt something stir under him whereat sleep forsook him and his reason fled. So he arose and cried, "Meseems there be Jinns in the chest. Praise to Allah who suffered me not to open it! For, had I done so, they had risen against me in the dark and slain me, and from them would have befallen me naught of good." Then he lay down again when, lo! the chest moved a second time, more than before; whereupon he sprang to his feet and said, "There it goes again: but this is terrible!" And he hastened to look for the lamp, but could not find it and had not the wherewithal to buy another. So he went forth and cried out, "Ho people of the quarter!" Now the most part of the folk were asleep; but they awoke at his crying and asked, "What aileth thee, O Khalifah?" He answered, "Bring me a lamp, for the Jinn are upon me." They laughed at him and gave him a lamp, wherewith he returned to his closet. Then he smote the lock of the chest with a stone and broke it and opening it, saw a damsel like a Houri lying asleep within. Now she had been drugged with Bhang, but at that moment she threw up the stuff and awoke; then she opened her eyes and feeling herself confined and cramped, moved. At this sight quoth Khalifah, "By Allah, O my lady, whence art thou?"; and quoth she, "Bring me Jessamine, and Narcissus." And Khalifah answered, "There is naught here but Henna-flowers." Thereupon she came to herself and considering Khalifah, said to him, "What art thou?" presently adding, "And where am I?" He said, "Thou art in my lodging." Asked she, "Am I not in the Palace of the Caliph Harun al-Rashid?" And quoth he, "What manner of thing is Al-Rashid? O madwoman, Thou art naught but my slave-girl: I bought thee this very day for an hundred dinars and one dinar, and brought thee home, and thou wast asleep in this here chest." When she heard these words she said to him, "What is thy name?" Said he, "My name is Khalifah. How comes my star to have grown propitious, when I know my ascendant to have been otherwise?" She laughed and cried, "Spare me this talk! Hast thou anything to eat?" Replied he, "No, by Allah, nor yet to drink! I have not eaten these two days and am now in want of a morsel." She asked, "Hast thou no money?"; and he said, "Allah keep this chest which hath beggared me: I gave all I had for it and am become bankrupt." The damsel laughed at him and said, "Up with thee and seek of thy neighbours somewhat for me to eat, for I am hungry." So he went forth and cried out, "Ho, people of the quarter!" Now the folk were asleep; but they awoke and asked, "What aileth thee, O Khalifah?" Answered he, "O my neighbours, I am hungry and have nothing to eat." So one came down to him with a bannock and another with broken meats and a third with a bittock of cheese and a fourth with a cucumber; and so on till his lap was full and he returned to his closet and laid the whole between her hands, saying, "Eat." But she laughed at him, saying, "How can I eat of this, when I have not a mug of water whereof to drink? I fear to choke with a mouthful and die." Quoth he, "I will fill thee this pitcher." So he took the pitcher and going forth, stood in the midst of the street and cried out, saying, "Ho, people of the quarter!" Quoth they, "What calamity is upon thee to-night, O Khalifah!" And he said, "Ye gave me food and I ate; but now I am a-thirst; so give me to drink." Thereupon one came down to him with a mug and another with an ewer and a third with a gugglet; and he filled his pitcher and, bearing it back, said to the damsel, "O my lady, thou lackest nothing now." Answered she, "True, I want nothing more at this present." Quoth he, "Speak to me and say me thy story." And quoth she, "Fie upon thee! An thou knowest me not, I will tell thee who I am. I am Kut al-Kulub, the Caliph's hand-maiden, and the Lady Zubaydah was jealous of me; so she drugged me with Bhang and set me in this chest," presently adding "Alhamdolillah—praised be God—for that the matter hath come to easy issue and no worse! But this befel me not save for thy good luck, for thou wilt certainly get of the Caliph Al-Rashid money galore, that will be the means of thine enrichment." Quoth Khalifah, "Is not Al-Rashid he in whose Palace I was imprisoned?" "Yes," answered she; and he said, "By Allah, never saw I more niggardly wight than he, that piper little of good and wit! He gave me an hundred blows with a stick yesterday and but one dinar, for all I taught him to fish and made him my partner; but he played me false." Replied she, "Leave this unseemly talk, and open thine eyes and look thou bear thyself respectfully, whenas thou seest him after this, and thou shalt win thy wish." When he heard her words, it was as if he had been asleep and awoke; and Allah removed the veil from his judgment, because of his good luck,[1] and he answered, "On my head and eyes!" Then said he to her, "Sleep, in the name of Allah." So she lay down and fell asleep (and he afar from her) till the morning, when she sought of him ink-case and paper and, when they were brought wrote to Ibn al-Kirnas, the Caliph's friend, acquainting him with her case and how at the end of all that had befallen her she was with Khalifah the Fisherman, who had bought her. Then she gave him the scroll, saying, "Take this and hie thee to the jewel-market and ask for the shop of Ibn al-Kirnas the Jeweller and give him this paper and speak not." "I hear and I obey," answered Khalifah and going with the scroll to the market, enquired for the shop of Ibn al-Kirnas. They directed him thither and on entering it he saluted the merchant, who returned his salam with contempt and said to him, "What dost thou want?" Thereupon he gave him the letter and he took it, but read it not, thinking the Fisherman a beggar, who sought an alms of him, and said to one of his lads, "Give him half a dirham." Quoth Khalifah, "I want no alms; read the paper." So Ibn al-Kirnas took the letter and read it; and no sooner knew its

---

[1] This sudden transformation, which to us seems exaggerated and unnatural, appears in many Eastern stories and in the biographies of their distinguished men, especially students. A youth cannot master his lessons; he sees a spider climbing a slippery wall and after repeated falls succeeding. Allah opens the eyes of his mind, his studies become easy to him, and he ends with being an Allamah (doctissimus).

import than he kissed it and laid it on his head; then he arose and said to Khalifah, "O my brother, where is thy house?" Asked Khalifah, "What wantest thou with my house? Wilt thou go thither and steal my slave-girl?" Then Ibn al-Kirnas answered, "Not so: on the contrary, I will buy thee somewhat whereof you may eat, thou and she." So he said, "My house is in such a quarter;" and the merchant rejoined, "Thou hast done well. May Allah not give thee health, O unlucky one!" Then he called out to two of his slaves and said to them, "Carry this man to the shop of Mohsin the Shroff and say to him, "O Mohsin, give this man a thousand dinars of gold; then bring him back to me in haste." So they carried him to the money-changer, who paid him the money, and returned with him to their master, whom they found mounted on a dapple she-mule worth a thousand dinars, with Mamelukes and pages about him, and by his side another mule like his own, saddled and bridled. Quoth the jeweller to Khalifah, "Bismillah, mount this mule." Replied he, "I won't; for by Allah, I fear she throw me;" and quoth Ibn al-Kirnas, "By God, needs must thou mount." So he came up and mounting her, face to crupper, caught hold of her tail and cried out; whereupon she threw him on the ground and they laughed at him; but he rose and said, "Did I not tell thee I would not mount this great jenny-ass?" Thereupon Ibn al-Kirnas left him in the market and repairing to the Caliph, told him of the damsel; after which he returned and removed her to his own house. Meanwhile Khalifah went home to look after the handmaid and found the people of the quarter foregathering and saying, "Verily, Khalifah is to-day in a terrible pickle! Would we knew whence he can have gotten this damsel?" Quoth one of them, "He is a mad pimp: haply he found her lying on the road drunken, and carried her to his own house, and his absence showeth that he knoweth his offence." As they were talking, behold, up came Khalifah, and they said to him, "What a plight is thine, O unhappy! knowest thou not what is to come to thee?" He replied, "No, by Allah!" and they said, "But just now there came Mamelukes and took away thy slave-girl whom thou stolest, and sought for thee, but found thee not." Asked Khalifah, "And how came they to take my slave-girl?"; and quoth one, "Had he fallen in their way, they had slain him." But he, so far from heeding them, returned running to the shop of Ibn al-Kirnas, whom he met riding, and said to him, "By Allah, 'twas not right of thee to wheedle me and meanwhile send thy Mamelukes to take my slave-girl!" Replied the jeweller, "O idiot, come with me and hold thy tongue." So he took him and carried him into a house handsomely builded, where he found the damsel seated on a couch of gold, with ten slave-girls like moons round her. Sighting her Ibn al-Kirnas kissed ground before her and she said, "What hast thou done with my new master, who bought me with all he owned?" He replied, "O my lady, I gave him a thousand golden dinars;" and related to her Khalifah's history from first to last, whereat she laughed and said, "Blame him not; for he is but a common wight. These other thousand dinars are a gift from me to him and Almighty Allah willing, he shall win of the Caliph what shall enrich him." As they were talking, there came an eunuch from the Commander of the Faithful, in quest of Kut al-Kulub for, when he knew that she was in the house of Ibn al-Kirnas, he could not endure the severance, but bade bring her forthwith. So she repaired to the Palace, taking Khalifah with her, and going into the presence, kissed ground before the Caliph, who rose to her, saluting and welcoming her, and asked her how she had fared with him who had brought her. She replied, "He is a man, Khalifah the Fisherman hight, and there he standeth at the door. He telleth me that he hath an account to settle with the Commander of the Faithful, by reason of a partnership between him and the Caliph in fishing." Asked Al-Rashid, "Is he at the door?" and she answered, "Yes." So the Caliph sent for him and he kissed ground before him and wished him endurance of glory and prosperity. The Caliph marvelled at him and laughed at him and said to him, "O Fisherman, wast thou in very deed my partner yesterday?" Khalifah took his meaning and heartening his heart and summoning spirit replied, "By Him who bestowed upon thee the succession to thy cousin, I know her not in anywise and have had no commerce with her save by way of sight and speech!" Then he repeated to him all that had befallen him, since he last saw him, whereat the Caliph laughed and his breast broadened and he said to Khalifah, "Ask of us what thou wilt, O thou who bringest to owners their own!" But he was silent; so the Caliph ordered him fifty thousand dinars of gold and a costly dress of honour such as great Sovrans don, and a she-mule, and gave him black slaves of the Sudan to serve him, so that he became as he were one of the Kings of that time. The Caliph was rejoiced at the recovery of his favourite and knew that all this was the doing of his cousin-wife, the Lady Zubaydah; wherefore he was sore enraged against her and held aloof from her a great while, visiting her not neither inclining to pardon her. When she was certified of this, she was sore concerned for his wrath and her face, that was wont to be rosy, waxed pale and wan till, when her patience was exhausted, she sent a letter to her cousin, the Commander of the Faithful, making her excuses to him and confessing her offences, and ending with these verses:—

> I long once more the love that was between us to regain,
> That I may quench the fire of grief and bate the force of bane.
> O lords of me, have ruth upon the stress my passion deals

Enough to me is what you doled of sorrow and of pain.
'Tis life to me an deign you keep the troth you deigned to plight
'Tis death to me an troth you break and fondest vows profane:
Given I've sinned a sorry sin, yet grant me ruth, for naught
By Allah, sweeter is than friend who is of pardon fain.

When the Lady Zubaydah's letter reached the Caliph, and reading it he saw that she confessed her offence and sent her excuses to him therefor, he said to himself, "Verily, all sins doth Allah forgive; aye, Gracious, Merciful is He!" And he returned her an answer, expressing satisfaction and pardon and forgiveness for what was past, whereat she rejoiced greatly. As for Khalifah, the Fisherman, the Caliph assigned him a monthly solde of fifty dinars, and took him into especial favour, which would lead to rank and dignity, honour and worship. Then he kissed ground before the Commander of the Faithful and went forth with stately gait. When he came to the door, the Eunuch Sandal, who had given him the hundred dinars, saw him and knowing him, said to him, "O Fisherman, whence all this?" So he told him all that had befallen him, first and last, whereat Sandal rejoiced, because he had been the cause of his enrichment, and said to him, "Wilt thou not give me largesse of this wealth which is now become thine?" So Khalifah put his hand to pouch and taking out a purse containing a thousand dinars, gave it to the Eunuch, who said, "Keep thy coins and Allah bless thee therein!" and marvelled at his manliness and at the liberality of his soul, for all his late poverty. Then leaving the eunuch, Khalifah mounted his she-mule and rode, with the slaves' hands on her crupper, till he came to his lodging at the Khan, whilst the folk stared at him in surprise for that which had betided him of advancement. When he alighted from his beast they accosted him and enquired the cause of his change from poverty to prosperity, and he told them all that had happened to him from incept to conclusion. Then he bought a fine mansion and laid out thereon much money, till it was perfect in all points. And he took up his abode therein and was wont to recite thereon these two couplets: —

Behold a house that's like the Dwelling of Delight;
Its aspect heals the sick and banishes despite.
Its sojourn for the great and wise appointed is,
And Fortune fair therein abideth day and night.

Then, as soon as he was settled in his house, he sought him in marriage the daughter of one of the chief men of the city, a handsome girl, and went in unto her and led a life of solace and satisfaction, joyaunce and enjoyment; and he rose to passing affluence and exceeding prosperity.

So, when he found himself in this fortunate condition, he offered up thanks to Allah (extolled and excelled be He!) for what He had bestowed on him of wealth exceeding and of favours ever succeeding, praising his Lord with the praise of the grateful. And thereafter Khalifah continued to pay frequent visits to the Caliph Harun al-Rashid, with whom he found acceptance and who ceased not to overwhelm him with boons and bounty: and he abode in the enjoyment of the utmost honour and happiness and joy and gladness and in riches more than sufficing and in rank ever rising; in brief, a sweet life and a savoury, pure as pleasurable, till there came to him the Destroyer of delights and the Sunderer of societies; and extolled by the perfection of Him to whom belong glory and permanence and He is the Living, the Eternal, who shall never die!